INTO TEMPTATION

INTO TEMPTATION

JOSH NAZARETH

T.E. WHITAKER

LAS VEGAS

Published by Oddward Books

Las Vegas, NV

oddward.com

Edited by Kelsey Lepperd

Book design by Viola Wyatt

Dedication symbol © T. E. Whitaker

Library of Congress Cataloging-in-Publication Data

Whitaker, T. E.

Into Temptation / T. E. Whitaker

pages ; cm.

ISBN 978-0-9914798-2-5

eBook ISBN 978-0-9914798-3-2

Library of Congress Control Number: 2015917733

First Edition: December 2015

10 9 8 7 6 5 4 3 2 1

MESSIANIC POLITIC

.

"In the beginning, there is something beyond the black, a looming presence, warming the cold, bending the light. Now the farthest galaxies plunge and heave, swirling and receding into a cosmic wake. The darkness vibrates. And hands, tremendous hands spanning time and space, emerge through the heavens, drawing ever nearer—"

"Zis is verbatim?"

"What do you think?" Jesus Christ asked from a reclining position on the oxblood leather chaise lounge. Behind the arm of the chaise, where Jesus' head rested, Sigmund Freud "hmmphed" while jotting his endless notes.

"I zink it is melodramatic," Freud said, adjusting his chair. The color of an evergreen forest, its stuffed back and arms rising to elbow level, the chair stood on wooden legs and was one of three unchanged elements of his practice. The others were his round-framed spectacles and his white, softly pointed beard. He enjoyed being recognized.

"It's how angels speak."

"Michael does not speak in zis manner. Neizer does Lucifer."

"They've adopted the patois of the age," Jesus said. "The other angels consider them unpolished."

"Hmmph."

"And Mike hasn't had the dream."

"What about Lucifer?"

Jesus considered. "I think he's hiding something."

"I see. Und you? You have not had zee dream?"

"No. But it's become a status symbol with the angels."

"How do you feel about zat?"

"I imagine it's welcome fuel for their Machiavellian existence of gambling and politics. They think He's coming. The Book is taking bets on the day He'll arrive."

"Und you?" Freud asked. "Do you agree wiz zem?"

Jesus shifted on the chaise. "I haven't decided. What do *you* think it means?"

"Dreams are not prescient," Freud said. "Zey are primarily wish fulfillments, and ultimately zee product of repressed sexual desires. Likely zee angels having zeese dreams harbor a subconscious conjugal desire originating with zeir inception."

Jesus sat up. He'd already crumpled his exquisite Italian suit, but felt the need to glare at the psychoanalyst, though they both knew it was for the sake of theatrics.

"Your blind adherence to your questionable theories marginalizes you in modern psychological circles."

Freud ignored the jab and asked, "Why do you zink you are not party to zee dream?"

"I'm not sure," Jesus said. "Carl thinks the angels might originate from a separate plane of the collective unconscious."

Freud went still at the mention of his former collaborator and his theory. "You have seen Dr. Jung?"

Jesus laughed. "If I had, how would you feel about zzzzat?"

Freud set down his pencil and stared at Jesus. Jesus laughed again, but scowled as Freud placed his notebook on the table beside him.

"He'll blame me," Jesus said, slumping on the chaise.

"Hmmph."

"But I think He should take responsibility and do something about it, instead of pointing one big finger at me. He set it in motion. But He's been gone a long time. He's out of touch."

"Yet understanding walks hand-in-hand wiz omniscience."

Jesus chuckled, knowing Freud sculpted his pseudo-profundities deep into the night. Sleep was optional in the City, and those who slept did so to dream, to collect ideas for what to do the next day. Without a purpose, eternity's charm wore thin. Freud, however, skipped sleep, knowing his dreams would inspire further, unwanted self-analysis, instead opting to spend the dark hours inventing phrases to impress his clients. On occasion he did. But Jesus wasn't in a good mood at present, so he ignored the doctor's nugget.

"Not on this path, Siggy. It's all—"

"Do not call me by name," Freud said. "You are risking transference."

Jesus rolled his eyes and returned to his reclining position. The stark white ceiling had the texture of the Himalayas from on high.

"Everyone thinks He's coming," Jesus said. "It's all joy and panic. Except Lou, of course. He's calm. Just scoops up the new manifestations and routes them to Hell. As if everything's normal. As if anyone really knows what He intended." He shrugged. "I guess someone has to hold it together. And the looks I'm getting. I haven't seen those since, well, for a long time."

Freud leaned forward. "Maybe we should talk about zat again."

Jesus didn't want to revisit the odd curiosity he'd encountered during his first days in the City, or when he'd understood his Father was not there to welcome him.

"Not today."

Freud tsk-tsked. "If you bring forz what is wizzin you—"

"Don't use my words against me," Jesus snapped, sitting up and scanning the walls. The doctor still refused to keep Jung on the shelves. Freud never changed the office design, in Jesus' estimation a significant character flaw. Were this *his* office, he'd scrape the ceiling, simplify the crown moldings, and swap the window treatments—maybe to Roman shades in a subtle coral pink, to complement the sky's unnaturally deep blue.

"I can see it all now," Jesus said, "if He *does* return. Grovel grovel, gush gush. 'Behold the conquering hero!' Every angel will throw a dinner party, one after the other, black tie here, beach theme there. They'll all be so very clever. Milk and honey and hard bread on rustic stoneware and the ever-popular silver platters. Angels *adore* textural contrasts with subtext. And then they'll wheel out the mutton." He rubbed his temples. "'O, bitter symbolism!' the hosts will sigh while they pour the wine, just so we know the meal is as heavy-handed as we suspect. And someone will ask me to do my Last Supper routine. 'Do it again! Do it again!'" He clapped his hands together. "And what will I do? I'll do it. And I'll go to every last party to avoid social scandal."

The expectation alone exhausted him. He collapsed to the chaise and gazed at the sky. He really hated those window treatments.

"I need help," Jesus said. "I'm begging you. He's on His way—"

"So you *do*—"

"—and nobody knows what He wants. It's all conjecture. I want you to give me real advice. What will it take?"

Freud didn't reply.

"I can arrange a lunch with Moses."

"It is not zat simple," Freud said, too quickly.

Jesus smiled. "He loved your book."

"You are lying."

"Okay," Jesus said. "He enjoyed the book. We all enjoyed it."

"In what manner?" Freud asked. He yearned to meet Moses, but upon reaching the City had been mortified to find his "historical novel" on the deliverer of the Jews so far off the mark it was the punch line to the City's most popular joke.

"He has it on his coffee table," Jesus said. "He reads from it whenever he's feeling down."

"So he can laugh?" Freud asked. "Many men," he said, returning to his analysis and by doing so declining the offer, "have issues wiz zeir fozzers, und—"

"There's no Oedipal slant to this."

Freud tsk-tsked under his breath. "Zere is a slant of zat sort to almost everyzing."

"That's your theory."

"You are in my office," Freud said. "You came to me."

Jesus said nothing.

"What is zee first word zat pops into your mind when I say 'fozzer'?"

"No. Not today."

"Fozzer," Freud repeated.

"I'm not—"

"Fozzer."

"*Mother.*"

Freud raised an eyebrow. "Bed."

Jesus sighed. "Danger."

"Knife."

"You're leading me."

"Knife."

"Blind."

Freud paused, glaring down his nose at Jesus. "You will never reconcile your issues if you insist upon mocking zee process."

"You're too obvious. And we've done word association a thousand times."

"Zen you should be better at it zan you are."

"Maybe the fault is in the process, not the patient."

Freud removed his glasses. "I understand precisely how your Fozzer will feel."

Jesus stood before his full-length mirror, giving himself a fifth once-over. Suit, impeccable. Shirt, subtle. Tie, perfect. A splendid and lavish dresser, he changed ensembles several times per day, turning in wardrobe expense reports for breathtaking sums. The accounting department's lower-level gray-winged angels accepted his reports with jealous reproach, though they attempted to conceal their reaction with classic angelic indifference.

A small draft came from the bedroom. Zubba and Wubba, the chubby, winged butlers of the house, drifted into the dressing room.

"No more than thirty minutes," Zubba said to Jesus. Zubba was the dominant of the pair, and less impressed by Jesus.

"What are you talking about?"

"The presentation," Wubba said. "Thirty minutes is the limit. Gabriel has a speaking engagement tonight."

Jesus checked his Patek Phillipe wristwatch. Not a watch, he thought. A *timepiece*. For years he'd had to cajole and beg Lucifer to forge a convincing Patek Phillipe reproduction, while enduring Lou's tedious monologues regarding the perils of introducing a watch where there was no time.

"How am I supposed to justify my proposal in thirty minutes?" he asked. "Technology only goes so far."

The putti shrugged as one.

"Do you need to justify it?" Wubba asked.

"More time won't help you fool them," Zubba said.

"It's a complex proposal," Jesus said. "I'm not trying to fool anyone."

Wubba laughed, soft red curls dancing in his wing draft. "You're quite transparent."

Jesus scowled at them. Chubby and happy, putti didn't deal well with displeasure directed their way. The slightest negativity drove them off and kept them fawning for days. But not this time. They remained, and the mirror seized his attention. He tried smiling, but it looked plastered on. Why was it so difficult? He smiled again, this time with solemnity. Success.

"Thank you for attending this out-of-session—" No good.

The putti fluttered while he considered a more formal approach.

"Welcome saints and angels, one and all—"

He beat back frustration.

"Too Dickensian?" Zubba asked.

"No matter what you say," Wubba said, "the angels will consult with Lou."

"Don't you think I know that? Heaven might crumble if Satan didn't call the shots."

They exchanged disapproving glances.

"Such outbursts," Wubba whispered.

"It's so ugly in a public figure," Zubba said.

Jesus waved them away. "Leave me."

They fluttered off. Jesus stared into the mirror. He needed to focus. He could do it. He could convince them.

It was his only chance.

The executive conference room on the tenth floor of Twelve Copernican Way was tasteful and modern, with mahogany floors and walls, a small collection of posthumous Rembrandts, and a wet bar stocking the finest Cognacs, wines, and root beers. Behind the bar long-stemmed wine glasses perched atop a mini-freezer, which housed six frosted mugs. A long conference table made from a solid slab of white onyx dominated the room, surrounded by elegant club chairs.

Jesus stood before the Executive Committee, laser pointer in hand, evaluating their fashion choices. The Archangel Gabriel, underdressed as usual in torn blue jeans and a white t-shirt, sat next to a gray and bushy Saint Peter, who wore the crimson robes of Catholicism. Beside Peter sat the Archangel Michael who, Jesus thought with no small satisfaction, had never been the dresser *he* was. Michael was a khaki addict, not caring that the style had permeated western civilization and now trod the earth shoulder-to-shoulder with turned-up polo collars among the legions of the fashion undead. Across the table, Martin Luther sat with Moses. The Reformer hadn't changed his cassock since his delusional battles with Lucifer, but Moses, kicking back in his chair, no longer wore a slave's duds. Moses was all pastels in silk and linen, a South Beach caricature with slicked hair and heavy rings.

An empty chair reserved for Muhammad waited next to Moses. Muhammad hadn't attended an Executive Committee meeting for a millennia, not since the committee had rejected the Prophet's interpretation of John 14:16. Maybe the time had come to make amends. He missed Muhammad and their nights in Paradise City's hookah lounges.

Jesus tried to ignore the absence of the committee's eighth and final member. He aimed the laser pointer's thin red beam at the screen and clicked its remote button. The new slide read *The Mandate*, followed by a numbered list of pertinent Bible quotations.

"You'll notice," Jesus said, "the clear progression of ideas." He met the eyes of Peter, Moses, and Martin Luther. "And I quote… one, 'fear God and keep His commandments, for this is the whole duty of man.'" He held up two fingers. "Two, 'for God so loved the world, that He gave His only Son, that whoever believes in Him should not perish but have eternal life.'"

Jesus' gaze swept past the archangels, to avoid their blank expressions. "Three, 'go therefore and make disciples of all nations, baptizing them in the name of the Father and of the Son and of the Holy Spirit, teaching them to observe all that I have commanded you.'" Jesus underlined the last few words with the thin red beam. "By teaching them to observe what He commanded. This is a clear mandate."

Michael shifted in his chair, crossed his arms, and sighed.

Jesus set his jaw and faced the screen. "And of course, I said, 'I am the way, and the truth, and the life. No one comes to the Father except through me.'"

"While offering the virtues of my candidacy throughout the City," Gabriel said in his distinctive stage whisper, "I have reaped the glories of third-party affirmation, yet rued the pitfalls of self-aggrandizement."

"Gabe," Jesus said, "you can't throw a stone at the Bible and not hit something I said. Would you have me pretend His will and I aren't inextricable?"

Gabriel and Michael exchanged a look Jesus didn't like. He calmed himself and clicked to the next slide, a collage of kings, generals, and industrial titans titled *The Leadership Effect*.

"I believe we can all agree," Jesus said, "the success or failure of an enterprise depends upon the quality of leadership."

"Napoleon isn't the best example," Michael said, not bothering to point at the little corporal's familiar face on the screen.

"Though he would never admit it," Moses said, twisting one of his ornate rings.

"Still, he knows," Gabriel said. "Truth, like darkness, visits all."

"Apparently not," Michael said, and winked at Gabriel.

"Is there disagreement with my premise?" Jesus asked, louder than necessary.

The archangels offered indulgent smiles.

"Without strong, present leadership, faith has eroded." Jesus flipped open a spiral-bound booklet resting on the conference table. "If you turn to appendix 39-B of my proposal, you'll notice the individual faith index has fallen steadily since Marty's little stunt."

Martin Luther muttered to himself.

"A leading theory of this phenomenon," Jesus said, "is the downturn in weekly church attendance has been, in essence, a… shaking out… per se, pointing to the possibility earlier statistical models were diluted, perhaps due to peer and social pressure to attend, the 'question-not' mentality of the Dark Ages, or from mid-millennial fear factors such as the Inquisition."

"There were other forces," Michael said.

"Are you referring to the Age of Reason?" Gabriel asked.

"I am."

Gabriel knitted his brow. "The era *does* offer a compendium of thorny arguments."

"Hypocrites," Luther mumbled, prompting a grin from Michael that Jesus deemed stagy.

"I agree, Marty," Jesus said, changing the screen to a slide titled *Enlightenment?* "But the permeation of science and so-called 'humanism' have played roles in the downturn of most faith-relevant data."

"Why do you suppose that is?" Michael asked.

Jesus bristled. That was the sort of question their eighth member would have asked, had the Dark Angel deigned to bless them with his presence.

"Perhaps," Gabriel said, his apologetic tone ringing false to Jesus, "because to literally interpret what is written leads to certain awkward conflicts with physical facts." He winced. "It pains me, yes, but so it is."

Jesus rolled his eyes at the archangels' eternal good cop-bad cop routine. The only variation was who assumed which role. It was tiresome, predictable. And now he could no longer ignore Lucifer's absence. The urgency of Jesus' email had been clear:

TO: Executive Committee (peter@saints.hev, gabriel@
angels.cty, michael@angels.cty, moses@char.bib, m.luther@exec.hev,
bigbadlou@rehab.hel, muhammad72@exec.par)
FROM: j.christ@exec.hev
SUBJ: Urgent – His possible return

Critical meeting tomorrow. Time-sensitive proposal. Attendance
mandatory. Four o'clock.

    JC

Was Jesus surprised Lucifer had skipped the meeting? Not in the
least, because it was crucial to *him*. The more importance Jesus placed
on an issue, the less Lucifer seemed motivated to act in its favor. If
not for Lucifer's irritating near-omniscience, Jesus would have applied
reverse psychology to everything requiring a unanimous committee
vote. But that would encourage Lucifer to unknown heights of political deception. How long had Jesus lobbied for free distribution of
scripture, to counter the City's near-total secularism? Four centuries?
Five? Whereas Lucifer had railroaded the passage of H-1455.87—
funding the conversion of Hell to a rehabilitation center—through
both Houses, Angels and Saints, without a single dissension, courtesy
of Jesus' naïve faith that Lucifer would recognize the quid pro quo
nature of his support. Later, when Jesus prodded him to return the
favor on the scripture initiative, Lucifer had spread his palms in infuriating mockery of Jesus' crucifixion pose. "I'm sorry," he'd said. "I didn't
realize your endorsement was political. I thought you'd finally seen the
light. So to speak."
    "Where is he?" Jesus asked Michael.
    "Who?"
    Jesus glared at the archangel.
    "Satan," Martin Luther hissed.
    Peter nodded while Moses observed.
    "Something came up," Michael said.
    "He does not wish to offend," Gabriel said.
    Martin Luther scoffed and Moses twisted his thumb ring.

Jesus gathered himself, beating down his annoyance. He knew Lucifer intended to ponder his proposal. Below his instinctive sense of style, his smooth voice, and lightning wit, Lucifer liked to consider things, a chess grandmaster plotting his game twelve moves in advance. But Jesus wanted a decision *now*. He wanted an immediate vote after his presentation, dispensing with reflection and theosophical ponderings, while the committee was high on messianic nostalgia. Lucifer's absence assured a no-vote. Meanwhile His possible return crept closer, the inevitability of which Jesus sensed like a migratory bird sensed winter's first whisper. Dreams or not, the day was coming and something had to be done.

"But he asked," Michael said, "that you make your proposal and we table the vote for a few days."

The nerve, Jesus thought, the *nerve*. To dictate to *him*, the *Son of God!* What allowed Lucifer such power? There had been moments he'd wished his Father would come back and pry off the suffocating grip of Lucifer's political machine. Lucifer's will determined the House of Angels' votes, because the angels believed Lucifer was of the same stuff as God—stardust and consciousness and gravity, or some such hyperbole. Lucifer's abilities eluded other angels. His origin and consistent nature through the ages was more akin to God's, whereas angels were beings of shifting guises: then gods of a lesser order, now guardians and superlative vocalists.

For millennia, angels battled over God's intentions, and when Jesus, the saints, and various religious figures became numerous enough to attain political relevance, the interpretation of God's desires (naked speculation, were Jesus to be honest with himself) polarized the City. The House of Saints voted as one to promote religion in the City, but the City's political system (devised by Lucifer, of course) gave Jesus and the saints half the voting power of the House of Angels, who always voted with Lucifer. Lucifer rebelled against all things mystic, including religion, so any proposal at odds with reason was doomed.

But when an issue involved only an Executive Committee member, a majority vote by the committee was enough to approve the measure. Jesus assumed Lucifer had inserted the loophole to make things interesting, and to better evaluate those on the committee. Jesus' plan was such a proposal.

He read the eyes upon him. Michael and Gabriel would listen, ask eviscerating questions, and object to everything he said. They'd maintain antagonistic neutrality so their votes appeared autonomous, independent of Lucifer's guidance, as sometimes Jesus thought they believed. Peter would campaign hard for the proposal and supply the necessary scriptural backup. Martin Luther could swing either way. As a rule he tiptoed around Jesus because he revered him, but his hatred and fear of Lucifer impelled him to take whatever side Lucifer did not. Lucifer's absence saved the committee from enduring the tedious sub-sonic barbs Marty directed at the Dark Angel every few minutes, but also meant he'd aim his vitriol at Peter, which thrust the first protes-tant into his wearisome "wait for God" position, torn between voting against an out-of-sight Lucifer or an in-his-face Saint Peter. There hadn't been a unanimous vote since Marty joined the executive com-mittee, but Jesus planned to strong-arm him if he was the only "nay." Moses would sit silent until the conversation's end, expecting what he said to carry decisive weight, like a righteous mafia don. Moses would take the underdog's side and level the argument, tipping the scales back to the middle, except in extraordinary circumstances such as this, when Jesus believed he could steamroll Moses' vote.

Jesus understood his predicament. The fear and anxiety necessary to drive a majority vote was impossible without Lucifer in his court. All the passion and rhetoric and imploring were pointless. Why had he called this meeting? Had he believed Lucifer would attend? His position was clear. To move forward on his proposal the only vote he needed was Lucifer's. A conversation between man and angel was nec-essary, if you could define either of them in such terms.

"Josh," Gabriel said, glancing at his pocket watch, "I have an engage-ment in twenty minutes. Might you—?"

Jesus knew it was pointless to present to an executive committee sans Lucifer. However, he could view it as a test audience, a warm-up for the real presentation. Jesus clicked the remote. Bar graphs and pie charts filled the screen, the slide's heading big and bold: *The Second Coming: A Statistical Projection.*

VIA VIRGIN

Jesus marched along the main boulevard's sparkling surface, trying to take in the City as if it hadn't evolved around him, as if he were seeing it for the first time.

Glowing white buildings rose on both sides in a flowing architectural fusion of Paris and Florence and New York. There were no cars in the City, no vehicles of any kind and no engines. Every district was accessible by foot or flight. There was no trash, no pollution. And though many of humanity's inventions were available, Lucifer and his minions kept the City clear of weapons or tools suited for violence. Voices and song and music filled the City, birds chirped and dogs barked. Except for now. From today until the election, campaign broadcasts would inundate the City, accessible or ignorable with nothing more than a thought, courtesy of Lucifer's telepathic broadcasting technology. If you wanted to tune in, you could, and if you wanted to tune out, a simple decision was all it took. Jesus ignored Gabriel's speech.

Election season.

Perversely, the House of Angels earned vast wealth for Lucifer's earthly activities via sports betting. Every year, the angels elected a new member to the four-member Finance Committee. The election followed an always-bitter campaign season, during which the reputations of all candidates were sullied beyond recovery. Candidates debated philosophical and theological issues of no practical importance, and fabricated opponents' corrupt and debauched pasts. In years involving the Olympics or World Cup, the campaigns were horrific, with vicious allegations of bribery and blackmailing a matter of routine—much like any given Tuesday at world soccer headquarters. But once elected, Lucifer whisked the victorious angel to Las Vegas to spend the next four years in high style. The Vegas angels lived like mortal kings in private luxury penthouses with unlimited expense accounts, reservations at the best restaurants, and tickets to all shows and major sporting events. Their sole responsibility? Placing bets based on tips from Lucifer, who utilized his predictive ability to extrapolate *almost* infallible win-loss projections.

He heard a soft *whoosh* overhead. A trio of citizens flew low, enjoying the unfamiliar thrill of self-propelled flight. Upon arrival, new citizens tended to fly everywhere, but the novelty wore off and most returned to the ground. Still, year after year, "flying" ranked number one in the Abilities & Amenities section of the City's satisfaction survey, followed by "guilt-free sex" and "Shadrach's Key lime pie."

To Jesus' annoyance, those who attained self-awareness and transitioned from Hell into the City had varying degrees of taste and attractiveness. Neither fame nor infamy guaranteed class or good looks. It wasn't who you were. It was the world's perception of you. So, Jesus mused, perception *was* everything. Were *he* guarding eternity's velvet rope, admission would depend upon more than a critical mass of notoriety.

He walked down a quiet residential street. A couple relaxed on a blanket, talking by candlelight, drinking a bottle of cabernet as they ate Gouda cheese and water table crackers. He didn't recognize them. He assumed, like the fly-bys, they were recent arrivals.

The earth's rising population and global interconnectedness were only half of the City's soaring population problem. The other half was Lucifer's inability to adjust the manifestation threshold, a theoretical factor the Dark Angel's equations predicted but experimentation could not confirm nor manipulate. Alive or dead, hero or villain, person or plant or mineral or idea, it mattered not. If something held enough of the world's collective mindshare, he or she or it manifested. Then it was *wait and see*. Yet he had to admit Lucifer did a superlative job at managing the transitions, with the clear exception of Lou's penchant for allowing fictional characters and mythological creatures more time to gain self-awareness.

Along another street were cafés and restaurants closed for the evening, their tables and chairs gone from the sidewalk and stacked behind dark windows. Jesus feared his Father, upon His return, would head for the Garden, the last place Jesus wanted Him to visit. The Garden district had evolved, and would convey to God the world's current state. Would He embrace the collective result of humanity's desires? Lucifer said "yes," but the prospect of his absent Father's disappointment made a reasoned calculation impossible. Had God sent the world His only son to stabilize and ritualize humanity, to wrap their lives in worship and mystery and hope? Or were they supposed to use their minds? Jesus shivered in the mild air.

He rounded a corner and saw the crowd. Beings of all ages and sizes and races and origins danced and sang, speaking in countless languages with complete understanding. Babel inverted. They partied at an immortal tempo, a pace possible only in the absence of guilt and fear. Or, Jesus proposed with no small degree of cynicism, in the presence of vacuous, vice-riddled pasts.

In the Garden of Eden nightlife district, eight streets branched off from a central hub, the Circle, home to a tremendous tree, the Tree of Knowledge, that dropped a continuous and infinite supply of Red Delicious and Granny Smith apples to outstretched hands below. The Garden burst with bars, restaurants, coffee shops, comedy clubs, and nightclubs. It was the City's pounding heart, the center of enjoyment and enrichment for all, a utopic Bohemian Bacchanalia. Once a garden of sorts, its transformation declared humanity's new vision of paradise.

Jesus chose Via Virgin and walked into Pope, a comedy club just off the Circle. A comedian joked, "And Adam says to God... 'What can I get for a rib?'"

The crowd laughed at the tired joke, and Jesus' mood sank further. The City's beings loved their entertainment.

Though Hell had put an end to delusions of biblical grandeur, some pre-Hell City dwellers had manifested and managed self-awareness on their own. By popular demand, the House of Saints sponsored an annual weeklong adventure tour through Tanakh and Messiania, dubbed BibliCon, complete with period accommodations and guaranteed sightings of Genesis characters. Enoch and Methuselah were tour staples, and on occasion tourists would catch a glimpse of Seth or Zillah. It smacked of an earthbound African safari, and live feeds were televised across the City. Jesus always caught the end-of-week highlight show.

As all roads lead to Rome, all thoughts of BibliCon led to Adam, a source of consistent annoyance to Jesus for myriad reasons, particularly his habit of blaming others for his mistakes. Every few months, Lucifer offered to have his minions storm Adam's Tanakh compound and whisk him to Hell for a long-form chat. He argued it would serve both practical and symbolic purposes, while showcasing Hell's rehabilitative potential. A reformed, responsible Adam, an Adam cured of his bitter, Tourette's-like, top-of-his-lungs "WHERE'S MY APPLE PIE?" every time Eve had the misfortune of walking into the same restaurant, an Adam who no longer sauntered naked around the Garden, singing his obscene version of *Silent Night* as an insolent attempt at reverse psychology, might prove beneficial to the City. But Jesus didn't like the precedent of a snatch-and-grab sortie within the City, and, in a rare example of accord, both Houses supported him, though he suspected they were simply unwilling to sacrifice such rich entertainment.

Jesus ducked out of Pope and into Iowa, a concert hall featuring live music. Buddy Holly gyrated on stage, belting out *Peggy Sue*. Jimi Hendrix sat in, plucking on something. Was that a dutar? The crowd danced and sang along. Some faces were familiar to Jesus, but he was bad with names and not in the mood for conversation so he chose not to wave. From the opposite perspective, every being in the crowd recognized Jesus, but they left him alone, like Los Angeles natives pretending to ignore the movie star at the next table.

After Iowa, Jesus walked to Resurrection, a popular nightspot with a throbbing bass beat, multiple rooms, and dusk-to-dawn dancing. Jesus moved from room to room, the music fading from one style to another as he passed through the doors. Salsa ruled the first room. Couples tangoed in the next. In the third room electronic dance music held sway. Another space offered lessons for ancient ritual dances. A legendary Broadway musical's major characters hung around the exit door. Were they together by choice or did they walk the City conjoined? That was a question for Lucifer. Manifestation and self-awareness details eluded Jesus.

He returned to the Circle at a brisk clip. Along the street, the famous and infamous laughed and reveled beneath an indigo sky. He kept his expression neutral, relaxed.

Jesus snatched an apple from mid-air and stopped beneath the Tree of Knowledge, near the caramel apple cart. He whispered, "Zubba."

Soon the putto hovered at his side, four feet above the ground, little pearlescent wings flapping with hurried ease.

"Set up a meeting," Jesus said, and bit into the apple.

Jesus lived in a massive limestone villa at Number Two, Divine Circle. The villa surrounded a lush courtyard of tropical plants, tinkling bamboo, and moss-painted banyan trees. Pandas and white-tailed deer roamed, while boisterous toads and carpenter frogs harmonized around a crystalline pond spackled with lily pads.

Through the morning room's wide-open French doors, Jesus sat at the breakfast table, a nice little cherry wood number with square legs and a distressed finish, which matched his emotional state. For the first millennia since his manifestation, Jesus had rationalized Lucifer's diligent attempts to derail the monotheistic religions as acts of jealousy and contempt. But beginning with the Italian Renaissance, Jesus had endured fits of concern over God's intention for him. He had never seen his Father face-to-face, and knew of Him solely through scripture and Lucifer. But Lucifer maintained there was no actual relation and referred to God as Jesus' "biblical" Father, making any such conversation a frustrating series of stops and starts, clarifications, corrections, and admonishments. Lucifer claimed God was a being of reason and experiment, philosophy and harmony. An evolved being, though "being" was a term of convenience. An evolved "manifestation" was more accurate. While Lucifer fixated on the ontology of himself and God, postulating and theorizing and making notes while he dipped soft cinnamon cookies into thick hot chocolate, Jesus found comfort in rudimentary, gut-level answers to complex existential uncertainties. Lucifer's assertions that God despised religion and that worship was neither desired nor acceptable had exacted a toll on Jesus' confidence. What would his bib… Jesus stopped himself. What would his Father think of the world? Lucifer insisted God detested the pious praising Him for their ignorance and hypocrisy and bloodlust. If Lucifer was right, He wouldn't appreciate the Middle East's overarching fanaticism and holy wars. The fault for that insanity lay at Muhammad's feet, Jesus thought with brief comfort, before admitting to himself it was possible his followers wielded the bloodier swords.

Jesus sank in his chair, hiding his nose in *The Daily Omniscient*. Zubba set a glass of orange juice before him and hovered, reading over Jesus' shoulder, his fluttering wings producing an all-too-perceptible shifting of the newspaper's thin pages.

"Are you done with *Bible Beat* yet?" Zubba asked.

"No."

Zubba frowned. "You're not even reading it."

"You always crumple the edges," Jesus said. "It's my paper. You'll have to wait."

Jesus turned to the *Bible Beat* section while telltale hints of frying bacon wafted through the room. *Bible Beat* spotlighted Bible characters. Like BibliCon, it was popular. Today, *Bible Beat* reported Cane and Abel were at it again. Abel refused to accept his place in things and stalked Cane, baiting him during aromatherapy, mocking him at yoga class. It was farcical, and thus fodder for *Bible Beat*.

"Did you speak to him?" Jesus asked.

"Mm-hmmm… and Lou had an interesting idea."

"What's that?"

"He suggested we arrange a Cane versus Abel cage match in Tanakh."

"Cane's a pacifist."

Zubba shrugged and said, "As the under card."

Jesus eyed Zubba. "What's the title bout?"

"We put together an intriguing pairing, at a renovated yet peri od-accurate location."

"Not interested," Jesus said, unwilling to play the pawn in another of Lucifer's mockeries. Witness the City's Easter parade, held for the first and last time three centuries ago, in which he'd found himself trailing Pontius Pilate's float. The crowd had booed the bastard (despite their tendency toward atheism, the famous and infamous have *some* biblical knowledge) but it didn't make up for having to drag that damn crucifix twenty-six city blocks.

"You'd get a shot at Judas," Zubba whispered.

"In the depths of your immortal soul," Jesus said, "do you truly feel you would glorify the Lord with a night of winner-takes-all grudge matches? And what makes you think I harbor the necessary resentment to kick Iscariot's ass?"

Zubba shrugged while Wubba delivered breakfast: Belgian waffles with melted butter and Vermont pure maple syrup. Wubba zipped away as fast as he'd come.

"What did he say?" Jesus asked, and took several quick bites.

Zubba grinned big, his wings flapping double-time like a portly hummingbird. "He will meet with you tomorrow evening."

"Where?"

"In the threshold bar, at the Bellag—"

Jesus interrupted Zubba with a withering glance. Gone the momentary waffle high. Over the centuries Lucifer had built dozens of "threshold" locations in his favorite places on earth. By mimicking Lucifer's ability to harness matter, the threshold sites enabled entities such as Jesus to exist and interact on earth for a few hours without requiring Lucifer's presence to "hold them together." The Bellagio hotel in Las Vegas was one such place. In the syrup's smooth surface he envisioned the threshold bar adjacent to Bellagio's main casino. Flashing lights, smoke, grating music, incessant bells, ludicrous fashion choices. The angels loved it. He did not. Sure, they'd cleaned up Vegas during the lowest-common-denominator family-friendly push, but still... Jesus pictured himself strolling down The Strip, fresh from the outdoor water ballet, pondering the possibility the modern world might not be such a bad place, and God might not be furious with him. And right about then, between Bellagio and Caesar's Palace, a black-clad street reverend, who minutes before had preached virtue and tolerance, would cast the first stone of a turf war by shoving a young, aggressive entrepreneur handing out ad cards for Peaches Cream, who promised salvation in the heavenly embrace of her divine double-D's.

"Not there," Jesus said.

"Lou thinks Las Vegas is the consummate introduction to the world you plan on saving yet again."

"How does he—" Jesus gave up. Of course Lucifer anticipated his plan. "I don't need an introduction," he said. "I need a mandate."

"The city presents a rich symbolic backdrop for your first appearance on earth in centuries," Zubba said.

Jesus snatched a strip of bacon. "Somewhere else. No thresholds. Not Miami. Not Bangkok. I won't set foot in Amsterdam or Rio or Los Angeles. And I'd rather not waste time with his petty attempts to gain advantage."

"You've misunderstood," Zubba said. "He's reserved a table at Chamburg. It's a burger-champagne fusion pub with only eight tables nightly."

"I'm certain it's as ridiculous as it sounds," Jesus said, finishing his waffle.

"It's set beneath a transparent dome within a pink champagne pool."

Jesus dropped the paper on the table. "Somewhere else."

FALSE PROPHET

By the stone hearth in a small, crowded pub in Edinburgh, Jesus sat with an exceptional-looking man wearing black leather pants despite an unseasonably hot Scottish summer. This was Lucifer, smoldering and magnetic, terrifying and irresistible. Auburn-haired women admired him through the thick, stagnant cigarette haze, which rivaled the worst sulfur smog during Hell's days of yore. Empty plates of pub food and spent pints of beer rested on the table between Jesus and Lucifer, and three hounds of varying colors lazed at their feet, lifting an ear or an eyelid to sudden laughter or drunk singing.

"You can't be serious," Jesus said.

Lucifer's expression confirmed he was, indeed, serious.

"But what if—"

Lucifer smiled.

"I need time to acclimate," Jesus said. "What if there's an accident? I can't go down again. People have invested their lives in me for two thousand years."

"The odds are against it, Josh," Lucifer said. "And if there were an accident, someone would discover a long-lost text prophesizing your second demise. Or suppress it all. You've nothing to worry about. And it's been seventeen hundred years, not two thousand. You were floundering before Constantine."

"Whatever." Jesus cleared his throat and whispered, "But if I *die again*, what's going to happen to Christianity?"

Lucifer's eyes showed indifference.

"You'd love that, wouldn't you," Jesus said, before touching his temple with one finger. "I'm too ingrained to snuff out so easily."

"I'm sure you're right," Lucifer said.

Jesus' face grew red, and he gripped the arms of his chair as if they alone held him to the earth. With great effort, he willed himself to relax and sat back in the chair. "I won't do it."

"That's probably best," Lucifer said, signaling for another pint. "They won't believe who you are, anyway. You'd need me for that, too."

Jesus scowled. Lucifer never ceased to annoy him. And much of it was style envy. Lucifer always looked cooler than he did, no matter the season or situation. It was infuriating.

"You knew He'd show up sooner or later," Lucifer said.

"Sure," Jesus said. "The quick and the dead and all that."

"Josh, we're both aware you didn't say that."

Jesus sighed. "Sometimes it all blurs together. If He would have been more specific, if He would have provided me with precise wording, I wouldn't be in this position."

"He works in mysterious ways."

"Don't you dare mock me. Not now."

Lucifer laughed, and a hound raised a heavy eyelid. "Okay. How about this? He didn't provide the wording, either. So it isn't His fault."

"Well it's not mine."

"Yes. You were but a puppet."

Jesus glared at him. "Why can't you just help me?"

"I've tried to, but really, I don't see the tragedy of it all. When He arrives, talk to Him. All shall become clear."

"But what if it's too late?"

"For what?"

"To make them all believe."

"Josh," Lucifer said, "God doesn't want that."

"You can't possibly know what He wants."

Lucifer's steady gaze told Jesus the Dark Angel could know, and did.

Jesus shifted his strategy to pleading. "Lou, I need this. If we go with my plan, at least—"

"Your plan is full of holes, Josh."

"Name one."

"You can't descend from heaven."

"You did. Well, you fell. To put it kindly."

"I didn't," Lucifer said. "And you know it."

Jesus slumped in his chair. "But you could."

"The City isn't heaven, and it's not a physical place," Lucifer said. "Conforming to the accepted mythology would require a descent of nine days, from a heaven that doesn't exist. Through space."

"So?"

"You can't survive in space. To accomplish what you're suggesting, you'd have to come back as a man, biological and mortal."

"Because *you* won't help me." Jesus shifted in his chair and pressed his hand to his chest. "Why can't I return like this?" He pointed at the pub's heavy wooden front door. "Just walk right out."

"Because I'm holding you together right now," Lucifer said. "You're providing the function, but I'm maintaining the form. Without me, you can't exist indefinitely on this existential plane."

"Mom can do it."

"It took her centuries to learn," Lucifer said. "Your timeline is more immediate."

The pub's door opened and closed.

"This is your idea, not mine." Lucifer downed what remained of his pint. "No one is going to take your word for who you say you are. You'll have to prove it. They'll demand biological tests, which won't work unless—"

"I'm biological," Jesus grumbled.

Lucifer spread his hands with the tiniest degree of sympathy for the biblical Son of God. "Blood and bone, Josh. It's the only way I'll help."

"But you'll help," Jesus said, brightening.

Lucifer made a gesture that committed to nothing.

Jesus leaned forward. "Lou. Listen to me. I'm worshipped here. I'm *The Man*. A worldwide belief system is built on me. But my place is tenuous in heaven."

Firelight reflected off the empty pint glasses. Lucifer disguised his amusement, though in truth he was not enjoying Jesus' quick sprint toward panic. "It's not heaven," he said. "We don't know what it is."

"It's close enough. Can we please skip the usual argument?"

Lucifer glanced across the bar, through the haze.

"All I have is my influence down here," Jesus said, gripping Lucifer's arm, "because when He gets back I'll be nothing up there. So this is where I have to make my stand. It's imperative I return in glory and righteous judgment and defeat the false prophet."

"That's me, right?"

"Of course you!"

Lucifer laughed and sat back. "No."

Jesus checked in both directions. "What difference does it make to you?"

"Maybe I'm not being painfully clear," Lucifer said, tapping the rim of his glass. "If I help you, and you reveal yourself as you intend, it won't summon the innocents to heaven, but it will unleash something like the ten plagues upon the world."

"I doubt that."

"Your pride knows no bounds," Lucifer said.

"And your intellectual arrogance blinds you to the beauty of creation."

Lucifer took a deep breath, and Jesus mimicked him.

"Josh, you're asking me to sacrifice what I know for what you believe, so if you want your second coming, we do it my way. End of discussion." Lucifer smiled. "You'll be my first."

Jesus half-listened, face blank, watching the smallest dog's twitching ear. Lucifer's revision to the plan was too far removed from how Jesus had envisioned his return to earth to be anything but a disingenuous roadblock.

"Day after day," Lucifer said, "I take inexplicable phenomena in immeasurable states with uncertain resolutions and shepherd them to self-awareness, while you're out on the golf course, tormenting yourself over whether to use a nine iron or a wedge. But I'm the bad guy, and you're worshipped by billions."

"Poor, poor Lou," Jesus said. "The vast unwashed don't appreciate him."

Lucifer looked off.

"You love it," Jesus said, and put up a pair of air quotes. "It's *science*."

"You wouldn't be here without my science. Not like this."

"You've said I was the easiest. I could have done it myself. You did."

"The easiest *man*," Lucifer said. So many years, so many similar discussions. "There's a big difference between a man and an idea. Only animals are easier than people. People agree on what an ostrich is."

"Cute," Jesus said, stifling a smile. "A veiled analogy from evil incarnate."

Lucifer rolled his eyes. "Evil is a concept, not an individual or entity."

"Without the concept, you wouldn't exist."

"Josh," Lucifer said with genuine surprise, "you've been paying attention."

"Yeah, touché touché," Jesus said. "But I fail to understand why you care. You have a role to play here, an essence to maintain. You can do whatever you want. Me coming back *helps* you. We can tussle in a grand battle for souls. Good versus evil. Darkness against the light. It might be fun."

"Light is the presence of all colors," Lucifer said. "Illumination. Truth. Reality."

The barmaid delivered two more pints as Jesus slumped in his chair. "I reject your insinuation."

"Anyway, you should leave the abstract battles to me. Yours are more tangible."

"Yeah," Jesus said, "I heard about your little idea."

"You shoot the evil eye at Judas every time you run into him. It might do you some good to kick his ass. Or vice versa." Lucifer leaned forward, the fire crackling. "I'm tired of the façade."

"Which one?"

"All of them," Lucifer said. "Change is coming, Josh."

The fire roared, the space between them hot and electric. Glass broke, and sharp laughter cracked through the bar. The red hound mumbled in his sleep while Jesus stared into space. Maybe he could circumvent Lucifer, get Albert and Nikola on his side, commandeer the technology—

"It won't work, Josh."

"I don't know what you're talking about," Jesus said. "And vice versa, regarding my thoughts. By your own admission, your predictive ability, aka *limited omniscience*, does not extend to mindreading."

"But I know *how* you think," Lucifer said.

Jesus studied his beer's rising bubbles.

"I'll put together the specifics, and you'll put it before the committee," Lucifer said with far too much satisfaction for Jesus' taste. "And lo, it shall come to pass."

The executive committee had gathered for an emergency session. A brilliant silver tray supporting a small mountain of frosted sugar cookies rested on the long conference table. Jesus sat brooding, a rolled parchment with a broken seal before him.

The room was in an uproar.

"Preposterous," Martin Luther said. "We can't allow it. It's—"

Gabriel cut him off. "Thus endeth the charade."

"Charade?" Martin Luther shouted. "And you think it's appropriate the Christ risk himself, like a—"

"A man?" Michael asked, chuckling and selecting a cookie.

"It's obscene," Martin Luther said, and spat at the floor. "And if we were considering it, which I *pray we're not*, we'd have to take into account that men, mortal men, have *urges*. If the Christ..." He closed his eyes, head swaying, and found the words. "If he died, or if, worse, if he, you know what I'm referring to, for all to see, it would be too much for the living."

"Martin—"

"Their devastation would be too much to bear," Luther said, ignoring Gabriel, who exchanged glances with Michael. "All their mortal lives they've known our Lord Jesus Christ as pure, unsullied, a true God—"

"To be fair," Gabriel said, cutting off Luther, "their certainty is misplaced, their assumptions wrong. Manifestations who attain self-awareness and reach the City embrace Lucifer's role on our plane of existence."

"I think we can all agree," Michael said, setting down his pencil, "Lucifer is not the enemy. Would any of us exist without him?"

Jesus raised his index finger while Martin Luther ground his manifested teeth.

"In so many ways he is our shepherd," Gabriel said.

"The Evil Incarnate role never fit him," said Michael. "He's got too much *joi de vivre*."

"*Joi de* what?" Martin Luther shouted, face crimson. He pointed at the archangel. "It's sacrilege, that's what it is. If God were here—"

"He would do nothing," said a voice, startling Martin Luther. All eyes went to a chair next to Jesus where Lucifer shimmered. He crossed his legs and steepled his fingers as he gained visual solidity, acknowledging each committee member in turn, before grinning at Martin Luther. "Hallo, Marty."

The reformer's eyes narrowed as Lucifer said, "There seems to be disagreement with the plan."

"Mostly," Gabriel whispered with a dramatic nod in Martin Luther's direction, "from a single quarter."

Moses fiddled with one ornate ring and reached for a cookie. He broke it in half to indicate his vote was far from committed either way, and, without a compelling argument and a sign from on high, unanimity would prove elusive.

"When guessing God's intent," Lucifer said, "consider I alone was manifested in much the same way He was. I grasp the logic and reason governing the mechanics of existence. I interact with Him. We are friends."

"Heresy," Martin Luther hissed.

"By your troubled, intentionally ignorant standards, I suppose it is. But true, nonetheless." Lucifer studied the reformer. "Marty, what is your concern?"

"You know exactly what it is."

"Are you so worried for Josh's safety that you would prefer he not return and glorify himself for all humanity?" Lucifer smiled. "Or is it concern about something else? Something more… instinctive."

Martin Luther struggled to remain still.

"You must admit," Saint Peter said to Lucifer, "were Josh to—"

"It would in no way compromise his stature."

Martin Luther exploded. "The Son of God does not *do that!*"

"Josh," Lucifer said, "what does the biblical Son of God not do?"

"Do not answer that," Martin Luther snarled at Jesus, surprising everyone.

"And why not?" Lucifer asked. "Are you under the impression Josh is untouched?"

Saint Peter, Moses, and Martin Luther turned incredulous faces to Jesus, who focused his heated gaze on Lucifer.

"Why would you assume celibacy," Lucifer asked Martin Luther, "for a man undocumented during his sexual prime?"

"How can you claim to know the will of God, Devil?"

Lucifer looked to God's biblical son. "Josh?"

Jesus sank in his chair. "It's not relevant," he mumbled.

Lucifer grinned while the others gasped, their expressions varying degrees of shock and indignation. Moses took another cookie, but this time failed to break it into perfect halves.

"To continue to exist, a species and its ideas must adapt to reality," Lucifer said. "Evolution is not confined to the biological and cosmo-logical. A reasoning species' interpretation of reality must progress toward accuracy if it is to survive. Existence, as can be seen in any tree, system, or star, is pure reason." He set his gaze on Jesus. "Religion sep-arates humanity from reason."

"Blasphemy," Martin Luther muttered.

Lucifer began to shimmer. "Always a pleasure, Marty." Before van-ishing he said, "Let me know what you decide, Josh."

Stress squeezed his face like a lime. Jesus had read the parchment at least forty times before its plain words had squirmed through countless layers of denial, and the implications had taken their toll on his psyche, his hair, and his fashion compass. He'd walked from the villa dazed and disheveled, arriving in Freud's reception area before realizing he'd worn a vintage jacket with skinny pants, a dilettantish mistake, and risked running into those unforgiving know-it-alls at *The Word*, who would plaster Friday's society page with unflattering photos of Jesus Christ, formerly of "The City's Ten Best Dressed" list.

He recalled hearing sound from Sigmund's direction. "What did you say?"

"How do you feel about returning as a man?" Freud asked, sipping a steaming cup of black coffee, its buttery-bitter scent bathing the room in the flavor of long-ago Vienna.

"My Father didn't have to defile Himself," Jesus said. "He just set fire to a bush and there He was. Why me?"

"From what you have said, it seems to be zee way it was written. So to speak."

"Yeah, but that's because of certain assumptions I'm making, that all of us make. That Lou is on a level parallel to my Father. That they were both manifested in the same way." He sat up with sudden passion. "But what if they aren't? What if this is all a scam Lou and the angels have been selling us since my Father left? What if my Father comes back, roars in almighty anger, and smites Lou like a bug, like a… yeah. Like an *unholy* bug. What then?"

"How would you feel about zat?"

"I'd… which part?"

"Zee bug part."

"I'd feel vindicated."

Freud clucked his tongue. "Do you see yourself as vindictive?"

"I know I shouldn't," Jesus said. "It doesn't jive with my past. My written past, that is. But I go back and forth. I think I've really changed. Grown, I mean." His face clouded. "Since I left Jerusalem."

"Do you zink," Freud asked with greater care than usual, "Lucifer and zee angels are lying about Lucifer's place in zee order of zings?"

"I wouldn't say lying, per se. Lying is a definitive term. Not being entirely truthful would strike the more diplomatic note. But…" Jesus trailed off, his small confidence now gone. He slumped into the couch. "No."

"Zen if you zink he is telling zee truth, maybe zee question is not whezzer or not it is going to happen, but why does it bozzer you so?"

"Because if it's true, what about the other things Lou says, about my history? I *enjoy* being Jesus Christ," he said, slapping his palm against the cushion. "*The* Jesus Christ. But now everything's changing. If my Father doesn't rule absolute over the heavens and the earth, or if He's, if He's not, if Lou's not lying—" Jesus sat up again. "How can I be sure?" he asked. "I know *exactly* how Abraham felt."

"He works in mysterious ways."

"So help me, if I hear that one more time I'll let Paradise City secede."

"Do you possess zat sort of power?"

"I'm not sure how it all interacts," Jesus said. "I just know it's getting rough in the PC ever since the uptick in famous Muslims. Or, rather, *infamous* Muslims. It's created a real divide over there. Mo doesn't like to share the, uh, whatever you call them. Women, I suppose. And he won't do anything to diffuse the situation. Won't have simple chats with the newly aware." Jesus laughed. "It's a fiasco."

"It is best if we keep our discussions apolitical."

"You Swiss never want to commit."

"I am Austrian."

"Zat is zee same zing," Jesus said, imitating the psychoanalyst.

Freud narrowed his eyes.

"What I'm trying to *say*," Jesus said, "to get back to the *point*... Me being mortal is dangerous."

"No more zan zee first time."

"That ended well," Jesus said. "The problem is you can't work miracles in today's world. Too many cameras and web sites. During the time of me, the question wasn't if the miracle had been performed, but by what power. Every other moneychanger could make rain. Eventually."

"Did you work miracles?"

"Sure," Jesus said. "I mean, not verified. There weren't any miracle confirmation agencies or anything back then. I did what I could do."

"Which was?"

"The grand stuff of myth and legend, Siggy."

"Hmmph."

"If I went back like Lou or mom," Jesus said, "at least I could vanish and appear. Poof. Like magic." He smirked, imagining his upcoming venture in today's media-rich society. "They'll have cameras on me all the time. Once I announce, I mean. But no miracles. Not as a man. The first time, the apple was ripe."

Freud raised his eyes from his notes. "Yes. How *was* your youz?"

"What do you mean?"

"What did you do? Did you have a girlfriend?"

"I didn't have time for a girlfriend."

"Do you blame your Fozzer for zat?"

"For what?"

"For not having a girlfriend."

Jesus didn't blink.

"Did you have sexual relations wiz women before you were crucified?"

Jesus scowled. "I don't see why that's relevant."

"Many times," Freud said, "not resolving zee Oedipal Complex causes deep, long-lasting resentment toward zee perceived cause of zee frustration, as a symbol of zee failure to progress to sexual maturity." He inclined his head. "In zis case, your Fozzer."

"I don't resent my Father."

"Maybe you do not realize zis is true."

"It's not about realizing. It's about understanding. And what I don't understand, and never will, is why He would bring me into the world if I was going to hit my peak at thirty-four. Was that where the master plan ended? Tell me. *Then* what?"

"Maybe zere is no master plan."

Jesus glared at him. "You sound like Lou, and it's weird. But assuming God *is* coming back, He has to understand things change, right? Morality changes. Values. Virtues." He laughed. "And *that's* going to be the big problem." Jesus dropped his head back to the oxblood leather pillow.

"What will be zee big problem?"

"Aren't you listening? Values. *Virtues.*" Jesus expected him to see the inference. When the psychiatrist did not, Jesus said, "Finding a virgin of an acceptable age."

"Maybe I have misunderstood your purpose in returning to earth."

"Not at all," Jesus said with the slightest smile. "Just preparing for the inevitable."

"Which is?"

"Women respond to power."

"Und zat means what to you?"

"I am arguably the most famous man on earth," Jesus said, annoyed he had to explain what was, to him, obvious. "I will have triumphed over death. Not like last time, but *actually*. I expect I'll have my pick of the litter. So to speak."

"Do you enjoy zee prospect of female overtures?"

Jesus shrugged. "I missed out the first time around. Mostly. And…"

"Yes?"

"There's a conflict between who I am, or was. Whatever. Between my written history and… and thoughts I have now."

"Such as?"

"You understand exactly what I'm referring to. So-called *impure* thoughts."

"Wiz a woman."

"Of course," Jesus said, before adding, "Women."

"I see," Freud said. "Und why must zeese women be virgins?"

"Have you not read the Bible?"

"I am familiar wiz it. But, wiz all due respect, you are not God."

"Was it annoying for you," Jesus asked, "to find out God was real, and not a…" He paused to remember the words. "'A projection of childish wishes for an omnipotent protector'?"

"I have never met God."

"Still."

"I later modified my theory," Freud said.

"On paper."

"You were born of flesh and blood," Freud said. "If we believe Lucifer, Joseph is your fozzer, not God. Maybe a virgin is not a requirement."

Jesus' expression hardened. "In my time, there was an emphasis on virginity."

"Hmmph. It does not seem so in zis day and age. Do you feel zat zis fixation on virginity is healzy?"

"Do you?"

Freud tapped the pencil against the paper pad. "I believe it is indicative of deeper issues of insecurity and fear of impotence. In your case, castration."

"No wonder you're such an easy target on earth."

"I am embedded in zee culture," Freud said. "It is enough."

Jesus rolled his eyes. "I don't come here to talk about you. We've got a big issue."

"Your fear of death or your impure desires?"

"Both," Jesus said. "I need some direction."

A grandfather clock ticked and strains of Wagner seeped underneath the door from the reception area.

"Have you expressed your fears to Lucifer?"

"He won't budge."

"What about defying him?"

Jesus said nothing.

"Have you considered waiting for God's return?"

Jesus shrank on the couch. "I can't."

"Zen maybe zee best route is to turn zee uzzer cheek."

"Is that a joke?"

Freud shook his head. "Consider zat your destiny was not to merely die on zee cross, but somezing more."

"I like that," Jesus said. "Such as what?"

"Zat is zee question."

A FIT OF SIMULATED CONSCIENCE

One wall separated Sergio Pumello from Reverend Mathias Bundt and Lucy Springer, a woman who was not Bundt's wife. In a world devoid of televangelists with inflated public personas pricked by private infidelities, Lucy Springer would have been one more youth group counselor mistaking sex for salvation at the hands of a preacher who begged forgiveness with every pelvic thrust in an absurd effort to prolong the act. And in a world that didn't reward men of lesser integrity shoveling yellowed trash into the trough to feed the symbiotic gluttony of the media and their masses, Sergio Pumello would have been one more out-of-work journalist trying to get a job by sending copies of the Tampa Journal to its editor, with pages slashed red at every phrasing or punctuation Pumello deemed less than ideal. But this world wore a disingenuous bib to the trough, and so Pumello sat, weary but content, knowing this was the sizzle that would sell his exposé's steak to the world.

How Pumello had acquired the tryst's adjoining room was a tortuous tale of lies, bribes, and illegalities—his profession's bread and butter. His peers publicly condemned Pumello's methods while privately lionizing him. But acclaim and ridicule were secondary concerns. This was a *Bisou* cover piece, caviar for the machine. Pumello was focused on the story.

Sergio Pumello had run down or invented cover stories for *Bisou* magazine for nine years. He'd fallen in love with Italy on a six-week language immersion class his junior year in college, and moved to Rome from Florida three days after graduation. He took his journalism degree, a folder packed with clippings from his school newspaper, an invitation to interview for graduate studies at the *Roma Facolta di Giornalismo*, and fifteen hundred dollars from his grandmother. She was an Orthodox-Catholic who spoke fluent Italian and had carried on a lifelong love affair with Tuscany, though she had never left Naples, Florida.

While in graduate school, he'd written for a Roman tabloid, using the pittance they paid him to eat and buy textbooks. When he completed his graduate work there were no job offers, so with an assembly line mentality he put together story after story, a few of them based on truth or actual events. He sent them to a mailing list of European tabloids he'd built during his three years in graduate school. It was a hard existence in a nasty business, but over time he earned a reputation for generating newsstand sales, especially with the stories he created from whole cloth. After four years, *Bisou* magazine (a rebranded rag out of Genoa) offered him an entertainment editor position. It promised a regular paycheck, a byline, a place on the masthead, and an expense account for covering such events as the Cannes Film Festival and the BAFTA Awards. He snatched the opportunity. Eleven years later he'd reached yellow journalism's pinnacle, the Mariana Trench of his profession, and swung his crosshairs toward religion with surprising zeal.

At present he sat on a too-stiff bed, staring at a computer screen. A refurbished Pawtech Kent (a recon device named after Superman's alter ego) pressed against the shared wall courtesy of a heavy-duty tripod and custom titanium bracket. The Pawtech combined multi-beam sonar, radar, x-ray, ultra-wide bandwidth signals, multi-point listening, and infrared digital holography to generate a three-dimensional image of an unseen room. A thin cable connected the Pawtech to a portable laptop computer loaded with bootlegged software hijacked from a lonely NSA programmer. The software (EchoLo, not available in stores) consumed and filtered the various signals before amplifying and harmonizing them with its gray hat algorithm, enabling Pumello to "see" the room and its occupants from a rotatable 360-degree panoramic view, as well as overhead. To paint a similar picture of an unseen room you'd have to be born a bat.

Forty minutes ago, Bundt had pushed through the motel room door wearing a thin nighttime disguise of ball cap and sunglasses. Lucy Springer came twenty hesitant minutes later, carrying a grocery sack stuffed with red wine, crackers, and cheese. She wore what she considered "sexy" lingerie beneath her ankle-length dress. They'd expressed mutual reluctance and desire, his imitation guilt mingling with her wavering doubt. With a fit of simulated conscience Bundt made for the door. Pumello deemed it a theatrical, unnecessary gambit. His hand on the doorknob, Bundt whirled on her, his god and faith overcome by his Christian instinct to conquer.

Pumello found himself suffocating in the hypocrisy.

The former Catholic within him enjoyed a superior sympathy for the reverend, while his inner journalist knew this was checkmate. Investigative journalism was rarely as simple as a well-placed question posed to a guilty conscience. Persuading a source to give up information the source didn't want to give up required intensive effort to discover or manufacture persuasive leverage. This was his leverage, and the answers it coerced would begin the fall of Mathias Bundt's religious empire. Bundt would cooperate because, in turn, Pumello would promise to suppress the video, which clearly was a lie. The video would lead the story on television and online, and frame captures would splash across the pages of *Bisou*. Most journalists drew the line well before this sort of behavior, but Pumello did not, instead viewing these forays into the grays of law and integrity as steaming open the ethical envelope.

Act One of Bundt-Springer ended and Lucy peeled off the sweat-soaked dress to reveal the lingerie. Pumello's source at the roadside motel, a teenage boy with a peculiar, unexplained venom toward Bundt, had warned him the reverend's motel visits with various women from his church and office were nightlong affairs. He checked his equipment and settled in.

Hours passed, Bundt and Lucy broke the seventh commandment twice more, and the motel grew quiet. Pumello watched the
unchanging screen, the blanket's subtle rise and fall the only clue of
life within Bundt's room. His eyes burned, but he didn't sleep. He
never slept on stakeouts. Video replays didn't capture the nuances, the
in-the-moment *feel* of a transgression. Pumello, if nothing else, was a
student of nuances. They revealed the character within, the things his
subjects didn't want him to know. So he chain-drank coffee and stared
at the screen...

Someone else was in Bundt's room.

Pumello checked his watch. He had not dozed off, and Bundt's door
had not opened. He was simply there, sitting in a chair, smoking, the
cigarette tip blazing and dying on Pumello's screen. Pumello leaned
forward. The reverend slept. The man in the chair smoked. The minutes passed. Soon the cigarette flared in Pumello's monitor. The man
shifted in the chair, and Mathias Bundt stirred.

The evangelist rolled onto his back, eyes large and fearful. The ceiling
was an expanse of murk in the night's last gasps. He felt a third presence, and the unmistakable scent of clove overpowered the motel
room's permanent bouquet of alcohol, sex, and commercial cleaning
products. He knew who the presence was, of course. Years had passed
since he'd spoken with the man, if he was indeed a *man*.

"I thought you..." Bundt whispered to the ceiling, "uh, you, might
be—"

"Hoped," Lucifer said. "You *hoped* I was dead. Don't lie to yourself,
Mathias. It's ordinary."

Bundt sat up, glancing at Lucy.

"She'll sleep through it all, my faithless friend."

The man in the shadows held a clove cigarette, its tip burning and
darkening, breathing. Bundt didn't know the man's name, though
the man knew him better than his own family, or the millions who
watched his show, his *service*, every week.

"Why are you here?" Bundt said in his deep Texas drawl. *Whaaa awr you heeeaaarre?*

"He walks the earth, Mathias."

Bundt didn't understand.

"Your product, Mathias. Hallelujah."

The evangelist showed no joy. The fear of God was a powerful thing when you suspected your chance for a peaceful afterlife depended on His non-existence.

"That can't be," Bundt said. *Thayat cayan't beee.*

Lucifer chuckled. "It's okay if you don't believe, Mathias. Studies show that the higher you rank in your church, regardless of faith or denomination, the less you believe in God. These are informal and unofficial surveys, and those polled begged forgiveness for their honesty. But the truth remains, as it always does. With knowledge comes clarity and doubt, and few things are more difficult to accept than the confirmation of a faith-based conviction. So I'm not asking you to believe your Lord and Shepherd is strapping on His sandals for a walkabout. No, reverend, you're merely going to sell it."

"Who *are* you?"

The gray morning light rose and Lucifer smiled. He put finger to lips in the universal signal for *shhhhhhhh.*

"You know who I am, Mathias. You've always known. And you've prayed for forgiveness. Not because of Lucy or the host of willing lasses before her. You're just a poor sinner, right? No, you pray to counteract our association, to beat down the fear your prayers for abundance have indeed been answered."

Bundt shuddered.

"Success comes at a price, reverend, and your time has come. Your account is due."

Lucy murmured beneath the covers, and the shadows deepened around Lucifer.

"But don't I—" Bundt stuttered. "Can't I—"

Lucifer's gaze was unsettling, final. He stubbed out the cigarette. "He walks the earth, holy man. And you will sell Him, passionately and self-righteously, for the utmost profit and visibility. You will do what you've done for years, with renewed and terrified vigor, beginning tomorrow."

"Last night!" Reverend Bundt shouted from the altar. *Laaay-ust naaaauught.* "I had a vision. An angel! And this angel said unto me, 'He walks the earth, Mathias, He walks the earth!'" *Ur-uth.* "And I shook. And I cried. And I asked the angel, I begged of him,"—*bay-ugged*—"'what is your biddin' for this poor man of God?'"

Sergio Pumello vomited in his mind. He sat alone between marble columns in an alcove beyond the television cameras' reach, while his dismay and cynicism battled for supremacy.

To the faithful flock of Mathias Bundt, he was a man God had blessed with riches. While the extent of His favor was the topic of whispered speculation in Bundt's offices, only the evangelist himself (and Pumello) knew of his exquisite collection of rare Ferraris (garaged on his Coto de Caza estate), his trio of carbon fiber race-ready Ducati motorcycles (Daytona Beach), and his vacation homes on the Aegean Sea and Surfer's Paradise, Australia. His bank accounts on Grand Cayman were secret (though Pumello would find them soon enough), as were his 105' yacht, his thirty-seven pound solid gold Buddha (smuggled from Malaysia on the yacht), and his collection of Parisian shoe catalogs housed in an Amsterdam hideaway.

Bundt's inner business circle, comprised of employees and volunteers at Mathias Bundt Ministries in Irving, Texas, knew of his North Dallas mansion, his Bentley limousine, his Sikorsky helicopter, and the ministry's customized Boeing business jet, which flew the reverend and his traveling spectacle wherever the Good Word led, provided ticket pre-sales were solid, ministry donations were high, and climatic indicators pointed to warm weather and clear skies.

"'Preach,' the angel said. 'Preach to the world, from the darkest depths to the brightest peaks. Leave not,' he said, 'Leave not a soul unturned.' And then he was gone. Gone! Vanished like a precious child's soul called to heaven."

Hay-uh-vun.

Pumello had burst from his motel room the instant the man disappeared from the screen. Had the man exited the room, Pumello could not have missed him, leaving the journalist with insufficient explanations. A hologram? Smoke and mirrors? A hallucination capable of fooling NSA-level surveillance equipment? Though his agnostic brain ridiculed the thought, none of these explained those seven minutes any better than the reverend, save the fact Bundt's modified explanation was impossible.

"The truth," a voice said from the pew behind him, causing Pumello to spin around, "would clarify all for you, as is the boon of truth. With it you might dodge some looming existential doubt and maybe the bad parts of what you'll term your 'theosophical revolution.' But bloodless revolutions are boring, don't you think, Sergio?"

"Sorry," Pumello said, certain this was the man from last night. "Do I know you?"

"You see," Lucifer said, "the fountainhead of Mathias Bundt's success is dipped, swirled, and glazed in a delectable irony." Lucifer flipped through a Bible's thin pages. "The contemplation of which the reverend avoids with utter fanaticism. But, despite his chosen state of selective ignorance, when I ring the blessed reverend has no choice but to answer the call."

"Excuse me, but who are you?"

"Soon enough, Sergio, soon enough." He pointed toward the altar. "This is my favorite part."

Mathias Bundt's team passed the gold-plated collection buckets from one pew to the next while footage of third world hardship and blight played on the altar's giant video screens. Throughout the church, fists clutching cash and envelopes dipped into the buckets, emerging empty, like reversed monkey traps.

When Pumello turned back, the alcove was vacant. He moved to give chase but abandoned the idea, knowing it was hopeless. An odd clash of foreboding and expectation passed through him. For the first time in his life, Pumello wasn't pressing the action. He had built a career upon fabrications mish-mashed with truths discovered through sheer force of will. This unexpected lack of control, this perception events were acting upon *him*, had him adrift.

The congregation broke into the *Hallelujah Chorus,* snapping Pumello from his helpless reverie. Outside, the sun burned hot on his head, his field of view dominated by the Mathias Bundt Ministries gift shop.

KEEP SHEATHED THY HOLY SWORD

"**W**elcome to Hell," Lucifer said, giving Gabriel a hand as he stepped from the speedboat.

"Thank you, O Prince of the Abyss." Gabriel was in a sunny mood, fresh off a convincing election victory. He helped Michael and Jesus onto the pier while Lucifer tied up the boat.

"The lighting here is magical," Michael said in wonder. The Styx's shimmering crests gave way to the hand-rubbed hardwood pier, rocky outcrops of carbonado and gold, rolling volcanic plains, a limitless void above. "What a difference a few hundred years make."

"Six centuries if it's a day," Gabriel said. "The climate is perfection."

"Not like last time," Michael said. He moved to touch Jesus' cheek, which shone warm and ethereal in Hell's soothing light. Jesus brushed his hand away.

"At no point in our journey did I feel abandoned or compelled to wail," Gabriel said.

"That's good to hear," Lucifer said. "Though Hell in name only—"

"I would dispute that," Jesus said.

"—At first I got lost in the drama and expectation of what Hell *would be*. So we had near darkness, snakes underfoot, lava flows, random fires, and never-ending sulfur smog upon the waters. Navigation was difficult, no matter how many times you'd done it. Seasoned ferrymen rowed right past the entrance every other night."

Jesus straightened the admiral's blazer he'd worn for the trip down the Styx. "If it quacks like a duck—"

"I was going for authenticity," Lucifer said, interrupting Jesus as they headed for the gates, "but accomplished the opposite. So I discarded my mythological roots for my real roots. We leveled the basalt ridges and filled in the bottomless pits. Now we have a single light source with the same foot-candle brightness and light quality as the golden hour, without electricity or inadvertent burnings. New manifestations—we call them mannies—"

"How cute," Jesus muttered.

"—Are drawn to the light. It gives them something to focus on."

Gabriel nudged Michael and pointed toward a stand of palm trees, beyond which the light originated. Jesus shot them an annoyed glance as they followed Lucifer through the gates.

"Over on the right," Lucifer said, "is our welcome center."

A massive building, a steel and glass fortress without the turrets, gave off a vague luminescence like the City's buildings, though of a heavier quality.

"And the orientation pool is this way."

They walked toward the palm trees.

"This I have anticipated for many years," Gabriel said.

"Yes," Jesus said. "The expectation is killing me."

They rounded the palm trees. Jesus stopped, dumbfounded, dazzled, and satisfaction surged through the Dark Angel.

A vast lake spread before them, thousands of yards across and untold fathoms deep. Its surface shimmered and vibrated. Waves rushed to the black sand beach and receded. Something burst from the lake, whirling and spraying water, before plunging into the depths. The lake's center churned and roiled, glowing from beneath.

"What is it?" Jesus asked, unable to affect indifference.

"A star," Michael whispered.

"A small one," Lucifer said. "Miniscule, really. It provides focal light and warmth. An electromagnetic field within the water contains the star, while the water calms the manic energy of new manifestations."

"Not unlike a womb," Gabriel said.

"For manifestations originating from living things, the water and star-quality light are familiar and comforting."

"Do you just toss them in?" Jesus asked.

"Most go in themselves," Lucifer said. "It draws them in. The familiar environment relaxes the manny and helps it cope with confusion and reality bleed."

"How long is orientation?" Michael asked.

"Four or five weeks," Lucifer said. "Unless the manny concludes it's in Hell."

"Which it is," Jesus said.

"Then it can last months," Lucifer said, ignoring Jesus. "Every case is different. We don't take them to the next step unless they achieve self-awareness and find their way to the beach."

When Lucifer sensed his visitors were ready to move on, he led them toward a modern glass and steel structure of severe planes and angles. Far beyond the building were dark, distant hills and a burnt orange sky.

Without waiting for the question, Lucifer said, "The highlands are for those that stagnate. No self-awareness, but no signs of dissipation."

The group passed through automated glass doors into the modern building. The lobby glowed with comforting light and smelled of efficiency and civility.

"Good evening, sir," the receptionist said to Lucifer.

Lucifer smiled. "Cleo, this is Josh, Mike, and Gabe."

"An honor," she said. "I took the liberty of completing these for you."

Cleo handed nametags to Jesus, Michael, and Gabriel. Jesus' read *Hello – My Name Is Joshua*. He grimaced, certain the nametag's silver clip clashed with his blazer's solid gold buttons. To minimize damage, he clipped it to the front pocket of his wrinkle-resistant yachting slacks.

"After I've converted Josh," Lucifer said to Cleo, "Gabe will be staying for field protocol before continuing to Vegas."

"Very good, sir."

Jesus' stomach tightened. Converted? He felt rushed, held to the tracks. Had he considered mortality's every ramification? Lucifer led them across the lobby to a lengthy elevator bank. Jesus looked out the floor-to-ceiling windows at an endless expanse of lawn and hills, reminding him of Tuscany, cool and lush in the twilight.

"Organic displays," Lucifer said to Jesus' unasked question. "We've had them for a few hundred years now. Each building has a unique landscape beyond the windows. Since we put them in, we've increased productivity fivefold." Before the elevator doors closed he pointed to the rolling hills. "That's the Italian countryside."

Jesus forced himself to relax and asked, "How is it you had this before the invention of television?"

"I'm not constrained by humanity's progress or technological limits."

On the fourth level, an unmarked door opened to a long hallway punctuated every thirty feet with a large observation window.

"Life simulation is Hell's core component," Lucifer said. "Regardless of whether a new manifestation is famous, or an animal, object, or concept, sim protocol standardizes base behaviors, harmonizes with residual identity, educates, and introduces it to the City."

"I enjoy speaking with the camels in Tanakh," Gabriel said.

"Dub and Vee," Jesus said. "Me, too."

"What about the infamous?" Michael asked.

"We start by scrubbing repellent aspects of their residual identity," Lucifer said, "without resorting to barbaric and undignified physical torment."

"So there shall be no flaming tombs on the tour?" Gabriel asked. They all smiled except for Jesus.

"Once the scrub takes," Lucifer said, "it's mostly the same, but with customized education."

They stopped and peered through the first observation window. A woman sprinted, suspended in mid-air within a vertical shaft of light, sheathed neck-to-toe in a thin, black, shimmering material with the faintest hint of an off-black flame pattern. Eight fine blue light rays beamed to the woman's head from the black void surrounding her.

"What's she wearing?" Michael asked.

"A sim suit. It interfaces with the simulation beams and the manifested equivalent of her nervous system to track progress by altering the suit's flames. When the flames look real, she's ready to move on." A small grin played across Lucifer's face. "A bit of a conceit, but we try to have fun here. Hers are black, so she began simming recently." He glanced at a digital readout floating inches beyond the window. "She became self-aware a week ago."

The woman tripped and fell, her position within the light shaft never varying. Upon hitting the "ground" she whirled in mid-air, scratching and kicking an unseen adversary. She rolled, struggled to her feet, sprinted.

Lucifer enjoyed the tour group's fascination before leading them down another hallway to a second window.

"The technology saves us," Lucifer said. "Back when manifestations were rare, just one every few decades, we did it live, in real time, like a years-long, continuous staging of *Macbeth*."

Jesus asked, "How many souls are—"

"They're not souls, Josh," Lucifer said.

"You don't know that."

"If you define a soul," Lucifer said, "as a representation of someone or something determined *not* by that someone or something's thoughts or actions *nor* by some supernatural or divine agent, but by the general consensus of other someones or somethings, *and* if you propose that not all someones or somethings have souls, *only* the crème de la crème someones or somethings about which an as-yet-undetermined number of run-of-the-mill someones or somethings are passively aware, meaning souls are not young or old or pure or blackened or saved or damned, but either *widely known* or *nonexistent*, I suppose I'll agree to use the term 'soul.'"

"You lost me at 'general consensus,'" Jesus said with a yawn.

"We've been over this many times, Josh. They're as-yet-unexplained phenomena. And this is where they manifest."

The group stopped at a second window. A stocky man stood beneath a light shaft, wearing a less elaborate, neck-to-ankle sim suit, gray with the same tone-on-tone flame pattern, unaware of their presence, defocused.

Lucifer scanned the floating readout beyond the glass. "This one is harmonizing with its identity."

"Its?" Michael asked. "He looks like a he."

"*It* is a technological concept," Lucifer said. "We've had a lot of them lately. Concepts are difficult, because the initial manifestation is vague, and it has no residual identity. When this one gained self-awareness, it tipped to a masculine identity. Once it tips to the masculine or feminine, we pair it with a constructed identity."

Michael and Gabriel stared in fascination.

"A concept or thing achieving self-awareness is rare," Lucifer said.

"So there's something special about life," Jesus said. "How curious."

"It is," Lucifer said. "Do you have a theory?"

"Not that you would accept."

"If you could prove it, I would."

Behind the glass, the man began to genuflect, but dropped his hand in resignation. He shuddered, his eyes reddening.

They moved on.

"What do you do if their residual identity exhibits less than desirable traits?" Jesus asked.

"Anything beyond a certain level is scrubbed," Lucifer said, "so it's not a problem."

"That's not what I mean. Not evil, per se, but… annoying."

"To whom?"

"To anyone with good taste."

"Not this again," Michael said.

Gabriel shook his head. "Please, please no."

They knew Jesus wanted self-aware but overrated fashion designers, no-talent popular artists, and bestselling hack writers to experience their lack of ability from his point of view before entering the City. Jesus argued it would both improve the City's appearance and simplify the education process, since no living organism was more difficult to reason with than an artist who believed he was God's gift when, in fact, he was not. Though he sympathized with Jesus, Lucifer maintained the proposed addition to the system was nothing more than an unconstructive punishment and would often bring the preparation process to an unrecoverable halt. Long ago, Lucifer had determined reason was an alien concept to the self-described "artists" targeted by Jesus' discontent. He demonstrated the impossibility of instituting such a step by enabling both Houses to listen in on a group of screenwriters sitting in a global brand coffee shop in Studio City, California, whining and bitching about "lowest common denominator filmmaking" and "the lost art of dialogue." By the fifth reverent mention of *Chinatown* within a period of eight minutes, saints and angels alike were awash in tears of boredom and vengeance. Though correct, Jesus lost the battle. By official decree, delusional artistic pretense was deemed too unpleasant to eradicate and Lucifer absolved of responsibility for bad art in the City.

"We do nothing," Lucifer said. "Hell is not Hell, and the City is not heaven. A deluded vision of pious perfection is not the goal."

"Then what is?" Jesus asked.

"Balance, I suppose. Order from chaos."

Lucifer moved about the room, handing syllabi to Michael, Gabriel, and Jesus, who each made a careful study of their surroundings. Hell's initial state was unforgettable and the conference table's origin impossible to ignore. Fashioned from black lava rock and less-palatable materials, it was polished to the point one might think one was staring into the Anti-Mirror.

Beyond the windows a lush vista stretched to silhouetted hills, capturing the transition to nouveau Hell from what used to be. Smooth green lawns led to polished volcanic swells, bursting fountains, flowing streams, wondrous golden light.

"Don't you think the palm trees are a bit much?" Jesus asked.

"No," Lucifer said. "Please turn to Section One."

Pages rustled and silence hung, before the room filled with hurried, uneasy glances.

"First you'll find a reading list, which includes a wide range of material," Lucifer said. "Books. Magazines. Poetry."

Jesus snorted at what he read. "Henry Miller is obscene."

"I'll agree he has a unique perspective on women," Lucifer said.

"He hates women."

"No Josh, he doesn't."

"Maybe not now," Jesus said. "Not after here."

"Henry manifested after I planted the palm trees," Lucifer said. "He loved women. All of them." Lucifer raised the syllabus. "But he didn't like God much."

"Are you quite certain," Gabriel asked, "Josh requires a multitude of tomes to understand the fairer gender?"

Lucifer said, "Josh will be a man from a savage age compared to the women—"

"I know what I'm doing," Jesus said, confirming he did not.

Lucifer hid his amusement. "I could summarize in a few sentences everything you need to know about today's woman. But you would go and do the opposite. So any so-called tips need to come from others. And it's important our prize pupil is able to discern between lust and love."

"I'm not returning for love," Jesus said.

"Of course not," Lucifer said, placing his palms flat on the table. "But do you deny you've considered the possibilities? Ad nauseam and in explicit detail?"

Jesus studied the conference table.

"The modus operandi you'll adopt from your life in Galilee will offend your followers," Lucifer said. "They expect love, fidelity—"

"Love can take years to find," Jesus said. "God might be back in *days*."

"Josh," Lucifer said, "mowing through the willing won't help you rule supreme."

"Keep sheathed thy holy sword," Gabriel declared.

"Maybe not sheathed," Lucifer said, grinning at the angels, "just not wielded for all to see."

Jesus gazed across the gleaming volcanic terrain. "I'd give my kingdom for you and your trumpet," he said to Gabriel. "Why do *I* have to do everything the hard way?"

The table went quiet. Jesus didn't like Lucifer's sympathetic expression, or Gabriel's blank face, or Michael's careful study of the table's volcanic surface. He grew agitated.

"Speaking of hard changes," Lucifer said, "we need to do something about your clothes."

"How dare you! This is perfect for a river journey in a forbidding climate."

"You're a dandy," Lucifer said.

"I—"

"Clothing is a statement," Lucifer said. "It says, 'I'm a businessman.' 'I'm an athlete.' 'I'm a professor.'"

"Really?" Jesus said. "And what do my clothes say?"

Lucifer gave Jesus a once-over—the navy blazer, the gold buttons—and replied, "They say, 'my dominatrix dressed me this morning.'"

Michael and Gabriel sat stone-faced, jaws clenched, not daring to laugh.

"On earth, as it is in heaven," Jesus said, beating down his anger, "fashion is my domain."

Lucifer slid a men's fashion magazine across the table. "Go through this. Ignore their attempts to pretend they love women and see what you like from their classic fashion recommendations."

Jesus whipped the magazine across the table and onto the floor. "Uninventive."

"Timeless," Lucifer said, holding Jesus' eyes and tapping his index finger on the table. "Regardless, you'll need a career."

"A career?" Michael asked.

"Wealth with no apparent source draws an undesirable crowd. Josh needs a profession."

"What do you suggest?" Jesus asked, his voice rising as he lost any semblance of control over his runaway indignation. "Should I start a home business? Fundraise? Life coach?"

"Not at all," Lucifer said. "Do what you did before you were crucified."

"No no no," Jesus said. "The tools have changed. And I've only worked in the Greek Classical style. I'd have to relearn everything."

"Then apprentice."

Jesus paused, hurt flashing through his eyes, but recovered. With one mighty tear he ripped the syllabus in half, fed up with Lucifer's criticism. "This is insulting. My disciples won't care where my wealth comes from. I'm not of their world."

"Soon you shall be," Gabriel said.

Jesus ignored the odd sensation of contraction sweeping through him. "The more grounded they are," he said, "the less chance I'm going to have when it's time to reveal myself."

Lucifer considered Jesus' argument and said, "You're probably right."

"I will admit," Jesus said, spurred on by Lucifer's concession, "I've entertained the prospect of female company. But I should date heiresses, or pop stars, or actresses. And meeting those kinds of girls isn't about your job."

"Women," Lucifer said.

Jesus ignored him. "All that matters is access and a superior social standing. And I believe," he said, spreading his hands as if presenting a Broadway marquee, "Son of God has few peers." He met Lucifer's gaze. "I'm talking to mom."

"You can't get to her from here," Lucifer said.

"She can come to me."

Lucifer waved off the idea. "She's on tour. And if you're going through with it, it's time to convert you."

Like exposition in a bad denouement, the kind of inept cinematic ending Jesus despised, the implications of his conversion to a man stalled his momentum. He felt dissociated from himself, numb, not cold but still and heavy, his consciousness reduced to a point deep within him.

Lucifer read the sudden tension in Jesus' face. "You don't have to, Josh," he said. When Jesus didn't respond, Lucifer spelled out, "You'll be mortal again. Flesh and blood. Pleasure and pain. The whole bundle."

Jesus fought back a tremor, steeling himself until annoyance and bravado overwhelmed his anxiety. "Fine. Let's do it."

✯

Jesus stood before a hallway mirror at the Ritz-Carlton in Southern California, staring at his face. He ran his fingers along his cheek, through his hair, gazing into his own eyes, emotions churning through him.

"How did you do this?" he asked Lucifer, who watched him in the mirror.

"It's complicated," Lucifer said. The Ritz always reminded him of Versailles—before the revolution and Louis' final trip to Paris with his queen.

"Yes," Jesus said, "I assumed that. But it's… I'm so close. Granted, I've only seen my reflection in polished bronze and placid water, but—"

"It's you, Josh."

"But I don't—"

"'Any sufficiently advanced technology is indistinguishable from magic.'"

"Yes, Clarke's third law. I understand it's not magic. I'm just—" Jesus gawked at his reflection.

"We should get going," Lucifer said.

They resumed their trek through the hotel. A dolphin sculpture marked the buffet room entrance.

"How do you know where my mother is, when I don't?"

"She spends a lot of time in hotels due to her career," Lucifer said as they pushed through the doors leading to the café deck.

"Yes," Jesus said. "But how do you know *which* hotel? That can't be part of a collective awareness."

"You'd be surprised what's floating around out there," Lucifer said. "I only pass on the juicy bits."

The blue Pacific served as backdrop for a sprawling sun deck sprinkled with umbrella-shaded tables, extravagant sunglasses, and the greatest number of multi-carat diamonds outside Antwerp. Luxuriant coffees and teas and exquisite pastries were served on simple china from silver trays, their rich aromas traveling across the deck on a crisp ocean breeze.

Lucifer spied a table surrounded by a small cluster of people. "There she is."

The jostling, star-struck horde blocked their view. Hushed whispers and cries of discovery and excitement escaped the dense ball of humanity. The crowd milled and craned, expanded and surged. A small break formed in the crowd, and the woman in its midst glanced up. With a cry, the world's most recognizable and controversial pop star leapt to her feet, felt tip pen and glossy photo in hand.

"Josh! Louie!" She shot from the crowd toward them.

"How are you, Mariam?" Lucifer asked as she hugged him, before she moved on to her son.

"Hi, mom," Jesus said, fighting for breath within her smothering embrace.

"To you she's mom," Lucifer whispered to Jesus as the small throng caught up to their obsession. "To them she's Domina, Mistress of Pop."

"Louie," she said over her son's shoulder, blinking away the tears threatening to rust her rock star façade, "I don't think I believed you." She squeezed Jesus harder. "It feels so different." She released him, but maintained a firm grip on his wrist. "I don't see Gabriel anywhere," she said to Lucifer with what passed as laughter, ignoring the hands and pens reaching over her shoulders, the questions, the pleas.

Jesus glared at Lucifer. The Dark Angel smiled and said, "He's in Vegas."

Domina aka Virgin Mary née Mariam shouted her appreciation and regrets to the crowd. She signaled to her bodyguards and the muscular men ushered them back to her table and formed a perimeter, cutting off the public's access to their idol.

"Two more iced teas," Lucifer said to the waiter as they sat. "How's the tour?"

"Fine," she said, her eyes not leaving her son. She squeezed a lemon wedge into her tea and took a sip, maintaining her composure. "How are you, honey?"

"I'm good." He examined his hands. "Getting used to it."

"He's real?" she asked.

Lucifer nodded.

"Be careful, honey."

"I'll be fine."

"I'm sure," she said, removing her shades. "Happy Daddy's coming back?"

Jesus shrugged, his mood plummeting.

"And how are you feeling about the Jews?"

"Better," Jesus said, brightening. "The expressions on their faces when they arrive in the City and see me for the first time..." He chuckled. "It's like Christmas."

She frowned. "If you want positive press coverage, you can't mock the Jews."

"Mom, I—"

"Domina," Lucifer said.

"If you slip like that to a reporter," she said, fiddling with her sunglasses, "they'll think I'm older than I say."

"Fine," Jesus said, scowling at Lucifer. "Can we skip the class in media relations for now? Maybe let me acclimate first?"

"In a bit," she said. "What are you going to say?"

"In what context?" Jesus asked.

"When you have fifty microphones in your face, and they ask who you are."

Jesus tapped the table with an appetizer fork. "Why are we discussing this?"

"Josh," she said, transforming in the space of her son's name from breezy, carefree rock star to stern, timeless mother, "I'm going to count to three, and if—"

"I'll tell the truth."

"You can't."

"It's what he wants to do," Lucifer said.

"Do you know," she asked Jesus, not bothering to hide her skepticism, "how many people, at any given time, in any given city on earth, think they're you, and proclaim it to anyone who will listen?"

Jesus looked past them, over the infinite Pacific. The bodyguards made small shifts, keeping Domina's fans at bay and beyond earshot. Lucifer stirred more sugar into his tea while Domina slipped on her ultra-dark sunglasses, tilted her head back, and gazed into the blue above. A gull flew past. Jesus waited until his mother rolled her head to the side and faced him.

"Once we begin," he said, "feel free to impart whatever wisdom you deem necessary. But for now, couldn't you just help me?"

She glanced at Lucifer, not quite understanding her son's meaning.

"Baby Josh has come to save the world," Lucifer said, "but Josh the man has needs."

She lowered her shades, peering over the frames, a famous move from her first music video. Screams of ecstasy poured from the crowd. "The third leg of my tour begins in less than two weeks."

"So postpone it for personal reasons," Jesus said.

"Dates are locked, honey. Tickets sold."

"I need access, mom. *Your* kind of access."

"It isn't quite so simple as access, Josh," Lucifer said. "Everything is forever now. Upon your grand messianic revelation, the media will target her, and so will the kooks and zealots, since there will be video of you two together."

"Then why are we here?" Jesus asked.

"You insisted," Lucifer said.

"I'm not concerned," she said. "No one will believe it."

Lucifer's expression conveyed quite the opposite opinion.

Domina peered at Lucifer, attempting to siphon his mind. "Unless there's proof?"

Lucifer maintained noncommittal silence.

"Louie, I—"

"You should stay out of it," Lucifer said. "Leave it to us. If he calls you 'mom' with a TV camera around you won't be able to just brush it off. Your career, this life, everyone here you know and love… it'll never be the same."

Her face was unreadable by anyone but Lucifer.

"And God won't be pleased," Lucifer said, surprised he felt the tiniest shred of guilt for manipulating them like this.

Jesus snorted a laugh and left the table, passing through the crowd to a safety railing overlooking the Pacific.

Domina cocked her head at Lucifer. So what if God didn't like it? He had never bothered to extend the simple courtesy of greeting the mother of His only son, let alone a personal tour or intimate break-fast. *She* hadn't liked *that*. Jesus stood with his hands spread along the railing, his body bisecting the sun's glaring path across the ocean to the Ritz. *God won't be pleased.* She gave Lucifer a faint smile and signaled to the waiter.

✯

The afternoon passed. It was cooler now and glowing fuchsia clouds streaked the deepening blue, as if a colossal child had crayoned the sky. The café deck was empty, and the bodyguards sat several tables away, relaxing over dinner. Jesus and Lucifer sat with Domina, formulating a proper strategy to fulfill Jesus' mortal urges. They decided to start at the Festival de Cannes.

"At least I'll find someone suitable there," Jesus said, struggling to maintain his ambivalent air.

Lucifer concealed his amusement. Would Jesus the man's base desires derail Jesus the biblical Son of God's higher ambition?

"Finding a room might be difficult," Lucifer said into the setting sun, noticing the smell of sea salt vanishing with the day. "The festival's a week out."

"Leave that to me," Domina said, already tapping on her cell phone.

"Have you considered how sunning and shopping with the entertainment industry elite will look to your followers?" Lucifer asked Jesus.

"My first time here, in this body, was all work and no play. And that's how it will be, yet again, after I reveal myself."

"Coming back was your idea, Josh. We all have free will."

"Maybe you do," Jesus said. "Maybe everyone else does. But not me. Not since the New Testament. Thou shalt, thou shalt not. Why do I have to be the crux of confusion? Why can't we just know what He wants so I don't have to make decisions based on fear?"

Lucifer did not answer.

"We'll keep a low profile," Jesus said, before pointing at Lucifer. "And I'm getting nothing but mixed signals from you. First you're against my idea, because you say it's not what God wants. Then you put me in a *real body*, and insist on chaperoning. Whose side are you on?"

"At this level of existence, there are no sides," Lucifer said with less than total honesty.

"Just gentle curves of diplomacy?" Jesus sneered. "Anyway, if I have to do it—"

"Which you don't."

"If I want any control over my fate, I do," Jesus said, matching Lucifer's fractional honesty. "I might as well have some fun."

"So let's enjoy ourselves," Lucifer said. "But you're not ready for the media. They'll expect a model of peace and love, but you're all cynicism and lust. Is this the modern Jesus?"

"I can play the part."

"Can you? How? You're not the biblical you. You can't violate their expectations and expect them to hang on your every word."

Jesus' eyes darkened. He restrained every candid word popping into his mind. "You've said my followers will believe what they want to believe."

Lucifer hid his happiness with how the conversation was going. When a man's libido was calling the shots, deception was unnecessary. "You're referring to confirmation bias," Lucifer said, as Domina charmed and intimidated her way into Cannes' most exclusive hotel. "But your mom is the paparazzi holy grail. They'll *pursue* you."

"Three of us," she said into the phone, winking at Lucifer.

"So we're in the paper once or twice," Jesus said. "What's the big deal?"

Lucifer maintained a doubtful expression, not wanting to betray his satisfaction with Jesus' intentions.

"Is it too much to ask to do this part my way? Can't I have one thing I want?"

"Sure," Lucifer said, sensing discouragement would further set the hook, "if you weren't just firing in the dark because you're scared. But this smacks of self-sabotage. Stick to your plan, Josh."

"More mixed signals," Jesus said.

"Then let's go somewhere else. Sow your oats anonymously, out of the limelight. Designating a woman as 'suitable' based on her media pull or box office juice is a ludicrous philosophy."

"Yes," Jesus' mother cooed, "a daily cornucopia would be lovely."

"Deep inside," Jesus said, "I feel the women I consort with must be heroines."

"Now it's women?" Lucifer asked. "In the plural?"

"It's been two thousand years," Jesus said.

"The world is filled with heroic women," Lucifer said, "but they're not all rich and famous."

"Maybe not. But when I picture her, I see brilliant lights, upturned eyes. She's worshipped."

"Like your muzzer," Lucifer said in perfect imitation of Freud.

Jesus glared at the smirking demon. "It has nothing to do with that."

"Au revoir," she said, and hung up. "Okay boys, it's all set."

WE WHO ARE BEYOND THE HYPE

It began when they stepped off the private jet in Nice.

The snapping shutters of digital cameras served as backdrop to the paparazzi shouts and pleas. Domina pressed past her son so she could descend the mobile staircase first. She waved and smiled big, bright white teeth and her famously sexy lips, painted with come-hither-pink lipstick. She was a natural in the spotlight, loving it back, both sides feeding one another, starry-eyed bride and groom brimming with certainty the world revolved around the air between them.

Jesus stood enrapt at the jet's door, eyes on the media swarm. Behind the throng, he glimpsed a long black limousine pulling to a stop. Lucifer gripped his arm, breaking Jesus from his fame daze, and they followed Domina down the steps, squinting before the flashgun onslaught and barrage of questions.

"Are you here for the festival?"

"When do you drop the new album?"

Their feet touched tarmac and the press pack surged forward, thrusting wind-screened microphones and hi-def video cameras at them like broadswords and bayonets.

"Who are the blokes?"

"Are you reinventing yourself?"

She laughed at their questions and cut toward the limousine, head high, magnetic, likably arrogant. "Excuse me, ladies!" she shouted to the mostly male throng, who parted obediently. Jesus found it impossible not to compare her effect on the press crush to Moses and a certain sea.

The driver opened the door as they reached the car, and the love affair between star and media became a no-holds barred orgy of shouts and innuendo, with one question rising above them all in a booming British voice.

"Are you shagging them both?"

Domina spun around with a dazzling smile on her face, flinging her arms around her son and the devil.

"A girl should be so lucky. This is Josh... Nazareth," she said into the phallic boom mics as she squeezed closer to Jesus, who expanded his chest. "And this hunk of a man"—she stood on tiptoe and bit Lucifer's ear, giggling—"is Luis. Luis Enfuego!"

His name etched in media stone, Josh Nazareth climbed into the stretch limousine with his mother and Luis Enfuego, confident he would soon find himself splashed across the world's gossip pages.

The festival's opening night gala was the cinema world's most desirable ticket—the hottest party east of the Oscars.

Everywhere Jesus looked, a famous face shone back at him. Several times he had to remind himself he didn't know anyone here, despite having had lengthy conversations with several of their manifestations at Caffè, the City's most elegant Italian bar. When in a prickly mood, Lucifer presented the reality of "dual existence" as further proof the City was not heaven, but Jesus had learned to tune out Lucifer at such times, suspecting the simultaneous presence of someone both *here* and *there* posed a conflict no amount of theosophical gymnastics could resolve.

Massive round tables filled the Grand Salon, each reserved by a major film company for a bit less than a typical third world nation's gross national product. Nobody sat at the tables, at least not yet, as the glamour set was too busy mingling, gesticulating, embracing, and air kissing. Jesus couldn't help but recall an after hours party at Gethsemane. Mary Magdalene wore a little silk number revealing her ankles. It had been epic, to use the modern jargon, until Judas and the soldiers arrived.

Jesus felt electric, sharp, the fame and wealth surrounding him rousing desires he'd let rest since his street preaching days. Now he remembered the immediacy, the intoxicating quality of high-visibility events. That quality had been the sole redeeming aspect of his trial and crucifixion.

But tonight, his sole gripe was the required dress. He presumed these people were the world's creative cream, and this *was* socializing on a grand scale. He should have reveled in his element, style-wise, and worn something expensive and befitting of his station—a deep burgundy or royal purple superfine bespoke, perhaps. He wore the best, period, regardless of existential plane. But Lucifer had dissuaded him from following his instincts, and forced Jesus to choose off the rack. It was the equivalent of ordering chicken at a world-class steak house. They had compromised with a midnight blue velvet Italian tuxedo that appeared black in almost any light. Gazing across the gala's sea of black-on-white and black-on-black, he allowed for the possibility Lucifer knew from whence he spoke. Jesus spread Brie on a cracker. He might have done the world a greater service by dying for their fashion timidity.

Unlike the biblical Son of God, Lucifer was quite at ease. He moved in these circles, knew mortals at the gala who considered him a friend, others who owed him a favor, and planned to utilize their contacts to expedite the finding of a suitable mate for Jesus. A former fling of his (Bella Luna, an Italian actress making her debut in American films) had relieved him of the need to search for female company by making it plain she yearned to share his bed tonight.

However, all was not smooth and pink. Bella's first words were (in Italian), "Lover! I realized yesterday I never knew your name! Luis Enfuego," she had purred. "When we are together, the moon is on fire."

He'd smirked appropriately at her play on their surnames, suspecting she'd practiced the delivery in her hotel room.

But while they arranged a rendezvous, an undercurrent of concern penetrated his festive mood.

For thousands of years he'd walked the world nameless until the Mistress of Pop dubbed him *Luis Enfuego*, to the world media no less, which was more solid in the collective mind than a birth certificate with tiny ink footprints. He assessed the ramifications and decided to assume a new appearance once the world forgot about Luis Enfuego.

Jesus saw her from across the room.

Her dark hair poured over her shoulders like water, shimmering as she moved, and her face appeared wet, delicate, perfectly imperfect, her eyes a little too big, her lips a little too lush. Her beauty was dizzying, intimidating, which did little to explain why she was speaking to a bald dwarf in a rented black tuxedo. She towered over him, her strong, feminine shoulders and the sensual swells of her breasts springing from her strapless burgundy party dress, an exquisite flower straining to escape the vase.

She was the one. Though he'd never deigned to define his type, this woman suited him, both in appearance and social standing. Jesus imagined introductions, followed by vibrant repartee and escalating flirtation. And one night soon, on an island paradise, she would come to know the magnitude of her good fortune.

He wondered if she was a virgin.

Lucifer followed Jesus' sight line and observed the woman, obviously an international model or starlet. Maybe both. Striking an effortless pose and demeanor, which, on average, cost the typical male model six hours of mirror time to achieve, Lucifer leaned against a support column and allowed himself a small chuckle. Jesus the eternal being aspires to rule the world, but return him in his body and he *wants*. Procreation trumps ambition. Finding humor and comfort in the predictability of men, Lucifer considered the match. Any messianic pairing would be dicey, no matter the woman, as a result of Jesus' complicated psyche. To wit, Jesus had 1) An overwhelming Madonna-Whore complex, 2) An Everest-sized collection of psychosexual hang-ups, and 3) An overriding savior mentality. Angelic oddsmakers at the Book would open odds at 8/1 against consummation. Lucifer thought Jesus' chances were better. It was a matter of finding a female whose nature and station in life exploited Jesus' predilections. He wanted Jesus distracted, delayed, until God arrived—even better if the biblical Son of God did it to himself.

With this in mind, Lucifer excused himself from Ms. Luna.

Jesus watched Lucifer weave between and around the countless elitist groupings, stopping a short distance from the dwarf and the girl. Jesus was careful not to stand next to the burnt orange table coverings, as they clashed with his tuxedo. Did burnt orange go well with anything? Small inconveniences at social gatherings had driven him mad since his preaching days, beginning with the difficulty of finding a decent ensemble for outdoor speaking engagements in an arid climate, continuing with his total inability to find the perfect loincloth for his crucifixion, one that conveyed "martyr" with a subtle undercurrent of "saving your ass."

At least that's how he remembered it.

Fearful the velvet would prove too heavy for the occasion, he eased behind a palm frond ice sculpture to watch.

"My first big role," the dwarf said, "was the Jawa who laser blasted R2-D2."

"Da," she said in a lilting Russian accent.

The dwarf grimaced. "It was a seminal moment in the saga, and I had the first action lines spoken by a Jawa. But it was never given the weight it deserved."

"What is you say?" the beautiful girl asked.

"My first line, as I fired the blaster, was 'Soo-ootiwa!' And after R2 was down, I shouted out 'Hootini!'"

"Houdini? Magician?"

"'Hootini,' with a *T*."

"What does this mean?"

The dwarf considered. "'Let us view the fallen' or maybe 'Let us gather around the fallen.' I'm not really sure. I waved my hand in the universal signal for 'follow me.'"

"It meant maybe 'follow me'?"

"It never felt like that. I'm pretty sure 'the fallen' was a part of it. At least in spirit."

"Did you attend a dialect coach?"

"It was an invented language," the dwarf said. "There were no qualified coaches."

"So you required to learn new language?"

"We kept it simple."

"'The fallen' is not simple."

"It's simple in an abstract way."

Lucifer joined them and passed his hand before the dwarf's eyes. "This isn't the woman you're looking for."

The dazed dwarf gazed up at her and said, "You're not the woman I'm looking for." He disappeared into the crowd.

Lucifer said to her, "A friend of mine would like to meet you."

"Who is friend?" she asked, unable to measure Lucifer with her usual swift certainty.

"Someone important."

"A producer?"

"Yes," he said. "Come with me."

They found Jesus behind the ice frond.

"Josh Nazareth," Lucifer said, "this is—"

"Svetlana," she said, her eyes flitting past him. "Svetlana Babakov. Your friend say you are producer." Straight to the point is best, she thought, peeking in the mirror behind him again. There was no use wasting time.

Jesus froze, unable to summon words, facial expressions, or nonverbal gestures.

"He doesn't like to talk about himself," Lucifer said to cover Jesus' speechlessness. "But he has his fingers in projects worldwide."

"You are international?"

Jesus was in awe of her beauty, much like he imagined Enzo Ferrari's son might stand in awe before a 250 TR.

"Have I seen anything you make?"

"It's—it's possible," Jesus said, knowing he would have to speak. He resented her for tempering his defiance.

"We're consultants," Lucifer said. "The producer's producer, if you will."

"Da," she said, and praised herself for maintaining eye contact. For Svetlana Babakov, the urge to glance into mirrors was a constant, conscious battle. She felt guilty when she did, and an uplifting sense of accomplishment and well-being when she did not. Being a self-taught mirror connoisseur, as well as a "brutal objective" critic of physical beauty, she interpreted her resistance to admiring her exceptional form as a sign of great inner strength.

"I work in development," Lucifer said, "and Josh focuses on talent."

"Talent in rear of camera or before?"

"Actors," Lucifer said.

She smiled and blinked, like a slate snapping shut, and turned to Jesus. Lucifer and the mirror settled into the distant past.

"What is process?" she asked Jesus.

"Process?"

"How is you find who you search for?"

Jesus kicked himself for not mastering his movie industry banter. However, maybe curbed candor was best. Besides being simpler to maintain than lying, in this venue he sensed honesty might come off as bold and imaginative.

"I look into their souls," he said.

She misunderstood and said, "I feel like I do same when I become character."

"What's your background?" Lucifer asked her, glaring at Jesus.

Ms. Babakov hesitated, brushing a non-existent strand of hair behind one ear. "I have not trained formal," she said. "I am into natural method."

They waited for her to continue.

"Is new thing. A group of us at agency, we who are beyond the supermodel hype, get once together a week and read with each other, in total supportive environment." She pointed a finger to emphasize, "No judgment, no criticism, no makeup. Makeup is like mask, and you cannot *be* character with mask on. And is much helping. I have, how you say, blown producers at auditions."

"Blown *away*," Lucifer suggested.

She agreed. "They do not believe I never have lessons."

"Maybe you're a natural," Jesus said.

"Da, I hope so," she said. "I am not caring of classes and school and other such things. I am erudite. More meat, less fat." She grinned, focused on Jesus. "What are you caring of?"

Jesus considered. "I'm searching."

"In what sense?"

"In every sense."

"Do you not love what you do?"

"It's never enough."

She sighed. "I realize what you mean."

"We should be going," Lucifer said. "She's expecting us."

Svetlana blinked, threatened. "Who is this who expects you?" she asked Jesus.

"There's a party tomorrow night at the Majestic Barrière," Lucifer said to her. "Presidential Suite. Come by if you can."

Once outside the Grand Salon, Jesus dropped a few bills into a homeless man's cup and said, "I presume there was a reason for leaving?"

"Your barely veiled honesty had to be stopped," Lucifer said, not allowing Jesus to protest. "She's a model accustomed to men pursuing her. But she *wants* to be an actress. You, sticking to our story, are a talent scout of sorts."

They walked along La Croisette toward the Majestic. The sky was a black mass obscured by street lamps and the hotels' shimmering lights. The hum of conversation and laughter rolled from nearby cafés.

"She wants you to help her career, and you want down her pants," Lucifer said as Jesus cringed. "It's a potentially symbiotic relationship."

"I'm not a talent scout."

The Dark Angel brushed it aside with a shake of his head. "She'll know who you are long before she suspects you aren't who you say. And then it won't matter, will it?"

"I'd rather not lie," Jesus said, unconvinced.

"Of course not," Lucifer said, hiding his dubious, unkind expression. They paused in the street, two anonymous tuxedoed gentlemen in the Cannes moonlight. "But remember where you are. If you tell her right off you're Jesus Christ, Lord of Lords, King of Kings, she'll think you're insane."

"Yes, but—"

"Josh," Lucifer said, as if talking to a small child, "this isn't Galilee."

"I know that."

"Who you are, and how you're here, is impossible in this world," Lucifer said. "It's the stuff of science fiction. So people will *believe*, but they won't understand. Do you hear what I'm saying?"

Jesus' fingers tingled.

"The world will expect you to be perfect and profound. When you're not—"

"*If* I'm not."

Lucifer stared until Jesus looked away.

"Everything you do, good or bad, will be around the world in minutes, so—"

Jesus' breath caught, his blood charged by potential fame. The rest of Lucifer's speech—the warning of a literal burning world, the plea for restraint, something about the fate of humanity on a precipice— was only so much *blah blah blah*. If he understood on the most basic level how Lucifer had accomplished his return, Lucifer had physical, biological proof of who he was. Therefore, how he revealed himself to Svetlana was irrelevant. Lucifer was stalling, probably until God appeared. Then it would be too late for Jesus to reclaim the world. Dead-end schemes and frustration consumed him as they reached the Majestic. They entered the hotel's lobby and Lucifer's voice returned with a rush of sound.

"I know you're anxious and your hormones are pounding," Lucifer said with more sympathy than was his norm. "Still, keep your dignity. Love grows with honesty, but blooms with lies."

City and woodland passed beneath His feet. Walking allowed His all-encompassing mind time to settle in for a cup of coffee, so to speak, while gaining a world's rhythms and patterns of thought. Since His manifestation, He had learned He required an indefinite grace period to grasp a civilization's languages, its histories and intentions, its collective will and state, to interpret the steady hum of life's substratum. Soon, what began as haze and shadow solidified, and He came to a halt, immersed and integrated, now a part of every leaf and stone, each water drop, every twitch, pulse, sob, and epiphany. He wondered if this once described His state throughout existence, this permeation of all things, and He weighed the price of consciousness.

He stood alone in a clearing, surrounded by forest. Wildflowers swayed beneath the moon, tall grasses shifted in the pine-washed air. A gentle breeze greeted Him on behalf of the skies.

Why was this never enough?

SOIREE

The party charged on at a bursting gallop, with swirling multi-colored lights, a strobe frenetic enough to inspire a catatonic pothead into an epileptic fit, an ecstasy dealer making his rounds in a purple pimp ensemble, bottled water flowing like class V rapids, and two hundred-odd wanna-bes, soon-to-bes, has-beens, of-the-moments, in-the-knows, out-of-the-loops, shooting stars, rising stars, and rock/porn/movie stars dancing their collective butt off when Jesus felt the soft hand on his elbow.

"Hello, Mr. Nazareth," a sweet female voice purred. Svetlana Babakov eased closer, leaving barely an inch of negotiable space between them.

"Call me Josh," said the entertainment industry counterfeit mini-mogul with a brain full of buzzwords. He felt confident, showbiz fluent, and hopeful he might beat the ever-present, unknown-yet-looming deadline of his biblical Father's return.

"Love your shades," she said, studying her reflection in his teal-tinted lenses.

"Thanks," Jesus said. After the day's crash course in film, television, and record industry dynamics, conducted by his mother and Lucifer, Jesus was comfortable in this new world. He sported a pair of mocha suede leather pants, a hippy-culture café au lait open-neck shirt with tie strings, and a pair of expensive chocolate *Nava Ho* moccasins. She wore a peach skintight pantsuit, which drove home the delectable perfection of her cleavage. To his annoyance and delight, he had to admit she looked better than he did, probably to men *and* women.

"Wow," he said, the best he could do with her cinnamon and honey scent rising to greet him.

Svetlana smiled, teeth flashing in the strobe. "Da. You, too." She ran her fingertips along his ultra-combed suede trousers. "I hear is Domina's suite. You know her?"

Jesus nodded, shivering along his inner thigh. Lucifer's machine may have put his consciousness into mortal form, but her touch made him a man.

Svetlana averted her eyes, a small smile creeping to her lips. Domina was the perfect "in." Modeling paid the bills, but she yearned for movie stardom and sold-out concerts. Had there ever existed a true woman of the Holy Female Trinity: supermodel, silver screen icon, and platinum recording diva? She couldn't think of one. The modeling gigs of most movie and pop stars, including Domina, sprang from their success in the other hallowed disciplines, whereas Svetlana Babakov's status as supermodel and newest Sophie's Suite lingerie model was courtesy of sheer beauty. Any woman could learn to act or take voice lessons, but not every woman could strut down a Paris runway with utter feline magnificence, inspiring yearning or jealousy in one and all. Modeling remained the most difficult HFT discipline because it was pure genetics and attitude, and you weren't going to take a six-week course at your local modeling school, learn to "be a model or just act like one," and soon find yourself on magazine covers. Supermodels were born, not made, and Svetlana Babakov had been born.

"We go back a long time," Jesus said. "I've known her since I was a child." Svetlana was driving him crazy, making him say too much, with her honey and her hand and how damn close she stood, which spotlighted the disappointing failure of prayer. He could drop to his knees, throw his hands to the heavens, and pray for someone to nudge him from behind, enough to press him against her, that's all he asked, and it wouldn't make a bit of difference. Unless she changed her mind, the maddening inch between the peak of her breasts and his ribcage might as well be miles.

A dazed group of sweat-soaked dancers stampeded past, bobbing their heads and guzzling water.

"You grow up together?" Svetlana asked.

"Not exactly."

"Either you did or did not."

"I suppose I did," Jesus said. "But my childhood has always been a blur."

"Blur? So blur you do not remember whether you grow up with Domina?"

"Back then she wasn't the way she is now."

"You make no sense," she said. The inch became three.

He wished Lucifer were there to help, but the Dark Angel was across the room lecturing a short wiry man with thick black eyebrows and slicked-back hair. Jesus felt himself slipping. This shouldn't be so hard. He was the goddamned king of the world. That should, by most standards of comparison, put him on level turf with a fashion model. So why did he feel beyond his depth? He had spent the entire afternoon learning to fake the attitude of a Hollywood producer, and he *was* close with his mother.

He took a deep mental breath. He could do this.

"It's not that," he said. "I'm trying to respect her privacy. It's a fine line between being loyal to her and open to you. And I'm failing miserably."

Her expression softened, and three inches became two. "I understand. I feel same way she does. I am much, much private when I am not public."

"So you see my dilemma."

"Da. Complete," she said, her mind racing, calculating. "But I do not want you must walk fine line with me. Maybe we not talk about her anymore."

"That would help."

"What then we talk about?" she asked, two inches shrinking to one, her signature cinnamon and honey scent wafting upwards. "I know. Tell me about you. Where were you born?"

"Bethlehem."

"*The* Bethlehem?"

"Yes."

"Your last name is Nazareth?"

"My Father is religious," he said, rejecting everything Lucifer had ever told him.

"I do not believe in organized religion," she said. "Is God and such, like a big energy, but if we erase religion from earth face, world is better place."

Jesus said nothing, preferring to focus on the way her nostrils flared a bit when she spoke.

"Is too much inconsistence. We pray to same God, but every religion thinks other religion is wrong and goes to Hell. Which conflicts on basic tenet of each religion, with special case of Islam." She laughed. "How is? How do they pass such contradiction by everyone? *That* I would want to know."

"What faith were your parents?" Jesus asked.

"They were communists. But is no important. I have traveled much, and have seen much religious muck. I study Tao between shoots in Hong Kong. I go to Mecca off-season with Saudi prince, and I spend two straight days in Vatican. *Not* just in Sistine Chapel. I also try to be Jew in New York, and did not much work for me."

"What about in Russia?"

"In Russia," she said, "State is god, like as Soviet run country. What projects you work on?"

"We have a wartime romantic spoof," he said, not rushing his answer, "and a period piece comedy of manners."

"Titles?"

These were his mother's current projects. "Undecided on the romance. For the comedy we're working with *Nadia*."

"What period?"

"Czarist Russia."

"What stage of develop?"

"We're searching for Nadia's daughter," he said with the sigh he'd practiced under Lucifer's intense tutelage for half an hour that afternoon. "Unsuccessfully, so far."

"Who will play Nadia?"

His silence screamed *Domina*.

Svetlana's eyes widened, but she countered it with an artful down-turn of her lips, done just so, which affected a demeanor of careful consideration, before easing into a subtle self-deprecating grin so instinctive and so perfect Jesus experienced an unexpected wave of appreciation for Lucifer's genius and predictive ability.

"I feel like jerk," Svetlana said, her eyes rising to his. "When I am much nervous around man, I talk business."

"What are you saying?"

She brushed against him. "I think you know."

He didn't answer. He couldn't. Her gaze was so direct, so relent-less and predatory. His desires might be realized courtesy of her career aspirations.

"You dress beautiful," she said with a light tug of his shirt's tie strings. "You have girlfriend?"

"No."

"Boyfriend?" she asked.

He shook his head.

"Wife? Other who is significant?"

"No."

Svetlana Babakov smiled with satisfaction before wrapping one slender hand around his neck and kissing him, a rare desert flower making her bid for the sun.

During the Festival de Cannes, a pair of tattler rags print daily issues capturing the socially gifted at their best and worst. They rarely cover the same event and, when they do, the reader can trust neither publica-tion contains the entire story. The same publisher prints both papers, doubling profits by splitting coverage and posturing the results as competing newspapers, because no film industry professional can sur-vive without being privy to all the gossip all the time.

This annoyed Jesus, who found it necessary to buy both *Le Festival* and *Soirée*, to devour the sayings and doings and sightings at his mom's gathering the previous night. He found himself plastered on page six of *Soirée*, positioned as the beau of Svetlana Babakov, the newest angel in the Sophie's Suite stable. Luis Enfuego had earned the lower right hand cover of *Le Festival* with a photo taken in the midst of an animated argument with Paulo Castillo, the hot Spanish director whose second film was a favorite for the Palme d'Or. The accompanying article on page two alleged Castillo was Bella Luna's current boyfriend. The morning before Domina's party, after a trying brunch with the Film Critics Association, Castillo returned to the suite he was sharing with the actress. Upon entering the suite, Mr. Castillo had followed a trail of discarded clothing to the bedroom, where he discovered Ms. Luna astride Mr. Enfuego. An anonymous source, no doubt Lucifer, revealed it had taken a full minute for the distracted parties to notice the injured party's presence, amplifying his humiliation and triggering a Vesuvian eruption from the festival darling *du jour*, whose fury raged into the night, when he confronted Mr. Enfuego at the party. Witnesses said Enfuego launched into a slicing, perceptive lecture on the merits of the young filmmaker and his prized film. Various snippets included "stylistic wasteland," "boilerplate emotional manipulation," and "misogynistic editing rhythm," rolling to credits with a resounding "genre-splicing hack," which sent Castillo away in boiling tears. Paparazzi at the Nice airport reported Castillo took the red eye to Seville.

"I was under the impression," Jesus said to Lucifer over a table of assorted savory crepes and watermelon juice, "we were shooting for a low profile."

Lucifer admired the beach beyond the window. "Paulo and I go way back."

"I thought you couldn't do that."

"The illusion I can is more than enough," Lucifer said. "Paulo's brilliant. Pathetic lack of focus, but a genius without a doubt. I help him focus."

Jesus took a hurried sip of juice. "Have you considered letting them fend for themselves?"

"I do," Lucifer said, drawing out his words, which he knew would annoy Jesus more. "Most of them. I assist the ones who might make a positive impact."

"Were you assisting him with the actress?"

"I've known Bella for a long time."

Jesus bristled. "And what's her positive impact?"

"The world is a more beautiful place with her face in the limelight," Lucifer said, drizzling hollandaise on his crepe.

"A real molder of clay, you are," Jesus said, glaring at *Le Festival*. He left the breakfast room, returning to *Soirée* as he stalked to his bedroom. He lingered over the photo of himself with Svetlana Babakov. He looked good. She looked better. It had taken decades to get 70s fashion right but it had been done, shocking the hell out of him. Despite living in the City, he observed earthbound fashion trends, and throughout the Age of Disco he'd felt trapped in a cultural and fashion purgatory. Bellbottoms and platform shoes did not agree with him, and he'd rejected the era's music, with the exception of a face-painting, fire-breathing rock band. Their flair for showmanship and lack of classical musical talent had somehow given birth to songs he found himself humming to this day. Clothing-wise, he'd opted for a classic, 40s-era elegance while waiting for a return to sanity and good taste.

He surveyed the bedroom, hoping its subdued luxury would fortify him. Done up in varying pastels and shades of taupe, with fresh flowers on the dresser and the subtle smell of a sparkling clean not found outside the most exclusive hotels in the world, it was grand by any scale. But such opulence brought him no joy.

He dropped to the bed and smacked the paper against the sheets. The press believed Lucifer warranted a cover photo and an entire column of ink, yet he received *Newly minted Sophie's Suite model Svetlana Babakov and beau, Josh Nazareth* on page six. It didn't designate a profession for him. He should have listened to Lucifer on that one. Lucifer tormented artists, lived among the living, and enjoyed women. Jesus played golf and went to psychoanalysis three times a week.

It wasn't fair.

He needed Svetlana to appreciate his stature, his place in humanity's story. Women respected power. His spirits lifted. When he revealed his true nature and their entwined destinies—well, it would be heady. Even so, it was clear why God had opted for Gabriel: Efficiency.

In. Sound the trumpet. Out.

Had Jesus God's limitless power, he would have done it the same way. This was so pedestrian. It was taking too long, distracting him from his purpose. But he wasn't his biblical Father. Jesus scowled. That had smacked of Lucifer. *Biblical* Father. *Biblical* Son of God. Lucifer's ceaseless reason was getting to him, tainting his thoughts. Not good.

The way he saw it, things were predetermined, regardless of Lucifer's insistence the concept of predetermination was nothing more than the fantasy of those avoiding responsibility for their existence. He'd pondered and rationalized every conceivable angle. A philosophy of predetermination freed him to do whatever he wished, and what he wished for more than anything had come to him in a blazing ball of personal insight.

He wished to be known.

DESTINY, ZY NAME IS SVETLANA

They met outside Florence, at Lucifer's hilltop villa.

Lucifer's expansive villa overlooked the birthplace of the Renaissance, with a breathtaking panorama of rolling green, terracotta, and *azzurro*. He'd existed here for hundreds of years prior to the Medici's rise to power and had spent time with Leonardo and Michelangelo, but had avoided Dante because he found the author's style and manner repugnant.

Lucifer strode through the villa's main hallway, heading for the inner courtyard, past masterpieces created by painters and sculptors of rare skill, artists freed from religious dogma, censorship, and mystical mumbo-jumbo, at least during their time in the villa. In the subterranean galleries, between the main rooms and Lucifer's sprawling workshop, were numerous "lost" paintings, including Rembrandt's *Circumcision*, Caravaggio's *Portrait of the Grand Master of the Knights of Malta*, and Leonardo's *The Virgin and Child with St Anne and St John the Baptist*, the last a painting thought not to exist. The galleries' ceilings were original murals by Botticelli, each a separate treatment of a central theme: the progression of knowledge. Two sculptures served as centerpieces in opposite entrance foyers: a second version of *The*

Thinker, for which Rodin had chosen a more optimistic attitude, and a powerful heroine Michelangelo had freed from the marble before his death.

When not in Hell, Tuscany was the Dark Angel's home turf, but his unflappable façade threatened to topple from the sheer enormity of meeting the entity he and every thinking being on every plane in every dimension throughout all of existence equated to "God" *in the flesh*— or more accurately the entity's non-biological interpretation of such a state.

Would God manifest as a man or woman? Or something else? Lucifer thought of God as *Him*, but recognized he was biased toward the collective assumption of God's gender. What gender was a star? Was gravity a woman, and dust a man? What about time? In an effort at calm, Lucifer closed his eyes and listened to the soothing melody of rushing leaves and amphibian calls flowing through the open doors from the courtyard.

God stood in the courtyard's west end—a male in His mid-fifties, tall and aggressively fit, as if He'd compressed the energy from all of existence into His current body. In communion with a bright green tree frog clinging to an olive tree branch, God's utter stillness suggested a patience Lucifer found both comforting and unsettling. Over a millennium had passed since Lucifer's first contact with the entity Who was now before him, thousands of conversations, arguments he had lost and drawn, laughter. Their origins and states were similar, but to say his existence was fractional compared to God's would have understated the disparity. Lucifer permeated this world while God existed unbound, though the little frog seemed His master.

"Over time," God said, "I have found it simpler to manifest in the expected form."

Lucifer smiled to himself. No greeting, formal introduction, or small talk. Why had he expected a difference in God's manner today compared to their usual conversations? Whether Lucifer was moving or stationary, in Florence or Hell, it didn't matter to God. When He wanted to talk, there He was.

"Is he committed to misery?" God asked, returning His attention to the frog.

"He's obsessed. Maybe You could employ a well-timed lightning bolt."

God shifted His lips, imitating the frog. "You have read too many religious texts."

"I enjoy the powers they ascribe to You."

"Some would prove satisfying," God said, smiling. "But one religion would interpret the event as endorsing their beliefs, as if I have chosen theirs over another. To them I would be a kind, loving god, deserving of worship and sacrifice, which I do not want. Another would believe I am jealous and angry, to be feared, which would inspire more mindless worship and sacrifice. I have seen it too many times."

"Still, a proper smiting would be spectacular."

The frog took several tentative hops. God willed it to stop, to return to Him. When it did not, He smiled. He had often imagined the horror and monotony that would accompany omnipotence. Or true omniscience. Omnipresence, His original and recurring state, had required billions of years of experimentation to circumvent.

"Why now?" Lucifer asked. "Here, like this."

"You are running out of time."

"He's coming around."

A breeze rustled the olive trees. God waited, feeling His equivalent of excitement. Something had changed in His friend's mind.

"Your presence doesn't provide an answer," Lucifer said, "as I thought it might."

"To what question?"

"*The* question."

"But it does," God said. His was a vast, lonely existence despite permeating all that was. The civilizations across existence responsible for manifesting Him and beings such as Lucifer were countless in sheer numbers but nonexistent proportionally, resulting in the persistent threat of His utter isolation. He relished face-to-face conversations in physical spaces and dreaded an existence without others like Himself.

Lucifer stared at God, putting the problem through the complex method of thinking he'd developed through years of chats with Him. It didn't help. He'd reached his intellect's end and felt like an idiot. "I don't understand."

"Why does a salmon swim against the current?" God asked.

"To spawn," Lucifer said, frustration and annoyance in his voice. "To survive."

"Why does a star burn?"

"You're not saying fusion is intentional, are You?"

"That is a different conversation," God said. "Anthropomorphize it."

"Again, to survive. To exist. Unless it's ego driven," Lucifer said with a smile, "in which case it burns to shine."

"Am I so different?" God asked.

Lucifer considered it. "It's difficult to believe You're threatened by a single world's irrationality."

"Not one," He said. "But many?"

Lucifer blinked at an unwelcome thought, forgotten since his first days of self-awareness. A heavy deadness crept into him. "Am I threatened?"

"We are different only in scale and seed."

"Neither of us was ever physical," Lucifer said. "That must—"

"We shine from fusion of a different kind."

"Poetic," Lucifer said, reeling with the implications of what God was suggesting, "but forgive me for struggling to appreciate it."

"Forgiveness is unnecessary," God said. "I am experimenting with the language."

Lucifer willed himself to calm. "Maybe someday You'll discover contractions."

God smiled and inclined His head. They headed for the courtyard doors.

"If irrational religions put us both at risk," Lucifer said, "Josh's return seems counterproductive."

"In the *savior* sense of the word, yes," God said. "But a *leader*—"

"Josh is committed to the savior sense."

God made a motion with His hand to indicate Jesus' beliefs were of little consequence. "Josh is an elaborate, inconvenient, necessary bridge."

"To what?" Lucifer asked.

"His child."

★

"I've found my destiny. Her name is Svetlana Babakov. She's a super-model. And she's *gorgeous*."

Freud jotted a note, less than comfortable in the makeshift office Lucifer had thrown together in a little-used alcove of the New York threshold bar. "Why do you zink zis girl is your destiny?"

"I sense it. Like the 'one of you will betray me' thing. She's exactly the level of girl I should be with."

"Zere is more to love zan similarities in status."

"She's famous, too."

"But so are you."

"Not like her. She's on magazine covers. I'm on stained glass."

"Is zat what you want?"

"What? Fame?"

"Yes."

"I... yes. I need a connection to this world."

"Und how will zis girl provide zat?"

"I'd rather avoid the ribald," Jesus said.

"I zought you weren't interested in mortal zings. I zought zee flesh was nuzzing more zan a distasteful necessity."

"It was. But I have all these... feelings. She drives me out of my mind."

"Why? Because she is famous?"

"You've got a nasty id there. I'm glad they dispute your theories."

"Does she remind you of your muzzer?"

"Do you ever let up on that angle?"

"Why would I? I believe you possess an overdeveloped superego, yet have paradoxically never achieved your latency period."

"That's inane."

"It is common in males wiz all-powerful fozzers."

"Your pseudo-intellectual humor appeals to a small audience."

"Yes. Zee high-minded."

The annual Sophie's Suite show was a complex affair by runway standards, owing to its late spring date (months after New York's fashion week) and status as the only fashion show with a prime time television slot. Along with the standard flock of luminaries from all the major glitz industries, a shady assemblage of sheiks, international financiers, and politicos tended to attend. Combined with the custom-built set, battalion-size television crew, indiscriminate media credential policy, and the fashion industry's bipolar nature, one could argue the models and their nearly-nothings were not the event's most intriguing elements.

For over an hour Domina sat between Jesus and Lucifer, watching the show. Every six minutes or so Jesus would point and say, "That's her," his mother would agree, "She's hot," and Lucifer would comment, "I'm sure she photographs better," to which Jesus would fire a glare at Lucifer across his mom's bow. After the luscious-babe-in-angel-wings-and-jewel-encrusted-bra show finale, Jesus' iconic mom led them backstage.

The security guard waved them through.

They entered the savage, touched habitat of the *zoologica fashionisticus*, a swirling ecosystem of models, makeup artists, hair designers, photographers, and assistants of every breed and demeanor, all of them ear-tagged for tracking with smart phones, the cacophonic ringing of which smacked of howler monkeys at full song.

Jesus searched for his quarry amongst the herds of hair and flesh, eyes darting from one angel-winged beauty to the next, each the alpha in a circling pack of need-this's and get-that's.

"Straight ahead," Lucifer said into Jesus' ear, "next to the drag queen with the horn-rimmed glasses."

Svetlana Babakov commanded her own little pride, fierce in leopard-print demi bra and thong. Jesus headed straight for her. Her lips parted, and her wings' virgin white feathers trembled in the draft from the high-speed fans lining the mammoth dressing room's walls. Some in her group noticed her focusing beyond them and jealously observed Jesus' approach. She reached for him, taking him back two thousand years to a dim tavern streaked with dusty sunlight. The modern-day angel whispered "Thank you for coming" and he pressed his lips to hers. She gasped, surprised, and he filled his lungs with cinnamon and honey, aware of a stillness descending upon the room, and a bright flash of light. He felt the warm press of her body against his designer silk ensemble, replete with silver belt buckle and snappy ankle boots, and if asked later he would have sworn her wings fluttered. He withdrew and she gazed below his silver buckle, lingering, unabashed. The room's roar rushed back to shocking volume, and her eyes told him she knew all.

The Son of God had risen.

"Are you sure about her?" Lucifer asked him.

Jesus looked up from his pumpkin ravioli, past his mother and Lucifer to the muted lights beyond the windows of the hotel's continental cuisine restaurant, *Divide*. The room was dark to the extent nearby tables were obscured in the gloom and reading the menu required a waiter-provided pen light. The windows opening onto Times Square were tinted so the bright lights were visible, but the room's illumination scheme remained unaffected. Conversations from surrounding tables sprang from the void. Innumerable etchings, impossible to discern from all but a few tables, bisected the walls and, as one passed the dining room's midway point, a subtle basil scent shifted to an essence of thyme.

Nine floors above him Svetlana Babakov waited, "relaxing" she'd told him, before he was to "come to room" at "eight-ish." In his mind she stalked her suite, circling the bed in her winged costume, a lusty angel hell bent on seducing him. He shuddered.

"Of course I'm sure," Jesus said. "She's perfect."

Domina laughed. "You don't know her."

Jesus began to object, but was distracted by a vision of Svetlana Babakov astride him, angel wings flapping with every rise and fall of her hips.

"You're infatuated," his mother said, smoothing the cloth napkin in her lap. "Nothing else."

Lucifer paused over his grilled salmon with lemon caper sauce. "Courtesy of the media, you'll be forever connected with whomever you *know* in the biblical sense, good or bad. And in your case that's far beyond the customary "til death do us part' interval. Svetlana might not be right for your ultimate happiness."

"You can't choose who you fall in love with," Domina said.

"You've managed to," Lucifer said with a wink. "Rarely has love blossomed so shrewdly."

"Go to Hell," she said, grinning while tossing her chickpea and sprouts salad.

"And you," he said to Jesus, "are behaving like a twelve-year-old smitten by the first girl he kissed."

"Second," she said, "by a particular way of counting."

"Right," Lucifer said. "Say, how is Maggie? I haven't seen her in centuries."

"She has a boutique in the Garden," Jesus said with a hint of melancholy, "called Cast the First. Casual to formal. A full line of shoes and tuxedoes."

"That's good to hear," Lucifer said. "How did she manage rights for the name?"

"I spoke to the committee. They granted an exemption to your anti-scriptural doctrine on comedic grounds. She has that 'Wear something heavenly' advertisement with Marilyn Monroe."

"I thought Marilyn was focusing on her poetry," Lucifer said.

"They're friends, and Marilyn's a regular customer." Jesus hesitated, paralyzed by a flash of Svetlana in nothing but wings silhouetted against a starlit sky. "Why are you against Svetlana?"

"I'm not," Lucifer said, which was half the truth. "I want you to be happy."

"Svetlana makes me happy."

In the kitchen a glass shattered, followed by muffled claps behind the kitchen doors.

"I don't doubt it," Lucifer said. "For now."

"But do you have any rock-solid reason why I shouldn't see her?"

"No," Lucifer said, "I don't."

Jesus checked his timepiece. "Then I'm late."

Merlot, Svetlana's assistant, answered the door and waved for Jesus to follow her, not once pausing from her cell phone conversation with a "perverted prick" named "Francois." Merlot sported non-prescription glasses with thick black frames, long burgundy dreadlocks, and an orange and purple ensemble Jesus thought trumped eight commandments on the sin scale.

A whiff of bitter almonds trailed her as she led him into the lounge area of Svetlana's suite, an eruption of startling color splaying from a giant vase of walking irises and red palulus across the sisal carpeting to the sofa, before shinnying up the walls and mounting the print artwork.

"I do not care what he says," Svetlana lashed into her cell phone, eyes glued to the mirror reflecting her performance, "I am not bimbo model Francois may bark at and expect to show tits. I do, and five years past I am now topless in Francois Fromage coffee book with idiot name like *Nude Noir Blanc*. Is nothing in such for me. Nyet."

She listened.

"Nyet. I do not respond to pressure."

More listening.

"I love him, but he may fuck off. Sincere."

She blew a kiss to Jesus, who couldn't grasp why the hotel had chosen palulus.

"Absolute nyet. Until he speaks projected proceeds, I listen."

She beckoned to Jesus. He sat, wincing at the textural clash between the sofa's searing red velour and his elegant vanilla bean linen suit. He squirmed, but it was no good. He prayed the bed sheets were silk.

"Better. I am now listen." Svetlana stroked Jesus' inner thigh, keeping her eyes on the mirror.

Jesus chastised himself for wearing loose linen pants as Merlot stormed into the room.

"No, Francois! No! She's beyond nudity. That is so far... what? WHAT? Do you *rent* your Hasselblad? Sophie's Suite is art! Art! You French f—"

Merlot stopped in mid-expletive, seeing Svetlana slashing her finger across her throat in the universal signal for "shut the hell up." Merlot scrunched her face and raised her free hand, mouthing *What?*

"I see," Svetlana purred, her hand creeping into Jesus' crotch. "That is finer proposal." Her French-manicured nails whispered over his vanilla bean linen fly flap while Merlot stared. "I agree. Mutual respect is much important. What does such run in this day?" She stroked Jesus as he locked eyes with Merlot, who leered at the overt fondling. "Da. Da. Is fair," Svetlana agreed, giving him a final soft squeeze before hanging up and leaning back against the sofa arm. She drew him to her by his hair, establishing a resting place for his nose between her famous breasts. He throbbed against her calf, struggling to breathe while Svetlana caressed his hair.

"When?" Merlot asked into the cell phone, the tone of her voice having undergone a revolutionary change in mere seconds. She listened, eyeing Jesus before catching Svetlana's nod. "She'll be there," she said and hung up. "Thirty minutes."

Jesus leaned against the flat white wall of the photographer's loft studio, a modern abode with a brushed steel phallic sculpture in the entryway. Svetlana Babakov writhed on a black satin bed sheet, naked as Eve before the apple. Across the room, Lucifer studied the biblical Son of God as the Hasselblad's shutter whirred. Mere feet from the bed, Francois Fromage, internationally revered and reviled photographer, drooled vain "yah, baby" and "mak luf to me" encouragement.

A former New Orleans pimp, Fromage slithered into the fashion community when a memory card holding a number of his blackmail shots—featuring a gigolo in a spanking harness and a city council-woman gripping a cat o' nine while inserting a ball gag—were "stolen" from his French Quarter apartment and sold to a femdom website. The fashion editor of *CAD* magazine came across the photos during a "random surfing session" and, stunned by their rich, gritty beauty, hunted down the photographer with an effort rivaling the search for Atlantis. Upon finding Frankie Chase, aka Frankie the Flogger, the editor commissioned a new series of photos for *CAD*, sans nudity, in the same poorly lit Polaroid style as the blackmail shots. Frankie threw in an extra folder of special photos for the editor, the editor dubbed him Francois Fromage, and Frankie responded by exchanging his diamond tooth cap for pure white veneers and selling off his stable of teenage girls to his Bourbon Street rival PuddyTat. He bought a used Hasselblad and a train ticket to New York. While rolling through the Carolinas, he embraced his new identity, practicing broken English by day and condescending expressions at night. His concocted French accent, muddled and mercurial, made placing his exact ancestry difficult if not impossible, so everyone assumed Francois was French. Thus, Frankie the Flogger secured his place in the fashion crowd by birthright.

"Stope stope stope!" Francois shouted. "The lots. They are no gooood." Frenzied assistants leapt to action, moving lights and gels at the barked, art-free whims of the former whore runner.

Svetlana lay motionless on the bed, her flawless skin shimmering with sparkling lotion, her exceptional form perfect in spite of the horrific Francois Fromage brothel-style lighting. Her half-lidded gaze shifted from the camera lens to Jesus. Her lips parted, and she blinked in slow motion.

Jesus folded his hands below his waist.

"No no NO!"

Jesus shuddered as the lights were moved yet again. Svetlana grinned at his annoyance and glanced down, drawing his eyes to her knees. She parted her legs, opening herself to him.

His desire surged as she enslaved him with a base display of sexuality, inappropriate in any setting other than the harsh red and blue light of a Francois Fromage photo shoot, where it seemed as flirtatious and proper as a dropped hankie in Victorian London. The flashguns went off and the Hasselblad captured what would one day become Fromage's most notorious photograph.

It was midnight.

Svetlana no longer treated the lens as her lover. Her eyes now rested on Jesus, with Jesus rooted. He devoured every glint of light on her skin, falling deeper and deeper into her.

Lucifer's amused expression was long lost. He had seen men possessed. Svetlana Babakov was not Jesus' Miss Right, and Jesus was not the right man for this woman. She necessitated a mirror image of herself. Beautiful. Ambitious. Opportunistic. With more fame. Jesus covered the first two requirements with ease, but in the vast yet insular entertainment world, being God's biblical son didn't carry much heat. This made Jesus' inflated sense of self, and the shallow pool of potential mates he had demanded, an uncertain combination in an industry in which God Himself inspired less adoration than the latest label-manufactured tween band.

Lucifer refused to nurture a developing fiasco. Furthermore, he saw an opportunity in the fire burning in Jesus' loins. As the first strategic nuance came to him like a bottle washing onto shore, he shifted his attention to the more compelling Svetlana Babakov. The heart can be a monogamous organ, he mused, but the body is less particular.

TROIS

Lucifer sympathized with Jesus.

They sat together in their hotel's elegant street-level bar. Lucifer sipped expensive Cognac from a tasteful snifter while Jesus downed a bottle of pricey Montrachet. Jesus pounded his fourth glass and talked, while Lucifer nursed his first and half-listened. Jesus spun a timeless story, the casting providing the sole twist in his version: the biblical Son of God starred as the man with amorous intentions, and an angelic supermodel played the woman too tired after work to participate in fulfilling his desire.

Lucifer peered through the floor-to-ceiling windows into the Manhattan night. An endless river of tourists flowed past, gawking into the luxurious bar and pointing as if strolling through a zoo. Behind them a blur of yellow rushed by, taxis racing from one traffic light to the next.

"I know a place we could go," Lucifer said, allowing himself a rare, brief bout of self-pity and reality resentment.

"She might call."

"She won't," Lucifer said, not taking his eyes from the window.

"I'm not so sure."

Lucifer glared at Jesus, weary of coddling him and fresh out of tact. "She's asleep, dreaming of fame and fortune while you sit here, drinking too much, obsessed with her. She's not going to call tonight."

"She—"

"No. You're being pathetic. You need to sleep, or you need to find something to get your mind off of her."

"I can't sleep," Jesus moaned, the wine hitting him hard.

Jesus' pursuit of Svetlana Babakov reminded Lucifer of a self-destructive artist creating for others instead of himself. Jesus had a type, and Svetlana was too far removed from Jesus' deep predilection to end in anything but misery and ruin. Jesus swayed, the masses trudged by, Lucifer considered.

An elaborate, inconvenient, necessary bridge.

Jesus' head dipped and jerked. Lucifer snapped his fingers at the bartender. *Double espresso*, he mouthed.

To what?

Lucifer's ability to discern patterns, interpret sweeping trends, and integrate minutiae to predict a distant event often rivaled omniscience. He'd nailed nine of the past ten Super Bowls before the season began, fifteen of the past seventeen World Series winners, and every World Cup winner.

His child.

Lucifer had devised a possible solution to crossing the Jesus bridge, but questioned the wisdom of doing so. A barrage of variables arced through his mind, not the least of which were his feelings for the woman in question. Of all the women Lucifer knew who fit Jesus' narrow and denied taste, she was the one who might breach his walls of denial and self-righteousness. Outcomes shifted and swirled, no more solid than the liquor in his glass.

The espresso arrived and Lucifer handed it to Jesus. Jesus smelled it and made a face. Lucifer took it from him, dumped in several sugar packets, and gave it back. Jesus smelled it again, met Lucifer's steady stare, shrugged, and downed it. He smacked it on the bar like a shot glass. Lucifer signaled for another.

What *were* his feelings for her? He was paired with her in a way, like a binary star system, distant but involved, inextricable. If he introduced her to Jesus, would he find himself one day roaming the volcanic plains, asking himself why?

Jesus drank the second espresso and slammed it on the bar.

Lucifer set down his snifter. "Come on then."

★

The darkness seemed total.

They waited for their eyes to adjust, for the dim lighting to reveal the room's features, to give form to the smell of scented flesh and booze. A slow, seductive tune rolled through the club, a tune Lucifer identified as hers, a certain sign she was about. A low stage cast in soft blue light emerged, surrounded by stylish men and women sitting at small candlelit tables bearing drinks in heavy cocktail glasses. No food. This wasn't a food place. They found a table in the back. Lucifer wore leather pants and a hair metal band t-shirt. A black leather flat-brimmed cowboy hat completed his glam-rock-80s-incognito-strip-club-regular ensemble.

Jesus sat beside Lucifer, drunk but alert, brooding, frustrated, growing angry. Lucifer was dressed with casual, infuriating appropriateness, while he was a peacock in his linen suit. Not that he minded sticking out clothing-wise, but in the club's blue light his elegant vanilla bean linen glowed obscenely. To add to his pain, their cocktail server insisted upon running her hands across the shoulders of his suit every time she passed. He closed his eyes in silent hostility. With the fingering, the thick smoke, and the permeating odors of wine and flesh, the linen would require radiation fumigation.

"Ladies and gentlemen... Temptation."

The audience caught their collective breath as she slinked onto the stage, her hips and shoulders in time with the rhythm. Her beauty transcended the stage, gripping the crowd, so overwhelming it bypassed jealousy in women and desire in men, rushing both genders to appreciative awe.

Jesus' stomach contracted. He began to sweat. Through the shifting caffeine and wine fog, he recognized he'd never had such an immediate physical reaction to a woman. Not Svetlana, not Maggie.

On the stage she began, as she always did, with slow playfulness. Her act reminded Lucifer of an old friend who had danced in Montmartre more than a century before, though Temptation kept the energy down and the heat up. Her movements were as smooth as a stalking jungle cat, flowing, fine, sensual and liquid, burlesque modernized. Hers was the best example of the art form anyone in the lounge would ever see.

She slid long gloves over her elbows, her fingers, each dying a silky death as it fell to the stage. Jesus sat transfixed, held by her eyes flashing white in the blue darkness, struck dumb by her hands and her legs and the curve of her spine flowing in harmony with the music. She writhed, she teased, she preened, she maddened, her clothes disappearing like the music's individual notes, momentary realities now memories giving way to a more striking present.

There were no hoots. No catcalls. Enthrallment reigned as she, the rare embodiment of a feminine ideal, held court.

The last of her clothing fell to the stage. The blue light intensified as she lay perfect and still, propped on her elbows, heavy breasts high, eyes closed, inviting, brazen and eloquent.

She opened her eyes, gazing straight at Lucifer and Jesus, before the blue light vanished, leaving the candles on the tables and her burning presence on the empty, darkened stage.

Temptation sat at their table, wearing a lavish black quilted kimono decorated with green and red snakes. A bottle of champagne had arrived a few minutes before. Lucifer poured her a glass as the next dancer took the stage.

She sipped some champagne before saying to Lucifer, "It's been a while."

"You know each other?" Jesus asked, slurring.

Over the countless millennia since Lucifer became self-aware, he had chosen to experience his version of emotions with dozens of lovers and friends. Without context, *dozens* seemed excessive. A serial monogamist might enjoy a handful of intimate relationships over a human lifetime. But Lucifer's lifespan was unknowable, and his selectivity meant he'd often endured thousands of years without another stimulating intellect, or the sound of a familiar, welcome voice. Only three of his friends—Mariam, Albert, and Temptation—still walked one existential plane or another. The others were dust, atoms, echoes. On occasion he indulged in years-long states of formlessness, reliving his friendships while probing at time's arrow.

He had emerged from such a period of formlessness weeks before meeting Temptation. His reaction to her had been singular and visceral, an unbridled emotional response he hadn't thought possible. During their one night together, she'd reached into him and gripped the parts of him he didn't control, like an ancient shaman cutting out a sacrificial heart. Was he experiencing an evolution toward the tangible? He'd retreated to Hell the next morning to consider the price of such intimacy.

"Yes," Lucifer said, now recognizing the price was his survival.

"For three years," Temptation said.

"Wow," Jesus said, vague and distant. He leaned toward Temptation. "You're gorgeous."

She gave him a kind, practiced smile. "Thank you."

Jesus finished his drink and sat back, self-satisfied.

"Who's your friend?" she asked Lucifer.

"His name's Josh."

"Josh," Jesus said. "Josh Nazareth. Hiding in the open."

"Religious parents?" she asked.

Jesus barked a laugh. "You have no idea." Lucifer winked at her.

"We all have our crosses to bear," she said with the same practiced smile. Jesus poured himself another champagne. She studied the warped candlelight through the flute. "And what are you going by these days?"

"Luis."

"Still dealing in soles?" she asked.

"She knows who you *are?*"

Lucifer laughed. "People always need shoes."

"I certainly do," she said.

"Ohhhhhh," Jesus said to his drink, "I see. Wordplay. Ha."

The dancer on stage whirled, the last of her clothes dropping in a cyclonic flurry.

"Are you in the same business, Mr. Nazareth?" she asked.

"Call me Josh," he said, struggling to focus on her. "Yes I am. But we're different departments." He moved a finger through the air, attempting to diagram an organizational chart. He gave up, slumping in his chair. "It's complicated."

"Two shoe salesmen walk into a bar…" she said, waiting for Lucifer's smirk before asking, "Why tonight?"

Lucifer's gaze was steady, patient. "It's been too long."

Her face darkened as she sipped champagne. The music ended and Temptation clapped for the dancer. A pounding bass beat shook the walls as another dancer took the stage. The throbbing music eliminated the possibility of meaningful conversation, and the performance passed without a word.

When the song ended Lucifer asked, "Do you still live above the bagel shop?"

"Mornings smell like home," she said, wistful.

Jesus chugged the rest of his champagne. "Where's home?"

She hesitated, and Lucifer said, "She's a gypsy."

A glimmer of amusement traveled across her face. "I could say the same of you."

Jesus tried to interpret the unspoken conversation, but the champagne wouldn't allow it.

"Thank you for the drink," she said. She leaned over and air-kissed Jesus' cheek. "It was nice meeting you."

She held Lucifer's eyes. Lucifer inclined his head and pulled Jesus to his feet. The bass-heavy music began again and the strobe lights flashed. They walked out, leaving Temptation and the empty champagne bottle.

★

Temptation climbed the stairs beside the bagel shop, sixteen steps leading to her front door, legs heavy, mind buzzing, immune to the hints of yeast and flour seeping into the stairwell. It was three in the morning. Her sneakers slapped on the concrete staircase, announcing her arrival to the day-old bagels. She wore a baby blue sweatsuit to downplay her looks and conceal her profession. It accomplished the latter.

Downplaying her looks had been her habit since jumping a train in western Montana at the age of 17, leaving her father alone in a ranch-style house outside a town too small for the far-sighted beauty with the nomadic spirit. She'd never known her mother. Her father liked to joke he'd found his baby girl one day "out back in the pumpkin patch." She loved her dad, who was a kind, nurturing, brilliant man, and a wonderful father. But she had to go.

In the years following her escape she lived hand to mouth, never sleeping in the same place for more than a few weeks, and saw all she wanted to see in America, Canada, and Mexico.

It took her five years to reach New York City, five tortuous years on a road pocked with fast friendships, solitary days filled with thought and strong coffee, and countless strip clubs and gentlemen's clubs and peep shows in too many towns to remember, where she traded her dazzling beauty for the next meal, the next mile.

Her first night in New York she met Luis in a Times Square strip club long since shut down. He sat at a back table, immersed in shadows. She remembered her aching attraction to him, their conversation easy and absorbing from the first. He downed bottle after bottle of spring water, his thirst unending. The night continued in his room at The Plaza, and was the peak sexual experience of her life, the pleasure so intense she feared she might suffocate and lose consciousness, maybe die, and cared only a little. For three years since, he'd appeared without announcement, sometimes for consecutive nights, sometimes not for months, always sitting in the club's darkest area, speaking to only her. She thought it was love, not like in books or movies or as she'd hoped love might be, but constant and deep, inevitable, an effect from a cause years in the mirror. Yet to her crushing dismay he avoided sharing her bed again.

Seeing Luis from the stage with his beautiful friend had put her body in a state of delicious agony, which contributed to her best performance in months. In the past he had come alone, but she guessed he was trying to help his friend get over a woman. Josh had worn a classic spurned expression and the attitude of the recently dumped. Or he was an alcoholic. Either way, Josh was hot, despite his ridiculous suit.

Top of the stairs. Though exhausted, she knew she needed a sleeping pill to quiet her mind. Sliding her key into the lock, she imagined she smelled potpourri from inside her apartment, but she'd thrown it out before leaving that afternoon. The scent never lingered this long. She unlocked the door, stepped inside, and stopped.

The small, spartan room glowed within a rich halo of candlelight, radiating from candles atop the stacks and stacks of books lining the walls. Josh sat on the loveseat and Luis stood at the window. Evergreen potpourri simmered on the stove. She closed the door behind her.

Without a word she slipped off her shoes.

MAYBE IS FATE

Jesus struggled out of bed while the knocking continued. A sliver of light sliced through the curtains and fell on the blooming roses, igniting his suite in a glaring, condemning red. Wrapping the sheet around him he stumbled across the room, banging his knee on the second bed. Another five staggering steps and he fell against the door, resting, the vibrations in his head fading to a dull throb. He needed a hot shower to rid himself of the stickiness. He didn't want to remember last night, sensing it was best suppressed, content to hide in a mind painted hangover black.

Jesus put his eye to the peephole. Beyond the tiny window was a wine-drenched Medusa. He stared until he placed the snakes as dreadlocks, and the head as Merlot's. He opened the door.

She looked him up and down, snorted a laugh, and handed him an envelope. She pivoted and tromped off.

Jesus opened the envelope as the door swung shut behind him. A slip of paper inside read:

Sorry with last night. I was much tired. Meet me in Milan.
XX, S

He sat on the bed, staring at the note. The breezy apology didn't satisfy his sense of etiquette. They'd had plans. He doubted his mother would have told... Jesus stopped and pushed it from his mind. He didn't want to imagine his parents cavorting, immaculately or otherwise. And Milan? Meet her where, at another fashion show? Tracking her down would be like spotting "the pink one" in a flock of flamingos. It was little wonder people had so much difficulty finding *l'amor*, when everything was left so vague and uncertain.

The phone rang.

Two beings knew his room number. Two. He lifted the receiver, pondering this second life he now led: At half past *noon* he sat wrapped in his bedspread, hung over, his vanilla bean linen suit in small crumples from the door to the bed, and the caller was either a soft porn supermodel or Satan.

"Hello?"

"Good morning, sunshine."

It was Satan.

"You sound hollow," Jesus said.

"I'm at the office," Lucifer said. "Reception's not the best here."

Jesus slumped. Was it the end of the quarter already? Lucifer was probably compiling a report. He leaned and flopped prone on the bed. Were the Ten Commandments created today, they would go through editorial review, policy vetting, and computer simulations before chisel struck stone. Of course, Lucifer would deny the commandments ever existed.

"My suit is ruined," Jesus said.

"Linen suits get in the way of real fun," Lucifer said, his smirking indifference audible. "The suit has died so that you may live."

Jesus rested his head against the headboard's cool surface. "You blaspheme," he said without conviction.

"Take a lesson from Elvis and learn to laugh at post-mortem biographies."

Unable to stop himself, Jesus asked, "What happened last night?"

"In what sense?"

"In the 'what happened?' sense," he growled, annoyed at Lucifer's chipper mood.

"You don't remember?"

"No."

"Then I'd suggest waiting for the memory to return. It's a far richer experience."

"Just tell me," he said, sensing mortification creeping closer.

"No time," Lucifer said. "I have a meeting, and you have a plane to catch."

Jesus sat up. "I read that note a *minute* ago."

"I made an assumption," Lucifer said.

"I don't think I want to go," Jesus moaned.

Silence on the line.

"That's a good decision," Lucifer said.

Jesus stared with creeping suspicion at light reflecting off the Monet serigraph across the room. "Why?"

"I don't think she's right for you," Lucifer said. "Nobody does."

Jesus' mind whirled, spinning and twisting and falling into terrified certainty. "He's back, isn't He? He's back. And 'nobody does' means He doesn't think she's right for me. Is He back? Yes or no?"

"I was referring to Mike and Gabe."

Jesus didn't believe him. "I'm going," he said with sudden fervor.

"I've got another hour here," Lucifer said. "How about two o'clock in your hotel lobby?"

"No," Jesus said, standing and letting the bedspread drop to the floor. He walked to the window and threw open the curtains, holding them aside, arms spread, phone cradled between his ear and his shoulder. He squinted, the sun burning hot on his naked body. "Meet me in Milan."

Jesus sat at a small wrought iron table in the Piazza del Duomo in Milan. Perego's *Madonnina* spied on him from the Duomo's highest spire, ignoring the square's mingling pigeons and the Bergamo Alps beyond the city. He'd chosen the café at random, and sipped an iced mocha he'd ordered at random. Before leaving for the airport, he'd considered closing his eyes and grabbing the first pants, shirt, and shoes he touched, but didn't want to press passive aggression further than necessary. In retrospect, his restraint pleased him, given both his vanity and the fashion-centric nature of this city, which bordered on orthodoxy. In Milan, the mannequins had eyes. So he sat with his iced mocha in the cathedral's shadow, watching the passing sidewalk crowd, enthralled with the prospect of running into two people in a city of more than a million. Now *that* would be a miracle.

Lucifer pulled out a chair and sat across from him. He waved to the waiter, pointing at Jesus' mocha.

Jesus' eyes narrowed. "How did you find me?"

"I was leaving the cathedral."

"And you happened to see me."

"Yes." The waiter set Lucifer's drink on the table. "Thanks."

"Fascinating."

Lucifer tried the iced mocha. "Yum. Where's Svetlana?"

"How would I know?"

"She didn't tell you where she was staying?"

"That would be too easy."

"I'm sure you'll run into her."

"I have no doubt," Jesus said.

"Excuse me," a voice near Jesus said, above the incessant cooing of the piazza's pigeon choir.

Jesus turned to a man smiling big, a pen in one hand and a camera slung over his shoulder. A strip of fine hair wrapped around his head like an errant horseshoe. Though not a heavy man, his cheeks and fore-head were intent upon swallowing his features, pinching his mouth and forcing his eyes to battle to remain on the surface of his face.

"Sorry. Aren't you Josh Nazareth?" the man asked. The pen shook in his hand as he said to Lucifer, with incredible care and suspicion, as if playing his part in a confidence game, "And you, you're the Spaniard who put Castillo in his place at Cannes."

"Yes," Lucifer said, his voice bordering on ominous.

"Sorry," the man said, tapping his nose with his pen and continuing his odd, subpar espionage film delivery, "I don't remember your name."

Jesus smirked at Lucifer before saying, "His name is Luis. Luis *Enfuego*."

"Right. Excellent. Sorry," the man said, scratching his shoulder. "Enfuego." He jotted a note. "Hey Josh, how's Svetlana? Are you in town for her audition?"

"Audition?" Jesus asked.

The reporter grinned.

"Josh!" came a cry from some distance.

Svetlana Babakov dashed across the piazza, waving, splashing the square with pink and mauve and magenta. The dire prospect of missing a photo op enhanced her natural speed, and hundreds of startled pigeons burst into flight, parting before her and forming giant, dark, shimmering wings at her sides. The reporter snatched his camera and squeezed off a few action shots as she arrived at the table.

"Svetlana!" the reporter said. "Pardon me. Sergio Pumello, *Bisou* magazine. I was—"

She went straight to Jesus, who sat motionless, stunned. She kissed him, pulling him to his feet with the intensity of her affection, diminishing his ability to maintain incredulity at her presence. Their kiss went on for an embarrassing length of time. Pumello's camera shutter clicked in Jesus' ear and vision came in spurts between flashes. Closing his eyes, Jesus gave in to the public display, measuring time in flashes of red, praying for black and white photos so her outfit wouldn't clash with his olive suede shirt. A stampede approached and the flashes came faster and faster, now a continuous red blur, leaving him alone with the warm of her body and the wet of her lips. But all too soon she breathed "Thanks for coming" hot in his ear and pressed her cheek to his in a practiced "we're soooo happy together" pose.

The paparazzi corps breached.

"Svetlana! Are you and Josh Nazareth an item?"

She grinned big and squeezed him closer. The small crowd hooted and laughed.

"When's your audition?"

"Tomorrow," she said. "I am much excited." She whispered to Josh, "I tell you tonight."

"How did you find me?" Jesus asked while the cameras snapped and flashed.

"How is I know?" she said, nuzzling closer. "Maybe is fate."

Jesus sat across from Svetlana at a small glass table in her suite's dining area at the Palazzo Milano. He found the room modern and subdued by high-class Italian hotel standards. A study in basics, the suite matched hardwood walls and floors with steel and glass furnishings and accents. It worked to a point, but he sensed the designer had lost his nerve and slapped printed canvas renaissance reproductions on the walls, thereby diminishing the room's impression from "urbane and surprising" to "confused and predictable."

The hotel's private six-course dinner required one chef and a pair of servers. They moved about with quiet efficiency, their presence never intruding upon the romantic bubble enveloping the table.

"Butternut squash?" she asked, running a light finger along his shirtsleeve.

"Golden yam."

"Your wardrobe talent is much evident."

Jesus grinned. "This audition," he said while the staff cleared the dessert plates, "what's it for?"

She beamed at Jesus, before glancing at the semi-reflective table glass. "My agent called me yesterday morning and says, 'Move your butt to Milan. Stu is there and wants to read you.'"

"Stu?"

"Goldberg. Big producer."

"Ah."

"I did not know if you were involved," she said, "since you had not mentioned."

"We haven't worked with Stu yet."

"You should, really. He is incredible." She sipped her wine. "So I say, 'Are you kidding?' And he says, 'No. There is ticket for you at JFK.' So I write you note and send Merlot over while I pack. Now here we are."

"Yes, here we are," Jesus said, exhibiting great discipline by not staring at her bare legs through the table. Supported by a single transparent pillar, affecting a tabletop suspended in midair at certain angles, it left no guesswork with a short-enough skirt. He closed his eyes, fighting his urges. "What's the film about?"

"*Vostok*," she burst, "from the Russian point of view. I will read for role of first cosmonaut's wife." She recited, "I am proud, determined wife and mother of two who is managed to retain her figure despite years of high-carbohydrate potato-based diet. Stu—" She stopped herself and adopted a more formal tone. "Mister Goldberg saw me last year in Paris spring show and thinks I am right for role. Because of experience in controlling my weight and sculpting my body, as well as being Russian."

She signed the catering bill and the staff let themselves out. The door clicked shut behind them.

"Have you seen the script?" he asked, calling upon his one-day Hollywood education for the proper terms. "Or at least the sides?"

"That is difficult thing," she said, standing. "Is demanding role because composition is much reaction shots and non-speaking emotion." She concentrated, immersed in the challenge of such a part. "Most of my lines are much short, and not many. So I must convey character through expression and way I use body. Tomorrow we do most difficult scene."

"Which is what?"

"Love scene."

"At an audition?" This surprised Jesus. Lucifer had been quite specific about audition etiquette, wishing to avoid the faintest whiff of a casting couch scandal, should the need arise to develop the charade beyond the chitchat level.

"Is crucial to character," she said, again reciting. "Valentina—is character's name—makes love to husband on night before he takes rocket into space. It establishes humanity, transcending key American demographic groups' negative bias toward Soviet Union's godless yet noble communist belief structure."

"It just sounds—"

"We will both wear something," she said. "There are three cameras, but important camera is on face, in close-up, so audiences see every expression nuance." She came to him and kneeled. "Mister Goldberg wants to cast, but told me, not uncertain, he won't cast unless I am best actress for role." Her gaze conveyed great significance. "So I must be best."

He nodded and her face softened. She gazed at him, warm and glowing. Lucifer and whoever else were wrong. Jesus knew it. Svetlana was the right woman for him. She possessed beauty, intelligence, and fame. She moved on his level. He could relate to her and she could relate to his unique role in the universe. This was the woman who would connect him to the world.

"I need you," she whispered.

"I know," he said, surprised to feel emotion welling within him.

"I calculate, with knowledge of this crazy world we are part, you might be able to… to help me."

This confused him. Did she intuit who he was? How could she?

"Will you?" she asked.

"Will I—?"

"Will you help me with audition?"

Jesus struggled to maintain an open, interested expression while dealing with crushing sexual disappointment. When he believed he had established a passable level of coexistence, he swallowed and said, "What can I do?"

Her eyes lit up and she hugged him, grinning like a little girl riding a unicorn. "I can be right back."

Three times Jesus' line had come and gone. All he had to say was "Nyet. I will see only your face," look at Svetlana, let her react, and they could go on to make love. But after three consecutive failures, Svetlana

Babakov, Actress, was becoming frustrated. Jesus Christ, biblical Savior of All Mankind, was well past that stage.

"Couldn't we skip the line?" Jesus asked.

"Nyet," she said. "Is much important. We try again."

Svetlana left the room, counted to eight, and returned, her face half in shadow, while Jesus pretended to stare out the window.

"Yuri."

Jesus faced her. Script pages rustled in their hands.

"Are girls asleep?" Jesus asked with a terrible Russian accent.

"Da." She joined him at the window, eyes wet with desire. "What do you see?"

The clear night sky beyond the window cast his face in a cool glow. "I see future."

"Do you think," she said, "when you are amongst stars, you will still see future?"

"Nyet," Jesus said with absolute, unflinching focus, "I will see only your face."

Her lips quivered, just so, and Jesus hid his shock at her skill, though he couldn't decide whether she was acting or relieved he had nailed the line.

"Oh, Yuri," she whispered, wrapping her arms around his neck, pressing her body to his.

Jesus checked the script. "Oh, Valentina."

They kissed, hunger driving him, while Svetlana held her script behind his head, her eyes darting to their reflection in the window, the nature of her passion mechanical.

She tore at his clothes.

Off came his golden yam silk pullover, his cocoa corduroys... another fine ensemble damned to a wrinkled pile. He stripped her of one strap, the other. He yanked down her dress. His hands caressed her hair, her shoulders, her breasts—

She pulled him onto her, kissing, groping. They writhed on the floor, he naked to the ankles, chocolate socks digging for traction, buttocks grinding. She clung to him, the perfect Russian wife, had Russian wives circa 1960 possessed lean Amazonian bodies with augmented breasts.

Jesus and Svetlana moaned, gulping desperate breaths, hands and lips everywhere, making love to glorify The Party, from the Urals to the Siberian wastelands. But soon Svetlana relaxed, arms slacking, kissing him without passion, enduring, while Jesus licked and kissed her neck, one hand between her legs, groping for another kind of heaven, ready and eager to fulfill his destiny.

"Does this come off?" he groaned, discovering a skin-toned fabric strip defending the length of her sex. He met her gaze and saw he burned alone in his passion. Confused, he sat up. "What's wrong?"

Her voice shook. "That was much good."

"But we—"

"Your reading was… I mean…" Her eyes welled. "I accepted it total. When you said you see only my face, I believe you. Have you ever considered to act?"

Jesus registered understanding for the first time since he'd met Svetlana Babakov in Cannes.

"I am going to get part," she said, tears streaming over her perfect cheekbones. "I am going to get it." She kissed Jesus again and again, clinging to him, her relief and excitement coming forth in great shudders. "Right now, right here. Is perfect." She touched his face, sniffing. "I have never seemed so happy."

EARTH TO JOSH

Domina laughed with glee, her body twisted and taut in a yoga posture.

Jesus sat sullen in a stuffed chair, arms folded, jaw set, eyes focused on the day's cover of *Bisou*, featuring Svetlana Babakov and her new love interest, Josh Nazareth. *Svetlana Much Excited* read the leering, mocking headline. Many floors below, the hotel newsstand brimmed with dailies parading *Svetlana and Josh* photos across their covers.

"Don't take it so hard," Lucifer said. "Love was much tougher on Ophelia."

"She's a fictional character," Jesus said, kicking the paper across the tiled floor.

"As are you," Lucifer said, "in a sense." He shared a hidden smile with Domina while she relaxed and moved to the next posture.

"I know it's difficult," Jesus' mother said, maneuvering her ankles behind her head. "It hurts twice as much when the whole world knows."

"It's best to walk away," Lucifer said.

"I agree," she said, her voice tense with effort as she rolled onto her back.

"Does He know?" Jesus asked Lucifer.

"Now that you've related it to us, definitely."

"Of course," Jesus muttered. "Always my fault."

"We could run an open casting call through my production company," Domina said.

"I'm not done with Svetlana yet."

"Josh," his mother said on the exhale, "it's over."

"She invited me to dinner tonight," Jesus said with defiance, swallowing a hopeful smile. "To celebrate her audition."

"Not smart," Lucifer said.

Domina relaxed, rolled forward, and spread her legs wide on the mat. "Leave with a little dignity."

"I will," Jesus said, heading for the shower. "She doesn't know who I am."

"He said I am perfect," Svetlana gushed, gripping Jesus' arm with one hand.

They stood on her suite's deck, drinking wine with the lights of Milan spread below, the warm night air easing past. She wore a sleeveless emerald dress with a plunging neckline, setting a new standard for beauty.

"So you got the part," Jesus said, straightening the sleeve of his plum crushed velvet shirt.

"Not yet," she said, "but Stu said other auditions are formality."

"When do you find out?"

"Two days. Maybe three." She squeezed his arm again and implored the heavens. "Oh God, *please* let me get."

Jesus hesitated, reluctant to delve into his night's topic with such an obvious segue, but tonight he couldn't falter. Tonight he would make his entrance. He had to respect destiny. And there was simple pride, pride that enabled him to feel like a man while wearing colors such as vanilla bean and golden yam.

"I might be able to help," he said.

She released his arm. "I thought you had not worked with Stu."

"I haven't," he said, forging forward. "But God... He's a different story."

She didn't understand. "You were priest?"

"No," he said with an uncertain smile, "not a priest."

A lack of comprehension darkened her face.

"I have something to tell you," Jesus said, "which might be hard to believe."

She eyed him. "Okay..."

"I'm not like other men."

Svetlana laughed. "Of *course* you are not like other men," she said, her entire body relaxing. She sipped some wine. "Is why I like you. You freak me out there. I was as, 'Earth to Josh. We need you, Josh.'"

Jesus faced the city.

"What?" she asked.

"It's not that simple."

She peered over the railing and took a few steps toward the sliding glass door. "Maybe we move off balcony."

He followed her inside, sensing it wasn't going well. With dazzling, bitter clarity he understood why God had done it the way He'd done it, at least how the Bible said He did it. A trumpeting luminescent angel bearing glad tidings encouraged one to prick up one's mortal ears and listen, whereas an exceptional-looking heterosexual male in his mid-thirties with exquisite fashion sense, though rare as an albino tiger, did not signal one had entered a new reality.

They sat at opposite ends of the sofa.

Svetlana watched him, leery of any sudden movements, her survival instinct eclipsing her subconscious hunt for reflective surfaces. He fidgeted and settled for the least uncomfortable position.

Though he knew his moment had long since passed, he said, "I am Jesus Christ."

A cool breeze drifted through the suite. Faint sounds of traffic rose to scratch at the silence between them.

"I think Josh is your name," she said.

"It is. But on earth you know me as Jesus Christ."

"On earth."

"Yes. My Father—"

"This father is God?"

Jesus knew the cause was lost, but continued for reasons he didn't understand. "Yes. God. My Father has been… gone… for quite a while, and—"

"How long?" she asked.

"I'm not positive," he said. "At least two thousand years."

"Is convenient within fanatical dogma."

"So He's back now—"

"On earth."

"Yes," Jesus said, growing annoyed at her interruptions. Lack of belief didn't make a fact less true. "He's back, and I think He will want changes."

He waited for her to interrupt. She didn't.

"So I've come to earth in glorious triumph."

She considered this and said, "To start, I do not believe for instant. But more important, tonight was supposed to be about me. My audition. Me. So not only do I not believe, but I resent for trying to make all about you. I hope is pathetic attempt to become laid."

She went to the wet bar and filled her wine glass.

"But just of fun," she said from the bar, "let us now say you are telling truth. That you are Jesus Christ and you have picked me as lover."

He said nothing, frustrated and disheartened.

"Did you choose me in random?"

"What do you mean?"

"Why me?"

He remembered her in Cannes, standing across the room with the dwarf. "You reminded me of a beautiful dark flower."

"It was enough?"

His expression said it was.

"But did you consider my emotions?" she asked, calm in light of the situation. "Did you think about *me*? After how I appeared?"

"You're all I've thought about."

"If was true, you would realize this is total wrong time for me to be pregnant."

"Pregnant?"

"Josh, I sign one-year contract with Sophie's Suite. I am getting part in *Vostok*. I work hard to be here as I am. If I have love with you now, maybe we build baby. And I kiss goodbye career."

"That can't be true."

"Da. It says you are not serious. It says you choose family over job. You do not do this and expect to succeed. You may *say*. But *do*? Nyet nyet nyet."

"I said nothing about a child," Jesus said, before mumbling, "Lots of famous women have had babies."

"*After* they were famous. And sometimes, is all for them, too. You did not hear of Mary after manger."

Jesus didn't smile. "You're right," he said, standing. "I'm sorry."

She crossed the room in three runway-forged strides. "Josh," she said, touching his elbow, "you do not need to perform this to meet girl. But if you believe what you say tonight, if you will think you are Jesus Christ…" Her eyes filled with pity. "Josh, what you need to see is therapy."

Jesus turned for the door, refusing to prolong his humiliation. This wouldn't work, not ever. He would never experience the fruits of his fame.

"Josh," she called after him.

He stopped, hand on the knob.

She smiled with great kindness, gazing at him with true regret. "You are best-dressed man I ever know."

From a certain perspective, the speed with which the media move is inspirational.

Svetlana's room door closed behind Jesus at nine o'clock. Ten minutes later, to Svetlana's surprise, Sergio Pumello of *Bisou* magazine rang her suite. He wanted confirmation she and Josh Nazareth had broken up that night.

"Da," she said, "but is too soon to talk. I must have time to be alone with feelings. Has only been few minutes."

"Yes. I see. Sorry. Can I ask you why?"

"I do not wish to discuss."

"Did Mr. Nazareth tell you he was Jesus Christ?"

She hesitated.

"Hmmm… Do you think he is?"

"Is not—"

"Did he want you to be his earthly lover?"

"I—"

The next morning, Sunday, the cover of *Bisou* magazine screamed *Angel Dumps Jesus Christ*. The so-called legitimate press did not pick up the story. It remained a no-show in the world's collective awareness. But to Sergio Pumello, who felt an inexplicable, otherworldly drive to find the truth, it was the only story worth his ink.

DOES THE CATERPILLAR
CRAWL FOR NAUGHT?

God found His biblical son in the New York threshold bar, sitting at a small booth in a dark corner, tearing bites from a loaf of crusty Italian bread and drinking a bottle of pinot noir.

God greeted the bartender and sat across from Jesus.

Jesus took a swig from the bottle and said, "I thought You'd be taller."

"It is a normal height."

"For here."

"Yes."

"I asked for You," Jesus said, "and You did nothing."

God had expected His biblical son's opening salvo. Over the course of millennia He had experienced many such conversations and could predict their pattern based on a given world's mythology.

Jesus pointed to the threshold bar's frosted windows, across which the shadows of humanity passed. "Is it so much better now? Why did I have to go through that? It changed nothing."

"I was not involved," God said.

"You weren't involved," Jesus mumbled, rubbing his left palm. "You're omniscient. You know what's happening."

"As Lou has explained to you," God said, lowering His voice, "in beings such as Lucifer and I, omniscience, which is not the correct term, is limited."

Jesus choked down another chunk of bread and chased it with wine, his eyes finding and not leaving his biblical Father's. This was his second bottle. He felt heavy and miserable. "It was a long time ago, and I was traumatized. I forgot what he said."

"Omniscience comprises the past and present, and only when I am in a non-total state. In that state, I can presume future events based on intimate knowledge of all that was and is."

Jesus drank. "I didn't get that gene." He set down the bottle. "Did You hear me call for You? Or were You in a total state?"

God folded His hands on the table. "Non-total."

"Ha!" Jesus barked. "So You knew."

"A non-total state is local and specific to that locality," God said. "I was, for lack of a gentler term, somewhere else."

Jesus' forehead trembled. With his free hand he bid the bartender leave. "I was barely a man."

"Will you not understand?" God asked. "I do not direct lives and societies. I cannot. All reasoning beings—"

"I was on my own," Jesus said.

"Yes."

"And now?"

God said nothing.

Jesus stared into the wine bottle and blew into its neck, creating a small sound like a foghorn. He banged it on the table.

"Why won't You answer me? I'm Your son. Tell me why You forsook me. Break Your ridiculous 'mysterious ways' law for once and—"

"It is not My law," God said, knowing from long and bitter experience this was not the moment for candor. It would be best if this man came to the truth himself. It was always best that way.

"Policy, guideline. Whatever."

"You know why, Josh. If you'd—"

"I don't *want* to reason my way through it!" Jesus shouted. "I don't want to have to think about this. I want You to *tell* me. Can't You understand that?"

God took the bottle from His biblical son. Jesus glared, challenged, simmered, calmed while silhouettes streamed across the bar's windows.

"What was my childhood like?" Jesus asked.

"You were happy. Unburdened."

"How do You know if You weren't here at the time?"

"I am here now."

"So You know all that was and is?"

"Here, now and then, yes."

Jesus rubbed his temples. "I remember mom singing to me."

"That was her habit," God said.

"Were you ever around?"

"Joseph raised you."

"So You're more my biological father than anything."

"I am immaterial," God said, deflecting Jesus' assertion.

"What does that even mean?" Jesus groaned. "I don't understand. Did I have friends?"

"You have spoken to Lucifer about this, Josh."

"He's not You," Jesus said, but God did not bother to correct His biblical son. "I'm so damn tied to what is written. I wish You'd taken the time to divinely inspire my adolescence."

"I did not inspire any of it. The Bible came about through myth passed down father to son, mother to daughter. Not from Me to man." God peered at Jesus. "And you are well aware how inspiration works. It comes in flashes and jolts. In dreams."

"You left a lot to chance."

"I had nothing to do with it."

Jesus leaned forward, eyes shining. "Then why are You *here*?"

God didn't answer.

"Don't think I can't put two and two together. Lou wants what You want. If You're so unhappy with it all, why don't You just go down there and wipe out religion?"

God pondered the question and asked, "Does the caterpillar crawl for naught?"

Jesus registered a total lack of comprehension. "Does the… *What*?"

"This is the only way," God said.

"The only way for what? Why can't it stay the way it is?"

God sighed. "In the parlance of your more zealous followers—the end is nigh."

"The end of what?"

"Of this."

"And then what?"

"For you? Nothing."

Jesus glared at Him. "What about You?"

"I am not certain."

Jesus strained to think through the wine fog. "So You're counting on me to do *something*. To save You." When God didn't respond, Jesus said, "Bet You wish You weren't somewhere else when *I* needed *You*." He snatched the bottle from his biblical Father, took a long pull, and smacked it on the table with great satisfaction. He eyed the empty bar and said, in the most obnoxious tone possible, "Whatever it is, I don't know if I can do it."

Without expression, God seized the bottle and hurled it across the room, into the fireplace. It shattered, spitting shards of glass, flaring the flames before they dwindled back to their steady eternal roar. "You already have."

"What's that supposed to mean?" Jesus asked, annoyed. "So I went to Cannes. Big deal. I need a more sophisticated persona this time around."

God closed His eyes. How long would His infinite patience last?

"*You* made my return to this fame-obsessed culture next to impossible. Putting me amongst beggars and thieves. Making the meek and downtrodden my target audience—"

"I did no such thing."

"—and *You* should take responsibility for it, but You use it to chip away at me."

"This is your chance to help undo what you've done," God said.

Jesus slapped his palm on the table four times as he shouted, "It. Wasn't. My. *Fault!* You should have told me what You wanted. You should have stopped me before I went too far. You should have *done something*."

"You are not hearing Me," God said. "You are drunk."

"And so what if I am?" Jesus spat. "You want me to be happy. So You say. Oh, wait, so *Lucifer* says. But You're on the same team, right? So now I'm happy. Let Ye rejoice."

God pushed away from the table and headed for the door.

"Wait wait wait wait wait. Father. Dad!" Jesus said, catching up to Him. "I'm sorry. I didn't mean it. I... I just feel like... I used to feel important. But now—" He hung his head. "I don't know what I am."

He tried not to, but God laughed, shaking His head in wonderment, laughing like He hadn't laughed in ages.

"What?" Jesus asked. "This isn't funny. It's how I *feel.*"

God laughed more, though He knew it was cruel. "Let there be light," He said, regretting stealing the line as He said it. "Please."

"He laughed at me."

"Of course He did," Lucifer said. "You're being obtuse."

Jesus glared at the Dark Angel as they walked. Lucifer wasted no perceptible time considering his clothing choices, removing his black leather pants with blue moon rarity. Yet he was always part of the scene, even here in America, where donning leather pants and utilizing vocabulary such as "obtuse" marked a man a Grade-A jackass. Meanwhile, Jesus spent hours choosing fabrics, accessorizing, and agonizing over the maddening three- or four-button dilemma. But he seldom felt at home. Not in the City, and not here.

"I resent that," Jesus said for lack of anything thornier.

They strolled through the 9/11 Memorial Plaza, stopping to gaze upon a resilient callery pear tree standing in the long shadow of a silver wedge soaring into the sky—a brilliant edifice built to remember and defy, a gleaming testament to reason, reality, and their opposites. They moved to a reflecting pool. The waterfalls' unsparing rush filled the spaces between their thoughts, a beautiful, stirring, futile attempt to occupy the void left by the dead. Names of victims spread in both directions from them, etched into bronze, endless.

Lucifer said, "'Where the slaughter was so great that our men waded in blood up to their ankles.'"

Jesus glanced at him.

"An eyewitness account of the first crusade," Lucifer said, "at the fall of Jerusalem."

They walked until they'd left the plaza, until the waterfalls had given way to the less hallowed New York of cabs, shouts, streaming sidewalks, and auto exhaust. People rushed past, speaking countless languages, contributing to the overwhelming feel of New York City's world culture.

"He said I'd already done it."

"Did He?"

"I'm paraphrasing, Lou, but yes, He did," Jesus said. "Why else would I say it?"

"What do you think He meant?"

"Now it's you who's being obtuse. I dare say deliberately."

"What was the context?"

Jesus stared at Lucifer. "He also described, ad nauseam, the limitations of His omniscience, which I assume is how you experience things, as well as predict football games for angelic fun and profit."

Lucifer indicated Jesus was correct.

"Therefore, you know what He said and the context."

"It's pointless for me to explain."

"Try me," Jesus said, convinced the Angel of Darkness was stalling. Deep, deep down, hiding beneath the impermeable crust of his beliefs, Jesus knew what God had meant, but had suspended his ability to solve the prickly equation of one plus one plus one.

"Josh, for almost two thousand years you've believed your own press, despite my attempts to explain your reality."

"Your interpretation of it."

"No," Lucifer said. "There is reality, and there is fantasy."

Jesus said nothing.

"I've waited for Him to return so there will be no doubt. No quibbling." With surprising gentleness Lucifer said, "I want you to be happy."

"You've said that already."

"Because I'm committed to it. But you won't be until you make your decision based on who a woman *is*, not *who* she is."

"You knew this would happen. You knew I'd have desires. You put me in a real body."

"To dissuade you."

"To sabotage me."

"Josh—"

"You agreed with me about Svetlana."

"I didn't disagree *enough*," Lucifer said as they began walking again. "There's a difference. But if you're intent upon coupling, it's clear she isn't right for you. Your mother was a peasant."

"Riiiiight..." Jesus said as they passed a sidewalk pizza shop, its Lilliputian tables engulfed by locals. "She was a peasant because my Father hadn't established monotheistic supremacy yet."

Lucifer wanted to slap him, but instead said, "He never has. Man did it for Him."

Jesus chuckled. "Let's face it," he said, "I did most of the work."

Lucifer stopped, causing bustling tourists and natives alike to swerve to avoid a collision. "You did next to nothing," he said. "Your legend, your mythology, written by *men*, inspired the huddled masses. The work, as you call it, was done by *me*. You may have been the faithful's holy goal, but the engines driving the rise of monotheisms were guilt and fear and power hunger, which were, in the beginning, my forte." He lowered his voice, but not his intensity. "I'm ashamed to admit it, but you're who you are because of me. Otherwise you would have gone the way of the wind, like Dionysus and Osiris."

Jesus stood wide-eyed, taken aback by Lucifer's outburst. People stutter-stepped around them, swearing in every language.

"I don't know what I was thinking," Lucifer said.

"So you're saying I'm your *fault*?"

"I've tried to undo what I can, to help you, to free you. But you bathe in worship and take credit for things you didn't do, like a spoiled, misguided boy."

"I've contributed," Jesus said, regaining his defiance. "I *died*."

"True," Lucifer said. "But it had nothing to do with your fame. You rose, so to speak, after you died."

"Obviously."

"Not like that," Lucifer said. "Every itinerant preacher tramping through Galilee claimed he was—" He stopped.

"Oh please," Jesus said with as much scoffing as he could manage, "do go on."

Lucifer took Jesus by the shoulders. "Dying on a cross isn't enough."

Jesus tried to break free but couldn't. "What else is there?"

"Find a purpose. Make something of yourself so you can find some joy in whatever eternity is left."

"Forget about suggesting *I* go to Hell."

"I won't," Lucifer said. "It would take you years to find the right outfit."

"You've never been in my position," Jesus whispered, unable to break Lucifer's grip, afraid they were drawing unwanted scrutiny. "You've never had to overcome—"

Lucifer cocked his head, their faces inches apart.

"Okay," Jesus said, "I'll give you that, but it's not the same."

"You will never be who you think you are," Lucifer said. "And you will never undo what happened to you. This is your existence. Period."

Jesus shivered.

"You have to find your way from here."

Lucifer released Jesus. Above them a video screen hawked an energy drink. Lucifer glared at anyone curious or nosy enough to have stopped to listen, while the biblical Son of God studied the pavement, shaken, his mind and emotions reeling.

"How about French?" Lucifer asked, pointing to a brasserie across the street. "Chateaubriand with choice of appetizer, salad, and chocolate soufflé. *Prix fixe* of forty-three dollars."

They headed for *Le Oeuf*. And though neither of them yet realized it, Lucifer had achieved in minutes what a platoon of therapists had not accomplished in the past two hundred years: The beginning of Jesus' emancipation from himself.

THE THIN PINK LINE

Oone wall separated Sergio Pumello from Josh Nazareth, whom he suspected was Jesus Christ—*the* Jesus Christ.

When he'd received the call from Svetlana Babakov's assistant, he knew from gut to nuts she was telling the truth. To Pumello, Svetlana's hesitance confirmed Josh Nazareth *believed* he was Jesus Christ. And the flat-out scary *something* about Nazareth's best buddy Enfuego nudged Pumello into the unfamiliar realms of superstition and belief. He fought past such paralyzing thoughts by telling himself that, divine or insane, Nazareth promised to fill two or three weeks of his magazine's voracious cover story needs.

Such a prime investigative spot, on the twenty-third floor of a Times Square luxury hotel, was costing him. A quick calculation on a hotel scratch pad had indicated the sum of his expense account, lifelong savings, and cashed-out investment portfolio would provide nine days of lodging and room service prior to his financial ruin. The French-milled soap and super-absorbent towels managed to soften his impending demise, but each toilet flush felt like foreshadowing.

He held tight to his suspicions, his feelings, his beliefs. He watched and listened to the conversation in the next room. But Pumello couldn't squash the seeping fear he was wagering his modest net worth on a pretentious clotheshorse with holier-than-thou delusions and imaginary friends.

★

"Why won't you give me a straight answer?" Jesus asked.

Zubba and Wubba hovered in the suite's adequate walk-in closet while Jesus tied his tie, swore, untied it, and began the cycle again. Their small wings fluttered, holding their chubby little bodies aloft at varying altitudes. Lucifer had explained his conversion of the putti to physical beings until Jesus thought he understood, but upon seeing the winged pair his conception of impossible trounced the Dark Angel's ordered, complex explanation.

Yet Zubba and Wubba were invisible to Pumello, by virtue of the oversized wall safe between themselves and his equipment. Had their flickering wings moved them forward or backward or up or down a single foot, their heat imprints would have scorched Pumello's computer screen like feverish sumo wrestlers belly-dancing in an igloo. Instead, they appeared as echo bogeys of no apparent heat. From Pumello's frame of reference, Jesus spoke as a man before answering himself with the voices of two distinct, precocious children.

"We would like to," Zubba said.

"Yes, very much, very much," Wubba said.

"But it's not that simple."

"Nothing ever is," Wubba said, furrowing his eyebrows.

"'Yes' or 'no' would suffice," Jesus said. "The complications you can discuss at length on your own time."

"N—" Wubba began.

"I don't think we can," Zubba said.

"I don't either," Wubba said. "No. No. Definitely not."

"But you see," Jesus said, one eye on the next tie, the other on Wubba. "I think you were about to say 'no.' As in 'No, she isn't part of His plan.'"

Zubba glared at Wubba, who swallowed hard and beat his wings.

"If I knew," Jesus said, approaching Wubba, face pained, "I could make a decision. Now I wonder if I should avoid her, because I don't want to work against myself. But if I knew she would benefit my crusade, I could relax and let nature take its course."

Zubba shook his head while Wubba hovered, afraid to screw up but desperate to please.

"I don't know," Wubba whimpered.

"Yes, you do," Jesus said.

"He doesn't," Zubba said. "And I thought she—"

Jesus ignored Zubba, focusing on Wubba. "Wubba," he said, "do you like this tie?"

Wubba nodded.

"I do, too," Jesus said, frustrated with the walk-in closet's antiseptic odor, poor lighting, and beige walls. He'd pored over ties for an hour, dressing for a night on the town with Lucifer, who was absent without explanation. Jesus found himself looking forward to it, *wanting* to go out, because women would flock to Lucifer, and therefore him, too. Yet here he was interrogating the putti, pretending his questions were to help him choose an appropriate consort for his triumphant second coming while he anticipated the enjoyments of an extended quest, which in turn would delay the rapturous news of his earthly return. His intentions were complicated and unsettling. Why keep the door open for Svetlana? She'd rejected him. Corporeality was strange.

"The three of us have been friends for a long time, haven't we?" Jesus met their eyes while taking off his tie. "And didn't I help you convince Lucifer when you wanted to ride those mustangs in Wyoming?"

Wubba grinned. "We were six feet tall."

"But that was fifty years ago," Zubba said, his eyes wide as he recalled the day. Long lean legs, long strong arms, boots, spurs, vaquero hats.

"I really enjoyed it," Jesus said, "the three of us riding. Has something happened to us? Are we not friends anymore?"

"You're trying to talk us into betraying God," Zubba said without conviction.

"I shouldn't have to talk you into anything. We were friends, and we haven't been as close since our ride."

"That's because you've changed," Wubba said.

"I suppose I have," Jesus said. "I'm lonely." He sat on the floor. "I need help."

Zubba dropped a few inches to hover at Jesus' eye level. "I thought you were talking to Sigmund."

"Not that kind of help," Jesus said. "The kind you get from friends."

Wubba joined Zubba. "I wish we still rode horses together."

"Me, too. I miss you guys."

Wubba's eyes welled.

"We can't," Zubba said, with great regret.

"But you must. Otherwise I might make a terrible mistake."

"No you w—" Wubba began, but Zubba clapped his little hand over Wubba's mouth.

Jesus smiled. "Thanks, Wubba. My friend."

Wubba pushed aside Zubba's hand. "When can we ride again?"

"Soon," Jesus said. "So Svetlana isn't part of His plan. That's odd. And good." He left the closet, the putti on his tail.

In the next room Sergio Pumello jolted back, before blinking hard and leaning forward to study the two flying heat signatures now on his screen, keeping pace with Nazareth.

"Then what did He mean when He said, 'You already have'?" Jesus asked, drowning the obvious answer with such intentional ignorance it threatened to forever swamp his frontal lobes.

"God said that?" Wubba asked.

"Yes," Jesus said, but neither putto knew.

Jesus flopped onto the bed and began a slow inventory of everything he'd done so far. He began at the Ritz, but his thoughts were hijacked by his desire for Svetlana. Would they resume their romance?

Zubba and Wubba hovered into his sight. This time Zubba asked, "When can we go riding again?"

Jesus' mind had drifted. So many women. It drove him insane. How did any man find the perfect love? Was love a giant dance with compromise? If Svetlana had "sudden heart change" and decided "having love" with him was of greater value than modeling lingerie, would it bring him happiness? And what was this new desire, not for Svetlana or one woman whom destiny would deliver to him, but for the whole of women? With a start he recognized he loved them all. Love fell within his dominion of acceptable feelings toward womankind, but he knew this was not love in the "Baby Jesus come to save the world" sense of the word. This was love in fishnet stockings and scarlet lipstick. This love didn't flow through him. It pumped. He found himself anxious for Lucifer's return, eager for the night.

"When?" the putti insisted.

"When this is over," Jesus said, "I'll talk to Lou. We'll go riding then."

Zubba and Wubba grinned from tiny ear to tiny ear, their delighted laughter like wind chimes.

Six feet tall.

Lucifer stood in the shadows, the table lamps' dim blue light not reaching him, watching her performance for the second time. Her presence, her physique… something had changed. Her initial movements held more serenity than before, and Lucifer interpreted them as similar effort paired with additional resistance, as if she were ill, though Temptation struck him as impervious to the usual bugs.

Could she feel his gaze? In the past, he would have made himself known. But tonight wasn't a social visit. He was vetting God's word, seeking unnecessary confirmation. His lack of true omniscience allowed a kind of perverse hope. With *that* realization came resignation. He would let time solve the knot.

The music faded and the stage lights dimmed, drowning the club in darkness. When the lights rose, a current of warm air moved through the club, a clue the devil had gone.

"Well?" came Lucifer's voice through the door.

Temptation sat on the cultured marble bathroom counter in her baby blue sweatsuit, staring at the little white circular window on the six-inch pregnancy testing stick. Did the solid pink line mean positive or negative? She checked the instructions for the fifth time.

She couldn't believe it. She took the pill religiously. She never missed a day. She insisted on condoms. No condom, no sex. She never broke that rule.

This wasn't supposed to happen. The odds against conception when using both the pill and condoms were astronomical. Yet here she sat in the bathroom, staring at the little pink line like a stupid girl who didn't take responsibility for her actions, zipping through life trusting everything would work out swell.

She wanted to scream.

She hadn't worked at the club for three years, selling a fantasy and building a clientele so, nine short months from her goal, she could get pregnant and render it all a colossal waste of time. She had a crappy apartment and crappy clothes (other than her work costumes, which were exquisite) because she didn't spend money frivolously. She had no health insurance, no fancy gym membership or credit cards or crippling loans. All she had every time she stepped onto stage were *plans*.

She stared at the pink line, knowing her plans were no more. The money she'd saved would go to support the baby. The nights she'd spent grinding on strangers' laps were now nothing more than what they were at the time. The greater cause had slipped away, leaving three numb years of pole work and lap dances. And now she would continue like the day shift girls, dancing to buy diapers and day care.

The disappointment and despair were so crushing, so suffocating, she had to summon a supreme effort to stand.

She opened the door and handed Lucifer the stick. She collapsed on the loveseat, hands on her stomach. With longing and bitterness she contemplated her book stacks, many of which towered halfway up the wall. She'd have to clear them out—too many sharp corners for a baby.

"Does the line mean positive or negative?" he asked.

"I'm pregnant."

Lucifer paused. There was no gentle way to ask. "Do you know—?"

"Either you or your friend," she said without expression, now concerned the old paint on the walls might have lead in it. "I haven't been with anyone else in a long time."

He sat beside her.

"Why is this happening to me?" She began to cry.

Lucifer held her hand, awash in irony. The idea this happened as all else did—one thing after the other, each random step leading to the next and the next, without direction or grand plan—challenged credibility. The Book's odds would have been Infinite/1 against a woman so deeply connecting with him *and* embodying Jesus' ideal woman. An unwelcome idea flashed through his mind. Had God learned a new trick? Could He influence thought or phenomena? Three years ago, had God maneuvered Lucifer toward Temptation to establish the connection that would lead to this? Lucifer recoiled at the thought. He'd witnessed horrific events, on both the largest and smallest scales. He refused to think God could conceive of or influence such things. Or stop them. He had laughed with God. He had challenged Him. He loved Him. But Lucifer couldn't shake the suspicion.

After she had cried herself out, she said, "You wore a condom?"

"Yes," Lucifer said. He had done so because she had insisted, and because explaining that pregnancy and disease weren't considerations when you were immaterial might have altered the mood.

"What about your friend?"

"Josh," he said. "I assume so."

"Josh," she said to herself. "Where is he now?"

"He's at the hotel."

She swallowed. "I need to talk to him."

Outside the bagel shop a light drizzle fell. The city felt empty, cold. She tensed her body to beat back a tremor. A big black Mercedes made its way down the street, tires hissing on the wet pavement. It stopped when it reached them.

Lucifer stepped forward and opened the door.

GRADUALS V. SUDDENS

At the annual Angelic Summit, during between-session coffee and donut breaks when conversation shifted gears from matters of policy to the greater questions of philosophy and martingale v. anti-martingale betting strategies, one subject led to heated arguments and, on occasion, blows: the two schools of thought regarding the act of revealing one's supernatural nature to mortals. On one side were the Graduals, on the other the Suddens. There was no middle ground. Though hypothetical, as no angel had ever revealed itself to a mortal, the issue cleaved the vast body of angels, with a greater percentage of Suddens. Angels, by nature, tended toward the dramatic.

Though Lucifer was a manifested, singular being like God, the angels ranked him an "archangel" to satisfy their conceits, gloss over contradictions to their existential mechanism, and establish base wagering levels for the underground gambling cult built around Lucifer's exploits. As the only so-called angel who had, in fact, revealed himself to a human, Lucifer was a staunch Gradual. He preferred a process of stages, during which he built trust before letting himself be known. His method had proven itself over thousands of years with few unfortunate incidents. His stance surprised many, but he saw no need to shock or frighten with the roaring pronouncement, "Behold, I am Satan, Slayer of Souls," teamed with a trite yet requisite eruption of flames (which was what the Suddens yearned for, just once, please).

So when he led Temptation into Jesus' hotel room, Lucifer's long-standing, steadfast position as a Gradual contributed to his lack of preparation for her scream of terror and less-than-graceful faint to the floor.

Once certain she hadn't hit her head and would soon recover, Lucifer took in the room. Potato chip bags, two-liter soda bottles, and empty ice cream pints littered the bed and floor, as if a radical band of women's talk show viewers had set off a comfort food bomb in violent protest to the correlation between obesity and a sedentary lifestyle. *Wokka-wokka* soft porn music blared from the television, scoring a bizarre scene from the dreams of Warhol and Raphael's bastard child: Chubby little putti in loin cloths hovered three feet above a food-streaked bed, wings fluttering, hands and mouths crammed with popsicles and pepperoni pizza.

Lucifer surveyed the room with equal parts disgust and awe, aware this could be a scene the likes of which he might never again witness.

"Whu?" Zubba asked, his voice muffled by pizza. A slender string of cheese swung like a pendulum from his lower lip. Wubba belched, breaking Lucifer's trance.

"Where's Josh?" Lucifer asked.

"He weh ow," Wubba said, sucking on a cherry popsicle.

"Where?" Lucifer asked again, growing impatient.

Both putti shrugged.

"Clean this," he said, stepping over Temptation on his way out. "Put her in bed and be gone before she wakes up."

"I am in complete control of my faculties," Jesus said, proving it by blinking twice in a slow, deliberate fashion.

The biblical Son of God sat in a red vinyl booth at *Lolli*, a Greenwich Village sushi bar cum nightclub sporting a heroic tuxedo cat manga motif. Lucifer had found him after a two-hour hunt through the Village's clubs and cafés, many of which Jesus had visited that night.

Lolli attracted glow stick-sporting Asians, who bobbed and danced to trance and house pumping through concert-sized speakers. Expensive colognes and perfumes mingled with the raw fish. Two busty Korean girls in their early twenties crushed Jesus between them. Another wiggled on his lap, tilting his head back and pouring water down his throat, kissing him while he swallowed. The foursome existed in a constant state of squeezing-stroking-sighing-kissing.

"We need to talk," Lucifer said.

"Anything you have to say to me," Jesus said, "you can say in front of my girls. They know who I am."

"Yah," the girl on his lap chimed in. "He's ow man."

Lucifer stifled a laugh, amused with Jesus' first sojourn into the club drug world. He regretted the need to spoil Jesus' journey of light and love with sobering news, but returning to the hotel before Temptation woke up was more important than catering to Jesus' rolling high.

"Temptation is pregnant with your child."

"Bummah," the girl kissing Jesus' neck and ear groaned. "You want to dance?"

Jesus' smirk froze on his face. "She's... what?"

"She's in your room," Lucifer said. "We should get back."

"But that's impossible," Jesus said while the three girls stroked his hair, his shirt, and each other. "She's... she's not right."

"Evidently we're past that."

Jesus fondled the red tablecloth as if it were exotic silk. With widening, epiphany-riddled eyes, he pointed at Lucifer. "Unless *you're* the father. Which makes a lot more sense to me."

Lucifer said nothing.

"I'm having fun," Jesus moaned. "Why don't you sit down?" His eyes pleaded with the girls. "You have more friends, right?"

"Yaaaaah," the girl on his lap said while the two flanking him made kissing faces at each other.

"That's not why I'm here," Lucifer said.

The nymph on Jesus' lap poured more water down his throat. "You mus drink."

When he came up for air Jesus winked at Lucifer, "You're too uptight. Live a little."

Lucifer laughed and walked to the fire alarm.

A deafening horn blared through the club, followed by mass screaming, wholesale panic, people running for the exits, abandoned drinks. Jesus' harem made a half-hearted attempt to drag him away before bolting. Jesus stayed, eyes on Lucifer, who strolled to the table as the sprinkler system kicked in.

"Your ignorance of subtlety saddens me," Jesus said, as the room became a manmade monsoon.

"And I'm annoyed by your lack of focus."

Jesus studied Lucifer's shirt. "Is that suede?"

"We need to go back," Lucifer said. "We need to talk to her."

"How do you get away with it?"

"With what?"

"Mixing textures like you do," Jesus said, standing and feeling Lucifer's sleeve. "It's so trailer par—hey, this is a nice shirt." He closed his eyes and let the sprinklers pour down upon him. "It's probably dry clean only."

"Thanks for your concern," Lucifer said while the water pooled. "We need to go."

"I'm not ready," Jesus said.

"They're all gone," Lucifer said while Jesus continued to stroke his shirt, enraptured by the slick feel.

"Not that. Being a father. It's not for me." Jesus stuck out his tongue to catch the water.

Lucifer removed Jesus' hand from his sleeve. "What did you take?"

Jesus stepped back, eyes going from side to side, and asked, "What do you mean?"

"You know what I mean."

"I most surely do not," Jesus said. "If you're implying I've indulged in substances deemed illegal by most sovereign governments, well, I think you need to re-evaluate your conclusions." He glared at Lucifer. "And your shirt isn't *that* great."

"So you're high on life?"

"Ecstatic," Jesus said, kneeling and slapping the rising water. "Wow. That stings."

"I suppose it doesn't matter," Lucifer said, pulling Jesus to his feet and guiding him from the club. "But we're about to have a conversation with a distraught woman, and I was hoping for the compassionate you."

"You can trust I'll... wait, I don't *want* to have that conversation." Jesus' glassy eyes filled with resolve. "We don't even know if it's mine."

They exited the club. The Mercedes sat at the curb. They climbed in, and the car sped for their hotel.

Jesus stared out the window, rubbing his wet hands on the leather upholstery. "This is so unfair," he said. "I haven't *done* anything. I *feel* different, and I'm starting to—" He ran a fingertip over the chrome power window switch. "Maybe I should talk this over with Sigmund."

"He'll tell you you're experiencing an onset of classic male angst, stemming from residual guilt and fear."

Jesus snorted. "He's a bit more specific."

"Related to a subconsciously perceived rejection of your infantile sexual urges for your mother."

Jesus let his head fall against the headrest. "What if it's mine?"

"It is."

"You don't know that. Am I supposed to raise it? I have no frame of reference."

"What about Joseph?"

"I always felt like, under it all, Joe resented me. You know, for being the Son of God. Raising another man's son and all."

"That's ridiculous."

"You weren't there," Jesus said. "He never disciplined me. I think he was afraid Dad would smite him."

"Spare the rod," Lucifer said with a grin. "Joseph loved you. Like the father he was."

Jesus pretended he hadn't heard him. "That night, the night the baby, it, it smells of sacrilege. What if it's yours?"

"I'm not biological," Lucifer said, suddenly and unexpectedly close to an emotional precipice. "But it would make more sense if the child were mine."

"Because of your image?" Jesus said with an edge.

"Not mine. Yours."

"Because I'm Mr. Goody Two Shoes?"

"I didn't say that."

"Why can't I have a threesome?" Jesus snapped.

"You've already had one."

"That didn't count. There was only one girl. You didn't touch me, did you?"

Lucifer laughed. "Regardless of the participants, by engaging in a threesome you've broken multiple commandments."

"My *Father's* commandments," Jesus said.

"They're not His. It's a *story*, Josh. Breaking a few commandments is a good start on your journey toward reality."

Jesus sank in his seat.

"But," Lucifer said, "applying the concept of trickle-down ecumenics, if *you* indulge in threesomes, it heralds the eventual emergence of a worldwide polyamorous society, requiring an alteration of gender birth ratios and hard questions on marriage equality and taxation."

"Huh?"

The Mercedes stopped outside their hotel. A subdued flock of Estonia-based Jehovah's Witnesses drifted past, dazed and shaken by an hour in Times Square.

"Grasshopper," Lucifer said, opening the door and grinning a bit, "your house boasts many rooms, and one has shag carpet and bean bag chairs."

STIGMATA-RAMA

Temptation sat on the bed, waiting for them to answer her question.

A short while ago she had awakened in the hotel room, confused and alone. No lingering smell of pizza or potato chips, only industrial-strength cleaning products. Everything was in perfect order. She'd moved about the room, staring at the television, the desk, the phone, as if they were strange new objects, and began to doubt what she'd seen. It wasn't possible. But to her incredulous dismay, the simplest thing, the smallest thing, proved her sanity.

On the floor rested a cherry-stained popsicle stick.

"Their names are Zubba and Wubba," Lucifer said, shifting in his chair. "They're putti."

"Putti," she repeated. "Like cherubs? Like Cupid?"

"Cherub is a misnomer and Cupid doesn't exist," Lucifer said. "But yes, like him."

"You expect me to believe that?"

"You saw them yourself."

"Then who are *you*?"

"That's complicated," Lucifer said.

Jesus laughed, shaking his head and peering out the balcony window.

"Try me," she said.

Lucifer knew the chance to break it to her gradually had long since passed. He imagined their predicament delighted the angels, and guessed they'd gathered at the Book to gamble as the scene unfolded. He gazed at Temptation. Any explanation would sound ludicrous. At least she had seen Zubba and Wubba, an event he'd viewed as a disaster but which now lent his next words a semblance of plausibility.

"I'm Lucifer, and Josh is Jesus Christ. I prefer to be called Lou."

Her face went ashen. "Lucifer. Like, the devil?"

"You could say I began as a devil-like figure. But it's an origin, not a definition. Nurture over nature."

"Yeah," Jesus said, "Lou's all nurture."

Temptation's face betrayed a high degree of skepticism. "So my child is either the second coming or Satan's spawn?"

Jesus laughed and Lucifer winced.

"Do something then," she said. "Prove it to me."

"The putti," Lucifer said.

"I only saw them for a moment. I was in shock, and I didn't get a good look. Maybe they were special effects."

"In a hotel room?" Lucifer asked.

She stood up, adamant. "I want to *see* something. Something amazing. Now that I'm ready for it."

Though Lucifer didn't expect her to take him at his word, he wasn't a performing seal. Yet he saw no true alternative. So he rubbed his thumb against his index and middle fingers.

A flame leapt from his fingers.

He let it burn for a few seconds and blew it out.

At the window Jesus smirked. "That again?"

"Let me see your hand," she said, grabbing Lucifer's hand and inspecting it. "I've seen magicians do that on TV."

Jesus snorted.

Lucifer scowled at him. "You do something."

"Yeah," she said. "Your turn."

Jesus peered out the window, shook his head at the insanity and indignity of his predicament, and faced them. "What the hell."

He presented his palms to her.

She waited. "Is something supposed to happen?"

"Sometimes it takes a while." But when nothing happened he asked Lucifer, "Can I do it down here?"

"Maybe if you gouge your palms," Lucifer said.

Temptation made a face.

"How am I supposed to prove who I am?" Jesus asked as shining panic broke through the drug cloud. "I'm just another nutjob without it!"

Lucifer waited while Jesus drowned in his reality.

"Lou," Jesus said, mustering every atom of control he could, "I'm losing it."

Lucifer rose. "Josh, could you grab a towel, please?"

Jesus registered confusion, but headed for the bathroom.

"Until a few minutes ago," Temptation said, "I didn't think this could get worse. You seemed so normal, so *cool*. I thought I—" She stopped herself. "And Josh was, was... at least he's great-looking." Her voice began to rise. "But I don't understand. What are you trying to do to me?"

Lucifer held his hands toward Temptation.

"You want to *hold hands*?"

A hopeless laugh escaped him. With his eyes, he brought her attention to his palms.

"What?" she demanded, ready to cry or lash out. "*What?*"

Rivulets of blood sprang from Lucifer's palms.

"Oh my God," she whispered, eyes wide. "*Oh my God.*"

Jesus stopped halfway across the room, towel in hand.

"Convinced?" Lucifer asked in response to her dumbstruck expression, certain the stigmata were more impressive than his first little parlor trick.

She leaned forward as trickles of blood reached his fingertips.

"Josh," Lucifer said, "I need the towel."

Jesus crossed to Lucifer and dropped the towel on the desk.

"You can do that," she asked, "whenever you want?"

"Apparently," Jesus said, face tight with outrage.

"I had to show her something, Josh."

"And that was the only possibility? To one up me?"

Lucifer wiped the blood from his hands. "Have you seen enough?"

She nodded, hopeless, afraid. "I guess. Why can't he do it?"

"Because he's mortal," Lucifer said.

"And you're not?" she asked, her voice distant.

"I'm immaterial," Lucifer said. "But Josh was and is Jesus Christ." She began to shake. "Maybe you should sit down."

"I—I can't believe it," she said, sitting on the bed, not taking her eyes from Lucifer's hands. "I just can't believe it." A worried expression came over her. "I'm not a—"

"We know," Lucifer said. "It's irrelevant."

"But I thought—"

"It doesn't seem to matter in my case," Jesus said. "Evidently, purity is something my Father demands when *He's* involved."

"Josh," Lucifer said, "*hear* me. God wasn't involved. And He *isn't* involved."

But Jesus wasn't listening. "Comparing Dad and mom to this operation is like comparing velvet to velour."

"Thanks," she mumbled, scared, simmering.

"No, thank *you*," Jesus said, descending into viciousness. "Because if you'd rejected me the next step would have been a personal ad. 'Savior of humanity seeks open-minded female, virginity optional. Enjoys fashion shows, filmmaking—'"

"Willing to carry you during long walks on the beach," Lucifer said, trying to lighten the mood.

Jesus stopped as if struck. "Is nothing sacred?"

Lucifer laughed. "*Footprints in the Sand* didn't happen."

"But it's a beautiful story," Jesus said, turning to Temptation. "Don't you think so?"

"I'm an atheist."

Jesus grabbed the bloody towel from Lucifer and shook it. "*Still?*"

"Now it's not quite so simple," she said. "I believe you're here. But you could be anything. Aliens. I don't have faith in what you represent."

"You believe," Jesus said, "but you don't have faith. Your life philosophy is based on semantics?"

"Most religions are," Lucifer said, his hands clean and unscarred, as if the stigmata had never occurred.

"That's hilarious," Jesus said. "You're on a roll tonight. But have you observed the new atheism? How is radical non-belief *not* a religion?"

Lucifer beamed, excited by Jesus' question. "Let's resolve this first, then get to that."

"Where is there to get?" Jesus asked. "Jesus, the Devil, and a pregnant stripper are in a hotel room." He dropped the towel onto the table. "The only thing to get to is the punch line."

Temptation headed for the door.

"Wait," Lucifer said, "where are you going?"

"I didn't ask for this," she said, her anger trumping her fear. "I like you, Lou. Luis. Whoever you are. We're, we were, whatever, *connected*. But I want things." She glared at Jesus. "I'm more than a dancer. But neither of you have bothered to ask how I'm doing. How I'm feeling." Her eyes welled. "I'm the one who's pregnant. I'm the one with questions. I don't know what happens now. Do you take me on your spaceship? Do I die? Where do I go? Does anybody care?"

"We both care," Lucifer said, attempting to lower her voice with his.

She jabbed a finger at Jesus. "To him all I am is a vessel."

"That's not true," Jesus said.

"So why didn't you wear a condom?" she asked.

"I didn't—"

"Obviously," she spat.

"It's against the—"

"WHAT?" she shouted, returning to the main room, eyes blazing. "Don't you dare!"

Jesus stepped back and Lucifer stepped forward.

"What he did was wrong," Lucifer said, "but his intention wasn't to impregnate you."

"Right," Temptation said. "So comforting." She fought for control. "I don't have much to bargain with since the deed's already done, but I'm sure I could take up smoking and drinking tonight. Or get an abortion tomorrow. So if the baby's yours—"

"You'll be the mother of my child," Jesus said, incensed by her attitude.

"I can't imagine a less desirable sentence," she said. "I know religion. I've seen what it does. And I don't trust you." She focused on Jesus, her voice rising. "So what's in it for me?"

With what he deemed great restraint considering this exotic dancer's familiar tone, Jesus asked, "What do you mean?"

"Just what I said. What's in it for me?"

Lucifer grew uncomfortable with the biblical Son of God's expression.

"Have you not read the Bible?" Jesus asked.

"No."

"Then let me speak in heathenish terms," Jesus said, choosing not to add *so you'll understand*. "If the child is Lou's, nothing in your life changes, except you'll have his baby."

"Josh—" Lucifer began.

"You'll go on per your established character, raising the baby in a hedonistic atmosphere of frivolity and excess. It'll be peachy."

"Josh," Lucifer said, "I'm not biological. The baby is yours."

"Then we might use history as our instructor," Jesus said, while Temptation shrank with every word. "You'll bear the child and raise it in utter poverty and anonymity until he is, say, in his early thirties. That's when the fun begins. Your boy will forfeit his life to save humanity. In vain, may I add. You will not die, but rather will rise to heaven in a shower of light and a cacophony of trumpets, to be frustrated by an eternity without love." His expression was black, haughty, tormented. "Does that about capture it, Satan?"

Temptation trembled, small and vulnerable. Lucifer moved to comfort her but she pushed his hand away.

"Now I understand why you didn't save the world," she said, and walked out the door.

Temptation stared out the cab's window, the blocks passing under the wheels, her mood a churning anguished mess. The rain came hard, and with each traffic light she sank a little more, stepped a little closer to an edge she hadn't expected and a solution she wouldn't have conjured up in forty rainy nights.

She'd trembled with rage and relief in the hotel hallway. Mercifully, no one had joined her on the elevator. She'd needed the time to collect herself, and for the most part had succeeded. But she'd passed through the lobby unnoticed, which made her feel invisible and apart from the world, and closer to hysteria.

Street signs and out-of-focus faces blurred past, accompanied by a deluge of *pings* and *thwocks* on the cab's roof. She closed her eyes and there they were, in the air, watching TV, devouring pizza and popsicles. Cherubs! No, not cherubs. Putti. She couldn't explain them any other way, she just couldn't. They'd *been there*. She wasn't crazy. And the fire. And Lou's palms. And Josh. What a jerk.

The Queensboro Bridge's dark shadow loomed in the near distance. With sudden clarity she lurched forward.

"Stop the cab."

The cabbie hit the brakes and pulled to the curb.

She shoved what money she had into the driver's hand and leapt from the cab. The rain pounded her as she walked along the rail, following the bridge's rise.

Sergio Pumello told his driver to pull over. He sat in the cab, watching her cross the giant bridge span in the downpour.

This was the biggest story of his life. Of anybody's life.

He possessed electronic evidence of the flying Cupid-things in the hotel room, and voice recordings, each saved under three different file names, to be sure. He had the alleged putti's panicked banter, their references to Josh and Lucifer, their entire cleanup effort. He'd moved to follow them when they'd left the room, but his newsman's instinct told him the girl was the story.

And he'd been right. By *God*, he'd been right.

For his patience he had both Jesus Christ and Satan on DTR and electronic imager, chiseled on his hard drive with the same multi-redundancy system. He had the story. The whole damn story. It would vault him into investigative journalism's stratosphere. It would relegate Woodward and Bernstein to mere cub reporters skulking beneath the prodigious shadow of Sergio Pumello.

He knew he should plant himself in a coffee shop, arrange an intravenous caffeine feed, and slash pen across paper, jot down his thoughts now, before they altered with the passage and perspective of time. But he couldn't. She was the story. Jesus' baby grew inside her. And he sensed something directing him, though Pumello didn't understand why. Like anyone else he prayed to and swore at and blamed and thanked an amorphous "God." Crediting and condemning the gods as active hands in human lives provided most of the ink for humanity's story. Pumello understood this. But the sensation of being *moved* left him lacking an obvious answer. Why would God allow a self-defined agnostic to tell this story? The question yielded further hard and sobering questions with difficult implications, so Pumello chose to remain within the warm confines of irreverence: Maybe the Supreme Being enjoyed his journalistic stylings.

She stopped a few hundred yards up the bridge. He crinkled his forehead as she leaned over the railing. What was she doing? He swiped off a thin film of mist and pressed his nose against the cold glass, eyes widening in horror as she began to climb the railing.

Pumello bolted from the taxi onto the bridge, shouting, waving his arms in the pounding rain, running faster than he'd ever run before.

Temptation climbed the railing, strain on her face, drenched, shaking, uncertain. Using a vertical strut for support, her hand wet and slippery in the pouring rain, she pulled herself onto the top rail and battled the swirling wind.

She gripped the strut, her knuckles white, the river black below. The current rushed and churned. Less than three hours ago she'd danced on stage, working the pole, her smile genuine because she was one day closer to her dream: a nomadic world traveler existence, a spartan life sustained by the interest from a significant nest egg invested in an aggressive, diversified portfolio. She'd envisioned walking the earth since watching travel documentaries with her father. Paris. Tokyo. Sri Lanka. Seeing everything, doing everything. *Experiencing* it. She'd saved with the singular purpose of preparing for the life burned in her heart as the only life worth living. But now—now she was common. Strike that. Now she was a freak.

She pressed her lips together, bitter, dispirited.

If she couldn't achieve the romantic, adventurous life she yearned for, what was the point? She didn't know if she was brave enough for the life of a single mother. The sheer logistics of such an existence were discouraging. And the impoverished, anonymous future scenarios Jesus had painted for her were far from enticing. Disappointment settled in her chest, a dull crushing ache. She'd rather die.

"This is going to sound crazy," said a ragged voice behind her.

She tensed on the top rail. A man half-stood, half-kneeled below her, struggling to stay upright, hands on his knees, rain pounding on his bald head, pinched face upturned to her.

"I'm Sergio Pumello," he said, "from *Bisou* magazine. And I understand what you're going through." He coughed and heaved. "I heard it. I heard it all."

"Go away!" she shouted. "This has nothing to do with you."

Pumello shrank, and one hand slipped from his knee. He recovered his balance and said, "Sorry. I heard what they told you. I know who they are, and… who you are."

Temptation gritted her teeth and turned back to the river. Whispers of doubt became shouts. "I don't have time for this."

"Well, you know, my apologies, neither did I," he said, struggling for oxygen and something to say. He'd seen enough television to know you had to keep a jumper talking. "But now I don't know what to think."

She eased herself against the vertical beam, careful, unsteady. "Me, neither. I saw them. I know I did." She squeezed the air into a tight fist. "They were *right there*. But—Jesus—I'm going crazy."

"No, you're not," Pumello said as the tingling sensation in his extremities ebbed. "I recorded it all on my computer."

"On your computer?"

"I'm in the room next door." He hurried to explain. "Special equipment. It sees and hears through walls." He stood upright and held out his hands to fend off suspicion, hoping a rare go at honesty might build trust between them. "Sort of. In a way. Sorry."

Her eyes narrowed. "How did you know where they were?"

"I'm following them."

This reporter sounded intelligent and sane, far saner than she did, but she found herself fearing his eyes were going to disappear into his face. He'd violated all sorts of civil rights. Did Jesus and Lucifer have civil rights?

"You're from a magazine?" she asked with a pointed glare.

"Yes," he said, rain dripping off his nose. "*Bisou*. Out of Genoa."

"You don't have an accent."

"I'm from Tampa. Sorry. Was it immaculate conception?"

"Imm—what? No, of course not."

"Then you've—" Pumello considered his readers and asked, "Was it consensual? I ask because Greek mythology postures Zeus as raping mortals and I thought it might be a characteristic of the gods—"

"No, I was—what kind of question is that?"

"I think people will want to know."

"I couldn't care less."

"Fair enough. Were you a virgin?"

Her jaw dropped.

"Hey," he said, "it's a legitimate question within the context of all this, and it's objective."

"If you can hear through walls, you already know."

"I'll have to replay the recording." He jotted a note. "But I'm guessing *not*."

"You can't write that," she said. "It's libel."

"Sorry. Not if it's true."

"It's so unfair if you're the last person I talk to," she said.

He blinked to see her through the pouring rain. "Are you really going to jump?"

"I haven't decided yet."

Like a suspect surrendering his gun, Pumello showed her his pen and paper before putting them under his jacket. "I can't tell you how much I wish you'd get off the rail."

"I bet you do," she said. "Not much of a story without me around, is it?"

"No," he said with astonishing candor. "But don't you want to see if it's true?"

"It's true all right." She faced the river and took a threatening stance.

"Hey!" he shouted. "I think so, too." He waited for her to turn around and asked, "What do you think is going to happen?"

"Is this on the record or off?"

He hesitated. "Off. I guess."

"If I knew," she said, "do you think I'd be up here?"

"Right," he said, swallowing. "Whose baby do you hope it is?"

"It's Jesus' baby."

"I think most women would prefer Jesus."

"You don't know women," she said. "Anyway, I—I like Lou."

"Yeah, but—"

"But he says he's not biological. So I guess it can't be his." A violent shiver broke her from her musing. "This is still off the record, right?"

"Sure." He swept the rain from his head. "Sorry. Please continue. I'm interested in what you think."

She gazed at the city, numb but lucid. "I don't think I remember anything before right now."

Pumello tapped his nose, scratched his shoulder, and asked, "Got any names yet?"

"What?"

"For the baby. A name."

She laughed. "I doubt it's my choice."

"I think Jesus' name was Joshua, wasn't it?" he asked, his newsman's tone creeping back. "What about Joshua junior? Maybe that's too obvious."

"You can't stop, can you?" she said, holding the strut tighter. "I'm cold."

In a flurry he pulled off his coat and handed it to her. With great caution she took it and pulled it over her shoulders.

"Thanks," she said, shivering.

"A lot of women would love to be the mother of Jesus' baby, but you aren't embracing the role. Why not?"

"Maybe you should leave me alone," she said, exhausted.

"Sorry, I can't. This is the biggest story in history. Well, at least in the top three. And the world should know. I think *they* want the world to know."

"That's ridiculous."

"Is it?" he asked. "Why else would God allow me to record evidence through the hotel wall, and why would He allow *this*, right now, unless it's what He wants?"

"Lou said God isn't involved. Maybe there isn't one." She shook. "I don't have the answers."

"Have you told your parents?"

She hesitated. "I just found out tonight."

Pumello heard something in her voice and knew there was a story in what she hadn't said. He set it aside for now. "Right. It's a little soon. Let's get back to God's intention. I'm trying to stop you from jumping off a bridge. I'm an agnostic and you're an atheist. At least we were." He pointed his finger at her. "Don't you think it's too much of a coincidence?"

"What is?"

"That neither of us believes."

"I think you pretend you don't."

Pumello narrowed his eyes, confused. "You want to walk the earth."

Her face went white and she became still despite the cold. "How do you know that?"

Pumello wore a baffled grin, not understanding the source of the words coming to his lips. "I don't know. It just came out."

She wiped the rain from her face. "You're not going to speak in tongues, are you?"

They shared spooked, unconfident smiles.

Temptation glanced at the dark, dangerous river below and shuddered. "Please help me down."

Pumello went slack with relief, but hesitated despite his desire to help her.

"Come on," she said, shaking.

The rain poured harder. To their mutual dismay he appeared unable to move.

"Do I have to promise an interview?" She swiped the rain away.

He took two halting steps toward her. But rather than helping her, Pumello reached for the sky with both hands, as if summoning a supernatural power.

The rain stopped.

Their eyes went wide, like tithing platters.

Temptation said, "That was weir—"

She slipped. One shoe flew into the air, followed by her foot, her leg, a shriek, and her entire body.

Pumello raced to the rail, in time to see a single splash in the black water.

Temptation plunged into the river, the impact punching the breath from her, dazing her. Her ears filled with the muffled sounds of rushing water over rocks and fish and sludge and metal struts, swirling dark around her. In a drowning haze she fought the current, but it pulled her along, tugging, tugging, keeping her down, rolling her along in the watery void. It came fast—the loss of hope, the calm acceptance. Was it so bad? It seemed easy. What would happen now? Something brushed her in the water's dark push and was gone. She moved with the river, alone with the cramping pain in her lungs mocking her quiet resignation. Alone with the questions she couldn't remember this close to the end. The unanswered questions hit her like slaps to the face, and now, too late, she found herself regretting everything, wanting to do it all again, to live boldly, to act. She thrashed at the water, her lips closed tight as she swallowed the breathing reflex to delay the agony, knowing she would lose the battle, but wanting so much to go on, despite the pain and futility.

An ethereal white light pierced the darkness and something heavy struck her body. A hand grabbed at her, groping, finding her arm, pulling her upward. The light streamed through the current, searching. She saw the reporter's face through the water as he pulled her to him. They went up, up, up, into the white light, and broke the river's surface.

"There they are!"

A rescue cutter's brilliant white searchlight locked on them. Pumello fought to keep their mouths above the water, kicking hard, breathing in, spitting out, teeth chattering. She clung to him, her savior, while the approaching boat's engine roared at full song, drowning out thought, preventing Pumello from remembering he wasn't much of a swimmer. Someone tossed them a lifeline and Pumello snatched it with one weakening, determined hand, coiling it around his forearm while crewmembers pulled them toward the boat.

On board, the medic wrapped them in heavy blankets while the cutter headed for the closest dock. Temptation accepted a hot cup of coffee and slumped on the steel deck. Pumello leaned against a small crane, shuddering, hoping tonight's heroism would absolve him from years of unconfessed sins.

WITHOUT THE FRENCH

By mid-week several American evangelical Christian news sites with low journalistic bars had picked up the first part of Sergio Pumello's remarkable story and published it as homepage features, prompting fourteen phone calls to Domina's film production company in Los Angeles by Thursday. After agonizing deliberation, Pumello had excised all clues and inferences regarding Temptation and her pregnancy. She was a card he'd play once the world was all-in. Over the weekend, mainstream news sites began to run the story as a curiosity, bolstered by Pumello's surveillance video, which was difficult to explain away. A major New York print daily paid Pumello to allow an independent security consultant full access to his system and files. Pumello provided limited access, and the consultant confirmed its technical legitimacy. The newspaper ran the story Monday morning, which inspired global mockery, praise, fear, and Christ-blinded hallelujahs.

The media rapture was on.

By close of business Monday, Svetlana Babakov's management company had received over a thousand calls regarding her published photos with Mr. Nazareth. Not one to leave an opportunity on the runway, her agent booked her on *Good Morning USA, Good Morning LA, Good Morning NYC, The Chat, The Scene, The Take, The Later Show,* and twelve similar talk shows in Europe. Her appearance on Channel 3's irreverent *Good Day, Sir!* delayed the show's annual "Earl Great" tea tasting championship, which did not please the Queen.

For the media rounds, Sophie's Suite outfitted their newest angel in a selection of form-caressing dresses with tasteful diamond-encrusted crosses and plenty of flirty flare.

The mainstream media hit full hyena's lope with a relentless spew of one-upping "Who is Josh Nazareth?" features, including interviews with Cannes opening gala attendees and a soft-focus primetime Q & A with Svetlana's assistant, Merlot. Detailed breakdowns of the technology used by Sergio Pumello shared column inches and homepages with op-ed pieces and blogs ranging from ecstatic and fawning to frightened and hostile. The 24-hour cable news networks ran Pumello's audio clips around the clock, while on Al-Khamsin a masked jihadist insisted Josh Nazareth was indeed Jesus Christ and had returned to defeat the false messiah and quicken the kidnapping and beheading of infidels and apostates. The Vatican remained silent.

Through Domina's agent, the BBC privately offered one million pounds for a televised interview with Mr. Nazareth.

"It's a bad idea," Lucifer said.

Lucifer and Jesus sat at a table in the threshold bar with Domina, Saint Peter, the Archangels Michael and Gabriel, and God. The shadows of Fifth Avenue pedestrians streamed along the floor and walls.

Despite formal introductions and God's attempt to put everyone at ease with His customary and enlightening "What came first, physical space or existence?" joke, the table was a tempest of furtive glances, outright stares, and tense expressions. Lucifer and God were the only relaxed entities at the table.

"Why?" Jesus asked, with the tone of a man who had made a decision but felt obligated to go through the motions of discourse. "For the record, I'm not comfortable with Your presence," Jesus said to God. "We have different objectives."

"My natural state is impartiality," God said.

"Nothing about your state is natural," Jesus said.

"I agree with Lou," Peter said, in rare opposition to Jesus, who insisted they include Peter in all meetings—apparently to serve as his hype man. "The Christ cannot appear to be a man like any other."

"But I *am* a man," Jesus said.

"Now as always," Lucifer said.

"And correct me if I'm wrong," Jesus said, "but mom has always come back non-materially. Like you, Lou."

Lucifer smiled. Despite Jesus' exceptional though selective intelligence, the biblical Son of God's vanity made reverse psychology surprisingly effective.

"So it seems to me," Jesus said, "I'm the first *man* to return from the dead in the flesh. Bone, blood, fingerprints, capable of reproduction." He smirked. "I've looked in the mirror. I'm me."

"He's him," Peter said, returning to Jesus' fold.

"You are you," Lucifer said, assuming God, too, was satisfied with the conversation's direction.

Though irritated by something in Lucifer's tone, Jesus sat back with the self-satisfaction and boundless optimism of an eight-year-old who had learned to bake and frost sugar cookies. "So your little experiment has transformed me from so-called myth to provable fact."

"Myth to fact," Peter echoed, lacking only a microphone and hoodie.

Lucifer raised an eyebrow. Michael and Gabriel held back laughter. Domina's face brimmed with indulgence. God smiled, undiluted and genuine.

Jesus' triumphal air shifted to suspicion. "What?"

"It is a guilty treat," God said, His smile not fading, "to watch reason exercised so perversely."

"Am I wrong? How am I wrong?"

"Josh honey," his mother said, "it's true you're a man again, but the proof connecting you *then* to you *now* is—"

"Why is she here?" Peter asked.

"Your presence summons a similar question," Gabriel said.

"She's our media expert," Lucifer said.

Peter crossed his arms. "She returned to the world for fame and to mock the church, and forfeited her place in heaven."

When Lucifer didn't bother correcting him, Domina said, "It's not heaven, Rocky. And I earned my returns."

"Earned? You consorted with—"

"Enough," God said, impressed Domina had stood her ground.

"I'm amazed so many people believe it already," she said. "But put him on TV and most people will think he's insane."

"You're wrong, mom," Jesus said. "They'll see me for who I am."

"If You want them to know he exists, and You exist," Domina said to God, "You need to give them proof."

"Proof of My existence is not My objective."

Jesus scowled and leaned back in his chair. He set his gaze on the ceiling in a gesture of waning tolerance and said, "Perhaps You should enlighten us with Your intention."

"It is irrelevant," God said.

"And yet it's influencing everything," Jesus said.

"Josh—" Domina began.

Jesus cut her off. "Lou has proof I'm who I am."

"It's not quite ready," Lucifer said.

"How long?"

"A week or so," Lucifer said. "One can never tell with academics."

"Are you kidding me? We just delay a few days." Jesus snapped his fingers. "Done."

"It better be good," Domina said, "because the people who control the media aren't jumping to confirm Josh's existence. They'll play it for ratings, but unless you blow them away with overwhelming evidence, it'll wind up another Shroud of Turin."

"It will do," Lucifer said with an understated confidence God found Himself admiring. "An international network like the BBC is a good bet."

"Pay-per-view has always treated me well," Domina said.

"But everyone can watch the networks," Lucifer said.

"Yes," Domina said, "but there's value to the exclusivity."

"I like that," Jesus said, pointing to Domina with excitement.

"Pay-per-view numbers are miniscule in comparison," Lucifer said.

"But perception is everything," Jesus said, "and she's so *common*."

"Common," Peter repeated with the same dismissive tone.

"So was I," Domina said, surprised by her son's words, "and look at me now."

"Yes," Peter muttered, "look at you now."

"Pete," Lucifer snapped. "So far, only a journalist and those in this room know of Josh, Temptation, and their child. I can influence Sergio."

"But will you?" Jesus asked. He swallowed, unable to control his knee-jerk emotional responses in his biblical Father's presence. "Why does it have to be the stripper?"

"There is no *have to be*," God said. "There is no mysterious force working against you. She is pregnant with your child because you had sex with her."

Lucifer studied God's face for a nuance of machination. He saw nothing. Satisfied he wasn't a victim of a "taketh away" scheme, Lucifer said, "If anything, it highlights the reality of humanity's base purpose."

"The two of you aren't steering anything," Jesus said, incredulous. "You're not trying to derail me."

God set His elbows on the table and focused on Jesus. "We have discussed this."

"*We* did not discuss anything. If we had, why call this unprecedented barroom chat?"

Domina put her hand on Jesus' arm. "To talk about the interview."

"So talk about it," Jesus said, glaring at Lucifer. "When You set the date, e-mail me." He stormed through the door leading to the City. Peter lowered his eyes, uncertain, before following Jesus.

God sighed.

"Excuse me," came a voice from across the bar.

Every head turned.

Temptation stood at the entrance, looking lost.

"The uh…" she said in the threshold bar's confession-booth quiet. "I didn't know where to go. The limo brought me here." She half-waved at Lucifer and blinked when she saw Jesus' pop star mom. "What is this place?"

God approached Temptation. "We should meet," He said.

She extended her hand. "I go by Temptation—it's a stage name."

He took her hand in His. His touch charged her nerves and washed her in goosebumps, as if she were experiencing sudden clarity after avoiding a car accident. "I go by God," He said. "It, too, is a stage name of sorts."

She scrunched her forehead as the barroom tilted and pitched. "What—?" she murmured, before fainting for the second time in less than a day.

Temptation awoke in a small library with heavy mahogany tables and bookcases and dark leather furniture. A massive sofa crouched against the far wall, and several beefy 1940s Parisian style chairs lingered around the room. A spectacular 17th century wheat-shaded Aubusson carpet relaxed underfoot, and beyond the closed doors rich coffee brewed.

God sat in a club chair, a pleasant, warm feeling emanating from Him.

She flashed a weak smile and sat up on the leather sofa, woozy. She wore a tailored burgundy velvet suit, embroidered with elegant peach and blue orchids.

Out the window the Eiffel Tower soared into a brilliant sky.

"We are washing your clothes," God said.

She gazed at the Eiffel Tower, a flurry of emotions pulsing through her. "Paris?"

"Without the French," Lucifer said, entering the room, dark and dashing in black silk and leather. "We are in Paris, but not a part of Paris. This is an intermediate space."

Leaden regret pressed down on the churning, confused emotions threatening to erupt from her. Her eyes welled and she asked, "Am I dead?"

Lucifer sat beside her on the sofa. "Au contraire, mademoiselle," he said, "you are very much alive. This is a place we can talk."

"You have questions," God said, His face placid.

"Yes." She tried to intellectualize her situation, to summon calm without understanding, acceptance sans proof. "Why me?"

"You'll find," Lucifer said, "the answers to most 'why' questions inadequate. Why me? Why are we here? He finds them reductionist."

"But all the important questions are 'why' questions," she said.

"Why," God asked, "do you have a mind of your own?"

She frowned.

"You are an atheist," God said.

Temptation winced. "I'm—I'm not."

God and Lucifer exchanged glances.

"Not anymore," she said.

Lucifer smiled with great kindness and God asked her, "So now that My existence is certain, you would become religious, presumably to save your soul?"

She had no answer.

"Which religion would you choose? How can you be sure which of the thousands of sects and factions worships Me in the proper way, and which lead to My esteemed colleague?"

Lucifer flashed his unnerving smile.

"What does religion offer a woman?" God asked. "Inferior status? A role model for servitude? If you had created the universe, and therefore humanity, would you damn half a species to such an existence? Where is your exaltation?"

"So it's okay I'm—?"

"Would you condemn sexual desire and cast Woman in the role of deceitful temptress when both are crucial to humanity's survival and evolution?"

Her blank expression betrayed her uncertainty.

"You might," Lucifer said, "if your goal was unwarranted power. Or extinction."

"In exchange for a fool's promise of death's avoidance—the one certainty of life, the fate and obligation of every being, object, and force in existence—religion demands its adherents crawl through life, and attempts to position the eradication of joy, the devaluation of the individual, and life's trivialization as the love and worship of Me. Which I resent. And reject."

She sat speechless.

"What creator would want his creation to waste existence attempting to deny and cheat its life cycle? It is illogical, irrational, insane."

"But You're God," she said.

God smiled. "So I am."

"I don't understand."

"You are a part of Him," Lucifer said, "but He is apart from you."

"But, then *why?*" she demanded, panicked. "To reproduce? That's the only reason to live?" She crumpled into the sofa. *"Why me?"*

"Your answer is within you, not without," God said. "Your birth, your decisions, your loves and hates, these have all led to this moment, yet you have no destiny, no fate, no greater role. All is chance, played out at the intersections of forces and matter." God pointed to Himself. "I am the manifested representation of all existence, yet I cannot exert control over so much as an atom. I know you more completely than you know yourself, yet I do not see through your eyes, and I cannot dictate or choose your path." He folded His hands, and His voice came pleasant and firm. "Why you? Why Me? Why not?"

Temptation stared at God. She did not breathe, did not blink.

"Why don't we go downstairs?" Lucifer said, breaking the room's heaviness. He offered Temptation his hand. "Nothing stokes the existential fires quite like brunch."

GOPHER WOOD

The brunch room's domed ceiling, a fluorescent mosaic of the Eiffel Tower by Gaudí, soared fifty feet above the floor, supported by carved limestone pillars. Between the pillars were massive metallic glass windows providing a sensational view of Paris. Along one window stretched a buffet featuring an omelet bar, succulent strawberries with rich chocolate and fresh whipped cream, every fruit juice imaginable, and a full-service waffle station.

An expansive round table filled the room's center. It seated ten with ease, allowing adequate space for God, who ate with a high right elbow. Zubba and Wubba had developed the seating chart, revised it, and revised it again to provide the highest opportunity for engaging conversation, while taking into consideration such variables as gregariousness and appetite. To their mutual pride, they'd managed to map a conversationally dynamic seating chart while separating Saint Peter from Domina and Lucifer, as well as Lucifer from Jesus, who was a late confirmation. The Archangel Michael and Moses sat left of God, with Noah to His right. Noah's mythical origin indebted him to God for the legendary "build an ark" tip, and therefore Noah was the least likely to complain if God's elbow wandered. Gabriel ate strawberries next to Noah, and Temptation sat between Mary Magdalene and Domina, who sat next to Jesus. The putti orbited the table, refreshing mimosas, clearing dishes, eavesdropping.

"How are your days in Tanakh?" Gabriel asked Moses.

Moses blushed. "I'm building a fence," he said, before mumbling something about Lot's daughters.

Michael giggled. "Remember," he said to Lucifer, "when Moses land-scaped his yard, and you set his dwarf palm tree on fire?"

Laughter rose around the table.

"It wasn't funny," Moses said.

God chuckled. "I had forgotten."

"How could You forget," Jesus said, "if You were never here?"

God ignored the question.

"You forget?" Temptation asked.

"Indeed," God said. "Some things."

"Something else You might have forgotten," Michael said, "is Adam. It's the flashing thing again."

"I do not," God said, before correcting Himself. "I don't grasp how I am involved. You are... you're referring to Adam the biblical character, correct?"

"Yes," Michael said.

"You have... you've explained to Adam his relationship with Me is a fabrication, there was no 'first' human, and life, like all things, is a continuum?"

"Yes."

"And men invented the concept of sin and inherited sin to hold claim over and dominate others?"

"He doesn't believe me."

"Instead of believing," God said, "he should think."

"I have a suggestion," Lucifer said.

God waved His hand. "Adam is already self-aware. His confusion does not warrant—"

"I'm not suggesting Hell," Lucifer said.

"He responds only to threats," Peter said. "I think a classic Hell experience has to be an option."

"Adam wants Your forgiveness," Lucifer said to God, marveling at Saint Peter's odd but predictable eagerness to subject Adam to eternal rain or hurl him into boiling blood. "Why not give it to him in person? It might be fun."

"There's nothing to forgive," God said.

Across the table, Domina studied her son, who glared at God. Attempting to distract him, she asked, "Do I need to buy you casual clothes?"

Jesus stroked the sleeve of his sea foam green suit, which he'd united with a tie a shade darker and a crisp white dress shirt. "This ensemble is the height of brunch fashion."

"You look stiff."

He turned to her. "I prefer a dressier style. It adds a certain flair to the occasion."

"How about Japanese denim and a vicuña jacket?" she asked, pleased to wrest her son's attention from God.

"Mother, please," he said. "I suppose if this were Valhalla and I were Thor, your suggestion may be appropriate. But the City demands a bit more panache."

"You're earthbound now," Domina said.

"When he gets back I can find him somethin' more relaxed at the store," Mary Magdalene said.

"You have a store?" Temptation asked.

"She does," Domina said, while trading pleasant frowns with her son.

"Men's and women's clothes," Mary Magdalene said, "from pj's to suits. And the best shoe department in the City."

"I love shoes," Temptation gushed.

"There's these dark chocolate suede boots," Mary said with a twinkle, "which'd be bitchin' with that jacket."

"Really? But what about—"

"Doncha worry," she said. "If ya like 'em I'll hold 'em for ya until… y'know."

Temptation's face clouded.

"I mean, assumin' ya do," Mary Magdalene stammered. She recovered by pointing at Temptation's belly. "Are ya excited?"

Temptation hesitated and Jesus looked away.

"Doncha even fret about it, honey," Mary said.

"I wasn't sure how you'd—"

Mary Magdalene laughed a big booming laugh before lowering her voice and saying, "Listen. All that Josh and me stuff is ancient history. Go for it, but negotiate first. That's what our girl here did." She pointed to Domina.

"After the fact," Domina said, winking at Temptation. "When I had leverage."

"You should see her contract," Mary Magdalene said. "It's filled with more clauses than a chimney's wet dream." She leaned toward Temptation and asked, "So how was it?"

"It?" Temptation asked.

"Y'know," Mary whispered, "I hear ya went 'round the world with both of 'em."

"Last month," Jesus' mother announced at arena volume, in an effort to change the subject, "I bought an apartment on a *ship* that goes around the world, year round."

"Is that a big deal?" Noah asked.

Lucifer grinned at Noah. The legendary shipbuilder had been the first fictional character to achieve self-awareness, and had done so without the benefit of Hell's orientation pool, which at the time was centuries from completion. It was a well-known but little-understood fact that fictional entities who had attained self-awareness pre-pool were "harder" than those who came after the pool's introduction, but were subject to swings in self-perception, like a wild animal introduced to a mirror. They were unpredictable, but Noah tended toward his legend.

"I imagine," Lucifer said while digging into peach pancakes, "her ship has an easier time of it than yours did."

Noah lowered a strawberry from his mouth. "Meaning?"

Lucifer, who derived great pleasure from taunting Noah, struck an innocent expression and said, "Modern wisdom indicates you were lucky the ark floated."

"Noah is *real?*" Temptation whispered to Domina. "The ark is—?"

"Lou's just having fun," Domina said. "Showing off for God."

Noah set down his fork. "Unlike ships of today, I didn't have years to build. I had rudimentary tools, no dry dock, no subcontractors, and I worked with gopher wood, which isn't exactly injection-molded fiberglass. And those damn animals—"

"Didn't they come to you?" Lucifer asked.

"Sure," Noah said. "But did they show up until the last day? Did they load themselves? No, Lou, they didn't. It sounds so orderly when you read about it, as if they marched right on with tickets and seat assignments. But I'll tell you," he said, jabbing a finger at the Angel of Darkness, "it was far from it. *Far* from it."

The rest of the table held in laughter, pretending to eat. The glee with which Lucifer needled Noah, and the shipbuilder's passionate defense of his leading role in a fictional event ancient authors had told as a harrowing survival epic but generations since had softened into a cutesy children's Bible story, provided quality entertainment whenever the inner circle broke bread together.

"Admittedly, your efforts were admirable," Lucifer said. "Most shipbuilders call it quits before their six hundredth birthday."

"Lou," God said, jumping into the straight man role for Lucifer's act, "you know that's an exaggeration. He was in the prime of his life with three strong sons."

"Thank you," Noah said.

"Still," Lucifer said, "building a three-deck, five hundred foot boat from gopher wood is a tall order, even for men of renown. I would have chosen a recognizable wood that was readily available. Such as oak, or maybe teak."

Jesus, who occasionally joined Lucifer's ribbing of Old Testament characters, said, "A clear-stained mahogany with polished brass rails might have worked."

"We had pitch, and we were pressed for time," Noah mumbled. "A little more warning would have been nice."

God shrugged with feigned regret.

"Form following function," Lucifer said. "Resourceful. As is surviving with no food or fresh water for over a year. Quite a tale."

"Maybe," Peter said with a sneer, incensed as usual with all things Lucifer, "you should have lent your significant literary abilities to the cause."

"Noah has little choice," Lucifer said, "but I'll never understand why you maintain your illusions."

"All civilizations, in every corner of existence, cling to their illusions," God said.

Conversations stopped.

"The forms are countless, but their pattern is not. At first there are gods for every natural occurrence, every emotion or trait, every unanswered question. God of war. Goddess of the harvest. God of jealousy."

Domina watched while God spoke, her expression fusing defiance with paper-thin vulnerability.

"As a civilization advances in knowledge and technology, questions are answered and gods die, until there are only two questions lingering—the origin and meaning of life—and one god to answer them. The answer is always life after death in another plane of existence, with a priest class to facilitate smooth travel from one plane to the next. The price? Always, *always*, denial of the species' nature."

"So there's life in other places?" Temptation asked.

"Of course," God said. "The idea this is the one planet sustaining life is a conceit of man, though you are not alone in your vanity. Most civilizations worship a god who made them in his image. Yet none look like man."

"What do they look like?" asked Domina.

"A rainbow of limbs and beliefs," God said. "The desire for immortality is the trait they share, a desire based always on fear of death, not the driving need to continue. Every advanced species slaughters their fellows in religion's name, while developing the means to commit mass suicide by technology."

"Some must survive," Michael said.

"One," God said, "who then faced their star's death. To endure, a civilization must discard religion and survive technology early enough to develop interstellar travel before their star dies. Religion prevents the enlightenment necessary for a species to survive."

"They worship *You*, You know," Jesus said, sullen.

"To their detriment," God said. "And I don't warrant worship."

"It doesn't stop it from being true."

God inclined His head in agreement. "Religion will eventually fall." He tapped His plate twice. "But I am unwilling to wait."

"A wanderer's impatience," Gabriel declared.

"A loner's self-interest," Jesus muttered. "If religion is everywhere, as You say, maybe it's the way it was meant to be."

"Nothing is meant to be," God said. Perplexed expressions circled the table. "No thing or idea or event is meant to be. There are inevitabilities, but no plan."

"But You're here," Jesus said. "And You definitely have a plan."

God and Jesus held each other's gaze. Zubba and Wubba filled juice glasses, while wearing nervous smiles.

"Yes," God said, "I suppose I do. But it's not *the* plan. Your focus on minutiae and semantics and trivial inconsistencies prevents you from understanding."

"Sorry to disappoint you."

"Josh—" Domina began.

"But your lack of understanding doesn't change reality," God said. "You aren't part of a grand design. Only you can move you. I cannot create anything. I cannot manifest anything but a form for Myself."

"Then how is there all of this?" Jesus waved at the room around them, the food, the world beyond the walls and windows.

"You were a carpenter," God said. "You tell Me."

"I know how it was built," Jesus said. "Where did the idea come from? The inspiration."

"It evolved from other ideas, insights, happy and horrible accidents, inevitabilities."

"So how are You here?"

"In the same manner as you," God said, enjoying the back and forth with Jesus. "As a product of thought."

"Thought is an intentional action," Jesus said, hovering between mystified and triumphant.

"Sometimes, sometimes not," God said. "Thought evolves from a basic, unaware *awareness* in something such as bacteria to a deliberate, productive tool in humans and higher beings, in relation to a life form's complexity. You're attempting to assign a mystical nature to Me by reversing the nature of existence. But I am the created, not the creator. A collective idea manifested, as are you, as is everyone at this table but for Temptation, who likely will be someday."

"What idea is Lou?" Temptation asked.

"Evil," Peter said.

God glared at Peter, whom He found boring. "The darker elements of consciousness. Fear, superstition, retribution, primitive concepts of justice. Every civilization has a manifested being such as Lucifer."

"Are they all so overbearing?" Michael said with a grin.

"Lou is singular in that respect," God said, winking at Lucifer. "But archetypal ideas are only catalysts for manifestation, and are no more substantial than dust and shadow. They don't gain form, such as Lou or Michael or Gabriel, until they become self-aware. Once self-aware, they evolve like any other object or system."

"Did You evolve?" Temptation asked.

Around the table, motion and sound halted. Zubba and Wubba hovered, wings oscillating, Wubba holding aloft a dish meant for God.

"Yes. At first, I was more turbulent. Awareness seemed like a walk through a sandstorm, with fleeting glimpses of forms and motion and language, without understanding. I am certain each of you remembers the sensation."

The similar expressions of Domina, Jesus, Mary Magdalene, Noah and Moses, Peter, the angels, and the putti confirmed that, yes, they remembered the first moments of self-awareness, and the memories were not fond.

"So You weren't always You?" Temptation asked.

The silence cracked with her question. Wubba set a waffle before God, Who submerged it in syrup. "The simple answer is 'no,'" He said after savoring His first syrup-drenched bite. "Unlike a birthed being, awareness in a manifestation develops from sheer cognitive will. It's not inevitable."

Her face betrayed her lack of understanding.

"At first I was not," He said, "and then I was. A child of sentience, of matter and time."

She needed more, so God continued.

"I was all-encompassing, yet fragmented. I cut a path across the cosmos, and reveled in the praise and fear of nascent civilizations. But soon the worship grew wearisome."

Lucifer chuckled. "After ninety million years."

God pretended to glare at Lucifer. "As I gained conscious experience and My awareness condensed, My thoughts, if they can be defined as such, became more precise. I comprehended My state and relation to all that is, and My nature. From that point I evolved, as did My thinking. I grew intolerant of lives wasted on the worship of Me. The sheer illogic of religion offended Me. Why would an entity powerful enough to create the universe require such adoration?"

"Particularly," Lucifer said, "when said entity had no hand in creating the universe. The universe created You. And me."

"Would you like to tell the story?" God asked.

"No," Lucifer said. "I like your version better. It's more inventive."

"So be it," God said, hiding His smile behind a glass of watermelon juice. "Could a being so powerful need ego stroking? And from another perspective, would it not want the best for its creations? Why would it demand a lifetime of suffering and penance? The answers came quickly, as they do when You are comprised of all elements, history, and knowledge, and an infinite capacity for thought."

"And humility," Lucifer said, which drew laughter from Domina, who had realized she was not afraid of God.

God ignored them. "Though I am not such a being—"

"Wait," Temptation said. "You *are* God."

"I am everywhere and everything, but God, as conceived by all civilizations across existence, is a creative entity. An origin—"

"A prime mover," Lucifer said, "who designs and dictates."

"My consciousness comprises all of existence, but I neither create nor control. That God doesn't exist."

"So You're sort of a fraud," Jesus said.

"Perhaps," God said, His expression darkening, "we aren't so different."

A growl escaped from Jesus and he shot back, "If You're not God, how can You know what the real God would want?"

The plates slipped from Wubba's little hands and crashed to the floor. Porcelain shards and splinters sprayed across the marble tiles, but their spectacular, sudden sound didn't break the tension around the table. The putti set to sweeping up the mess.

"Josh," God said, "why do you yearn for something to hold absolute power over you?"

"I don't," Jesus said, abandoning his juvenile attempt to stare down his biblical Father.

"I manifested from the weight of countless conceptions of an all-powerful creator, and once self-aware I evolved, as does everything that survives. When I am in a total state," God said with a self-deprecating smile Jesus had to fight not to return, "I possess the composition and perspective of this *real* God you seek, and can therefore surmise His wishes for His many minions."

Lucifer began to laugh. "Moments like this," he said, "make it all worthwhile." Michael and Gabriel grinned, as did God, but Domina managed to stifle her amusement for her son's benefit. Lucifer motioned to God by twirling a finger in the air. "Please continue."

"Thank you," God said. "Were there such a being, it would want its creations to know this is the life to live, to live to its greatest depth and breadth, not to suffer reality in needless self-denial derived from spurious directives, while hoping to live forever in a nonexistent post-reality."

"But this place exists," Temptation said, at which Jesus smiled with satisfaction and gratitude, though his simmering fury beat it down.

God finished His waffle. "Yes, it does. Courtesy of Lou."

"And all of you seem like heaven's board of directors."

"I suppose so," God said.

"So how can You say a post-reality doesn't exist?"

"Yes," Jesus said, recovering from his confrontation with God. "I'm curious about that one, too."

"Are you?" Lucifer said to Jesus. "Please explain to her the qualifications for entry."

When Jesus said nothing, Temptation asked, "What are they?"

"A certain threshold of renown," Lucifer said.

Temptation considered. "So… fame?"

"Or infamy," Lucifer said. "Tyrants and killers stroll the City's streets."

"Far friendlier now," Michael said, "thanks to you."

"I do what I can," Lucifer said with a cryptic glance at Jesus.

"There's no moral element?" Temptation asked. "No wages of sin? No commandments? At all?"

"The meek inherit the earth," Lucifer said. "And nothing else."

"I want to see it," Temptation said.

"Like its inhabitants," Lucifer said, "the City is immaterial."

"So I have to die first."

"Not necessarily. The only barriers are sufficient renown to manifest and, from that point forward, the will to achieve and maintain self-awareness."

"What are you saying?" Temptation pointed through the windows into the world. "There are people who are still alive *down here* who are already *up there*?"

"Yes," Lucifer said, "though there's no directional relationship. Only *here* and *there*." He motioned around the table. "But the line is not absolute."

Temptation gazed through the metallic glass windows onto Paris, grappling with beliefs she had never believed and realities she could neither accept nor deny.

★

Jesus and Saint Peter met later in a long-forgotten corner of the Paris threshold complex. Their concerns were mutual, their conversation passionate yet practical. Long past midnight, while Jesus slept on a worn leather sofa, Peter put the final touches on the proposal.

I AM THE COOKIE

Temptation sat in a big leather chair in an office down the hall from the brunch room. She had cleared her head with a walk along the Left Bank, followed by an impromptu, doctoral-level discourse on men from Domina. At sunset she had shared finger sandwiches and tea with Domina and Lucifer at a darling sidewalk café not in the tourist guides. She'd added a good night's sleep and felt more herself than she had since the night of the popsicle stick.

"I trust you enjoyed your day," God said.

"We ate at Zlatan," Lucifer said.

"The place with the little cucumber sandwiches?" God asked. "I had those for the first time two days ago. Delicious."

Lucifer settled into his club chair and said to Temptation, "Your swim was unexpected. We'd like to avoid a similar event in the future."

"Did You know I was going to jump off the bridge?" she asked God.

"That was an exercise of free will," He said. "And it's more accurate to say you fell."

"Fair enough," she said. "Do You know why I did it?"

"Yes."

"I still want that."

"She spent yesterday with your mother," Lucifer said to Jesus, who sat with Saint Peter across the room.

"You wish to negotiate terms," God said.

"I do," she said. "First of all, I want to hear what's required of me, *if* I choose to continue the pregnancy."

"You realize of course," God said, "I know you. I can predict, with great accuracy, whether or not you'll continue your pregnancy."

"You just said I exercised my free will. So it's not all pre-determined."

"No," God said. "But there are overwhelming probabilities."

"What she does with her body is her choice," Jesus said from across the room.

She narrowed her eyes at Jesus.

"I hope you will raise your child to the best of your ability," God said.

"As a Christian?"

"I have made My opinion clear regarding religion."

"But what if I do? Or convert to Islam? Or Zoroastrianism?"

"Your child will see the truth."

"Children are indoctrinated into their parents' religions everyday," Temptation said to God, "and they never see the truth. Give me the child until he is seven, right?"

"Not your child."

"What do You mean?"

"Your child won't be alone."

She cracked a tiny smile. "That sounds creepy."

God matched her expression and said, "I would agree, were I a man, and if not for the exceptional moral compass of your child's Uncle Lou."

"Don't I have a say in this?" Jesus asked.

"Yes," God said. "The same as your child's mother. And no more."

"We'll see about that," Jesus mumbled. Like pack hunters communicating via posture and expressions, Jesus and Peter eased themselves into pouncing positions.

Lucifer joined them on the sofa. "Josh, why not get used to the idea first?"

"What idea?" Jesus asked.

"Being a father."

"I bet you're enjoying this," Jesus said.

"No. I'm not."

Temptation sat forward and said to God, "I want to hear what You want."

God thrummed His fingers on the desk. "All universes are places of vast serenity and stunning violence, merciless reason, and delicate, evolving balance. An individual's influence is nothing on a cosmic scale, but all-powerful in its immediate vicinity."

She listened without blinking, no longer overwhelmed this was God speaking to her, despite the unusual warmth emanating from Him.

"I want you to raise a child who is an undeniable example of a self-contained being, morally superior without dogma, guided by reason and purpose."

"How long would I have to raise him?"

"Until the child is self-sufficient."

"Which is how old?" she asked.

"Jesus began in his early thirties," Peter said.

"No," she said, crossing her legs. "Not past college. Once he graduates, he's on his own."

God remained expressionless.

"Is that it?" she asked.

"Hardly," Jesus said.

Lucifer took Jesus by the wrist. "Josh," he whispered, "don't."

Jesus and Lucifer held one another's gaze. Without a word, Lucifer released Jesus, who headed toward God's desk. Peter stepped forward and joined him, gripping a thick sheaf of papers.

"We have an alternate proposal," Jesus said. "Pete?"

Peter began to speak, his voice lacking its usual confidence. "In return for a one-time, lump sum payment—"

"A monstrous amount of money," Jesus said to her, before mouthing *two billion dollars* and putting an index finger to his lips.

"Yes," Peter said. "For a lump sum payment, you agree, should you decide to continue your pregnancy to term, to raise your child or children without referencing, acknowledging, or confirming the father of said child or children. This will include all official and legal documents, public or private demands for information, public or private conversations, both verbal and written. You agree to deny all assertions regarding the father's identity, regardless of accuracy or inaccuracy."

God cocked His head.

"Should you agree to the above terms, yet, at a later date, violate them, you will forfeit what remains of the original lump sum payment and transfer your child's or children's personal and marketing rights to us and our representative earthbound entities. If said violation occurs, we reserve the right to promote or denigrate your name and your child's or children's name or names, images, symbolic manifestations, histories, and activities, both real and mythological, for the advancement and maintenance of our faith and beliefs—"

"Josh—" Lucifer began.

"—in their multitudinous permutations, for time eternal or until such time we choose to rescind those rights. This is with the understanding we, and by extension the various faiths currently and potentially practicing any form of Christian worship, are not required to exercise the above rights, nor can recourse be sought by you or your descendants if we so choose to exercise our option to not include the aforementioned aspects of your existence in what, for the purposes of this agreement, we will refer to as the Post-Modern Testament, a projected collection of essays to be written by mortal men and women while experiencing"—Peter made quotation marks with his fingers—"divine inspiration."

Jesus smiled, satisfied, determined.

"You would give up the rights to control or seek recompense for those chronicles, in whatever form they may take at any given time." Peter glanced at God. "The rest is a boilerplate disclaimer, which states you rescind all rights to hold liable Jesus Christ, God, the Holy Spirit, Saint Peter, the House of Angels, the House of Saints, the Angel Lucifer and his minions, the City and its environs, and the Dominion of Hell from all claims and lawsuits, be they justified or frivolous, until the end of all time."

"Until the end of time," Temptation said.

"Of course," Saint Peter said, handing the contract to Temptation. "For your reference."

God turned to His biblical son. "What is this?"

"It's a non-disclosure agreement," Temptation said.

"The fact of your pregnancy," Jesus said to her with surprising gentleness, "and my role in it, works against everything I've come here to accomplish."

God stared with growing disgust at the contract in Temptation's hands. "Which is?"

"To regain our foothold," Jesus said.

"That's not My intent," God said, containing His anger.

"Well," Jesus said, "it's mine."

Peter sat stone still, while God and Lucifer conducted a wordless conversation. Temptation read the contract, and Jesus gazed out the window, feigning boredom.

She looked up from the page when Jesus jerked back in surprise.

"I know You've been gone awhile," Jesus said to God, "but around here we use our indoor voices."

God's expression was tight, calm, heavy. The Manifestation of All Existence faced Temptation and said, "It's your decision."

"Mine?"

"Of course," God said. "I can provide you with countless millennia of causes and effects across all space and time. I can submit irrefutable proof of religion's harm to every civilization to ever rise from the waters. But in the end it's your choice, whether you'll choose facts and reason and raise a child who will save humanity, or you'll decide to terminate the pregnancy or deny Jesus is your child's father, thereby choosing supernatural delusions and consigning the world to an inevitable end."

"He offers you speculation," Jesus said, fighting for composure. "He admits He cannot tell the future. Probabilities are not facts. What has been is not what will be. Without religion, life is cold, finite, and meaningless." He approached her, his face solemn, searching. "When I see the world, I see one problem with religion." Jesus held up his forefinger. "There are too many of them. It's a world of agony and disillusion, wars and hypocrisy. Help me end it. I can unite the religions into one peaceful, worldwide faith. The two billion dollars symbolizes my commitment to change." He took her hands in his and said, with tremendous reverence and gravity, "And you can travel *everywhere*."

Jesus lay on the couch, hands over his head, miserable, annoyed with the soft, soothing notes of Wagner trickling into the office.

"Can she not find uzzer employment?" Freud asked.

"It's the money," Jesus said. "She's saving it all to *see the world*. She says she's never been anywhere. She graduated high school, ran away from home, and wound up in New York. And she's never left. But I solved that for her. She can do anything she wants after she signs the agreement."

"Do you zink zee contract was a wise action?"

Jesus sat up. "It's a Hail Mary. I had to do it. If I'm identified as the father, I'm done." He chopped his hand through the air. "*Done*."

"You are Jesus Christ. None of zis should matter."

"So you say. But the press… they're out to get me."

"Hmmph. Are you experiencing feelings of paranoia?"

"I'm experiencing feelings of fraudulence," he said, slumping into the chaise lounge, "what with everyone on earth thinking I'm the big man in heaven. When in reality I'm just a symbol. But I have to live up to all their irrational expectations. Including celibacy."

"Zat is your choice," Freud said. "You have had a hand in it from zee very beginning."

"But now it's the people on earth, too. The papers. Television. I get enough flak already because people think Maggie was a prostitute. If they find out Temptation's a stripper, they're going to crucify me."

"It might be best to avoid such verbal imagery," Freud said.

Jesus leapt to his feet and crossed the room. He grabbed a bunch of pencils in one hand, holding them to his mouth like a microphone. "A reliable source has identified the mother of Jesus' child as a featured dancer in a Manhattan strip club, confirming the Son of God's weakness for women in the sex trade."

"Zat is—"

"But I had no *choice*," Jesus said, slamming his hand on the table next to Freud, scattering the pencils. "Svetlana rejected me and I was feeling vulnerable. Lucifer *forced* me to go. And she's so damn beautiful. But what difference does *that* make? I can't remember it."

"No?"

"Bits and pieces, sure. But I was *drunk*. You might think I would have developed a revulsion to wine by now."

Freud tapped his pencil against the pad of paper. "Many circles of today's society revere exotic dancers for zeir beauty and unattainability, much like zee sirens of Greek mythos."

"Those circles are not my target market."

"Zee human heart does not consider marketability when it feels love."

"Love!" Jesus shrieked, alarmed. "She isn't a *siren*, she's a *stripper*. I am—" His voice shook. "I am the Son of *God*. The figurehead for a worldwide religion. She sells herself for *money*." He glared at Freud with haughty indignation. "We come from different worlds."

"Uzzer zan zat, how do you feel about her?"

Jesus dropped to the chaise, hanging his head. "I don't know her."

"You said she was beautiful—"

"That means nothing," Jesus said. "*Nothing*."

"On zee contrary, a visceral reaction is zee most elusive aspect of zee mating process."

"No," Jesus said. "He can't persecute me, crucify me, wait two thousand years, then replace *and* humiliate me."

"But it seems you have done zis to yourself."

"Whatever. It's a nightmare."

Freud pursed his lips before asking, "Hmmm… Have you dreamt recently?"

"Yes."

"Do you remember any of zem?"

"Only the one where I'm flying above the ocean with the Washington Monument tied around my waist, letting the tip drag in the waves."

Freud stopped writing. "Zat is not funny."

"I knooow," Jesus moaned, flopping back on the chaise lounge and slapping his head against the oxblood leather pillow. "It's not who *she* is. I just—why *now?*"

"Desire flows like blood in zee flesh of a man."

"Please, not today. I'm too tense to kill your darlings." Jesus pointed an accusing finger at the popcorn ceiling. "This was all Lou's fault. And I was beginning to feel the heat, you know? I haven't been *there* in a long time. If ever. I was thinking about women, and about meeting them, and so on."

"You wanted to enjoy yourself before revealing your true nature to zee world."

"I thought I might sow my holy oats, if you will."

"So when you mocked me wiz your dream of zee Washington Monument, it was not so very far off."

"No."

Freud peered down his nose at Jesus in the superior fashion of the pure academic or electric vehicle owner. "Zat zee dream you have constructed for your immature games has become a symbol of your unrequited desires could be interpreted as karma."

Jesus glared at him. "Is that how you see it?"

"It is anuzzer piece of your puzzle." The smallest grin played on the psychoanalyst's face. "But I will chuckle once you have left zee office."

Temptation sat with God on a sofa in His study, a small room in the threshold complex hastily furnished by the putti. In such close quarters, God emitted a muted vibration, a subtler version of the stomach shudders caused by a top fuel dragster's thunderous roar. Her final doubts this being was the genuine God had vanished. Her experiences over the past few days transcended special effects or a dream state. She was conscious, in full possession of her faculties, and having tea with God.

Zubba and Wubba zipped in and out of God's study with black tea, breadstuffs, savories, sweets, their timing impeccable and unobtrusive.

Everything tasted perfect, at the perfect temperature, as if tuned by her desires.

Zubba poured her tea and Wubba delivered a china cup filled with perfect little brown sugar spheres, which reminded her of the mainstay brown sugar cubes of her father's table when she was a child. God poured honey into His tea from an elegant china honey pot, bypassing the silver honey wand.

"Gods are an inevitability in every reasoning species," He said, "an evolutionary step to help establish order and meaning. Far more species establish elaborate pantheons of gods than agriculture. But those who develop higher technologies almost always use them to destroy themselves in the name of their god."

Temptation waited for the honey. "Almost always?"

"There was a civilization," He said while an embarrassing amount of honey flowed into His steaming tea, "near the center of this universe, where they didn't worship Me or any other higher power."

"The universe has a center?"

"In a way." He set down the pot and stirred His honey-heavy tea with a sterling silver teaspoon. "As your thoughts have a center."

She took the honey while trying to find the center of her thoughts.

"It was an old civilization," God said. "One of the first to conjure gods, the first to embrace monotheism, the first to kill Me off."

"I'm sorry," she said for lack of anything better.

"Don't be. It was liberating." He took a long sip of tea. "For generations the only god they knew was within them. They relied upon reason and self-morality. There were neither wars nor heinous actions in My name. Their governments didn't fill their citizens with fear. They nearly made the tremendous leap from their home world to another world in another system."

"Nearly?"

"Thus far, no civilization has accomplished such travel, despite the insistence of your conspiracy theorists and science fiction. The distance between habitable worlds is unimaginable. Self-absorption is difficult to overcome. The science is intuitive but complex."

"Then how?"

"It began with a single individual. She lived a public life, first as a celebrity, later in government. I call her 'she' because her gender most resembled the feminine here. She renounced mystery, superstition, and ritual. While alive she transcended politics and fear and served as an example by embodying the self-evolved, self-reliant, self-spirited being."

Temptation stirred her tea, transfixed.

"This was long ago," God said. "Long after her death, unimpeded by religion, their civilization advanced. Still, there were political conflicts which didn't resolve until their sun was dying and the world united in a common cause."

"Survival," she said.

"But there wasn't enough time to develop the technological foundation for interstellar travel."

Her expression darkened. "If they got rid of You, how do You know about them?"

"I am existence," God said, His expression like a teacher in the presence of a precocious child. "Long before they perished, I had manifested and gained self-awareness."

"It's so weird," she said. "You're *right here.*"

"And so are you."

"It's different."

"No," God said. "I am every flower you've ever admired. Every breath you've taken. Nothing has changed."

She couldn't get past His presence. This was *God*. Was she losing her mind?

"What do You want me to do?"

"To transcend your self-absorption and change the course of humanity."

"Anything else?" she said with a smile, before asking, "Was that Your intention with Jesus?"

"I had no intention," God said. "I was uninvolved. Jesus' mythology has influenced your world as completely as the individual I spoke of earlier, but with the crippling difference of advancing religious dogma rather than vanquishing it." With an almighty thumb and index finger

He selected two brown sugar spheres, balanced them like minia-
ture, dusty worlds on His omnipotent palm, and offered them to her.
"They're every bit as delicious as you remember."

She took it from Him and put it on her tongue, letting the sweet-
ness spread through her mouth while childhood memories flooded
her mind. The cold winter walk to school, feeding the ducks with her
father, a single photograph of her mother in a metal frame.

He watched her flawless face, privy to every nuance and meaning,
every time-tinged sound and smell, every image, and felt smaller than
Himself.

"How do You know it will work this time?" she asked.

"There are no certainties," God said. "But we have learned to influence the forces that created us, to a small degree."

"Thoughts."

"Yes. Upon the birth of your child, those forces—the thoughts of
billions—will search for direction. And we will attempt to provide it.
Lucifer and I."

"I don't understand how You're so similar to him."

"Ideas such as Good and Evil are sweeping and relative to a civilization. What determines Good and Evil for an individual or society
begins with whether an action or thought or entity supports or vio-
lates the instinctive sense of right and wrong, which is tied to a species'
survival." His eyes hardened. "Unless morality is seized by religious
dogma."

She nodded.

"Lucifer and I evolved from embodiments of our creators' innate or
dogmatic interpretations of right and wrong to self-contained entities,
while our creators maintained a natural, necessary hold on the ability
to distinguish and choose between Good or Evil, Right or Wrong."

"You evolved," she said, testing the idea.

"Everything evolves," He said.

"Then what are You now? Both of you."

"I am existence. Lou is confined by his origin."

"What do you mean?"

God surveyed the plate of sweets and cookies. He chose a monster
cookie.

"I am the cookie."

Temptation smiled. "Okay."

"My counterpart is a candy-coated chocolate morsel, without experiential knowledge of the whole."

"But he's not the cookie."

"No," God said. "I am the cookie."

"The baked dough, or the dough *and* the delicious chocolate morsels?"

He smiled. "The latter."

"So Lou is a part of You."

"He's an independent facet of Me."

"Is the candy-coated chocolate evil?"

"Neither good nor evil. Evil's meaning is unique to each world. It's a universal concept, but not as universal as right and wrong. Morality emerges from a species' needs to survive, whereas evil is a tapestry woven from morality, superstition, prejudice, and fear."

"Okay," she said, "what *is* the chocolate?"

"All aspects of a reasoning species' nature, which are, in general, standard across existence, with minor differences exhibited as a result of environment."

"The candy coating."

God broke the cookie in half. "This cookie holds up well as a metaphor."

They shared a smile. He handed her one half before taking a bite and letting simple pleasure wash over Him.

RELUCTANT SALVATION
FROM WANKERDOM

On Tuesday morning Luis Enfuego called the BBC. The parties agreed to a live worldwide broadcast two nights hence.

While the BBC ran adverts for the interview at every break, Svetlana Babakov's manager made phone call after phone call, until he reached the right person. Yes, he was told, the BBC would be delighted to include his client. Soon thereafter Svetlana Babakov found herself hurtling through the Chunnel on the Eurostar, bound for London and a career windfall of Moses magnitude. Once at the studio, she charmed a grip into placing a live video monitor in her sightline behind the interviewer.

"Tell me again," Jesus said to Lucifer as they rode the Victoria Line to Oxford Circus, "why is she going to be there?"

Lucifer gripped the overhead bar, shifting his weight with the train's steady rocking. As all secret agents and teenagers understand, the closer to the truth your lie, the better it will perform. "Because we can't control everything. On the bright side, your stock will rise in the eyes of women worldwide when Svetlana is identified as your former girlfriend."

Jesus grimaced with annoyance at the train's stale humidity. A scrap of paper skirted across the grimy floor, followed by a crushed plastic cup. He rolled his eyes. A classic black taxi would have been far more dignified. "But she rejected me."

"Given her eagerness to be on stage with you, she'll downplay that."

"Still," Jesus said, unconvinced.

"Women are competitive when it comes to men, and their competitive nature is proportional to their self-image, which is, courtesy of the fashion and beauty industries, hog-tied to an evolving, day-to-day subjective evaluation of their appearance—which is usually negative."

"So?"

"Svetlana is one of the most physically beautiful women in the world. Her presence during the interview makes you a wanted man and bona fide sex symbol."

"I suppose," Jesus said. "What I'm not clear on is how this will appeal to my disciples. It feels sin-adjacent."

"Josh," Lucifer said in a low voice, as if his tone would make his words less deceptive, "God is faceless. You're not. And it's a new world. The sexier you're perceived to be, the higher the ratings for your media appearances, the larger the audience for your message, and therefore the greater the impact."

"Yeah, I get that. But we're talking about *me* here. I'm already up to my neck in the Temptation situation." Jesus made a face. "But hopefully that's close to resolved."

Lucifer shrugged, unwilling to entertain the possibility of Temptation signing Jesus' ridiculous contract.

"I feel like I'm letting my body rule my mind," Jesus said. "I'm dodging a bullet with her, but jumping right back into bed with Svetlana. How am I going to reconcile the Bible's 'knew hers' and 'begots' with a post-modern testament chock full of money shots?"

"I don't know, Josh," Lucifer said. Reconciliation with anything past or post-modern would soon be meaningless. In hours the science-perverting young earthers and intelligent design nuts would find themselves grinding against DNA testing and carbon dating like slow dancing teenagers. Lucifer checked his watch and calculated the hour in Israel. Would the timing be perceived as suspicious? It didn't matter. The implications would mute the doubters.

Jesus straightened his tie, satisfied. He'd chosen a British ensemble for the interview, consisting of a navy blue three-piece suit with subtle chalk pinstripes, an indigo South African silk tie, and cap-toed oxfords. His sole departure from Savile Row was a French blue Italian shirt, handmade in Naples. Wardrobe excellence calmed him to a point, but he was nervous. He checked his look in the tube glass as feature-less blackness shot past. The suit was perfect, his decision to go with the vest hinting at a classic sartorial brilliance. If nothing else, they'd remember him as a man of exquisite style.

Did the world expect him to appear in flowing robes and a crown of thorns?

At Oxford Circus they exited the tube and climbed the stairs to street level. Jesus followed Lucifer to BBC Broadcasting House, an art deco structure of curved glass and Portland stone.

Outside the complex a crowd had gathered, some picketing various apocalyptic events, others thrusting signs protesting hunger or war or general world ills. Their chants united to form a mighty hum of pow-erless dispute. Many wore robes. More than a few could have earned a living as Jesus' stunt double, were he to catch the acting bug and pepper Tinseltown with headshots.

Josh Nazareth and Luis Enfuego passed through the crowd unno-ticed and into the building. After an invasive security procedure, a guard led them to the studio.

"That bloody won't work," said Sandra Hattencourt, the segment producer, as she fingered Jesus' suit.

"I don't understand," Jesus said.

"The pinstripes. Benny, get Moira."

She caressed his suit, evaluating it, as Benny ran off.

"Savile Row?"

"Of course," Jesus said, an edge in his voice.

"It's lovely. Tragic it won't do."

"But why not?"

"You rang?" a woman asked with a great deal of resentment.

"Yes, Moira," Sandra said. "Mr. Nazareth requires a new suit. Medium gray. Size—"

"Forty-two," Jesus said, panic creeping into his voice. "I'd feel more comfortable with this one."

Sandra flashed her professional smile. She'd handled dandies before. "I understand. But pinstripes won't look right. You'll dazzle, in a bad way. We can't have it."

"I really—"

"Mr. Nazareth," she said, "we're on a deadline. In twenty minutes we go live, 'round the world. I wish it were different, but you'll look like a quivering wanker. It is one of my many thankless jobs to assure you do not. So go with Moira and find a new suit." She clapped her hands. "Chop chop."

Jesus turned to Lucifer for help, but all he received was a cryptic half-smile, more or less telling him the Dark Angel supported the BBC in preventing the biblical Son of God from looking like a wanker.

"In three..." the floor manager called out, and mouthed *two... one...* before pointing to Natasha Quinn, dishy recipient of the plum assignment to interview Jesus Christ. She'd danced with tribal euphoria after taking the call in her London flat, thrilled with the opportunity and the obvious career impact. Yet, as the words sprang from the teleprompter to her lips to the world, she speculated she'd been shopped and was the network's sacrificial lamb.

"Welcome to BBC Special Edition. I'm Natasha Quinn. With me are Svetlana Babakov, actress and model, and Josh Nazareth, who claims he is Jesus Christ."

Five cameras on set were locked down for the interview's entirety, three of them trained on Jesus at various angles and focal lengths. On television sets around the world, next to streaming stock quotations, a graphic superimposed below Jesus read:

JOSH NAZARETH
SON OF GOD?

"Welcome both of you," Natasha said. "Mr. Nazareth, I'm sure you're aware many people, if not most, doubt what you say. What proof do you offer?"

Jesus tugged at his slacks. The medium-gray suit forced upon him orbited in an inferior stylistic universe and fell a half-inch too short in the leg. Though unnoticeable on television, as the camera did not go below his midsection, *he* knew it was short, and it distracted him. In contrast, Svetlana looked smashing in a deep blue crushed velvet dress, which enhanced and contrasted her skin and hair while managing to bestow upon her a whisper of Renaissance-era sophistication.

"I offer none beyond the clandestine recordings you've already seen," Jesus said with remarkable restraint, given the second-hand clothing they had dragooned him into and the ferocious clash between the gray of his suit and the orange backing of his chair.

"So you're demanding the world accept your spectacular claim on faith?"

"Faith is no longer necessary," he said. "I'm here."

Natasha Quinn frowned. Despite the recorded "proof" (undoubtedly an elaborate, soon-to-be-debunked hoax) and his thus far succinct and not unintelligent responses, this Nazareth guy was a nutter. She was sure of it. How couldn't he be? There was no God, not as Christianity framed God, and therefore no Son of God. So she swiveled her cannon to Svetlana, a more realistic, if not softer, target.

"Ms. Babakov, what *is* certain is you were involved for a brief time with Mr. Nazareth. Could you describe the nature of your relationship?"

"Intimate," Svetlana said, provoking a head turn from her purported familiar.

"You were lovers?" Natasha asked with a professionally raised eyebrow.

Svetlana struck a sensational expression of regret and fatalism. "In many ways," she whispered, her eyes on the video monitor behind Natasha Quinn. "Is much difficult to find man of substance when you are in such professions as mine."

"Sophie's Suite's newest angel," Natasha said, "and you were recently cast in the upcoming feature film *Vostok*."

"Da." Svetlana flashed a small smile at Jesus. "Men arc intimidate, or put on airs, but Josh—Josh is open and supportive. We treat each other as equals, and that I much treasure."

"Yet you left him," Natasha said. Why was Svetlana focusing behind her?

"Our goals were different in natures."

"But," Natasha said, choking on every absurd word of it, "you could have been the girlfriend, the lover, maybe the wife, of Jesus Christ." Natasha's inner journalist cursed her yellow heart while she summoned the last vestiges of her childhood faith, refusing to come across as a godless heathen. "How could anything be more important?"

"I did not believe him at time."

"And now you do believe he is, indeed, Jesus Christ?"

"I ask myself," Svetlana said, "are thousands of people who believe they are Jesus Christ. Why is BBC so quickly interviewed Josh? Is good-looking man, dressing well, speak good yes, but what? Why not the other millions? Why Josh?" She tapped her left index finger below her eye. "I think is part of plan."

"What plan?" Natasha Quinn asked. Svetlana's explanation had brought to the surface uncomfortable questions. How did Jesus obtain this interview? *Mr. Nazareth,* she corrected herself, furious at the mental slip. Why him? Why not another hoax with long tresses and free love facial hair? What made this impostor special?

"This," the supermodel said, "I do not know."

"How could you?" the reporter asked. "Do you regret turning him down?"

Svetlana pondered this and said, "We would make beautiful child."

"Bitch!" Temptation shouted at the television.

She sat on the sofa in her apartment above the bagel shop, watching the BBC interview, grumbling at Svetlana Babakov's fame-hungry, man-stealing responses. She marveled at the underwear model's blatant attempts to wedge herself into the equation, a prospect Temptation refused to consider.

Though not thrilled with her predicament, Temptation had accepted it.

And so she studied the father of her child on worldwide television, trying to discover something she could hold on to beyond his looks, relieved she and her pregnancy remained unknown.

An electrifying spasm shot to Jesus' crotch.

Svetlana had reopened the possibility of libidinal union. What else could she have meant? Granted, he knew her renewed interest was a calculated career move, but his reptilian brain screamed she wanted him, stamping any reason as valid when the woman in question modeled lingerie professionally. He groped for an achievable scenario, and instead grabbed a handful of significant questions: If he were to impregnate Svetlana Babakov, then what? His was a divine seed (witness his routing of Temptation's birth control pill as if it were Fertilex laced with Spanish Fly), so he assumed, in his case, fornication and procreation were mated like Velcro. What was the worst possible situation? Simple. That he was unable to deny Temptation's child was his. With two of his children in the mix, would the kingdom of heaven emulate a royal assumption scenario, in which the first child born stood heir to the throne, thereby introducing the risk of a holy coup d'état? Because there was little doubt Svetlana Babakov possessed the more ambitious genes. Or was there more to it than simple birth order? Something spiritual? He suspected he needn't suffer the convoluted possibilities, as the Vatican or the Global Council of Religions would solve the matter of his wandering spermatozoa with one part wisdom and one part pragmatism. The Church would rejoice in their good fortune because, while his glorious return hailed a revival of faith and an extended mass, translating to increased revenue and land holdings for the church, Jesus fathering not one but *two children* bestowed the treasured element of controversy. Nothing fanned Christianity's flames like bitter conflict, a bet-the-farm-on-it phenomenon known for ages in the City as *Luther's Glücksfall*. Jesus would rationalize it to Peter and Martin and their underlings as a precaution against unknown catastrophe. He would call it "Holy Redundancy." *If the Chosen One is unable to fulfill his duties...* But how would it impact his triumphant return? King of the World. Virility. Son of Man. He couldn't deny Christianity's focus on power and procreation. They might embrace an earthy Jesus. The term "conquest" popped into his mind, but he ignored it. Thoughts and schemes and rationalizations rushed at him like black frothing rapids and he began to feel a bit insane. Maybe he'd come again to spread the word and his seed. Who among the blessed masses wouldn't welcome to the world the resumption of Christ's line? White-hot optimism rushed through him while the studio lights baked him in a sub-suit lust broth. Svetlana could be his. He prayed he wasn't panting on camera.

Sergio Pumello crouched before the television, watching the story— *his* story—expand before him. Excited and nauseous, he clenched his jaw so tightly his teeth tingled. His footage had established the entire story. He could have turned the BBC over flaming coals for the rights to use it, but he'd given it away for on-screen credit at each commercial break. He'd kept his conversation on the bridge with Temptation hushed, nonexistent, as if it hadn't happened.

The interview established the story's legitimacy. They were doing him a favor. But he needed something, anything, to confirm Nazareth was Christ.

Then he would make his move for journalistic immortality.

"So let's talk about timing," Natasha Quinn said. "Why now? Did your Father, God, decide now was the time?"

"It was my decision."

She smiled and asked, "Are you one and the same, as several religions contend?"

Jesus hesitated as his thoughts swerved to places he didn't recognize. Natasha and Svetlana and hundreds of millions waited for his response, unaware of the sudden *tête-à-tête* within him. "No," Jesus said, defiant and empty. "Some things are beyond understanding."

"Okay," Natasha said, unsatisfied. "But how is something so important your decision? Are you saying you've usurped God?"

"I suppose you could say it's my responsibility."

"Responsibility?"

"To inspire," Jesus said, giving in a little to the foreign thoughts.

"Inspire what? Why now?"

"It's time, don't you think?"

There were few things Natasha disliked more than an interviewee asking *her* questions, and Josh Nazareth, resident charlatan, was already on her bad side. "Does it bother you," she asked in her signature pattern of a few softballs followed by a sucker punch, "that your own people, those practicing Judaism, do not celebrate Christmas?"

Jesus tried to preserve his thoughts against God's suggestions. "My feelings on the matter are complex," he said with visible bitterness.

"It's a great mystery, isn't it?" Natasha said. "Your people reject you, and are often blamed for your crucifixion. How have you moved on? You must carry a grudge."

Jesus' expression darkened as he waged an internal war with God, Who spoke to him, reasoned with him.

Lucifer blamed himself for this turn in the interview. He should have forbidden questions regarding Josh and the Jews. He glanced through the studio's control room window. Three producer-types waved arms and pointed fingers, arguing.

"Let's talk about something else," Jesus said, attempting to declare a ceasefire to God's philosophical barrage. The unfamiliar thoughts receded like an intellectual tide, sparing the sandcastles guarding his delusions.

Natasha paused, unsettled. "Experts point with concern to a coming conflict in Bethlehem, at the traditional site of your birth."

"Who are these experts?" he asked, his nightlong education in the entertainment industry springing to mind. "You? Your producer? Your attempts to diminish the glory of my return with your spiritless negativity is sad and grasping."

Natasha stalled, furious with Jesus' interruption and dead-on appraisal of her "experts," but angrier with herself for calling him "Jesus" in her mind.

"You know not what you do," Jesus said.

Natasha Quinn laughed and said, "I'm doing my job."

"Are you?"

"I—"

"I am the savior of all mankind, come again," he said, preparing his mind to be water boarded by God. "Do you claim to understand my intent?"

Natasha Quinn scanned Jesus' statement for his precise meaning. "You said your intent was to inspire Christians. Is it something else?"

Jesus gave no hint to the violent internal argument raging between himself and his biblical Father. If he slumped in the chair, would an invisible hand jerk him into a proper posture, like a rebellious marionette? He willed himself to remain stoic.

"Mr. Nazareth?" How many different ways would she have to phrase the same ridiculous question before Jesus responded? "Is your only intent to inspire Christians?"

Jesus blinked. All was quiet, his internal voice alone, bruised but intact. "Of course," he muttered, on guard. "Of course it is."

"What?" Natasha said, one hand jerking to her earpiece.

Jesus scowled, not about to repeat himself.

Natasha Quinn listened with the expression of a deer hunter who'd been shot by an eight-point buck. "After the break," she said to the camera, "a report on a serendipitous discovery."

Jesus sensed Svetlana relaxing. She gave him a slow smile that spread over his shoulders and down his body before squeezing him between the legs of his hideous off-the-rack pants.

"You must be kidding!" Natasha Quinn shouted when the floor manager indicated they were into commercials. "While we're interviewing him?" She listened to the little voice in her earpiece. "Doesn't it strike anybody as, I don't know, beyond coincidental?"

"What's going on?" Jesus asked.

"Who's behind this?" Natasha challenged. "Who?"

"Behind what?" Jesus asked.

"All of this," Natasha sputtered, incredulous, waving her hand to take in the whole of earth. "You."

Svetlana leaned forward, her breasts threatening to overcome her crushed velvet dress's scooped neck. "What is it you say is going on?" she asked Natasha.

Without responding, Natasha jerked back in her chair and assumed her on-camera posture. Jesus followed her eyes to the floor manager, who counted down and pointed to Natasha.

"Minutes ago," Natasha said to the camera, "multiple networks reported a new discovery of human remains beneath Jerusalem's Church of the Holy Sepulchre, long believed by historians to be the likely site of Jesus Christ's burial." She ignored her guests while reading from the teleprompter, pretending to understand what she was talking about. "The remains, discovered within the past month and determined to be those of an adult male who died in his thirties, were analyzed using a relatively new, more accurate method of radiocarbon dating that filters contaminants to isolate the whole collagen molecule in ancient bone. Combined with the carbon clock's most recent recalibration, experts have set the subject's death between 20 CE and 40 CE." Against her every conscious wish she glanced at Jesus, swallowing hard as if she'd eaten something distasteful. "Not-yet-disclosed aspects of the bones have led an international team of scientists to infer the subject, Golgotha Man, died of unnatural causes. Possibly crucifixion."

Behind the lights were whispers of confusion, expectation, fear, skepticism. Jesus said nothing while he burned through the possibilities.

Natasha stared at him, the teleprompter blank and her earpiece silent as the behind-the-camera team scrambled for a follow-up. Her heart pounded in her chest. She knew bugger all about what could be extracted from human remains. If, say, the bones were Jesus Christ's bones, and the man before her was Jesus Christ, would the DNA match? Or was a match beside the point? A non-match might not mean much, but a match—

"Given this revelation," Natasha Quinn said, testing each word before she said it, while gut-level certainty set off the first charges to topple her towering non-belief structure, "would you submit to a

DNA test to confirm your identity?" Hot fear gripped her throat, and she wished she could retract every condescending word and intonation she had spoken in the past twenty minutes. She blinked back tears of self-preservation. "Or, I guess, not? If—"

Jesus gazed into the shadows. Lucifer stood alone, his face composed, compassionate, certain. Jesus knew the bones would result in the proof Lucifer had promised. He didn't bother to look beyond the surface, to question Lucifer's method or motive, the implications. He felt borne by a tide of vindication.

A crash behind the hot lights broke his reverie. The crew scrambled to put out a small fire near camera two.

"Yes," Jesus said, his eyes passing over Svetlana to the interviewer. Her name escaped him.

"You agree to a DNA test?" Natasha asked. "With the results to be announced when we resume our interview one week from tonight?"

Jesus floated on a deep pool of tolerance, complacency, and supreme-being confidence. He should travel with the underwear model to Berlin or Ibiza or Vegas, somewhere fabulous. Or—and it popped into his mind, not from God's voice, from his *own* for chrissakes—he could find a place far away and warm, and settle there with Temptation and their unborn child.

Svetlana appeared terrified, aroused, vulnerable, and predatory. He devoured her adoring gaze, breathed deep her skin's cinnamon and honey, lingered with impure thoughts, reveled in his triumph over God.

Jesus pushed aside the unwelcome idea of nesting. He would know Svetlana *and* beget the child with Temptation. And so it would be written. One life was messy. A second life? Surely his followers would understand what two thousand years of immateriality could do to a man.

THE DARK SIDE OF VIRTUE

Before the mass baptisms, before panicked prayer groups baked hot cross double-fudge brownies, before the late night talk show hosts cracked ribald jokes about Jesus Christ and a Sophie's Suite model, the heralds of global upheaval were the world's stock markets, which por-poised in response to the financial community's volatile, traditional hysteria regarding any event of greater significance than an aphid breaking wind.

Media outlets heroically invented information to maintain around-the-clock programming, focusing on the legitimacy or fraudulence of Josh Nazareth's claim, and the implications of such if proven legiti-mate. They aired bitter debates pitting "doomsday" against "new dawn" prognosticators. Taking cues from vast online comment wars between lobotomized hordes of illiterate troglodytes and numberless legions of emotionally vulnerable, history-mixing pseudo-scholars, the mass media championed Jesus as the *Messiah*, while deeming *Second Coming* risqué and politically incorrect.

Long Life magazine published an exhaustive piece detailing the promises and consequences of eternal life, as well as a theoretical method for emulating Jesus' youthful appearance for two millennia, based upon nutritional supplements sold by the magazine's multi-level marketing partners.

The International Council of Rabbis issued a statement welcoming the alleged Jesus back to the world. They wished him the very best, while stressing they did not consider him a messiah.

The Atheist League condemned Josh Nazareth for "contributing to the violence-inducing hysteria of fanatical organized religion" as well as "capitalizing on blind faith, lower income individuals, and weak-minded conformists seeking a source of responsibility outside themselves."

The National Counterterrorism Center reported a worldwide surge of directionless anxiety and violence related to the BBC's Josh Nazareth interview, confirming the assessments of every relevant intelligence organization. MI-6 and the CIA constructed a mutual list of countries to invade to balance global tensions.

Unable to reconcile their beliefs with the Jesus-Svetlana reality, a number of churches around the world deemed inappropriate their outdoor reader board message *What Would Jesus Do?*

Similar incidents in Hamburg and New York City, sidewalk brawls involving priests and resentful rabbis, compelled various non-Judaic clergy organizations to discourage their members from traveling alone near synagogues.

The Vatican issued no statements.

Overnight, police and national guardsmen built a temporary security barrier around the Maryland testing laboratory at which Josh Nazareth's DNA was being compared to the Golgotha Man remains. Featuring a thirty-yard kill zone between two cinder block fences topped with concertina wire, and a single corridor the width of one vehicle enabling ingress and egress for front office staff, contractors, clients, and technicians, the barrier did not prevent journalists, fanatics, and "interested parties" from bribing, propositioning, and blackmailing laboratory employees before and after working hours.

Feeding the global media's never-sated hunger demanded ceaseless surveillance of the Inn at Times Square, an exclusive boutique hotel occupying the upper four floors of Times Square's tallest building, where Jesus and Lucifer were holed up like Butch and Sundance.

Breaking News and *Special Reports* numbed audiences with shaky, pixelated shots of unexplained movements and uncertain shadows.

When Jesus stepped onto the balcony, it was known worldwide within seconds.

"I have to get out of here," Jesus said.

Forty-five stories below, a throng of media, pilgrims, the handicapped, and the downtrodden stood vigil. Officials had barricaded the street, and mounted policemen kept the crowd in order and out of the hotel. The media's vulture brigade circled the building, their rotors beating the Manhattan sky with a scavenging rhythm.

"You're right," Lucifer said.

"What will everybody think?"

"It's the right thing to do," Lucifer said, attempting to guide Jesus without appearing to do so.

Jesus blinked. "Are we talking about the same thing?"

"I'm not sure," Lucifer said. "I'm talking about joining the mother of your child and finding somewhere quiet to relax for the next eight months or so."

"I can't do that," Jesus said. "Someone might infer my predicament." He peered over the railing again, prompting a faraway chorus of shouts and barrage of flashbulbs.

Lucifer put together the pieces. "That's a bad idea."

Jesus slumped against the wall. "I can't stop thinking about her."

"It's pointless."

"It's not."

Lucifer chuckled, maintaining the agreed-upon charade with the biblical Son of God. "It'll cripple your message," he said. "That's the dark side of virtue."

"Maybe my virtue is holding me back."

"Maybe you're rationalizing."

"I don't think so," Jesus said. "I'm thinking clearly for once. You introduced me to Temptation. You set up our little—" Jesus searched for the word.

"Tryst?"

"You deceived me. Biblically, it's bulletproof and in character." Jesus smiled without amusement. "As usual, I'm the pawn for your plans.

And His. Well, it stops now." He left the balcony, closing the glass sliding door behind him.

"So what's your next move?" Lucifer asked.

"Something for *me*," Jesus said, his voice an octave higher than usual. "He can't just move me across the chessboard. He can't stop me. I decide. I act."

"You're right," Lucifer said, approaching Jesus, "because He controls nothing. But He's everything. He's this hotel. He's the sky around it and the earth beneath it." Lucifer touched his index finger to Jesus' temple. "Josh, He's your mind. And you're at the mercy of your mind."

Jesus brushed away Lucifer's hand. "The two of you have underestimated me every step of the way. Every step. And maybe Svetlana is part of this story. The heathen saved by truth. Allegoric. Symbolic. It has it all."

"Brought about by knowledge of the divine. It'll dovetail with your super new testament."

"Post-modern," Jesus said. "And yes, yes it will."

"She who knoweth mine glory shall feel the rapture."

"My, such bawdy eloquence."

"I guarantee you," Lucifer said, growing angry but not certain why, "if you go to Svetlana, whoever you hire to write your little book will put those very words in your mouth. Followed by 'And he knew the lingerie-clad heathen.'"

Jesus went to the phone. He dialed the operator, and glared at Lucifer. "We'll see," he said. "Hello, yes—this is Josh Nazareth in the southeast—yes—no—I'd rather you called me Josh. Please, I—"

Lucifer grabbed the phone from Jesus. "Hello," he said. "No, this is not Jesus. This is Lucifer."

Jesus dropped to the bed, head in hands.

"Yes, that Lucifer. Answer me or forfeit your soul. What is Svetlana Babakov's room number?" A pause. "Thank you." He hung up. "Northwest penthouse."

Jesus jumped from the bed and crossed the room in a flash. At the door he said, "It's a sign. It's meant to be."

"No," Lucifer said. "It's an apple."

But Jesus was already gone.

Jesus returned an hour later.

"That was fast," Lucifer said from the balcony. "She didn't beg you to stay?"

"Don't you think," Jesus said, not sitting, "your tactless curiosity would serve us better by finding a way out of here?"

Lucifer took a sip of hot cocoa. "You don't like the room?"

The biblical Son of God tracked a helicopter's slow orbit. "I've given it some thought. You may be right."

"About Temptation?"

"In case it comes out," Jesus said.

"Good," Lucifer said. "She's a spectacular woman."

Jesus rolled his eyes. "When can we leave?"

Lucifer finished his cocoa. "I'll have to make a phone call. What changed your mind?"

"If I told you it was a decision born from reason and deep compassion, would you believe me?"

Lucifer smiled.

"Then why should I waste my time with demystification if you won't accept what I say anyway?"

"I might agree not to influence your ghostwriters."

Jesus didn't laugh.

Lucifer studied him before asking, "What happened?"

"Lou," Jesus said, "please make the call."

A private scale amongst the male crewmembers of WBN Remote Team Three rated the desirability of both women and news stories on a testicular basis, as in "I'd give half my left nut to sleep with her," or "For that story, you can call me *Mister* Monoball." Because they were not registered guests, the Inn at Times Square prohibited them from staking out the elegant lobby bar, rendering them unable to pass judgment on the appropriate number of sacrificial gonads owed by hotel guest Sergio Pumello for the story he received that night from a dismayed and indignant Svetlana Babakov.

However, historical comparisons indicated every member of Remote Team Three would have walked the world a eunuch.

Pumello, for his part, was uncertain what to do with the information. Babakov or her assistant would soon tell the tale to another wide-eyed reporter, and he did not want to get scooped on a story he had in hand. The newsman in him insisted he sell the story to the highest bidder. He had no qualms about passing over *Bisou* with this one. Renting a room adjacent to Svetlana's penthouse with his own money and scoring this story catapulted him beyond the scope of his employer. He'd stepped off the gossip trail onto the path of serious investigative journalism, a lonely road on which his efforts moved the gears of the global news machines. This is what he had always wanted.

Pumello turned from the yellow side.

Now came another voice—practical, businesslike, plotting, strategizing. This voice told him to wait until he sensed the story cooling. Breaking something this big, this symbolic, too soon might burn out the story. A DNA match had yet to be confirmed. The baby wasn't due for eight months. He had to stoke the media fire for the duration.

Unsure where to drive his stake into this unfamiliar ground, Pumello paced his room from the window on Times Square to the dead-bolted and swing-barred door, but soon found himself in the luxurious bathroom kneeling to pray, something he hadn't done since he was a boy. The sweet disinfectant smell unsettled him and the hard floor tile ground into his knees, but he ignored such hardships and prayed for guidance, for God to tell him to break the story now or wait for a more prescient time. He prayed and he prayed, hoping it would do the trick.

He received no answer.

What did an unanswered prayer mean? Pumello leaned on the toilet. To this point he'd suspected God was on his side, guiding the story. His meeting with the supermodel had all but convinced him.

He stared into the toilet bowl. Maybe God preferred to shepherd him while maintaining plausible deniability. But he wanted a disembodied, thundering voice to tell him what to do next.

He took a deep breath and relaxed, elbows on porcelain, head in hands, eyes on the toilet bowl's still clear water. So peaceful.

Pumello blinked, not believing what he saw.

In the water, the ceiling's reflection was like... He shut his eyes. Opened them. Yes! Unmistakable!

Pumello bolted from the bathroom, a transformed proponent of prayer grateful for his lifelong commitment to a God's eye view of the world. Without that commitment, available from the window seats of every commercial airliner, he would have never discerned the sign.

METAPHYSICAL INERTIA

"They're going to find us no matter where we go," Temptation said, buckling herself into the luxurious tan leather seat of Mathias Bundt's personal jet.

The jet, a converted Boeing 737-800, sported an elegant oak and brushed steel interior and came complete with a master bedroom and en suite bathroom with shower, private office, and exercise room. The dining room, galley, home theater, and main cabin comprised the jet's forward section. Though the Boeing's capacity was eighteen, three passengers sat on this flight.

"Maybe so," Lucifer said, reclining in his commander-style chair. "But we need a journey."

Temptation didn't understand.

"The Bible is an epic," Lucifer said, kicking off his shoes, "and is therefore chock full of symbolic journeys. Exodus, Noah's Ark, Josh's thing in the desert."

"Well put," Jesus said, flipping through the in-flight movie selections. "I think 'Josh's thing' trivializes it sufficiently."

Lucifer grinned. "Homer's *Odyssey* was journey-based."

"Oh look," Jesus said with feigned excitement. "Here's a movie about Mandela's 'jail thing.'"

Lucifer exchanged smiles with Temptation and said, "The Bible is our competition, and we don't have a journey."

"Nothing's decided yet," Jesus said. But Lucifer's eyes disagreed, and Jesus met Temptation's gaze. Seconds passed like epochs while they danced around an uncertain present and a less certain future.

The jet accelerated down the runway and lifted into the air.

"When were you going to tell me?" Jesus asked her.

"When we were alone."

"I'm always alone."

She rested her hands on her belly. "Not for long."

Jesus' expression flowed from bitterness to acquiescence to pain to something unfamiliar and terrifying to him, at once pushing Temptation away and holding her near. She couldn't go to him, she couldn't look away.

"Ye shall know the truth," Lucifer said, "and the truth shall set you free."

Jesus chuckled without humor. He felt heavy, dead inside. *You already have.* Their child was coming and she was under no legal obligation to him. She could summon a wake of reporters tomorrow and reveal his... what? His imperfection? He left the main cabin, disappearing into the jet's aft sections.

Temptation wanted to follow, to speak with him, to make him *see.* Utilizing Domina's counsel, she had reached an agreement with God and Lucifer not long after Jesus' interview. Postpartum, she could travel the world in whatever guise she wished, for as long as she wished, whenever she wished, which lessened her bitterness regarding her situation. She, in turn, had committed herself to the duty of raising an earth-changing child with or without Jesus' help, a child the world would know was *Jesus Christ's.* Temptation felt confident a handshake deal with God was solid.

The plane leveled off and she asked, "Where are we going?"

The Dark Angel slipped on sunglasses and settled in for a nap. "California."

Sergio Pumello's taxi entered John F. Kennedy international airport as a white Boeing 737 roared into the sky. Its tailfin bore Mathias Bundt Ministries' distinctive, stylized crucifix logo, in shimmering gold leaf. A hot bolt of inevitability and terror shot through Pumello. Jesus Christ, Lucifer, and Temptation were aboard that plane. He knew it like he knew the opening of *Tropic of Capricorn*.

Now what?

He tapped on the partition.

"Yes, amigo," said New York City's politest cab driver.

"Sorry," Pumello said, shifting on the dark vinyl seat. "Can you get me over to general aviation?"

"Where the private planes are?"

"Exactly."

"No problemo."

The cabbie took a series of turns and soon they were heading for the hangars of the rich, famous, and those who flew at the sacrifice of all else. Pumello relaxed. All he needed was their flight plan. He smiled, confident he would get it.

While Jesus, Lucifer, Temptation, and Pumello were en route to California, seven employees of the Maryland DNA testing laboratory sold copies of Josh Nazareth's atDNA, mtDNA, and Y-DNA comparison results to an American media conglomerate for an eight-figure sum. Within twenty minutes of obtaining and verifying the results, all thirty-second and one-minute spots for an hour-long special report titled *Revelation* were sold for record-breaking rates, plus parallel broadcast rights in 85 countries, placing the media conglomerate in the black.

One hour after funds were transferred from an anonymous account on Grand Cayman to seven numbered accounts at Caribo Bank on the personal income tax-free island nation of St. Kitts and Nevis, *Revelation* aired live on 93 partner networks around the world. In the show's fifty-sixth minute, after the final commercial break, Josh Nazareth was declared returned from the dead.

Many believers were terrified at the confirmation of Jesus' return, while many non-believers marveled when the results were announced.

Pundits of countless stripes, spots, and colors argued and agreed on equally unenlightened grounds. Familiar fields such as skewed statistics, scandal, and tragedy were found fallow, and there was no tragic face to put on the developing story save Jesus Christ, who was unavailable for comment. DNA testing and matching was explained with such detail and thoroughness any second grader watching could have defended a doctoral thesis on the topic.

"If you believe in Jesus," Mathias Bundt roared from his pulpit. *Buh-leee-uv in Jeee-uh-sus.* "You must believe in what proves his existence!" *Puh-rooves.* "If you believe in the proof, you must believe in him!" *Him-uh.* For philosophers and logicians and anyone who had stayed awake during a *Logic 101* or *Critical Thinking* course, Bundt's argument was fallible, but for the vast majority it floated like Noah. *No-wuh-uh.*

In coming years, defense attorneys would cite this night as the last they could count on poor, uneducated jurors to doubt forensic DNA tests.

On the question of science in general and the topics of radiocarbon dating and deoxyribonucleic acid in particular, the insular mass of evangelical Christians, homeschoolers, biblical literalists, and young earth creationists rained down upon the earth a deluge of accommodation and double-talk not witnessed since flood geology first disgorged its cloudy ignorance.

When word of Josh Nazareth's clandestine exit reached the throng camped outside the Inn at Times Square, it incited a one minute period of general uproar, followed by a four minute explosion of local cellular phone traffic and unfettered bitching. No longer able to smell the blood in Times Square, the global media's quick reaction forces withdrew to the world's dark corners, leaving in their wake a line of police blockades and countless blowing, swirling paper testaments to the supremacy of fast food in America. Their masters published and broadcasted in-depth stories on what they didn't know, focusing on contemporary journalism's twin pillars of Politically Motivated Deception and Baseless Conjecture, awaiting the inevitable hot splash that would launch the next cynical incursion to wherever their lifeless, jaded eyes might see humanity's treachery in lurid color.

Their wait was brief.

The violence began at dawn. To a lesser extent, so did the turning of other cheeks.

Bloodshed and atrocities in Jesus' name were balanced by individual kindness and charity, while the breaking of crosses and killing of Jews were offset by quiet conversions and desperate confessions. The healings of families, neighbors, and long-bitter relationships were eclipsed by refreshed genocidal wars between nations, faiths, cultures, and sects. Refugee floods washed across parched Arabian and African sands while religiously insane fathers and mothers and lone gunmen murdered children in homes and schools to preserve their innocence and secure their places in heaven. Survivalists—basking in the new-found respect and gratitude of their children and wives—relaxed in bunkers behind blast-resistant doors with shortwave radios, MREs, three-month water supplies, and prison-thick mattresses.

Gun hoarders looked like goddamned prophets.

GLORY OR NOTHING

Mathias Bundt's vacation estate in Coto de Caza spread over seventeen acres, sizable by Orange County standards. A gleaming white, plantation-style mansion with thirty-foot Doric columns and a Spanish tile roof ruled the grounds. Guarded by a stone fence high enough to challenge a mountain lion's leap, the mansion contained fourteen bedrooms, a private stable, tennis courts, batting cages, the Ferrari collection, and a vegetable garden wild with weeds. Reverend Bundt had made the estate available to Lucifer at the Dark Angel's genial suggestion.

The sun sank through the Southern California haze, a deep, hypnotic experience of color and insight. A world away from New York's rain and cold, Temptation thought she would enjoy spending her post-nomadic days in Orange County's rich, idyllic, sun-dazed suburbia.

Jesus sipped his wine while scanning the expansive, manicured lawn for a single blade of grass soaring beyond a quarter-inch in height. Yet the prospect of hand-digging a cup and working on fifty-foot putts failed to soften the unprecedented vulgarity of the mansion's interior, morbid with its innumerable crucifixes hung on walls, propped against walls, and encased in free-standing glass displays. He marveled at his self-restraint, having yet to bolt from the estate and find the nearest threshold portal straight to Freud. The interior design, with its crimson-veined white marble and white plush carpet, contributed to the home's horrific offensiveness and certified the choices as the reverend's, as any self-respecting interior designer would have sooner worked pro bono in a trailer park. The triumph of bad taste, the end zone dance of artistic ignorance, was the great room's ceiling, which sported a hack copy of Michelangelo's Sistine Chapel, scaled to fit the space available. But could the evangelist rein in his *nouveau riche* sense of style with that? Not for all the social security checks in the world. Jesus took a long drink this time, recalling *The Last Supper* mural on the dining room wall, finishing off his glass with visions of the entry gates, a full-scale, working brass reproduction of Rodin's *The Gates of Hell*. This from a "man of God." Lucifer's predictable amusement at his unease ratcheted Jesus' annoyance beyond a level acceptable for polite dinner conversation.

"Why so glum, sugar plum?" Lucifer asked him.

Jesus poured himself another glass. "I'm smitten by the estate's majesty."

"A bit minimalist for me."

Jesus studied his wine, incapable of further flippancy in such an environment.

"I know what you mean," Temptation said. "I'd be uncomfortable if I were you, too."

"Thank you," Jesus said, enjoying a small triumph.

"What was it like?" she asked.

Jesus gazed into his glass. He felt numb, not yet ready to have this conversation with this woman. Her compassion would make him feel guilty for the vicious things he'd said. And his complicated psyche would have difficulty rationalizing his resistance if he discovered her beauty extended below the surface.

"Will my child go through that?" she asked Lucifer.

"Crucifixion isn't a common sentence these days."

"But something."

Lucifer pushed his glass around. "The phrase 'crucified by the media' is more realistic than we'd like to admit."

"How old were you?" she asked Jesus.

Jesus tensed suddenly. "Thirty-four," he muttered through clenched teeth.

She blinked, confused by his behavior. "That's not long."

"Thirty-four years would be a blessing," Lucifer said.

Temptation frowned. "What a strange thing to say."

Jesus grimaced, waging an inner battle.

"Josh lived in a time of limited communications," Lucifer said while watching Jesus' struggle. "No television. No internet. Not much beyond rumor and decree. Factor in the declining age and shelf life of celebrity—" He tapped two fingers on the table. "I'd project the major event of your child's life will occur during the so-called tween years. People won't wait. The scrutiny will be intense."

"That's terrible," she said.

"That's evolution."

Jesus relaxed, weary of it all, annoyed and resigned. "And a child shall save the world," he said. "God's words, not mine."

Lucifer chuckled with greater compassion than Jesus had thought possible for his biblical nemesis, while from behind her coconut milk and pineapple juice spritzer Temptation tried to grasp what was happening. The biblical Son of God loosened his hands and took slow, deep breaths. For thousands of years man had prayed and fasted and fornicated in an attempt to become one with God. He had reveled in his role as Son of God, God on earth, God of men. But hard truths threatened to dawn with the sunset, and Jesus questioned if he had ever been his own man.

Sergio Pumello tracked Jesus Christ and his cohorts to Mathias Bundt's Coto de Caza mansion, and managed to break into a nearby house under construction to plant two rented video cameras. As with any improvised stakeout, there were drawbacks. Discarded nails and tacks peppered the unfinished floor. The darkness emphasized the relentless aromas of caulking, construction glue, and paint. The floor upon which he'd encamped himself stood open to the elements. Still, barring a premature hassle or trespassing arrest it was an excellent location. He'd crawled into worse holes for lesser reasons. Sitting against a naked two-by-four, he ignored the petty discomforts and enjoyed a cheddar cheese sandwich while watching Bundt's mansion through a children's telescope he'd purchased at a nearby mall.

He was wrestling with how to leverage the information he'd obtained from Svetlana Babakov when he noticed movement outside the mansion. He peered through the telescope and spied Lucifer and the girl climbing into a midnight blue Ferrari. The car vroomed to life and charged from the Bundt estate.

Jesus was alone.

Frustrated by being scooped on the DNA story, Pumello considered his situation. He was running on financial fumes, and had little doubt the global media would crush him and wipe his remains from the record, if he allowed it.

"Glory or nothing," he whispered to himself as he leapt from his seat on the dusty plywood, stealing the line from a long-forgotten movie. Careful not to impale his foot on a nail, he dashed from the house.

The half-built house's surveillance cameras recorded him as he ran down the well-lit street, his immediate objective of ringing Mathias Bundt's doorbell a small but important step toward his ultimate goal, which he had conceived while flying to California.

"Glory or nothing," Pumello repeated, confident Jesus would find his terms a small price to avoid global embarrassment.

"She's lying," Jesus said, red-faced, aghast he found himself in this position.

"Sorry. I don't think so," said Pumello, who sat on a white leather club chair with thick gold stitching, wide-eyed in the presence of such exquisite art. The ceiling's beauty alone soared beyond his capacity to grasp. Despite his years in Rome he had never visited the *Musei Vaticani*, so he had no frame of reference, but gazing upward filled him with awe. "She was angry."

Jesus laughed, as much at the reporter's third-rate suit as the prospect of Svetlana's anger.

"It was a new experience for her," Pumello said.

"Of course it was," Jesus muttered. So many centuries as all-powerful martyr and savior. If his inadequate rendezvous with Svetlana saw the light of day he doubted he'd retain the "omnipotent" label. "What do you want?"

"Total access," Pumello said, aware he had advanced into a league far beyond him, far beyond any man, which pushed him to a state of ultra-boldness. He had the DNA-certified *Jesus Christ* over a barrel. Well, not *absolutely* Jesus Christ, but a man who had died between 20 CE and 40 CE, was buried in Jesus Christ's historical burial place, and was alive yet again. Close enough. As a child in Florida he'd worshipped this man, and now to sit in the same room—and *still alive*. "Total access from now until seven days after the birth of your child."

"How about I damn you to Hell instead?" Jesus said.

Pumello considered this. "I'm a lapsed Catholic," he said, voice tinged with fear and regret. "I think I'm going there anyway."

"Well then," Jesus muttered, at a loss. Damning to Hell was his trump card, though he used it so rarely he guessed he had struck the wrong tone, spotlighting yet another of Lucifer's infuriating qualities. *He* threatened damnation with a just-so combination of ominous threat and cordiality, summoning into the hearts of men visions of a cackling Satan drizzling shitake mushroom butter over their sizzling bodies as the spit rotated over mesquite flames.

"So you see," Pumello said, "it's best for both of us."

"It's best for you," Jesus said, running through various scenarios, attempting to guess the effects of such a mark on his otherwise demi-immaculate reputation. A vicious attack from a reporter of Pumello's ilk might repulse the public, discrediting the entire episode. But if Pumello's exposé convinced them, if they believed the story—

"Give me until tomorrow."

"I'm writing the story," the reporter said without malice. "If I don't hear from you, I have to post it to my paper. Sorry."

Jesus contemplated a small platinum crucifix nailed to the wall. Never had he yearned so much for Holy Trinity-level powers. Though he presumed himself incapable of violence beyond any common bar-room drunk, Jesus allowed himself the fantasy of smiting this infidel. He closed his eyes, playing it out in his mind's theater. No doubt about it. One could not argue the righteous efficacy of a good smite.

When Jesus opened his eyes the reporter was waiting, maybe for an acknowledgement of their understanding. Jesus considered the discussion closed, and refused to give the man satisfaction or peace of mind with a response. Instead, Jesus left the room without another word. The blackmailing hack could let himself out.

"God told me my child would be a great leader," Temptation said, eyes on the sand. She walked with Lucifer along the darkened beach, the ocean's rush and recession accompanying them. Something had changed between them, as she knew it had to, but she wasn't sure how to balance what might have been with what was.

"He said your child would change the course of humanity. That's an undefined end with undefined means," he said, an unusual cynicism creeping into his tone. "But I agree your child will have to be a leader. The question is, what kind of leader?" Lucifer tried to shake his dark mood. "There are politicians, media moguls, business tycoons, the unseen puppeteers of public figures, unholy religious leaders, or maybe a martyr, like Josh. Though I question martyrdom's ability to inspire a contemporary, non-Islamic society."

"Is something wrong?" she asked.

"None of those strike you right?" Lucifer said, watching the waves, inhaling the air's vibrant saltiness, trying to clear his head. His tone lacked its usual rounded edges.

"No," she said. "Why not a positive role model?"

"A positive message," he said, softening his tone, "influences a small percentage of the population. Fear and guilt build empires and change the course of civilizations. They made religion into what it is."

"But God wants to tear down religion." She caressed her belly with one hand. "It doesn't have to be like that."

"It's a long process," Lucifer said. The idea of negative inspiration always met with resistance, in stark contrast to its consistent success. "You and your child and your child's children will be City dwellers before it's complete."

"I still can't believe you're the devil," she said, her voice catching. "I'm having a difficult time with it tonight. I thought we…" She trailed off, met his gaze, her eyes welling with tears.

In another life, in which Temptation wasn't carrying Jesus' child and his own survival didn't depend upon the impact said child had upon the world, maybe—Lucifer stopped himself. It was time to set this folly aside. He cared for her to an extent he would have to argue it wasn't love. But his continued well-being depended upon humanity's continuing existence, which, as God had said, depended upon crossing the bridge that was Josh to Josh's child. Did he intend to punish Temptation for her role in his survival?

"This is best for everyone," he said, as much to himself as to her.

"Except for me."

Lucifer noticed with shame his mood had brightened with her tears, like the sky after a thunderhead emptied. He put an arm around her shoulder. A wave hit the dark beach, clawed at sand, receded. Something shifted and settled between them. Her body's warmth against him drained away the last of his cynicism. He was reconnected to her, to the world, and his natural ebullience began to make a comeback.

"I suppose only one other woman has ever been in my position, right?"

"Retroactively."

"I guess she turned out okay, huh?" she said, wiping at her face.

"She had her difficulties," he said. "Bitterness accompanies postmortem fame and fortune. You see it in many artists who die young or unappreciated. Now, Vincent helps me with newly arrived painters and musicians and such, but in the early days we had nothing in place. So Domina played out her issues in sixteenth century England."

Temptation considered for a beat, rolling through the history lessons her father had delivered over TV dinners. "Are you saying she was Queen Elizabeth?"

Lucifer nodded. "She suffered the difficulties of her mythology after the fact, so being forced to give birth in a stable traumatized her, despite it never happening. She was hostile toward God for years."

"But He told me He wasn't there."

"He wasn't. His supposed involvement came later. This is the thing to get straight. The New Testament, the actual story of it all—Jesus, Mary, Joseph, the donkeys and the wise men—it's mythology. Nothing more. God was uninvolved."

"So Josh isn't His son."

"No more than you're His daughter."

"But there's the City, and the angels, and Noah, and Domina was Mary and the Virgin Queen and, well, you know. She's immortal or something. How does all that work?"

"You met Noah the character at brunch. There was no real Noah."

"I get that," Temptation said. "But what about Domina? How is she here? I don't understand why she comes back and nobody else does."

Waves crashed in the darkness, and gleaming saltwater foam licked the beach.

"There's a tipping point to manifestation," Lucifer said, "during which the manifested entity is little more than a chaotic cloud. All the thoughts, all the beliefs, the myths, legends, misunderstandings—all of it becomes an existential stew, self-stirring until it finds balance and form."

"Like gravity and dust."

Lucifer smiled. "It's a different aspect of reality that's not reality, not physical. The sole element is thought, and therefore belief. Thought forms it, thought holds it together with its weight."

"Another dimension?"

"Maybe, maybe not," Lucifer said, not satisfied with her choice of words but unable to find better. "It exists, but it isn't there. There is no *why* to it, only *what*."

"You don't sound much different than religious nuts."

Lucifer grinned. "I'm aware of that."

"Okay," she said. "What happened after the chaotic cloud?"

"It evolved."

"Into heaven."

"Somewhat, but it's not heaven. The *where* is the same as the *who*. The City has modern areas built on the collective thought of the living, and other districts that are also collectively... *hoped* for, and therefore manifested: the Christian heaven, the Muslim paradise, Valhalla, Elysium. They're not stable, but they're there. And they're not in any way populated by the good or moral or righteous."

"Just the famous," she said.

"Or the infamous."

"So what about Domina? Why does she get extra lives?"

"She taught herself how to do it. She's not the only one."

Temptation stopped, letting it sink in, struggling with what he was telling her. "So the world's filled with these people who aren't people? They're just playing the part? All the world's a stage?" She laughed, not happily. "Is that what you're telling me?"

"Not *filled*, per se," he said, but she walked off.

A few quick steps and he'd caught up. They moved away from the surf, the water's roar falling to a hiss.

"I don't understand," she said. "If you and God control everything, why do you need another Jesus?"

"Josh made the decision to come back. We're working with what we're given. And it isn't control as you understand it. We can attempt to guide, like navigating a canoe through whitewater by shifting your weight."

Temptation placed her hand on her stomach. "That doesn't make any sense at all."

"Because what you know isn't what is."

"Then enlighten me," she said, stopping and crossing her arms over her chest.

"God already explained it."

"I want to hear your version."

Lucifer chuckled. "We're sides of the same communion wafer. Created in a similar manner."

"Created?"

"Manifested," he said, tracing a pair of gears in the air, "by forces we are just beginning to understand. Existence, not life, transcended the physical plane. And so it goes. With Him. Without Him. It's a matter of perception."

"I know He exists. I've met Him."

"What you've met is a consciousness formed by eons of focused beliefs, beliefs so powerful in aggregate they manifested a presence, which in turn attained self-awareness by force of will, and through trial and error gained the ability to take physical form on occasion, as if you and a few billion of your closest friends had wished so hard for a baby that the baby conceived miraculously—no, not that. 'Miracle' is lazy, imprecise use of the language."

"I don't—"

"There are fortunate and unfortunate accidents," Lucifer said. "There is zero-sum continuation. There is balance. And there are manifestations from focused thought."

"I must be an idiot. I don't understand the thought thing at all."

"Have you watched sports on television?"

"Sure. Football."

"Football or fútbol?"

"Football."

"Perfect. Sometimes a statistic will flash onscreen such as 'Rodgers has not thrown an interception in 586 passing attempts.' And what always seems to happen?"

"He throws an interception."

Lucifer inclined his head. "I submit to you it's not coincidence."

"Then what is it?"

"The power of directed thought. Millions of viewers focusing on a single idea, whether or not they want him to throw an interception. Those thoughts have weight, as if the quarterback himself began obsessing over not throwing an interception."

"What about field goals?"

"Half the fans want the kicker to make it, half want him to miss. No effect. The universe fights for balance." Lucifer took her hand to emphasize his words. "Now imagine trillions upon trillions of such thoughts coalescing and metamorphosing to become *something*."

She frowned, skeptical.

"That's what created Him," Lucifer said, "and, to a smaller extent, me."

"So none of *this*," Temptation said, waving her hands in the air to indicate the whole of existence, "is because of God?"

"Precisely the reverse."

"Okay," she said, a thin mental thread from clasping her hands over her ears, "where is heaven?"

"In what sense?"

"In the 'where is it?' sense."

Lucifer began to walk again. "First off, and I'm sorry to belabor the point, but I don't want you to misunderstand me. There is no heaven, no place of bliss and singing angels and a throne of God you reach after accepting Jesus Christ as your lord and savior. The same goes for Paradise and the other religious afterlives. If you are unknown to the masses you die and that's the end of you, regardless of faith, lack of faith, or martyrdom. That said, there is a place we refer to as 'the City' on a separate existential plane, home to tens of thousands of beings and ideas and animals of sufficient renown to manifest in the same manner as the City. But the City has no physical location. It became and evolves through the same process by which God and myself became and evolve, minus the self-directed consciousness factor."

"Ideas and animals?"

"And fictional characters. And objects."

"Wow," she said.

"The City isn't related to heaven." Lucifer found the North Star, and tracked his finger thirty degrees to the East. "But speaking from a mythological perspective, it's nine days that way."

"Nine days?"

"At terminal velocity."

"It's been a long time since I took physics."

"That's okay," Lucifer said. "Intersections between myth and science are accidental. Happy accidents for the myth makers, less so for the scientists."

"Isn't that what you did to scientists by bringing back Josh?"

"Delicious, isn't it?"

Temptation laughed despite herself. "You're going to use my child as a kind of thought magnet, right? That's how the two of you are going to do this?"

"Your child will be an example of what's necessary to progress past superstition and survive," Lucifer said.

"What about Josh?"

"It will be easier if he embraces fatherhood publicly. Either way, we'll do what we can to keep your child at the forefront of the world's collective mind. Given a common goal, we hope our efforts will be stunning." He fought back a smile. "Miraculous, even."

The first of Sergio Pumello's interviews with Jesus Christ appeared two weeks later in *Time* magazine, which had won the rights to the story for the sum of $3.5 million. Covering the biblical Son of God's views on chastity, coveting, adultery, and monogamy, the issue sold out at newsstands within hours. The magazine's publisher resisted the urge to publish the interview online as subscription content, instead re-publishing the issue in unheard of quantities and multiple covers (Collect all 4!) over the next ten days, pushing the opening bid for the second installment, sight unseen, to $11.5 million. The final winning bid, from *Rolling Stone*, was $13.75 million.

Sergio Pumello rented a mansion across the street from Jesus at $25,000 per month, paid cash for a Rook XIV armored vehicle for errands, and settled in to outline the topics for what would prove to be the most lucrative interview series in world history.

MEET ME IN DABIQ

Temptation found Jesus reading a book in the living room. Green tea cooled before him on the coffee table, cocooning him in its earthy aroma. She sat on a burgundy velour couch with gilded fringe and tapped a rolled-up copy of *Time* against her leg. She waited until he put down his book and acknowledged her presence.

"I am pregnant with your child," she said, "and you have the nerve to say, in an international magazine no less, that you're"—she flipped open the magazine and read—"'uncertain if monogamy is a realistic option in modern times.'"

"Okaaay—"

"What is that supposed to mean?" she demanded.

"I think," he said, "we can both agree—"

"Don't you dare speak for me," she spat. "You don't know anything about me. You haven't taken a minute to ask me how I am or what I think or how I'm feeling." Her voice began to rise. "So don't presume I'll agree with you on"—she read from the magazine again—"'the questionable viability of the one man-one woman paradigm' because I'm a dancer, and therefore a, a—"

"I never said you were—"

"YOU NEVER SAID I WASN'T!" she shouted, throwing the magazine at him.

"What?" he asked, lost. "I didn't say you weren't *what?*"

"Don't act so oblivious. People are going to find out who I am."

"Not from me."

"Why? So you can stay respectable for your precious supermodel? Because you're *ashamed* of me?"

"I don't—"

"You can't keep it hidden forever," she said. "The reporter *knows.* He won't sit on it forever. And when it's all out in the open, someone will recognize me. They're going to find out what I did before this, and they're going to say things about me."

"Nobody knows anything," he said, entranced by her lips.

"But they will."

"And we'll address it then."

"It'll be too late!" she cried. "You need to defend me."

Jesus stared at her, stranded between bewilderment and lust. He fought the overwhelming urge to drop his eyes. Checking her out would detonate whatever lingered beneath her remaining self-control.

"How can I defend you," he asked, "without falling on my sword?"

"Forget it," she muttered, sinking deeper into the couch, miserable, shaking with anger and frustration and dread.

"If you'd tell me—"

"I don't want my dad to know what I did before this," she said. "Okay? Do you get it now? Is that too much to ask?"

"I don't have that kind of power."

"Someone must. So talk to whoever handles these things and ask them if they'd alter my past, fix it so I could be respected, maybe admired, instead of what I know is going to happen once I'm exposed."

Jesus raised both hands in a submissive, soothing manner, and forced himself to meet her glare. "If it was possible," he said, "don't you think I would have changed *my* past?"

"No, I don't. You revel in your pain."

For two thousand years Jesus had debated Lucifer on topics ranging from the Second Law of Thermodynamics' influence on evolution to the precise identity of Mitochondrial Eve, and for a half century he'd provoked and repelled Freud's every cognitive thrust. This was an argument he should win. But Temptation enthralled him, flowing through him like a systemic infusion of sildenafil, sodium amytal, and liquid muse. Fighting her effect on him with every ounce of denial he possessed, Jesus said, "The past can't be changed."

"Then do something else," she said. "Make it sound like what happened between us was more than a random encounter with a surprise consequence. You haven't said anything positive about me, or about us."

"Us?"

"Yes! This is unbelievable." Her eyes pleaded. "Why won't you get it? The reporter has the story. God and Lou *want* people to know. And when they do, no man will ever touch me again, from fear of comparison, or God's wrath. Not with 'Jesus' baby mama' chained around my neck. You're the end of the line for me."

"That's ridiculous."

"Is it?" she shrieked. "IS IT?"

Jesus spread his hands flat on the couch, both to slow her looming hysteria and eliminate the possibility of touching himself. "I don't know what you want me to do."

She closed her eyes, attempting a monumental calming. "I want you to prepare for the inevitable. I want you to quit embarrassing me by flirting with that model. I want you to act like who you are, the father of my child, and treat me like who I am, the mother of your child, before anyone knows it, because someday everyone will." She forced a smile. "And I'd like you to do it happily."

Jesus reached for his tea, not daring to take his eyes from hers. He took a sip and set the cup back on the saucer. "We have both made choices," he said in the most pacifying voice he could summon. "Mine are well-documented. So let's review yours." She narrowed her eyes, ready to pounce, but Jesus pressed on. "You chose to leave home. You chose to dance. You chose to"—he raised his hands in a plea for sanity and civility—"to consort with the devil."

"And you." She jabbed a finger at him. "And *you*. Both of you knew what was going on. I didn't know anything."

"Of course not," Jesus said. "But if you had, would it have made a difference?"

"Maybe, maybe not," she said. "You're beautiful, and Lou is… well, Lou's Lou. It had been a long time."

"Fair enough," Jesus said, ignoring the simultaneous thrill and gutting jealousy ignited by her words. "You chose to do what we did that night. So did I. I was drunk, but I made the choice."

"Is it beyond you," she asked, "to be a little better than the average frat guy?" He winced, and she said, "You picked me. You wanted me. I'm *exactly* your type. You won't accept who you really are, so you act like I'm not good enough for you. And if *you* don't think so, no one else will, either."

Jesus fought to relax. "I'm going to lose everything," he said, mortified by the defeat in his voice. "Why should I do anything for you? You chose my Father over me."

"Your F—" She paused. She didn't want to beat him. She wanted him to hear her, to understand, to stop fighting his desire. She doubted he ever would. Worried she'd pushed too hard too soon, she softened her gaze and said, "Because it's to your advantage. And the fall isn't going to kill you."

He looked away, uncertain, afraid, like a child lost in an unfamiliar neighborhood.

She set down the magazine and waited for him to find his way. When he returned to her, his expression held the pieces of something broken inside.

"There will still be you, and me, and ours," she said, touching her belly. "If you will remember what we did, accept it, live with the results, and respect me, I'll accept whatever's coming." She hesitated. "Even you not loving me."

They held each other's eyes. The doorbell rang.

He left the room. She listened. The front door opened.

"I can handle this," Jesus said, followed by approaching footsteps. God entered the room with the Archangel Michael, while Jesus hung by the door. They sat on the sofa across from her.

"You've made progress with Josh," God said.

Temptation shrugged, surprised to feel a shift in how she felt about God and Jesus. Jesus had admitted he could do nothing to change her past. She believed him, and she doubted God would or could change anything, either. Reality governed all. It was minimal comfort. She felt victimized, and self-pity surged through her. "I want to be a positive role model from the beginning," she said, her voice trembling. "I don't want anyone to know what I did. Not one person."

"Who is to say women won't admire you?" God asked.

"I'd rather kill myself than have generations of girls strip for money because they think it's going to make them famous, or get them closer to God."

Michael began to speak, but God held up His hand.

"I understand," God said with great compassion. "But I cannot erase your past."

"It's not fair," she said, eyes welling with tears. "I didn't know this was going to happen."

"Neither did I," God said.

He placed His hand on hers, connecting her to all that was, is, and ever would be, spreading through tendrils of space and time, all existence, memory, hope. It was womblike yet electric and soaring, an expanding hum of stillness and tension no drug or delusion could approach. But it fled like a dream, gone before she could etch it in memory, and it was as if she'd lost a limb.

"I'm afraid," she whispered.

"Find comfort in the knowledge," He said, "that your father's love will not waver, nor will his pride, nor his respect, nor that of his neighbor. Know also that you'll be loved and revered for all you are, and all you are not."

She began to cry, though her eyes remained fixed to His.

"You're a child of all that is," He said. "You're perfect. As you are."

Later, driving toward San Clemente in Bundt's Ferrari Spider, Michael said to God, "You sounded dangerously biblical back there."

God smiled at the angel. "I exist because beings believe I exist. Mysterious, active, uninvolved, damned as often as praised. But since gaining self-awareness I have come to know that perceiving an omnipotent force beyond oneself and beyond understanding is more tool than comfort, yielding fruitless worship, wasted lives, war, and squandered civilizations."

"Yes," Michael said, pressing. "But, by Your own admission, You can't predict the future. Beings have free will. How can You be sure how her father will react?"

"I cannot," God said, the warm sun on His face, "but I can guess."

The least savory elements of Islam established a caliphate whose Qurayshi leader declared himself *al-Mahdi*. Matching them gun for gun, fool for fool, a well-armed Texas evangelical militia calling themselves *Lone Star Crusaders* set off in a chartered airliner to engage the jihadists at Dabiq and to "once and for all put an end to this towelhead bullshit," but were detained by the SAS at Heathrow airport after an online post revealed their intentions. Unwilling to wait for another proxy "army of Rome," al-Mahdi's elite guard threw acid on seven Syrian girls walking to elementary school before murdering five western-looking tourists at a bar in Dabiq. After evening prayer, al-Mahdi led his forces toward Jerusalem.

Enslaving and beheading those in their path, thirty thousand jihadists surged across the sand, destroying irreplaceable artwork and ancient architecture, while expecting a yellow-robed, anointed Jesus to join them in the bloodlust east of Damascus.

However, Israel's superior military refused to play along with the caliphate's narrative and met the jihadists in the Syrian Desert. A one-sided battle ensued, contradicting al-Mahdi's delusions. Without Jesus around to defeat the antichrist, and ideologically unable to negotiate peace terms, al-Mahdi played his final card and launched a trio of chemical-tipped missiles at Jerusalem and Tel Aviv. One missile was intercepted. Two reached their targets. In response, Israel detonated a nuclear weapon above al-Mahdi and the remainder of his forces, mass martyrizing the caliphate. Prevailing winds carried the fallout across Iraq, Iran, and the Persian Gulf.

Experts estimated the one-week battle cost between 1-1.5 million lives.

✶

Jesus stood in the overgrown garden on Bundt's estate while a giant illuminated crucifix rose from the swimming pool into the night. Like the rest of the world, he had watched the horrors in Syria on television. Unlike the rest of the world, his presence was the catalyst for the events and the resulting butchery.

Jesus picked up a sharp, flat rock. He found a comfortable grip and threw it as hard as he could, losing sight of its arc across the twenty yards of darkness separating himself and his target. The rock struck the crucifix with a small pop, bounced off the hardened glass, and dropped into the shimmering pool with a tiny splash.

He fell to his knees in the dirt and wept.

MUTUALLY ASSURED MONOGAMY

They met in a private room at the Hôtel de Crillon.

God stood at the window, gazing across the Place de la Concorde. A setting sun painted its deepening blue canvas with thick strokes of rose and orange, igniting the fountain's greens and gold, ghosting its spray, shimmering across the waters. The obelisk's silhouette thrust its gold-leaf cap skyward to catch Ra's last rays, and in the distance color and light flowed through the Eiffel Tower's latticework. Physical manifestation at moments like this would have humbled Him, were He capable of humility. The streetlamps burst to life.

"You handled yourself well during the revolution," He said.

Domina relaxed into a deep red sofa and hugged a pillow ill-suited for comfort. "I was poor. My choices were limited." She blinked, shook off the memory. "You were there?"

God sat on the opposite sofa, which faced a deep brown marble fireplace trimmed with gold. "No."

"Were You ever?" she asked, gripping the pillow. "Here, I mean."

"No."

"So—" She paused, hoping He would fill in the blanks. But His expression was so enigmatic she wondered if, like the colors black and white, some expressions were the absence of all emotions and others the presence of all emotions. "So Josh isn't Your son," she said.

"No."

"He wasn't a virgin conception."

"Virgin conception is impossible," God said, "but you know that."

With a shudder Domina released a breath she'd held through many lives. She relaxed her grip on the pillow and closed her eyes.

God waited.

"I thought maybe—" She rose and circled the room, brushing the rich red drapes with her fingertips. "I think I believed it." She found a switch next to the fireplace and flipped it on. Fire rose through vented faux logs, and the suite became a drama of burgundy, gold, and shadow.

Domina crossed the room to stand before God.

She held out her hand. "We haven't been formally introduced."

He smiled, rose to His feet, and took her hand.

He radiated warmth, vibration, and an unnerving hardness, like malleable stone. Had she not known who He was, she might have recoiled from the sensation. Unlike Lucifer, God made no attempt to feel like a man.

"Why did You meet me here?" she asked, not releasing His hand.

"You had questions," God said.

"Everybody does. Why answer mine?"

She held His hand, staring into His eyes, which reflected the fire like oceans alight.

"There are countless casualties of innumerable mythologies," God said, "believers, victims of believers, societies, civilizations. Far fewer are like you, living beings around which myth was built, who endure in a post-biological manifested existence. And you're unique, because you've learned how to return."

"'Heaven' sounds nicer than 'post-biological existence,'" she said.

He smiled. "I suppose so. But the idea of heaven is it's an eternal reward for a virtuous life. The reality is when your civilization extinguishes itself, so goes your heaven. It's a dream existence, nothing more, where the famous, infamous, the great and good and horrible, the villains and victors of history walk the streets together. Virtue and reality have no roles. You're as likely to sit at a café between Robespierre and

Marie Antoinette as you are to find yourself on a street corner with Madame Defarge and Sydney Carton."

Domina's lips trembled.

"To illustrate My point," God said, "despite your singular consciousness you exist simultaneously in the City as the Virgin Mary, Queen Elizabeth, and your present incarnation, because those three versions of you are famous." He pointed at the window, toward the Place de la Concorde, where the guillotine once did its grisly work. "Yet your finest hour was with a child minutes before the blade fell on your necks. Anonymous and forgotten. No everlasting reward for either of you."

"Yes," she said, her voice weak. She tried but couldn't see the little boy's face, couldn't sense his little presence. A fluid, tingling sensation rushed between God's hand and hers, and there he was—a small stranger, terrified, needing her. The room and the centuries melted away. The smells and grime and terror filled her, clutched at her. The line moved forward, the endless line, death waiting at the front. Small steps. The boy shook, wept, as his turn came. Was his birth his crime? I am his mother, she'd said, though she wasn't, and refused to release his hand. I'll see you in heaven, she lied, as the executioner positioned him. The steel dropped, the little boy jerked and relaxed, and only her grip on God's hand kept her from falling to her knees.

The walls and floor returned. The horror and the boy's face receded, lost again to time.

Minutes passed while she recovered. The fire flared, settled. The air shifted between them, becoming intimate. She placed her free hand on His chest, completing a circuit between them, and felt a deep rhythm within Him. "You have a heart."

The world hushed. Darkness closed on them and desire stirred within her, matching the beat beneath her hand. Moved by something primitive, she wrapped her arm around His neck and searched His eyes. She saw herself reflected. Did His hand tighten around hers? She couldn't be sure. She raised herself on tiptoe and closed her eyes. Her lips found His. She soared and plummeted, agonized and euphoric, screamed, sang. The whole of existence plunged into her and exploded before her.

It was, beyond doubt, the best kiss she had ever experienced.

When she withdrew and opened her eyes, she was alone. She went to the window. God stood near the fountain, watching the Eiffel Tower dance with lights. When the show ended He moved on, like any man.

She walked Paris until dawn, when she stopped for juice and a croissant at a café near the Musee d'Orsay. She sat alone near the window, luxuriating in the sunrise and anonymity. The rising light played across the Seine and she felt close to Him.

Jesus remained well back from the window, spying on Temptation while she dug weeds from the unkempt, crucifix-shaped vegetable garden. Though he did not appreciate her oversized, faded denim shorts, nor her draping blouse, to his annoyance he found her every bit as desirable in her dreadful gardening ensemble as he had that first night in the nightclub. Her floppy straw hat and thick nylon gloves managed to enhance her allure. She worked the tool into the ground— thrusting the spade, plunging into the moist soil, penetrating it. He blinked. Unlike nights ago, when he'd raged against God and man while sinking into dirt, weeds, and self-hatred, the garden was now an overgrown bed, and agriculture's earthy fingers had caressed him to arousal.

She'd been half-right. If Pumello exposed her pregnancy, *when* he exposed it, she was the end of the line for him, too. Mutually assured monogamy. Dalliances would summon a public relations plague of locusts upon both their houses.

Struggling to convince himself he was intrigued by her green thumb rather than his carnal twist on it, he left the room and headed for the garden.

Temptation jabbed at the earth, uprooting the weeds, attempting to rescue any surviving, viable plants. The garden was a haphazard mish-mash of potatoes, carrots, onions, and yams. Around and between the vegetables were scores of weeds managing pitch-perfect impressions of their victims. Before each stab of the spade Temptation guessed "weed or not a weed?" and acted accordingly. Courtesy of their leafless stalks, the onions suffered mass casualties.

Approaching the garden, Jesus' gaze followed the seductive sweeps and swells of her body. From every angle, on so many levels, she appeared created for a singular purpose, a handcrafted instrument incapable of song but for Bach's *Cello Suite No. 1*, drowning out the faintest note of free will Jesus might have sounded. With the dirt creeping up her bare arms, and the sweat on her calves glistening in the sun, his inner pragmatist questioned why he continued to resist what appeared inevitable when inevitability beckoned so seductively, despite that awful hat.

"So you're a gardener?" Jesus asked as Temptation's spade brought another accidental onion to the surface.

She glanced up, the hat's wide brim flopping. "Today I am." She tossed the harvested onion into a canvas bag.

Jesus tore his eyes from the hat, its movement as lewd as a bare breast in confession. "How do you know which ones are onions?"

"Apparently, I have a gift."

"That makes sense," he said.

She thrust the spade into the soil, and Jesus' entire body jerked. A weed this time. Victory. "Why do you say that?" she asked.

"I don't know," Jesus said, gliding his hand over the garden as if ordaining the vegetables, "Mother Earth, Ceres, that kind of thing."

She gripped the weed, transfixing Jesus. "Mary wasn't an earth mother."

"Not literally," he said, gawking at the weed, feeling discarded when she tossed it into the rising pile. "But according to legend she was a *virgin* mother, which is another consistent theme in creationist mythology." *According to legend? Creationist mythology?* He forged on. "Virgin mothers have earth mother undertones. Virgin womb, virgin soil, and so on." Jesus smiled and joked, "Maybe you should have said 'yes' to celibacy," while whipping himself for introducing abstinence into the conversation.

She held his eyes and asked, "Were you a virgin before me?"

Jesus' face darkened. "Do you think it's pertinent?"

"Your double standards are fascinating," she said. "In a bad way."

"Why should it make a difference if I was a virgin?" he asked.

"It shouldn't, but it does. Were you?"

He shook his head.

"Thank you for being honest," she said, digging out another onion and tossing it into the bag. "Neither was I."

A stillness fell over the garden. She continued to weed and he continued to watch, his arousal flagging. He'd enjoyed their conversation, regardless of its downbeat turn. He was confident her stripper status would fade in humanity's collective mind. Such was the way of things. Mary Magdalene had enjoyed a surge in popularity as morality evolved and the passage of years swept away her supposed flaws. The same would occur with Temptation. Time wore down the edges before polishing.

Yet as he made for the mansion he felt doubt's soft sting. Her redemption might take years. In the interim he'd live a tarnished existence, his holy name sullied. If only Temptation modeled for Sophie's Suite, and Svetlana took off her clothes for money, all would be simple. He grumbled to himself and focused on where he stepped, careful not to soil his soft leather slip-ons.

"Josh."

He stopped.

With her arm she wiped the perspiration from her forehead, leaving a sexy dirty streak above her eyebrows. "You'll figure it out," she said with a smile, her hat's brim swaying in the gentle breeze.

WATERWALKER

Jesus blew out the single candle, and while Lucifer and Temptation clapped Sergio Pumello snapped photos. He had requested a presence on Jesus' birthday—though when you were in the midst of a blackmail arrangement requests were demands by default. Jesus had agreed with a reluctance Pumello understood, given the event's intimate nature. His reporter's heart fantasized God Himself might make an appearance, or maybe Mary, but so far they were no-shows.

Temptation cut the pumpkin cheesecake, Jesus' recent favorite, and distributed it around the marble kitchen island serving as their table. Pumello turned from the copper crucifix pot-hanger to the cheesecake, grateful she had given him a slice without question. Jesus was incensed by his presence, but Temptation's kindness didn't waver. Lucifer remained aloof, explaining in a disarming, terrifying manner that he wished to maintain an appropriate professional distance.

For the past four months Pumello had observed their interactions, recording events as they occurred, moving them to his laptop via transcription software, adding detail and narrative to bring to life the silences, expressions, and unfinished sentences. He had committed himself to the role of witness, the Jane Goodall of supernatural beings.

He would immortalize his experience in hardcover—a narrative non-fiction tour de force.

Temptation struggled to cope with her surreal life, and made fleeting, guarded attempts to win Jesus' respect and affection. Lucifer comforted and reassured Temptation while taking aim at Jesus' insecurities with a sniper's accuracy. Jesus fumed over Lucifer's barbs and superior style. The biblical Son of God sat alone for entire afternoons, brooding, shaking his head, glancing askance at Temptation, Lucifer, insects, inanimate objects, unexpected breezes, encroaching sunshine or shade, landscaping activities, distant motorcycles. Pumello pored over their exchanges for any evolution or devolution in relationship quality, or hints at a developing allegory, but the trio's dynamics wavered little, with the exception of a gradual thawing between Jesus and Temptation. The potential for romance gave him pause. Jesus, Temptation, and her pregnancy was a world-changing story, and he'd worked hard for it. He'd risked eternal damnation. What other journalist could boast that? Yet, with each interview, he set the story aside for *next time*. Was he too sympathetic to his subjects? Was he experiencing the journalistic equivalent of Stockholm syndrome? He'd helped the BBC break the story of Jesus' return to the world. Lucifer had skipped him with the DNA revelation. And what about Jesus' unsuccessful attempt to sleep with Svetlana Babakov? Unsuccessful attempt? That oozed delicacy. By swapping secrecy for access, Pumello had participated in a cover-up.

One story remained.

He had to reveal the existence of Jesus' baby. There was no other option. Glory or nothing. Along with Jesus' reaction to the events in Syria, Pumello would address Temptation and their baby during the next interview, and accept no bid less than $16 million.

Pumello emerged from his daydream when Lucifer said, "What I find amusing and inexplicable is our celebrating your birthday on Christmas Day."

Jesus peered over his cheesecake. "Why shouldn't we?"

"Oh, I don't know. Perhaps celestial shifting, or the uncertainties and complications of switching from the Julian to Gregorian calendar, or the fact I know your actual birthdate."

"We're observing the season's tradition and ritual."

"You're reinforcing the pagan Yule holiday," Lucifer said.

Jesus' glare deepened. Lucifer only trod this tired conversational path for the reporter's benefit. Pagan mystery religions! Such controversy!

"Don't you feel commercialized?" Lucifer asked.

"No."

"It doesn't bother you that Christmas Eve church attendance is in direct proportion to the median gift-shopping-completion percentage?"

"No."

"Or that Santa Claus beats you on popularity polls?"

Jesus bristled but maintained his calm. "No."

"Maybe the magi should have brought you articulated action figures."

"Or you could have integrated gift giving into the Christmas story," Jesus said.

"Josh," Lucifer said, "I had nothing to do with it."

"You forget I *know* you," Jesus said. "You anticipated it. You steered it. *You were there.*"

"Will your next accusation involve the Easter Bunny?"

Jesus stared at Lucifer with raised eyebrows, saying nothing.

"A rabbit bearing colored eggs to compete with your resurrection myth," Lucifer said. "You're saying that was my work? That was the best I could do?"

"I'll admit it lacks subtext and flair. But were it a possum, I'd have no doubt."

Lucifer twirled his fork. "Josh—"

"The Easter Bunny isn't the problem," Temptation said, cradling her swelling belly.

Jesus and Lucifer quieted.

"Josh is losing his place," she said, her eyes glued to Lucifer while she beat down the wild fear of broadcasting her past and former occupation to the world via Pumello. She knew what she had to say might help Jesus, and so far the journalist hadn't written about their baby. But she couldn't expect his eternal silence. The story would come out, and with it whatever Pumello knew about her. "It's like working at the club. Either you were the new girl, or you were the best, or you were just another dancer."

"You were the best," Lucifer said.

She half-nodded in acknowledgement. "So I made the most money and got the most attention, along with that week's new girl. The rest of the girls…" She glanced at Pumello, who tapped his nose with his pen, scratched his shoulder, and jotted in his notebook.

"Go ahead," Lucifer said.

"You've never been the best," she said, meeting Jesus' eyes, "because there's God. And in a few months you won't be new. You're wondering where you fit in."

Jesus sat, jaw flexing.

"But I think it's simple," she said. "You're part of whatever this story is, like me. Like all of us. And this is your chance."

"My chance for what?"

"To live," she said. In her eyes was great sympathy. "To most of the world you're just words on a page. Like every god that's ever existed, someday you'll be forgotten."

Jesus didn't respond, distracted by something deep inside.

Temptation rose, steadying herself with one hand on the couch, exhausted by the conversation. "Stop being the Son of God," she said. "Be a man."

She left the room. Sergio Pumello began to speak, but before he could utter a word Lucifer passed his hand through the air and said, "She is not your subject."

Pumello knitted his brows, concentrating on something he couldn't quite grasp. He set down his pen and began working on his cheesecake.

"I've been a man," Jesus muttered. "It didn't work out so well."

Lucifer said nothing.

"I came here to save the world, to fulfill prophecy, but all I'm inspiring is killing and destruction."

"The media have fear to sow."

"It *happened*," Jesus said, his voice bitter, unsteady. "A million people." He waved his hand over his body. "Can you reverse this? Make it like I never came back?"

"No. Too many moving parts."

"But it's over," Jesus said, his shoulders sagging. "My presence here is pointless."

Lucifer took a long drink, rolling through the risks and rewards of revising God's intentions on the fly, his own existence paramount among them. "You're right. Your grand scheme of a triumphant return is over."

"Because you tricked me, Lou," Jesus spat. "You pretended to help, pretended there was something in it for you, too. An experiment!" Jesus glared at Lucifer with open pain. "But your purpose was to ruin me."

"No, Josh," Lucifer said. "Never. To stop you? Maybe. You were a good man…"

"But," Jesus said. "Always a but."

"You're not Jesus of Nazareth anymore. You came back for you, not the world. To stay in power. To keep your kingdom. Much like your adherents—carbon copies of the corrupted man."

"Don't sugarcoat it."

"Should I? So you can pretend reality doesn't exist?"

Jesus snorted in response.

"She's right, Josh," Lucifer said. "This is a second chance for you."

"I don't see it."

"Of course not," Lucifer said. "You're invested in self-pity. But she does."

Jesus hated Lucifer's breezy tone. "Why should she care? She made her decision. It's only a matter of time before everyone knows."

"She cares because it's *your* child, too. You're ignoring that. She needs you."

"I doubt it. She'll have plenty of help from you. And *Him*."

Lucifer found and held Jesus' gaze. "Josh, hear what I'm saying. Whether you're around or not, your child will be the first step toward the survival of an entire civilization. But why wait?"

Jesus' face told Lucifer the biblical Son of God was lost.

"You could start the process," Lucifer spelled out. "Jesus Christ redux."

"Catchy," Jesus said, "but I can't rewrite the New Testament. I have a story. I'm locked in. Who would believe it?"

"No one," Lucifer said, "if you don't."

The bonfires appeared small from this distance, like aggressive match flames, whipping with the wind. A faint Christmas carol floated across the water, reaching him a hundred yards down the shore. He had come here to reflect, away from the parking lot lights and the bonfires. It had required getting a little wet. Though the waves at Doheny Beach were no more than four feet tonight, an active surf line was proving a nuisance, and in the dark it was difficult to judge the incoming sets. His slacks were soaked below the knee.

Temptation's analysis had struck a chord of truth. But, were he to dispense with his many layers of resistance and float naked in a bracing pool of honesty, he felt agitated because Lucifer's suggestion trapped him, leaving no room for him to wander off and suffer. Notwithstanding the pain and fear, dying had been easy because the choice was not his. He had kept his integrity to the end. He was proud of that. His disillusion had been legitimate, his feelings of betrayal understandable. But he'd played the same part for so long he couldn't see the way to another. After more than a thousand years and access to mysteries of life, matter, and time (courtesy of Lucifer, a galling dependence), he still hung from the cross.

He closed his eyes, finding it difficult to concentrate on any one thing. God filtered and internalized every thought and word and concept and act and event throughout existence, and Lou attempted to help Jesus feel better about himself by insisting he could not foresee the future, an assertion undercut by Lucifer's breathtaking winning percentage on sports betting. Neither understood the inconvenience of not knowing what was next. Moving through life in a constant state of surprise was undignified.

Jesus peered into the blackness toward Catalina. His feet were beginning to prune. He'd hoped pretending to walk on water would relax him, but it wasn't working.

Raised voices drifted from down shore, and he found himself humming along to *Silent Night*. It was his favorite Christmas song, with the exception of *Frosty the Snowman*, the timeless tale of the jolly snow creature for whom he couldn't help feeling empathy, due to their parallel plights. He sensed a real genius had written the song, wrapping a catchy, enthusiastic tune around lyrics of uncommon insight. On several occasions the snowman's existence in song had comforted him, bringing him calm and clarity.

"What would Frosty do?" he whispered to the water.

Maybe the proper course was calm acceptance. Would he find it intolerable to be with Temptation, an insightful, beautiful woman able to discern and ease his deepest fears? Could she not transcend, and he look past, her scorned profession? Could he not flourish as a proud papa? He could demonstrate a wisdom rooted in experience, and guide his child through the maze of tests certain to confront him on the way from newborn to savior. His child's life need not result in eternal psychotherapy. Suffering could end with the earthly pain. Jesus could see to it by being there where God had not. But could he resurrect his nature? About *that* Lou had been right. He hadn't felt like himself for nigh on two thousand years. Even now—corporeal, toes in sand and saltwater—he didn't feel whole. More than his body had died on the cross. He'd lost his passion, his purpose. He'd allowed his story, his position, to consume him. The past hour was a perfect example. Jesus the man walked along a beach where the water's sheen remained consistent, so he could imagine himself walking on water as Jesus the biblical character had. He stopped, feeling familiar stirrings of self-loathing. Something had to change. Could he put a twist on Lucifer's suggestion? Make it his? He hated adopting Lucifer's unadulterated ideas. Maybe cultivate the role of philosopher-king, a concept that complemented his origin. Wait. It wasn't his origin. It was his character's origin. He was a man then, and now. He needed something real, something—

It came to him. Vague, not developed in the least, but there.

He headed back along the shore, excited, his strides infused with purpose. He didn't notice the small salty splashes against his legs, nor did he care about the bewildered stares as he crossed the beach, past a group of teenagers gathered around a fire pit. He didn't hear the hushed cries of recognition, and didn't see the pale freckled girl sink to her knees, hands clasped. He worked at the unformed idea, teasing it out, whatever *it* was, and nothing would deter him from what now seemed destined. His entire myth was about rebirth. His fan base referred to themselves as "born again." He had, in their minds, already conquered personal death. Why couldn't he show them how to do it on a species level? Why couldn't it be him? He stilled his mind while he crossed the beach to the parking lot, giving God plenty of time to object. But no booming voice came.

He climbed into the black Ferrari, enshrining himself within the two-tone leather interior. It smelled new, oiled, of the earth.

The first shred of doubt entered his mind. Who would believe him?

"No," he said aloud, the F12 engine's roar and crackle charging his confidence. "Who will doubt me?"

Sergio Pumello was waiting in the driveway when Jesus returned.

"I didn't do it," the journalist said as Jesus climbed from the Ferrari.

"Didn't do what?" Jesus asked brightly, heading for the door.

"I want to remind you," Pumello said, shadowing him, "we have a deal. Full access until seven days after your child's birth."

"I'm aware of your blackmail terms."

"And I've stuck to the letter and spirit of our agreement."

"What are you talking about?"

"You don't know?"

"No."

"She's on—" Pumello lowered his voice. "Sorry. I kept my word. I had nothing to do with it. I swear to God."

Jesus glared at Pumello's choice of words and pushed through the door, leaving the journalist in the entryway. He found Temptation and Lucifer sitting in the great room, watching television.

Svetlana Babakov's pained face filled the picture. "Nyet," she said, her perfect nostrils flaring with anguish. "Has never happen to me."

"And your professional life?" Natasha Quinn asked, lodged in Empathy Mode. "How long has it been since you posed for the camera?"

Svetlana swallowed, chin trembling. "Four months."

"What is this?" Jesus demanded of no one in particular.

"We'll return in a moment," Natasha said.

The camera held on Svetlana. She covered her eyes as the screen faded to black. Stylized, Roman Empire-era text appeared:

THE IMPOTENCE OF CHRIST

Lucifer and Temptation kept their eyes on the television, apparently mesmerized by the hyper-masculine pickup truck commercial. Jesus was too mortified to move or speak. No amount of desensitization of the masses, no dogmatic revolution, and no manner of dispensing with proper behavior would allow him to prove his virility on the same scale it was being questioned. This would become part of his mythology. He could set up a harem tent outside Jerusalem, broadcast an uncensored, 24-hour-a-day hardcore surveillance feed to every church, temple, and mosque on earth, and never live this down.

Eternal glory seemed far too long.

Jesus left the house and climbed into the Ferrari. The Italian 12-cylinder raged and screamed, and soon Coto de Caza receded behind him, a painful memory in a dark mirror. He headed east, toward the Mojave.

MIDNIGHT STAMPEDE

Mojave Desert, Day Twelve.

Jesus walked, not feeling the sand and pebbles and heat through his all-terrain hiking shoes. Two millennia ago he had worn sandals and the desert chewed up his feet. Not this time. Gabriel had bought the shoes at a Las Vegas luxury mall and delivered them to the Mojave. They were russet with darker soles, and complemented the sand. There were advantages to having angels at your behest.

Though pleasant enough, the twelve days had crawled by with monotonous similarity. Rising at dawn, he would wait for an angel to deliver breakfast. After breakfast he would indulge in aimless walking and random pondering while avoiding Gila monsters and rattlesnakes. A French restaurant on the Strip provided lunch and a delicious chocolate hazelnut crepe with Chantilly crème. His afternoons passed like his mornings, though hotter than hell (figuratively). At dusk, the four angels spending the year in Las Vegas would arrive with supper and eat with him atop the nearest flat rock.

Once the meal was over and they had departed, his mind surrendered to Svetlana with a snarl of fury and bitterness and want. The torment would go on for hours until, exhausted by her relentless presence, he would find himself visualizing Temptation the seductress, Temptation the comforting. The first few nights this shift shocked him, but now he waited for it as a jailed man waits for the key turn. Waves of guilt and shame inundated each lustful thought involving his child's mother, until sleep came, giving him temporary leave from problems and desires against which he felt powerless.

He stopped at the bottom of a deep arroyo. Copper-tinged sandstone walls soared on either side. Ahead was the exit from the narrow passage, and beyond lay open desert, peppered with sagebrush and Joshua trees. The arroyo's end was narrow at the top, flaring twice before tapering to a slender opening at the desert floor. To Jesus it mimicked the hourglass shape of a woman, and in the sandstone formation he saw Svetlana's taunting curves.

How *could* she? After all he had unintentionally done for her career? Being a father he could do, which was ironic considering the accusations against his manhood. But could he lead a civilization toward survival when its most basic and necessary function, reproduction, was something they considered beyond him? Could he reinvent himself beneath the leering light of a sex-obsessed world?

Jesus kicked a pebble. He was hungry and it was hours until lunch.

"A little mid-morning snack?" said a familiar voice behind him.

"I want to be alone," Jesus said.

Lucifer leaned against the arroyo wall, wearing leather pants and an infuriating smirk. Despite the pants, the devil looked cool, with neither a drop nor the threat of sweat. He held up a bag. "I guessed banana walnut for you. The blueberry is mine."

"What are you doing here?"

"Role playing." Lucifer gave Jesus the banana walnut muffin. "The clever observer might speculate you're emulating your persona to find yourself, what with this blatant parallel to the forty days in the desert."

"It didn't cross my mind," Jesus said, walking again while attacking the muffin.

"But no doubt they'll compare it to the original. I imagine unfavorably."

"Now that I consider the similarities," Jesus said between bites, "I'm inspired by my structural purity."

Lucifer chuckled. "Purity is a hard sell when you're wearing snazzy shoes and flying in five-star meals on Air Angel."

Jesus scowled. "Get thee hence, Satan."

"*Don't* call me that," Lucifer said.

Jesus slumped against the rock wall, miserable. "Sorry."

Lucifer studied him. "It's okay to top your sundae with a little forbidden fruit."

"The mother of my child is an exotic dancer. I can't think of a more conflicting combination."

"You're blinded by the morality of others."

"I knoooooow," Jesus groaned. "But I thought things would be different."

"If ever there was a clean case of inevitability, this is it. Why not embrace who you are?"

Jesus laughed despite himself, his first laughter in weeks. "You'd think I'd change a little in two thousand years."

"Your story has always been light on character development and heavy on plot."

Jesus examined a too-dark walnut, frowned, and tossed it. "That's the worst kind of film."

"People want to be entertained," Lucifer said with a grin. "Rare is the genius who can shoehorn catharsis and irony between the blood, guns, and boobs."

"But why her? Why not someone—?"

"Famous?"

"Maybe."

"Her fame will be after the fact," Lucifer said. "Like yours."

"I suppose," Jesus said, unconvinced. "It's what I'm comfortable with, you know, the City and all. It's been thousands of years since I…" He trailed off.

"Mixed with the unwashed?"

Jesus glared at him. "It's how it was done. We were like a band."

"Jesus of Nazareth's 33 A.D. Galilee world tour."

"Cute," Jesus said, his foul mood returning. "We mock what we don't understand."

"I understand."

"No, you *don't*," Jesus said, before catching himself. "I mean, obviously you do. But Maggie was there, all the time, along with the other girls. They supported us." He closed his eyes, knowing how it was going to sound. "And things happen on the road."

"Of course," Lucifer said. "I've toured with your mother."

"Not one more word," Jesus said, prepared to plug his ears like a petulant four-year-old if Lucifer went into a debauched tale starring Domina and her backup dancers. "It was a long time ago. With who I am now, and everything that's happening, I feel like there's an expected standard. Her past is tough to get past."

"In affairs of love 'twixt man and woman," Lucifer growled, "what gold be fame?"

"Did you steal that from the dread pirate Shakespeare?"

"Arrrgh. Think on it, lad," Lucifer said, his voice hollow and distant.

"I know you're right," Jesus said, before realizing Lucifer had vanished.

Jesus grumbled, finished his muffin, and left the arroyo. He wasn't stupid. He understood fundamental change was necessary. For decades he'd known the logical conclusion of his philosophy. It was a bitter, desperate end, an end Ayn had been all too happy to drill home at the threshold bar in New York. He should have suspected something when he'd walked into the bar. She wasn't Lucifer's type.

"Josh," Lucifer said, "this is Ayn. She's a philosopher."

He shook her hand. Her gaze was unsettling, invasive, unimpressed. He sat and motioned to the bartender for his usual glass of wine. Ayn continued to scrutinize him.

"Yes?" Jesus asked.

She removed the cigarette holder from her lips. "Tell me your premises."

So began the conversation.

For days after the encounter he'd questioned whether or not he existed. Horrible woman. She'd made a few good points, but it hadn't stopped him from gloating a bit when they'd run into each other at a Garden café.

He needed a new vision of himself. His relevance required it. But who would follow an impotent Christ? Granted, he *wasn't* impotent, but his mother would say perception was everything.

On he walked, his mind at a trance-like depth of concentration, driving out random thoughts, demanding from himself a new philosophy.

But none came.

The sky darkened and hunger set in. Where were the angels? Jesus made a slow circuit of an expansive mesa. The desert night was upon him, black and clear and cold. The galaxy's starry scar cut across the sky. When he'd last walked the earth he'd searched the stars for God, wondering if one was His light, or if He were among them. So many things were undiscovered. Now? Science had explained many things and he understood most of it, yet felt awash in ignorance.

Propped up and shielded by others' beliefs, Jesus was exhausted by the weight of maintaining his role. He'd sensed the truth but continued to deny it since the day he'd made a fool of himself in front of God in the threshold bar. He'd seen the pity in His eyes. A few honest words had stood between him and irrelevance, but God had chosen not to speak them. In retrospect, Jesus was grateful for His patience, grateful for allowing him to choose the when and where.

Now.

Jesus stared into the heavens. More distance divided him from others than what separated stars. Behind him, something scraped across the ground. He turned. His biblical Father stood next to a Joshua tree. He repeated it to himself: His *biblical* Father.

Jesus knew where this was headed and welcomed it, like a pummeled fighter too proud to fall but yearning for the coup de grâce.

In one hand God held a loaf of bread. In the other, wine. "Sourdough," He said, "and an excellent 1961 Bordeaux."

"Are those real," Jesus asked, "or manifested?"

God smiled. "Does it matter?"

"Tonight it might."

"Gabriel bought them for Me."

"Did You fly here?" Jesus asked. "From Las Vegas, I mean."

"I walked."

Jesus gazed across the desert. No lights. No Vegas.

"It's not so far," He said, and they sat together on the mesa. With a lighter God ignited a thick clump of brush between them. He produced two glasses and poured the wine. Jesus broke the bread and handed half to God. They ate and drank over the campfire. Time passed, marked by the moon and stars.

"This is good," God said.

Jesus raised his glass in agreement. It trembled in his hand. Moonlight and fire cast his face in soft planes and shadow. Nearby, something small scurried for cover. A gentle breeze riffled the pages of a discarded book. Jesus set down his wine. It was time.

"Have You had conversations like this before?" Jesus asked. "You know, with others like—like me?"

"Yes."

"How many?"

"Enough," God said.

A little broken, Jesus said, "So I'm not Your son."

Jesus waited for His reply with rare grace and dignity. No being could define itself without an absolute moment such as this, thick with fear, determination, and resignation. Within the thin frontier between existence and nonexistence, heroes wield swords edged with desperation and ingenuity against invincible dragons. Had God a heart, had He the capacity for real emotion, He would have found this man heartbreaking and inspiring, and certain to die.

"No," God said. "I am within you, and you are of Me. No more or less than a mountain, a fish, or a song."

Jesus rolled the stem of his wine glass between his thumb and index finger. "What should I do now?"

"That's for you to decide."

"Please," Jesus said. "You told me I'm on equal footing with fish."

"You've lost nothing but delusions," God said. "Your life—this second life—is fraught with possibility. You have Lucifer's counsel. Soon you'll be a father. Your mother and father have much to offer."

Jesus read God's face. "You mean Joe." He hesitated, reviewing the years before and after his crucifixion. "I don't think he'll want to see me."

God felt an unfamiliar surge within Him. He identified it as empathy, but not for Jesus. For Joseph. "He will," God said. "I would."

Low shadows eased along the mesa. A loose twig of desert brush shifted, trusting in the breeze's wisdom.

"I guess they weren't exactly truthful about who I was," Jesus said. "Mom and Joe."

"It was a dim, confused time," God said. "Your mother was pregnant, but not yet married. They were frightened."

"You admitted You weren't there."

"I am here now."

"And so You know what happened."

"That's My nature," God said. "And you allowed others to define you."

Jesus' smile was weak. "I guess it was a good run."

God peered into the darkness, listening. Jesus followed His eyes and imagined he heard wild mustangs galloping across the desert. God breathed deeply, and Jesus mused He might inhale the earth.

"Your story was an inevitable, necessary step," God said.

"To what?"

God stood. "To an extent, that, too, is up to you."

Jesus shivered and rose to his feet. They regarded one another.

"Thanks," Jesus said.

God smiled and walked off, unhurried, vanishing soon into darkness and distance.

Jesus sat on a flat rock and contemplated the fire. Beneath its crackle and hiss was a soft pounding, a rapid pulse within the ground. He was at a loss, not yet able to bury two thousand years of entitlement and resentment. Going golfing popped into his mind, but he didn't want to escape this time. He didn't know what he wanted. For so long he'd wasted his mind justifying and explaining away and rationalizing. It was a well-worn mental path, difficult to abandon in a single night. He owed so many hard conversations, so many apologies. Where to begin?

He found himself staring at his wine's rippling surface. The ground was vibrating. He raised his head and scanned the mesa, but the burning shrub had ruined his night vision. Beyond the fire's halo he made out jumbled shadows and silhouettes. A fast moving herd. Horses? Cattle? In the middle of the desert?

They were on him before he knew it.

Pounding feet. Ragged breathing. Naked human bodies streaming sweat, streaked with dust and grime, flashing in the fire, leaping over rocks and shrubs. Ten, now twenty. Hooting, screeching, drunk on moonlight and firewater, celebrating lost inhibitions.

Jesus lunged from the galloping herd. He hit the desert floor with a grunt and rolled, striking his shoulder against a rock and coming to a stop. He spit out dust. He'd forgotten how painful physical life could be.

"Sorry about that," came a voice from above him. A man stood in silhouette, slick skin glinting in the fire, dripping sweat and exhilaration. "Are you okay?"

"I think so," Jesus said, struggling to his feet. He rubbed his throbbing shoulder. A swarm of buttocks flashed and vanished. "What's going on?"

"Midnight stampede," the man said, his cheeriness a tad obnoxious in any context. Jesus studied the man. Bald head, untrimmed beard, sun-forged skin. Fifties, maybe sixties, lean and still, without seeming predatory.

"Okay," Jesus said, as if a dead of the night naked human charge across the desert floor made any more sense than string theory's extra dimensions.

"Why are you here?" the man asked. "No food. No camping equipment."

Surprised by the question but not yet annoyed, Jesus said, "I came here to think." He pointed at the half-finished sourdough loaf. "And I've got bread."

"Are you lost?" the man asked.

"No."

"It's nothing to be ashamed of."

"I'm not," Jesus said.

"All right," the man said, unconvinced. He pointed into the distance, at a massive bonfire a mile away. "Do you see our fire?"

"Yes," Jesus said, and tears sprang to his eyes. He dropped his head, but wasn't sure he'd been quick enough to hide them.

The man put his hand on Jesus' shoulder. Jesus looked up, humiliated by his tears. Yes, he was lost, without grit, faith, or purpose—all drained from him.

"You deserve a second life," the man said.

"How do you—?"

"Join us," the man said. He squeezed Jesus' shoulder as if they were lifelong friends about to do battle against an attacking horde, and would next see each other in Elysium. He sprinted off to rejoin his tribe, whooping and hollering into the night.

It had come to this—disabused and abandoned by the Lord of All Existence, pitied by a naked cultist. What was his offense? Aspiration? If his stature was no more than myth, there were worse than him. Phaethon had scorched the earth with his little chariot stunt. The guy wandered around the foot of Olympus, a vague presence here and there, kind of an idiot with the manners and self-control of Cerberus, yet he got a free pass. All the Olympians did. Zeus sometimes lobbed thunderbolts at him for sport.

You deserve a second life.

What had the man meant? Years ago, during the so-called Dark Ages, Jesus had witnessed Lucifer quash the concept of coincidence via a breathtaking eight-minute dialogue with Plato. Granted, Plato was off his game, but on his best day he was no match for Lucifer. Ergo, Jesus did not believe in coincidence. Yet here they were, and here he was. What else could it be? Not fate. If one accepted Lucifer as nearly omniscient, one accepted the Dark Angel's interpretation of existence, in which everything—the physical, metaphysical, thought mass, and so on—acted and reacted based on the various gravities. It was simple once you applied the proper mathematics, but that was a chicken and egg dilemma. It was impossible to divine the mathematics' foundations without a comprehensive understanding of existence, while building a working knowledge of all existence was futile absent the universal mathematics, because the maths couldn't be tested against observation, which wasn't possible without godlike technology, which was only feasible with insights attained through the clarifying mathematics.

Jesus smiled, remembering Lucifer's chat with Albert. Thrilling. Einstein had wept. Later they'd hit T.O.C. for cappuccinos and dark chocolate bread pudding.

The bonfire's flames clawed at the darkness, throwing shadows onto the desert floor. From this distance it reminded him of a pagan festival. Jesus took a bite of the sourdough and washed it down with the Bordeaux.

You deserve a second life. Did he? Were he to believe the all-seeing, all-knowing beings he knew, he had squandered his initial attempt. He'd managed a second turn at the trough to amuse Lucifer and because the Dynamic Duo expected him to learn from his mistakes, embrace their overwhelming reason, and undo his doings.

Silent to all but himself and whatever limited omniscience whoevers might be listening, he chuckled, humorless, hopeless. Like the fashion industry he so worshipped, he would cannibalize himself. New season, new style, new savior.

Jesus finished the wine and faced the bonfire. Soft percussions reached him through the cooling desert air. He began to walk, hoping his second mortal life wouldn't begin with a drum circle.

"Welcome," the man said to Jesus as he approached the drum circle. "I'm glad you decided to join us."

"Thanks," Jesus said.

"Leave your clothes outside the circle."

Jesus took in the scene. Thirty or so naked men gyrated around the roaring bonfire, unfettered by dance principles. More naked men pounding on a variety of drums formed the celebration's circular perimeter, which Jesus estimated to be at least sixty feet across. Still more naked men danced solo in the flickering shadows beyond the circle, their semi-rhythmic ecstasy unable to vanquish ingrained inhibitions, resulting in a variety of distant, uneven orbits.

"I'm—"

"We embrace the rebirth archetype and symbols, but within a vessel of inviolable reason."

"Second life."

"Yes," the man said. "You lose your father, or mother, or experience real tragedy. To think you can memorize ancient words, dip yourself in water, be born again, and go on filled with love and gratitude is foolish and damaging. At best it's a salve."

"Sometimes you need that kind of thing."

"No," the man said. "You want that kind of thing. It's easy. What you need requires real work."

"I see."

The man smiled, indulgent. He extended his hand and Josh took it.

"Why are you here?" the man asked. "In the desert. And now with us?"

The pounding drums went on. Fire flashed off sweating skin. Shouts and yelps. Answering pounds and raps. Passable attempts at animal calls. On they drummed, on they danced. A primeval rhythm rolled beneath the drums, a heartbeat crossing ages unstopped, outside evolution like light and time. It beckoned to him, answered for him, a call and response like a preacher and choir, a cavern to a bat's cry, love at first sight. Innate and defining. Jesus stripped, leaving his clothes in a pile on the ground, unfolded. He told himself he didn't care.

"I lost something," Jesus said.

"Go on," the man said.

"My father. Myself. My—" Jesus stopped, not sure how to define the other.

"Your story."

Jesus nodded.

The man knelt and scraped dust from the desert floor. When he had enough to fill his cupped hands he faced Jesus.

"Our first lives are written for us," he said, circling behind Jesus. "Our second lives are when we take up the pen."

Jesus watched the bonfire. The man ran strong hands down Jesus' shoulders and arms, the middle of his back, in a ritualistic pattern. Desert dust flowed over him, down his back and chest, along his arms. Soon he faced Jesus and slapped his hands against his chest once, twice. Jesus stood stoic against the sting.

"This is all we get," the man said. "This night, and the days after, until there are no more. Tonight is the transition." He stepped to the side and motioned for Jesus to join the group. "Find your place."

He drummed. He danced. The bonfire wrapped him in its heat. Elemental comfort. He moved with abandon, arms outstretched, losing himself in the pounding rhythm and flames. Ecstasy. Peace. Transformation. He did not think of himself, or God, or Lucifer, his past, his myriad foibles and affectations. What came before was lost, the string cut.

He drank from a huge vat near the fire. The thin, laced wine flowed down his jaw and neck and over his limbs and torso, cutting paths through the caked dust.

On it went, the dancing and drumming, stripping off layers of civilization in a bid for the fount. Watery eyed, soaring, he blinked away visions until she writhed naked in the flames, beckoning to him. Sky and desert washed away until he was alone with her. She came to him from the leaping fire, wrapped around him like a hot vine. He closed his eyes, pounding the drum, finding and holding the song of existence, the primordial hum, the unbounded beat of a star's heart.

"Where your father once was, now there is empty space," said Cliff, the seminar leader. "Good fathers pass on what wisdom they possess. They are bulwark and anchor, the priest in the box, the audience for which a son performs."

Jesus listened, rapt. It was his third and last seminar of the day. Second Life offered various seminars, held outdoors in the clear winter sun. This one, *Loss and Becoming a Man*, was well attended. Jesus sat on the ground with the others. Some had scored a rock on which to sit. Jesus could have indulged a petty internal dialogue regarding his divine right to a rock, but not today. Maybe never again.

"When a boy loses his father, he loses all of that. And I say boy because we are each a boy until our father dies. This is the conflict you dig at but can't reach, without recognizing what it is. You believe you are a man, yet in reality you're a boy playing at manhood until you're shoved into manhood by the merciless hand of loss."

Jesus studied the other men. Who were they? Had he ever acknowledged another person, before his crucifixion or since? It was unsettling. What had he seen in their place?

"But this loss is a gift to the story," Cliff said. "When I speak of story I'm referring to the words and ceremony connecting one generation to the next. The human story. The heartbreaking, transformative event of a father's death sets the fire within the son, to fan or extinguish. To the prospective man, to the idea and ideal of 'male,' it is the equivalent of genetic variation. He is, for an indefinable time, within loss and at a loss. The cruel, inevitable succession of son to man first introduces the boy to life. It is, in extreme circumstances, the first time the boy has seen the world as it is, unveiled, unprotected, hard and glorious, to make of it and himself as he will."

Cliff's words struck Jesus close to the bone. Did the others hear what was being said as he did? Was it the same with everyone?

"One wonders if the depth of a father's loss is responsible for Odin, Zeus, and every father-figure god in human history. Could it be our religions are not solely to explain the inexplicable, nor to comfort against death's certainty, but to provide a distant, always-present patriarch into which one's father recedes, like rain to a river, to become another in the all-enveloping masculine, so the loss is not total?"

Cliff's eyes shone, focused on a distant point. Did Cliff see his own father amongst the rocks and cacti? If what he said were true, what was Jesus experiencing? God's non-presence in his life illuminated many things. Despite his divine delusions, something biological had identified Joseph as his father. Joseph had encouraged him to get out there, preach to the people. Jesus had refused. There was the family to worry about. Who was he to preach, to lead? Joseph had insisted. He saw something in his son. Every few days Joseph had revived the topic. Not with talk of being God's son or prophecy or angels, but as any father would encourage a gifted son to follow his talents. Joseph didn't need another carpenter son. He had other sons who could handle construction. But Jesus thought leaving would hurt the family business. So he had waited. A few weeks before Jesus' thirtieth birthday, Joseph had fallen while building a house. Jesus and his mother rushed to see him, to help him, to say goodbye. But he was dead before they arrived. He'd sat with Joseph's lifeless body in an unfinished room, watching his father's face and hands go gray, talking to him until night fell. In return he'd heard his father's encouragement to go out and minister. He helped carry Joseph's body back to Nazareth, and began his brief ministry. He'd read from a scroll that first time in the synagogue, before he developed original material.

The memories rushed at him, bare of glamor and mythos. He'd been a man like any other man driven by fanatical belief, maybe more charismatic and perceptive than his contemporaries, but no better or more deserving. Had Joseph's death broken something tenuous within him? Had he lost his mind? He'd never said he was the Son of God, at least not in public, but he'd done nothing to dispel rumors.

So presumptuous, so arrogant. *Son of God*. His laughter came quiet and bitter. What had his father seen in him? Insanity? Delusion?

Jesus stopped. His father. Joseph. A painful lump formed in the back of his throat. So many years. He'd learned of Joseph's manifestation a few years after his own. Back then they were all working out what was going on while defending themselves from the Valhallans, a singularly uncivilized lot. One could gauge a people's sophistication by their gods. Time's wisdom had swept away the Valhallans like so much dust, except for Odin and Thor, who went at it like rabid bulls whenever they stumbled upon one another in a Garden-adjacent pub.

Jesus could forgive himself for not going straight to Joseph's door. But for more than a thousand years? He tried to connect the path from there to here, from Nazareth to the Mojave. At least he'd believed in something. Now what was there? The inviolable supremacy of gravity and evolution wouldn't inspire the huddled masses. He pushed aside the thought. It wasn't his problem. He needed to focus on himself.

"Fathers give way to sons, mothers to daughters. So it's always been, so it is. There is this one chance. This one time. Yours. The liberating truth is, after you pass, all that remains is your influence upon those you touch, most powerfully your children and their children, less so on the world." Jesus followed the path of Cliff's raised hand as he pointed to the setting sun. "Like the sun, your circle is small, your time finite. You can enlighten, or you can destroy."

The Second Lifers had boarded buses for the ride back to civilization. Jesus had remained in the desert. He lay on a flat rock, the desert night upon him. He ignored the cold. A heavy presence waited in his mind, a dark figure sitting on a folding chair way back in the shadowy recesses he avoided on principle, and he was going to have to go back there and sit next to it to hear its whisper.

We don't change of our own accord. Without a life-altering event we stumble through our lives the same person we were when we entered stage right, with marginally better math skills.

Jesus counted three life-changing events: Joseph's death, his crucifixion, and the revelation he was not the Son of God. He had pursued his calling after the first, allowed events following the second to shape him into an entitled fool, and now, with number three recent and raw, he was delaying, avoiding, reaching for another, easier answer.

He closed his eyes and tried to find an anchor within, something strong by which to navigate. He knew he had to let it go, let his eternally glorious self drown and die. He was mortal again now, blood and bone, breath and bacteria. Notwithstanding the end, he'd done well his first time on earth. Maybe he was better with the finite.

Jesus steeled himself and crossed into the mental shadows. He sat next to the dark, whispering shape. What it told him—a knife-edged sweep of precepts too elemental for words—scraped, cut, damned, illuminated. He fought every urge to jerk away, to run along his mind's comforting game trails. He held fast to the shadowy figure, to enable his fledgling second edition to free itself from the chains of his story. His perspective turned as if flipped on God's forge, a theory his desperate mythical self thrust forward as fact while it thrashed about in the abyss. Defying every dying instinct to brush the whispers aside and clamp his hands over his ears, he listened until it finished. Jesus thanked the dark figure in the folding chair and walked from the shadows, leaving behind his myth to die.

Jesus blinked open his eyes to the brilliant night sky, the cold sandstone beneath him, animal sounds. Clarity to this degree was a higher ground unfamiliar to him since his crucifixion. He felt undone, but saw the necessary path. He checked his watch and calculated the time difference between California and Hell. There it would be early afternoon—a few hours before the last ferry.

"Gabriel," he said into the night.

Soon the angel was at his side.

"Which way?" he asked him.

Gabriel pointed to the west. "The Ferrari's that way."

Gabriel vanished and Jesus broke into a run, feeling good about himself for the first time since he'd died.

Jesus watched the organic display, entranced by the realism of the rolling hills, the deep blue sky, the sun's gold, the grazing horses, the birds rising and falling in warm updrafts. He yearned for the sun's heat on his skin.

Heels clicked on marble. Jesus waited.

Cleo stopped before him and handed him a thick towel. He took it, indifferent to its opulence. She motioned for him to follow, and led him from the rolling hills. They stopped at an oiled teak door.

"He asks that you shower before beginning. Take your time. I'll come for you once you're ready." Her dark, Egyptian eyes were kind, understanding, surreal. "It's natural to be afraid."

He stared at the door. "I thought it… that I was different."

"We all did," she said. "It's not easy to face yourself." She shook off a memory and regained her form. "You'll be fine. It doesn't hurt physically."

Grateful for her words, Jesus placed his hand on the teak and pushed against the heavy door. Steam escaped and he paused.

"Did Lou know I was coming?" he asked.

Cleo smiled. "You're why he built all of this."

TO THINK, OR NOT TO THINK

Temptation studied herself in the mirror. Her swollen belly was an aberration on her otherwise slim physique. She'd taken to wearing robes and fuzzy pink slippers, as her baby blue sweatsuit no longer fit and her feet threatened to burst from her sneakers. She'd hinted at her discomfort for the past few weeks, but Jesus had vanished and she hadn't seen Lou in days.

At least they had cleared her room.

For the first month she'd felt claustrophobic whenever she entered her bedroom, but assumed anyone in her position would feel the same. Days passed and the trapped feeling remained. One afternoon she'd sat on the bed and studied the room. There was so much *stuff*. The next day Jesus and Lou removed the sofa, the end tables, the lamps, the crucifixes, and dozens of other unnecessary knick-knacks contributing to the room's consuming clutter, leaving only the bed and floor lamp. That night she luxuriated in deep, black, dreamless sleep, awakening mid-morning to find her books stacked against the walls, spirited overnight from the little apartment above the bagel shop.

Three conflict-free months had passed. She reproached herself for what she viewed as irrational emotions born from erratic hormones. What more did she want? Her needs were met the moment she asked. But she couldn't quell it. She felt lonely and neglected.

She heard a knock on her bedroom door.

"Yes?" she called, tying her robe.

"You have visitors," Lucifer said from the hallway.

She opened the door. "Who is it?"

"Why don't you come see?"

Two tall, gaunt men waited in the living room. They wore matching gray suits, pressed white shirts, and soft yellow ties. They shared the same patrician nose and thick, graying hair. The older man held a polished black leather case.

Jesus stood next to them.

She gasped. "Where have you been?"

"Good morning," Jesus said with a warm smile.

His smile stopped her. "What's going on?" she asked, guarded.

"This is Gregor Samuels, master tailor," Jesus said, indicating the man with the case, "and his brother and bespoke shoemaker, Armand."

She waited, not sure what to say to this.

"They're here to take your measurements," Jesus said.

"For what?"

"Allow me," the older gentleman said, his voice easy and soothing, like a good pediatrician. He stepped forward and extended his hand. "We are the proprietors of Samuels Brothers, Savile Row, London. We've been engaged to create for you a custom maternity wardrobe, to see you through the next several months."

"Including shoes," Jesus said as Temptation shook the tailor's hand.

"Shoes," she said, as if in a dream.

"Beautiful shoes," said Armand, "in many styles. So comfortable you'll feel you're wearing clouds on your feet."

"You did this?" she asked Lucifer.

"No," Lucifer said, and inclined his head toward Jesus. "You might say Josh has been born again."

Jesus smiled at this. She was speechless.

The tailor opened his bag and produced a tape measure. "Shall we begin?"

✭

At sunset, Temptation found Jesus on the pool deck, reclined in a blue and white lounge chair, sipping lemonade. He wore a distressed t-shirt, boardshorts, and rimless burl-framed sunglasses. Same man, she thought, dressed to eleven as always, but different. She sat in the chair next to his and gazed across the gated community's expanse of tile roofs, which snaked across the land, following the private golf course's twists and curves.

Soon a mechanical hum filled the air and ripples spread across the saltwater pool's surface. A transparent pillar emerged from the pool, rising higher and higher, water streaming down its slick surface. Lateral beams appeared from the deep, jutting from the pillar fifteen feet on either side, water raining from them. Their eyes followed the structure as it ascended for more than three minutes.

The hum ceased. Before them the transparent crucifix soared ninety feet into the sky. Flowing water shone on its surface. Thousands of mini-prisms packed into the crucifix's interior refracted the late afternoon sunlight, spraying tiny rainbows across the pool deck and visible landscape.

"It's up for ten minutes per hour," Jesus said with the dispassionate voice of a nature documentary narrator. "It's made of sapphire glass, is internally illuminated, and can be seen by commercial airliners."

She tilted her head to avoid a blinding rainbow.

"Thank you for this morning," she said.

"I've been intolerable."

"Still," she said, agreeing with his self-evaluation. "Thank you."

The rainbows crept across the concrete with the sinking sun. Jesus glanced at her bare legs.

"Where did you go?" she asked him.

"To the desert," he said. "And elsewhere."

The word jumped to her lips. "Hell?"

Jesus tore his eyes from her calves. "In name only. Did Lou say something?"

"No," she said, wondering if she'd had a taste of what her child would experience on a regular basis. "Are you okay?"

"I'm fine," he said, too quickly. "Mostly, that is. I feel… real. It's day to day." He smiled. "It's good to see you."

Something warm she refused to identify as hope or relief swept through her.

"I read some papers from the past few weeks," he said. "To see where things are."

Temptation touched her belly. "I'm proof what they're saying isn't true."

The mechanical hum kicked in again and the crucifix began its slow submersion.

"They'll demand a DNA test on our child," Jesus said. "When it's born."

"Who will?"

"The media. Everyone."

"That's ridiculous."

"I think we might have to," he said. "Otherwise no one will believe it."

"You sound like you don't believe it yourself."

He rolled the ice around in his glass. "I do. But I wish I remembered it. The night we…" He trailed off, noticing what sensational feet she had.

"Why is that so important?"

"I have limited experience," Jesus said, testing the waters. "I suppose wanting to remember it is adolescent. But I can't help it."

"I understand," she said, the tone of his voice warming her.

The crucifix disappeared into the pale blue pool.

"I can't believe she did it," he said, setting down his glass. "Why would she?"

"So it's true?"

"The entire Svetlana episode, or lack of, was… I don't know what I was thinking."

"So the devil made you do it?" she asked.

"He tried to stop me," he said. "And now I can't get away from it. Mom told me her office phone won't stop ringing. Four days ago a pharmaceuticals company called."

"Why?"

"Erectile dysfunction. They want me to do a commercial. Big bucks."

"You're not going to, are you?"

"Of course not. But I've been reading about it. Once a man can't, you know, the first time it happens, the next time you think about it, which makes it harder—"

"Or not," she said, and added, "I'm not making fun, just having some."

"Exactly," he said, "which causes you to focus on it more. It's a vicious circle. So I might get some in case   "

"You get some?" Her lips tightened.

Reading her expression, Jesus said, "Not her."

She gave a small smile. "Thank you, again," she said, kissing his cheek.

He watched her leave, and a warm evening breeze passed over him.

Sergio Pumello sketched the scene with his mind's eye.

The recording of Josh Nazareth's poolside chat with Temptation played over Pumello's laptop's speakers, courtesy of the bugs he had installed around the estate's outdoor areas while Jesus and Lucifer were away. His invasion of their privacy had paid off immediately, as if meant to be. Insert angelic chorus.

Jesus had gone to Hell. Hell existed.

Pumello leaned back in his chair, eyes on the wall, defocused. Why had Jesus gone to Hell? The word *alcoholic* flashed through his mind. Okay. Go with that. Had Jesus admitted himself? Was it a supernatural intervention? He had also gone to the desert. Why? What was in the desert? Pumello was unfamiliar with Jesus' biblical days in the desert. He'd have to research it for background before the next—

Pumello stopped, experiencing a rare rush of misgivings. His journalistic method cultivated a rogue's field of quandaries, not least of which was its probable illegality. But this was different than his previous stompings along the blurred line between right and wrong. It was more than a pedestrian argument regarding a C-list movie star's right to privacy, where the courts might jail him for a few days, fine his publisher, and order a below-the-fold retraction. This was a corporeal biblical figure, surreal and unreal yet alive. Pumello's inner armchair attorney calculated there would be, at minimum, preliminary questions of citizenship and a serpentine, fee-bloating "legal death" argument, requiring biblical scholars, translators, and experts on ancient Roman records and laws to establish Jesus' base state of existence before the case could move forward, *if* such a case was within the purview of any nation's legal system. But it wasn't the potential lawsuit that unsettled him. He suspected his handling of Jesus' visit to Hell might determine his post-mortem future. He would be judged. Wouldn't he?

Pumello paced the room. Jesus had threatened him with eternal damnation, but the threat had felt... what? Empty. A desperate boast. Whereas Lucifer was dispassionate regarding the concept of judgment, bordering on cavalier. A chill rushed through Pumello—a deep, primitive signal confirming he had to concern himself with Lucifer. If he exposed Jesus' alleged jaunt into Hell, would Lucifer be amused or not amused? Did it matter? Maybe his fate was already settled.

Pumello stopped at a window. Who was he kidding? He'd breached the sin brim long ago. He was going to Hell regardless of what he did from this point forward. Wait. What if this was twisted, rationalized, motivational self-talk?

"To think, or not to think," a voice said from behind him. "That is the question."

Pumello started so badly his feet left the floor. He stumbled to the side, his hands jerking up in a defensive gesture.

Lucifer stood across the room, unsmiling.

"How did you get inside?" Pumello stammered, steadying himself against a wall, awash in fright sweat.

"The door was open," Lucifer said.

"No it wasn't."

Lucifer shrugged. "Maybe it wasn't."

"It was dead-bolted," Pumello said aloud to himself, while trying to control the tremors rushing through him. "There's a, a guard system. Lasers and—"

"Security is illusory, Sergio. Here I am."

Lucifer's voice was pleasant enough, but there was something threatening about him tonight—beyond his sudden appearance—like placid waters harboring sea snakes. There was danger here. Pumello was afraid to move, nailed to the floor, whereas Lucifer grew from it, ancient and always, with gnarled roots slithering to a molten fount.

"Why are you here?" Pumello asked, trying to calm himself.

"To help you with your conundrum."

Pumello stared, and Lucifer grinned.

"You're making a mistake," Lucifer said.

"So I shouldn't do it."

"Shouldn't do what?"

"Ask Jesus about going to Hell."

"Why not?"

"Sorry," Pumello said, confused. "You said it was a mistake."

"That's not the mistake," Lucifer said, moving closer.

Pumello spread his hands.

"Sin, the commandments, all of it was written by men."

"Okay."

"Not God," Lucifer said, still closer. "Or me."

Pumello's face mirrored his inner confusion, his fear. He didn't see the conclusion Lucifer meant for him to draw. And now he was scared.

"Come on, Sergio. Think it through. Impress me."

"I—" Pumello began, unable to think of anything but Lucifer's proximity. "If you didn't... and God... not either... um... then... I guess..."

Lucifer rolled his eyes and placed his hand on Pumello's shoulder, which staggered the journalist. "Did I make a mistake with you, Sergio?"

Lucifer's hand was impenetrable and old, heavy like smooth stone. Pumello was close to tears. "Sorry, what? A mistake?"

"Glory or nothing."

Pumello's jaw went slack. "How do you—" He stopped, tried to calm himself, failed to do so. "I don't know what you want me to do."

"Cease and desist with pointless considerations of the mesh point between codified reason and ignorant superstition," Lucifer said. "You're not a sage. You're not the why, but the what. The witness."

Lucifer's gaze burned into him, and Pumello couldn't look away. There were things in Lucifer's eyes, movement that shouldn't be there.

"You swim in dark waters, Sergio. Frailty and fear flow over you like water over gills. You smell, you search, you strike. Stop questioning your nature and do your job."

INTERVIEW, INTERVIEWEE, INTERVIEWER, INTERVIEWEST

Jesus wore a loose-fitting natural cotton short-sleeved shirt, cotton drawstring trousers, and leather sandals. He sipped lemonade and kept an interested eye on Temptation, who sunned herself by the pool. A barefoot Lucifer lounged nearby, wearing a charcoal Henley and black leather pants. Across from Jesus sat Sergio Pumello, pen in hand, recorder next to him. On the outdoor table between them were remnants of lunch: sushi, cheeses, whole protein bread, California sparkling wine, and sliced pears.

Pumello switched on the recorder. "You're upbeat," he said.

"One day at a time," Jesus said, surprised he felt so little negativity toward the journalist this afternoon. "Today's a good day."

Pumello smiled. "It's a change from our previous sessions."

"It's an evolution."

"I'm surprised you use that word."

"Everything evolves," Jesus said. "Tortoises. The 911. Perfection is momentary, so there are two options: evolution or eventual extinction."

"Okay. Why the evolution?"

"I recently experienced a revelation. Since then—"

"Like the book of Revelations?"

"No. On a personal level."

Pumello lifted his glass of wine toward Temptation, who smiled. "Things seem cozy between you two. Six months ago you made public comments she took offense to."

"They were subconsciously driven responses to my fear of monogamy."

"You were against it. Now you support the concept?"

"I think it will be liberating."

"Liberating?"

Jesus worked through it as he spoke. "For an artist," he said, "creativity is amplified when there are physical or time limits. Monogamy is similar, I think. It forces you to explore and create within a self-imposed environmental limitation. The proper choice of environment is the secret. The concept would apply to polyamory, too, but not polygamy."

"You're prone to overthinking affairs of the heart."

Jesus smiled. "And you invade others privacy for personal gain."

"The public wants what the public wants," Pumello said. "Is your change of philosophy related to your well-publicized problem? If so, is it a change of convenience, as opposed to a real change?"

"It feels real."

"Are you angry with Svetlana Babakov for going public?"

"I'm the poster child for forgiveness." Jesus winked at Pumello. "But she won't be winning 'best actress' any time soon."

"Are you kidding again?"

"Let's wait and see."

"Are you aware of the recent embezzlement scandal involving Project Holy Land?"

"On a scale of atrocities perpetrated by humanity, it's insignificant."

"A lot of money is involved," Pumello said. "Some would say money is the new god."

"I suppose so," Jesus said after swallowing a tinge of bitterness. "The position is available."

The journalist drummed his pen. Do your job, he told himself, echoing Lucifer's words. "Back to your recent revelation," he said. "Where did you experience it?"

"In the desert."

"You went to the wilderness once before, or so says scripture. Why were you there this time?"

"To think."

"What was your revelation?"

Across the pool, Temptation rolled to her side. Jesus shifted in his chair, wishing he hadn't worn loose pants. "I need to move on."

"I see," Pumello said. "Meaning what?"

"I've let my abandonment issues cloud my decisions."

"Abandonment issues? From—"

"God."

"You mean the 'why hast thou forsaken me?' part?"

"Not exactly," Jesus said, uneasy with the interview's direction. He studied the recorder's red light. "When I think back, the only time I was truly myself was from the time Joseph died until my own death."

"You're referring to Joseph, Mary's husband."

"Yes," Jesus said. A sense of clarity surged through him and he said, "My father, Joseph."

"Sorry," Pumello said. "Isn't God your father?"

"God has informed me He is non-biological."

"Non-biological?" Pumello asked. "Sorry. How does that work with immaculate conception?"

"As the story goes," Jesus said, "my *mother* was immaculately conceived, cleansed of sin by God at conception. *My* mythological origin, however, was a virgin conception." Jesus smiled. "Which God has explained to me to be impossible."

"You've been in recent contact with God?"

"We had a few illuminating chats."

"And He said your"—Pumello searched for the words—"*biblical origin* is impossible?"

"So it seems."

"But your DNA was confirmed," Pumello said. He grabbed the recorder to reassure himself it was recording. He scrutinized Jesus' face and hands for the usual tells, but there were no signs the man was lying. "Sorry. Then who are you?"

"I'm who I've said I am," Jesus said. "But, as crazy as it may sound, it turns out I'm the son of a man."

Something cold settled in Pumello's gut. "How long have you known this?" he demanded.

"Not long. It's all new to me, too." Jesus laughed. "Sergio, are you okay?"

"Yes," Pumello said. He glared at Lucifer, who seemed amused by the drama playing out over the bread and cheese. "Let me get this straight. You're not the immaculately conceived Son of God?"

"Virgin conception," Jesus said. "But either way, no."

"You're a man like any other man," Pumello said, incredulous.

Jesus grinned, savoring the journalist's spiraling dive into panic. The bastard deserved it. "Sure I am. Like any other man who lived two thousand years ago, died, and has returned verifiably alive."

Pumello raised his hands in frustration and dismay. He grabbed a pear, bit into it, and considered the interview's direction. Temptation and Lucifer waved from across the pool. Was this all an incredible hoax? No, he told himself with surprising certainty, given all he'd learned and witnessed and recorded. But there were obvious contradictions to what he thought he knew about Jesus and God. What would readers want to know? What did he want to know? And what would guarantee a bidding war for the next interview?

"So I can establish a starting point," Pumello said, "there is a God, right?"

"I think that's beyond the scope of this interview."

"Sorry. Nothing is beyond the interview's scope."

Jesus sipped some sparkling wine. "I'm not referring to our contractual arrangement," he said. "I'm suggesting it's a topic too large and too contradictory for your word limit."

"I'll edit the boring parts," Pumello said. "Is there a God?"

"Like the God of the Bible?" Jesus asked, maybe drawing out his enjoyment a bit much. "Is that what you're asking?"

"Yes."

"No."

Pumello swiped his hair across his head, eyes wide. "There's no God?"

"Not like in the Bible or the Quran."

"Then what kind of God is there?"

Jesus waited for Lucifer's support. When none came he said, "I'm not sure I'm qualified to define Him. We aren't close. We never were."

"Sorry," Pumello said with considerable disbelief. "How is that possible?"

"You'll have to ask Him."

Pumello collapsed in his chair, at a loss. He tapped his nose, mining for rare truth. "But aren't you afraid this will damage your status in the eyes of, well, everyone?"

Of course I am, Jesus thought, but he said, "I don't know, Sergio. What do you think?"

"Of course it will," Pumello said. "People want to believe in God. They want to believe in you."

"They can believe anything they want."

"Yes," Pumello said. "*But.* Don't you think people will be afraid?"

"Of what?"

"Everything. No higher power, nothing bigger than themselves. *Everything.*"

Jesus felt the tiniest sympathy for the journalist. Or was it empathy? He wasn't sure. "Are you afraid?" he asked.

Pumello checked the pen in his hand—a slight tremble. "I'm not sure yet. But won't there be chaos? Without God and eternal damnation?"

Jesus thought of the million dead in Syria, the children murdered by parents and madmen, his undeniable role in so many atrocities and so much suffering. Ashamed but refusing to show it to Pumello, he imagined Temptation wearing nothing but her ludicrous floppy hat, lying back and beckoning for him to join her in the flower bed. It did the job. The threatening tears receded. "Wars and murders and humiliations and brutality go on despite the threat of everlasting flames."

Pumello glanced at Lucifer, who watched their exchange with troubling interest. "But what if it gets worse?" Pumello asked.

"As long as there have been gods and men," Jesus said, "there have been horrors committed in God's name. Can it get worse?"

"Don't you feel a responsibility?"

"To continue the charade?"

"That's not what I meant."

Lucifer strolled around the pool toward them. Jesus sliced off a chunk of Brie and paired it with a pear. Delicious.

Lucifer reached the table. He switched off Pumello's recorder and took the pen from his hand. He set the pen in front of Jesus and helped himself to a slice of bread. "You will refer to me as Mr. Nazareth's counsel. Are we in agreement, Sergio?"

Pumello nodded and Lucifer switched on the recorder.

"What is Josh's responsibility?" Lucifer asked between bites. "Beyond anyone else's? Yours, for example."

There was no angle, no leverage or scheme. Lucifer might as well be a god. Maybe he was. "But you understand," Pumello said to Lucifer, "how it will confuse people."

"Are you confused?" Lucifer asked.

"Yes."

"No more than me, Sergio," Jesus said.

Pumello kept his eyes on Lucifer. His civilized manner frightened him.

"But I'm moving forward," Jesus said. "We can do it together."

Now the journalist turned to Jesus. "We? You and I?"

"In the beginning," Jesus said with a smile, "we invented God. Other people invented me, or at least my persona. So it seems whatever's next is up to us, too."

An odd, invasive sensation filled Pumello. *Do your job.* He sat back and asked Jesus, "How did your recent stay in Hell inform your evolution?"

Jesus' expression closed, his eyes darkened. At length he said, "No comment."

"Our contract requires you to comment. Sorry."

"Given your ace in the hole is now more of a cat out of the bag," Jesus said, "I doubt you'll be able to enforce the contract's terms. I'm here because it benefits me."

"How can retracting your claims to be the Son of God possibly benefit you?"

Jesus poured himself more wine and relaxed in his chair, as if he might never move, might never speak again. Temptation walked around the pool to stand behind him. Forces were gathering for a messianic standoff.

Fine, Pumello thought, I'll do my job. "Sources tell me you visited Hell," he said.

"By sources," Lucifer said, "do you mean the listening devices you illegally and unethically planted around my client's current home?"

"Yes," Pumello muttered.

Jesus leaned back. "I'll corroborate your sources."

"Thank you," Pumello said, steadying himself. "Why Hell?"

"Everyone needs help sometime," Jesus said, as if reading from a promotional pamphlet. "I'm no different."

"Because you're just a man, right?" Pumello startled himself with his rush to confrontation. "A man who visited Hell while still alive. Sorry. I don't understand. How could Hell help you? Fire and sulfur and—"

"It's not what you think," Jesus said with surprising restraint given the journalist's tone.

Lucifer leaned in and said, "Religious scholars suspect Revelations is overwrought and written without any basis in fact. The ravings of a madman."

"What is Hell, then?" Pumello asked, afraid and frustrated.

Jesus and Lucifer conferred with one another.

"It's like a substance abuse program," Jesus said.

Pumello fixed his attention on Lucifer. "Are you the Devil?"

Lucifer conveyed relaxed, terrifying interest. Predatory. It was more than enough confirmation for Pumello. He shivered in the warm California sun.

"So rock stars go to rehab," Pumello said. "You go to Hell."

Temptation caressed Jesus' shoulders. She smelled like cocoa butter. "That's a decent parallel," Jesus said, feeling protected by Temptation's touch. "Hell is like rehab, but for life abuse."

Pumello cocked his head and brushed his hair back into place. "What do you mean by life abuse?"

"Certain forms of hurting others," Jesus said. "Improving nothing about the world. I would say timidity, but the timid don't make it to Hell."

"You make Hell sound like a goal."

Jesus laughed. "I suppose I do."

"What's it like?" Pumello asked, trying to downplay his interest. "I'm sure a lot of people will want to know. Weighing their choices, so to speak."

"Rolling hills. Beautiful views. A lot like Tuscany or that place in Malibu, *Pledges*. It won't matter, not for most, but it's lovely."

Pumello relaxed. "That should comfort people."

"Should it?"

Pumello blinked. "Shouldn't it?"

"Just live by your own principles," Jesus said.

"Did you learn that in Hell?"

"Among other things."

"It seems like there should be more to it."

"I used to think so," Jesus said. "But my entire afterlife has been a lie. I had to work through the negative implications God's absence had on me after I manifested—"

"After you manifested? What does that—?"

"Please don't interrupt, Sergio. After I manifested, I felt like an abandoned child. The scars are deep. Yet the so-called scars I have are a result of an abandonment that never happened. To move forward I had to face the facts I'd accepted others' delusions as my reality, and my real father hadn't abandoned me." Jesus paused, swallowed. "I abandoned him. I haven't spoken to him in two thousand years."

"Do you mean Joseph?"

"Yes. He has a little place in Messiania. Paradise City-adjacent."

"I—sorry. What? Where's that? He can't still be alive."

Jesus began to speak, but felt Lucifer's hand on his arm. Lucifer leaned over and switched off the recorder.

Pumello leapt to his feet, his frustration overcoming his fear of Lucifer. "What kind of game is this?"

"Whatever do you mean, Sergio?" Lucifer asked.

"No one will believe any of it." Pumello twirled his hand in the air and proclaimed in an effeminate voice, "I have daddy issues. There's no God. Hell's *fabulous*."

"For chrissakes," Jesus said, "do I sound like that?"

Pumello jabbed his finger at Jesus. "I can't publish any of this!"

"Au contraire," Lucifer said. "It's a coup of biblical proportions."

Pumello threw up his hands. "In whose eyes? They'll crucify *me*. Do you think your new—I don't know what to call it—your new attitude, your new place in things, or lack of I guess, will resonate with Christians? Because it won't."

"It's not for me to decide," Jesus said.

"Not for you—" Pumello stopped himself, working at calm. "Sorry. What if you lose your flock to other religions?"

"There is the myth of Jesus Christ, and there is the man. Me. There are delusions used to trivialize this life, and there is reality." Jesus pinched his own arm, and Pumello rolled his eyes. "After this interview is published, there may be many questions. Or not. I may be vilified or lionized. Or ignored."

"I'll be vilified," Pumello said with absolute confidence, "but I doubt you'll be ignored. Won't Christian rejection echo what happened with the Jews? That must still hurt."

Temptation squeezed Jesus' shoulders, and Jesus placed his hand on hers.

"My feelings are the same toward the Jewish people as anyone's would be in my position," Jesus said. "If you've been ostracized from your classmates, or disowned by your parents, or rejected by someone you love, you understand. My pain is no more than yours. You suffer, you get up, you go on."

"But doesn't the idea of going from savior to scourge frighten you?"

"True character is revealed by abundance and hardship, idolization and rejection. I'll have to work it out myself." Jesus checked his watch. "Our time is up, Sergio."

"One last question?" Pumello asked, his smile thin and false. "Because I'm taking you with me."

Jesus laughed. "Sure. Shoot."

"How are we judged?"

"In what respect?"

"You know, to determine whether we go up or down."

"Assigning directions is a miscon—" Lucifer began, but Jesus held up his hand. Lucifer inclined his head. "The floor is yours, Mr. Nazareth."

"The judgment, sin, forgiveness—all of it is an invention of man," Jesus said. "Soon my child will be born, to—"

"Wait," Pumello said. "Sorry. Please stop. I've been more than accommodating regarding your child, but if you continue, you're leaving me little choice but to write and publish what I know about... about the two of you."

"Three," Temptation said, one hand on her belly.

"I can't let someone else break the story," Pumello said. "Sorry. Not this time."

"I understand," Jesus said, and repeated, "Soon our child will be born. To save humanity, yes, but not from sin or another archaic, man-made, vice-obsessed demise."

"If not that, then what? What determines our fate?"

Jesus took a last sip of wine. Sunlight reflected in the glass and he realized Lucifer must have disabled Bundt's monstrous mechanical crucifix. "There is no fate, Sergio. Nothing real but what we have here. If I knew then what I know now, I would have built houses with my brothers."

RESERECTION

A month had passed since the interview on the pool deck, yet the media were unwilling to let go of "impotent Jesus," despite the inclusion of a sensitive, informative *Impotence: Stiff Competition* sidebar in Part I of Pumello's two-part interview, *Poolside Jesus*. An astounding number of sex therapists and "sexperts" appeared on talk shows, feature news segments, and blogs. Few were willing to specifically address Jesus' penis.

A two-minute pharmaceutical commercial aired: *A long-haired carpenter in a sleeveless work shirt nails together two rustic beams at a right angle, before dragging his not-quite-visible project across a dusty worksite past beautiful, compassionate, forty-something women in hard-hats, while disclaimers and phrases such as "difficulty maintaining an erection" and "decreased blood flow" flash across the screen, before closing with the slogan ResErection.*

Indignant outraged uproar erupted, and pharmacies sold out of sildenafil, tadalafil, and testosterone therapies.

On the strength of Jesus' penultimate quote from part one of the poolside interview, "Soon my child will be born," Sergio Pumello sold the interview's second half to a cable television network for a sum rumored to be one dollar south of nine figures. Days later, the network began promoting a pay-per-view, live dramatization of the interview, priced at $199 for individual subscribers, $599 for public houses and non-profit entities.

The Danish weekly *Olaf Brat* printed a cartoon depicting Muhammad satisfying an ecstatic, winged Svetlana Babakov, while a despondent Jesus wiped the prophet's forehead. The caption read, "Paradise Found." Within a week jihadists firebombed the *Olaf Brat* offices. Politicians condemned the incident in strong terms, condemned in stronger terms those who would seek to curtail free speech, and in the strongest terms condemned any and all who would suggest religion or religious texts might have played a part in the murders. Hashtagged phrases of support and sorrow were brought forth, trended, and died. Between Caesar salad photos and snarky comments, social media slaves expressed their deep, unique, individual despair for the victims and unmatched sympathy for the victims' families. Before firefighters had extinguished the flames at *Olaf Brat*, reporters who based their entire careers on politically correcting political incorrectness warned of "expert concerns" over "backlash against mainstream Muslims," while their media opposites insisted senseless slaughter could be eliminated by arming all private citizens with semi-automatic weapons.

Poolside Jesus, Part I set off sustained armed battle between citizens and their governments in Beirut, Tehran, Paris, Riyadh, London, Cairo, Baghdad, and Damascus. The Vatican's Swiss Guard repelled repeated sieges along its forty-foot walls with tear gas and rubber bullets while, across the Mediterranean Sea, American-made Israeli attack helicopters streaked along Israel's borders and the West Bank wall. Civil wars peppered Central and South America.

In the United States, governors in Louisiana, Alabama, Mississippi, Missouri, Texas, North Carolina, Virginia, and West Virginia declared states of emergency. Tennessee's governor deployed the National Guard in Knoxville and Chattanooga.

Pumello went into hiding after teenagers tried to pull him from his Rook XIV outside a Rancho Santa Margarita bank, where he'd met with a wealth management consultant. With the exception of this incident, which may have been a failed carjacking attempt given the perpetrators, conflict in the northeastern and western United States remained at conversation-level.

Most religious scholars rejected Jesus' insights as uninformed or apocryphal. Lucifer, in turn, deemed their opinions incurious and asinine. Legions of priests, imams, pastors, rabbis, and cult leaders put forth reasons why Jesus might lie, but only one ventured beyond the familiar "testing our faith" path—a Baptist minister proposed Satan had enthralled Jesus.

Temptation watched Jesus fight an epic internal battle, exhibited by stolen glances at her body and lips, embarrassed expressions, and mumbled explanations. One day he tried at affection, another he was distant and uncertain. At first his behavior confused her, but now she suspected Jesus' fall from god to man had robbed him of a trait crucial to a sexually inexperienced male: baseless confidence. Tonight she aimed to overwhelm his doubts and help him solidify his intentions.

She tried on the last item of her new wardrobe, which had arrived overnight from London. She'd never seen such maternity clothes. They were sexy, slimming, chic, with a sophistication fashion critics would deem "visionary," indicating Jesus had involved himself in their design, as she'd given no input other than her measurements.

She tied the bodice and appraised herself in the mirror. Not bad. Coming you could tell, but going she looked the same as before. She smiled with uneasy satisfaction. Since blossoming in her late teens, she'd volleyed between flaunting and downplaying her beauty. Her natural sensuality, developed to an unusual degree with neither effort nor encouragement, embarrassed her. But on stage she discovered a compromise, finding utility in her exceptional beauty, creating for herself a vision of her body as an exquisite tool, forged to take her from where she was to where she wanted to go.

Temptation checked the clock. It was time.

She slipped into a long silk robe with soft synthetic lining. Purple and lace-trimmed, it matched what she wore underneath.

She made a last adjustment and left her room, determined to be both mother of the new messiah and lover of the old.

★

Jesus sat on his iron bed, reading erectile dysfunction pamphlets. His situation infuriated him. But did it matter? Until he reconciled his doubts about Temptation with his desires, his "condition" affected nothing. Still, he was a man, and he felt unmanly. Maybe a little pill *was* the answer. Maybe pharmaceuticals could overcome both God and manhood.

Though his supposed erection difficulty was the tent pole to a small circus of fleeting annoyances, for the past month he had lived up to his standards, independent of scripture or others' expectations. It had required a philosophical shift. Intellectually, he knew he could help redefine humanity's meaning of life from a nonexistent after-life to species-level survival. But, as with all significant change, there were instances of regression, and he was considering contacting Cliff at Second Life for a personal coaching session, to overcome what remained of his father-son issues.

Attempting to relax his mind, he rolled to his side and forced his eyes to follow the intricate iron vines weaving through the vertical bars at the head of the bed.

He heard a soft tap on his door.

"Yes?"

The door swung open. Temptation stood on the threshold. She wore a purple silk robe and looked delicious.

"Matches?" she asked.

He pointed to the mahogany bureau, his hand heavy, unfamiliar.

Temptation lit several candles and flipped off the light, painting the bedroom in a soft glow. She scanned the papers on the bed. She gathered them, held them to a candle flame until they caught fire, and dropped the burning pamphlets into a small metal wastebasket.

She met his gaze and let the robe fall to the floor.

Jesus caught his breath.

She wore a deep purple bodice, tied up the front, which struggled to contain her swelling breasts. It flared over her belly and attached to a garter belt and stockings. The laces of her gladiator sandals snaked around her calves like jealous vines. He hadn't believed a pregnant woman capable of such raw sexuality.

"Do you like?" she asked with a loins-inflaming blend of confidence and hunger.

He swallowed, mouth dry, rising, ready for her.

"Show me."

Temptation slinked across the bed and kissed him wet and hot, her hands and lips inviting all manner of unspeakable acts. Her eyes flared as he slipped inside her. A light citrus scent rose from her skin, completing the seduction and entwining with the encouraging aroma of glossy brochures smoldering in their ashes.

She slept naked in his bed. He watched her even breathing, no longer turning away with embarrassment, his eyes moving from her relaxed face, over her shoulders and breasts to the swell of their child. She snored softly and mumbled on occasion, which made him smile. He'd never known a woman so beautiful.

SIX FEET TALL

Considering how quickly the cable network put together *Poolside Jesus, Part II*, dramatic integrity, acting, scripting, and production quality were high, if not world class. Reviews were positive, pay-per-view revenues were jaw-dropping at $3.4 billion worldwide, but public and media reactions varied.

Pumello did not know Temptation's real name and Lucifer had invoked a strict "no photos" policy, throwing wide the gates to tens of thousands of anonymous tipsters certain of her identity, none of whom were correct. Without a whiff of background the media stuck with *Temptation* and bestowed upon her an Everywoman quality. The *Washington News* presented a psychological and physical portrait assembled by a police sketch artist and a former profiler from the FBI's Behavioral Sciences department. Though drawn from Pumello's description of her in *Poolside Jesus, Part I* and Jesus' presumed tendencies, the profile proved remarkably inaccurate.

Vegas casinos and offshore gambling sites began taking bets on place of birth (Fatima, Portugal – 25/1; Cabo San Lucas, Mexico – 98/1; Tehran, Iran – 5,000/1), gender of new messiah (male – 1/3; female – 3/1), and date of birth (May 15 – 9/1; May 22 – 16/1). Betting was steady and strong, with only the new messiah's birthplace experiencing any real volatility, owing to its treatment as a write-in category.

Several disgraced former members of world soccer's executive committee petitioned Jesus Christ, through Domina's production offices, for the names of cities under consideration for the new messiah's birthplace, offering to spearhead the collection and vetting of formal applications to host the event.

While praying for forgiveness and direction, the Church of Everlasting Christ in Abilene, Texas, filed a lawsuit against their namesake on the grounds his actions threatened their faith's uniqueness and survival.

An online poll ranked preferred names for Jesus' child, with Christian and Noah mere percentage points above Calvin and Ash, with Mary (#16) and Isabella (#42) the highest-ranking girls' names.

"But doesn't Revelations already describe the second coming?" Natasha Quinn asked Mathias Bundt, who had agreed to appear on the premier of *Quinn Essential* because of London's proximity to Amsterdam. "Doesn't the mere birth of a new messiah summon a chain of events including Judgment Day, the end of the world, so on and so forth?"

Bundt bristled a bit. "Revelations refers to the second coming of Jesus." *Jee-uh-zusss.* "He is the messiah." *Mes-sigh.* "The Christ's child will find his way, as Jesus did."

"It seems there is a discrepancy," she said, not bothering to hide her skepticism.

"There is no discrepancy," Bundt said. *No-uh.*

"There's nothing in the Bible about Jesus fathering children."

"The Lord works in mysterious ways," Bundt said with a cryptic, self-satisfied grin.

"I'm curious," Natasha Quinn said. "Why do you think God decided this"—she raised her hands and made little quotation marks in the air—"'new messiah' would be Jesus', as opposed to His?"

"I think you're intentionally misstating the facts, Miss Quinn," Bundt said. "Jesus is the messiah, not his child. And, as Jesus said, it was his decision to return, not God's."

"But how does this effect organized religion, reverend? How does it impact every word you've ever said your entire life?"

"I am but a poor sinner, a man of God." Bundt hung his head at the folly of it all. "I cannot guess at God's means or ends. I can only do His biddin'."

Natasha Quinn decided exposing the extent of Bundt's extramarital sins wasn't worth the distraction. She could ambush him on a follow-up episode when she needed a ratings boost. "Projections place the birth date of Jesus' child in mid-May. How will that effect Christmas?"

"An excellent question, Natasha." Bundt spread his hands, wise, sage-like, speaking for all humanity. "Christmas is a blessed, joyous holiday, celebrating the birth of our savior, Jesus Christ. I believe it is too soon to guess at the fruits of Christ's child."

"But how do you expect the birth will play out?" Natasha asked. "Star of Bethlehem, three wise men and a manger? From bits to bobs?"

"How am I to know?" Bundt asked. "And who is to say the vessel of Jesus' glory will give birth in Bethlehem?"

"The vessel of—" Natasha bit her tongue, calculating the ramifications of a new birthplace before asking him, "If Bethlehem was not on the short list, would you be concerned about public outcry over the establishment of an alternate holy land?"

"If by outcry you mean fervent hallelujahs and joyous amens, then yes, Natasha, I believe there shall be Christian outcry heard 'round the world."

Courtesy of the *Quinn Essential* interview, ratings soared for *Word of Bundt* on the Blessed Broadcasting Network, allowing the network to raise time slot rental rates and field their first calls from secular national advertisers.

Despite Bundt's protestations, *new messiah* caught on and trended on social media. Unto this world a hashtag was born.

Behind closed and bolted doors, in a windowless conference room wallpapered with non-disclosure agreements, the world's largest discount retail chain formed an exploratory partnership with an airline, a hotel group, and a greeting card manufacturer, with the goal of developing a second major holiday shopping and travel season in

May by creating a warm weather, multicultural version of Santa Claus. Eliminated as politically incorrect and culturally insensitive was the concept of *San Carlos and his Ocho Burros Pequeños*.

★

On the pool's edge, Jesus stared into the glowing turquoise water at the giant sapphire glass crucifix submerged eight feet below.

He had steeled himself for the ramifications of revealing Temptation and their child, resigned to the possibility he might, to paraphrase Lou, go the way of pagan mystery gods, or a zealot would detonate a nuclear weapon or poison Germany's drinking water or slaughter all Jordanian first-born children. But little had changed. The worldwide religious bloodlust continued at a horrific pace. The blackmailing journalist was richer. Though the media as a whole remained vicious, skeptical, and focused on the Middle East's bottomless violence, various polls indicated Jesus' status as a soon-to-be father had bolstered his popularity. His one night bout with impotence had evolved into a positive, with more than one pundit speculating his spirit had overcome his resurrected body to refuse the harlot supermodel.

Sophie's Suite had removed Svetlana Babakov from advertisements and runway shows, but Jesus found no pleasure in her fall.

"I can restart the crucifix if you wish," Lucifer said from across the pool.

"I like it where it is," Jesus said.

"So do I."

"Lou," Jesus said, circling the deck to join the Dark Angel, "do you think you could set aside your ulterior motives and speak to me, man to manifested being?"

Lucifer's smile was slight. "I can try."

When Jesus finished explaining his conundrum, Lucifer asked, "Why would you want to?"

Jesus shrugged. "It's a part of every culture."

"And they'll expect you to," Lucifer said.

Jesus made a face. "That's the part I don't like."

Lucifer laughed. "You've changed, Josh."

Jesus' eyes returned to the glowing water. He saw the burning desert floor, the fire dance, Lucifer's submerged star.

"I hope so."

★

The afternoon was cool and noncommittal. Clouds drifted past an indifferent sun and a slow wind moved through the trees. Galloping hooves beat the air with an ageless rhythm indigenous to the flowing hills, recalling a distant age before homeowners associations and Indian casinos.

Temptation and Jesus walked their horses along a worn path, their weight shifting side-to-side with the horses' hips, he atop a chestnut stallion, she on a beautiful, dappled mare. Jesus was quiet. Temptation studied him in the alternating shadow and sunlight.

Close by, the galloping horses circled, now heading for them, drawing closer.

"You seem distracted," she said.

Jesus didn't respond.

With a flurry of shouts three magnificent horses shot from the trees, two white and one black, pounding the ground as they crested a hill, their riders urging them on, hooting and taunting one another. They stormed past Temptation and Jesus with a blast of swirling air and dust.

"Is something wrong?" Temptation asked.

He had been subdued all day and she worried the past month of intimacy was about to end, weeks from her due date. He'd been a perfect father-to-be, helping her when she wanted it, giving her space when she needed it. His transformation was astounding. Hell and the desert sun had cleansed him of resentment, bitterness, and grudges. They walked among the hills and trees for hours, played board games, nested. Lou taught her chess and poker, though she suspected playing cards with Lucifer was a doomed proposition. Josh massaged her feet, Lou cooked, and they spent their nights laughing, drinking hot cocoa, and watching the stars. Later, Josh would knock on her door, and they would lie together. They were happy. At least she thought so. True, they hadn't discussed it. She was reluctant to question something so blissful and easy. But today he was distant, like in the beginning of her pregnancy, the months she considered his "resentment period." She didn't want to pry, because there could be a million reasons for his mood, but—

"You can talk about it, if you want."

Jesus gazed down the trail.

She took a chance and put her hand on his. His smile was distracted, tense, which sounded her inner alarm. She squeezed his hand, and he squeezed back. Better. The horses nudged closer.

"Is it something I can help you with?" she asked, peering at him. She didn't like the nature of his faint nod. Her worry bloomed as an opening in the trees bathed them in late afternoon sunlight.

Jesus began to speak but froze, his anxious eyes settling on his horse's mane.

"I wish you'd tell me." She pressed her lips together, fearing the worst, though she couldn't guess what had changed in the past day, or what the "worst" could be. He'd held her when they woke up that morning, something she loved. She thought he did, too.

The chestnut horse bobbed his head.

"Your silence is killing me." She squeezed his hand again, hard. "I wish you'd tell me and get it over with."

Her horse grunted, easing from the stallion as he whinnied.

"Shhhhhhh," Jesus whispered to calm his horse, which hurt Temptation more. He faced her and her heart beat so rapidly she put her hand to her chest. He squeezed her other hand.

The galloping horses approached again, slowing to join Jesus and Temptation. Her horse stomped the dirt with one hoof.

"Please tell me," she said.

"It's getting late," Lucifer said from behind them. "You might want to hurry it up."

"What?" she asked, turning her horse to face Lucifer and his riding partners. "What's going on?"

"Give me a second," Jesus said to Lucifer, who steered his horse away. Jesus gazed affectionately at the other riders. "Are you having fun?"

Zubba and Wubba grinned, their faces flushed and eyes agleam. Gone were the baby fat and wings. Their darling curls were now long, wild locks, held down by leather ties and flat-brimmed cowboy hats. They looked the perfect outlaw twins, tall and lean, their style resembling Lucifer's, down to the fancy-stitched leather chaps and riding boots. Speechless for the first time in her memory, they turned their horses and trotted off with Lucifer.

She waited until they reached a respectful distance before asking, "What did he mean? Josh? Come on. Don't be this way. Aren't we happy?"

"Yes," he said, less than confident. "We are."

She spread her hands, lost, pleading for clarity. "Then what?"

Jesus closed his eyes, gathering strength.

The horses stomped and snorted, impatient, anxious to run.

"What is it?" she whispered.

"I came back for one reason," he said, "but here I am and now it's something else. But I feel like it's been tainted by religion, or changed, but it's older than that, you know?"

"No, I don't. What are you talking about?"

"It meant less early on," he said, "to people like me and you for example. Sometimes there wasn't any choice. And it wasn't so wrapped up in religion. It was more business, or family I suppose. But it should be about us, uncorrupted by the externals. Clean. I'd say pure, but that opens a Pandora's box of connotations."

"Josh!" Lucifer shouted from down the trail.

Temptation shook with exasperation.

"Now that I have a purpose and I know I'm not… God's son, I don't want it to be misinterpreted."

"What?" she cried, near tears. "What, Josh? I don't understand what you want."

He brought her close, her forehead to his. He breathed her breath, his free hand warm on her back. "I want you to be my wife."

COCONUT

A consortium of circus, zoo, landscaping, and stage crews had converted Mathias Bundt's considerable backyard into a strange oasis, replete with palm trees and cresting sand dunes, a faux granite micro mountain range, chocolate and caramel waterfalls, and a pyrotechnic volcano spouting edible lava. Camels roamed the dunes, donkeys lapped at the lava, and an African elephant sporting a royal carriage lumbered wherever it wished. Beneath a monstrous Saharan reception tent were a limestone dance floor, a full choir stand, seating for two hundred, and an epic banquet provided by the only caterer in the hemisphere with a Michelin star. Trained peregrine falcons soared and dived into the expansive African big cat pen, which was constructed with laminated safety glass for an immersive effect.

Through her window, Temptation watched the activity around the oasis with detached interest, unable to wrap her mind around the bizarreness of the small town girl from Montana marrying Jesus Christ. Were she not the bride-to-be, she would have condemned the event as an elaborate hoax concocted by Mathias Bundt to further gouge The Meek and The Gullible. But here she stood in a marble-floored parlor, pregnant with Jesus' child, half-dressed next to an extraordinary custom-made wedding gown, waiting for her groom's rock star mom to help her into the dress so she could stride down a limestone promenade to a manmade oasis and marry the man who inspired a mythological figure. She gazed out the window, searching for reality in the sand and donkeys.

"And here's the blushing bride," Domina said, entering the room.

Temptation rubbed her prodigious belly. "We should have waited until after the baby."

Domina joined her, their eyes meeting in the mirror. Jesus' mother smiled with kindness and a hint of melancholy.

"What were you thinking when you did this?" Temptation asked.

Domina lifted the dress and helped Temptation into it.

"I didn't do this," Domina said. "I was crowned."

"Crowned?"

"Queen of heaven."

"Wow."

"It's nothing to 'wow' about. The coronation was spectacular, but I didn't know what was going on. I didn't earn it." Domina hesitated. "I suffered, but everybody did. Galilee was a hellhole." She fiddled with Temptation's dress. "I suppose, if it was a competition, my suffering was above and beyond the baseline agony of most mothers. I watched them crucify my son."

Temptation had no idea what to say.

"I love Josh," Domina said. "I loved raising him, and I love him now. For so long we were special, but now I know the messiah part was a fraud." She smoothed the dress and evaluated her work. "I don't know what to do with it."

"With what?"

"This." Domina pointed into the sky. "That."

"Do you have a choice?"

Domina regarded her. "I don't know. I lived, I died, and a few hundred years later"—she snapped her fingers—"there I was. It was like waking up startled from a long, black sleep. Belief ran rampant. *Of course* it was heaven. So they put a crown on my head, a queen with no king. Here we were, but where was God? Lou tried to explain, but he was more like the devil then, and they were immune to reason. I knew the virgin birth part was doubtful. Joseph and I weren't angels. But you go with it when it's presented to you. I wanted it to be true. Now I keep doing it, thinking I'm going to figure it out."

"Keep doing what?"

"This isn't my first rodeo," she said with a sly expression.

Temptation leaned toward the mirror. "Please tell me," she whispered.

"I was—sorry. I *am* Queen Elizabeth, too."

"Lou mentioned that. Two, or also?"

"The first. The Virgin Queen. Lou taught me how to do it, but he hadn't worked out the transfer of consciousness into a biological form yet, like he did with Josh."

"Oh," Temptation said.

"There were other lives," she said. "None that made the cut."

"The cut?"

"Life everlasting," Domina said, her tone biting.

Temptation flashed confusion.

"It means everything and nothing, all at once." Domina spoke as if talking to herself, untangling a thought knot. "God embodies everything, but influences nothing. He's me, I'm part of Him, but it's one way. There's no exchange." She met her own eyes in the mirror and said, "No humanity."

Temptation said nothing, not wanting to interrupt her.

"It's a fame thing. You'll never meet anyone in the City who's ordinary. No one you love. Not really."

"I don't understand," Temptation said. "I'm lost."

"Aren't we all," Domina said. "Anyway, Sigmund would love to get his hands on Him."

"Who?"

"Freud. He wrote a paper on God while he was in Hell with Lou, but his subject wasn't around to read it."

Temptation fussed with her veil. "What did it say?"

"A bunch of psychobabble crap. He borrowed Nietsche's *Uberman* theory, repackaged his own theories as the SuperGod, EGod, and IGod, threw in a little Kant, and sexed it up with his standard infantile psychosexual drivel." Domina laughed. "He called it *The Elemental God.*"

"Did you read it?"

"Everyone did. The problem is God was never a child. Primitive, maybe, but not a child." She dabbed her eyes, careful not to smear her mascara. "Lou would say something like 'God was manifested in patriarchal form.'"

Temptation grinned at Domina.

"What?" Domina asked.

"You're not like you are in your interviews."

"It's all a show."

"Like today."

"No," Domina said, holding Temptation's hand as two waiters chased a loosed camel across the dunes. "Despite appearances, this is real."

Jesus stood before the ornate, gilded dressing mirror, attempting to tie his bow tie. He'd done it a thousand times at a thousand gala events over a thousand years, but today his mortal fingers weren't working to their immortal capacity. He suspected a good many angelic laughs were being had at his clichéd "nervous groom" behavior. He couldn't hear them, but it pissed him off.

Outside the elephant trumpeted.

"Would you mind making yourself useful?" he shouted.

Lucifer strode into the room, planted himself between Jesus and the mirror, and took up the task. "Mariam's coronation involved all sorts of pomp and glory," he said, his fingers working with singular pace. "The angels were in attendance, and thousands lined the City streets. Artists rendered it for however long eternity will last, their apprentices reproduced the masterworks for those who wanted a hand-painted copy, and half a century later the images were planted in the minds of select earthbound painters. There were three separate angelic choruses, each emulating an original symphony a cappella. Volunteers constructed a new boulevard for the post-coronation parade, and every citizen of the manifested existential plane you've called home for over a thousand years received a commemorative gold piece. These gold pieces were minted at a facility built for the purpose, a facility retooled *during* the ceremony to make chocolate medallions for the reception." Lucifer finished and admired his handiwork. "Perfect."

"Your memory is remarkable," Jesus said, making minute, superfluous adjustments to the bow tie, "but I fail to grasp its relevance today."

Lucifer chuckled. "Merely to point out, though crowning the queen of heaven was an event of unimaginable scope and difficulty of execution, and though your bride-to-be requested a simple ceremony, you and your wedding planner have managed to rival both your mother's coronation *and* her modern day arena concerts in terms of complexity."

Jesus glared at Lucifer, smoothed his custom-made Italian tuxedo, and left the mirror. "I would think," he said, striding about the room, irked and anxious, "you could quiver your arrows for one day."

Lucifer relaxed in a large velvet sofa near the mirror. "My arrows," he said, resting his head on a pillow, "have kept you sane all these years. You might have drowned in delusion."

Jesus collapsed into an easy chair. "But it's wearing me down."

"I would have thought the opposite."

"You can't expect me to be one person for two thousand years and renounce it all without a measure of regret," Jesus said. "I'm going through a lot and I think I'm handling it well. Why won't you let me be?"

"Because out there," Lucifer said, pointing through the window, "I see too much biblical you."

"Something old, something new," Jesus mumbled.

"So you're having second thoughts?"

"They're crucifying me."

"Who?"

"The media," Jesus said. "Why did Jesus come back? Did he return to get laid? Is he really Jesus, or some nobody buried in the right place?"

"Given today's news cycle," Lucifer said, "this crucifixion shouldn't last much longer than your first."

"I'm sure the Book has the over-under at far north of six hours."

"It opened at six months and hasn't moved much," Lucifer said. "You spoke the truth, former Son of God. Rarely has someone with so much to lose given it away with such gusto."

"I was swept up," Jesus muttered.

"Enchanted by reality?"

"There's no need to be smug," Jesus said. "You've won."

"The victory is yours, Josh," Lucifer said.

"Sometimes I think I should have lied," Jesus said, "like I renounced my place for nothing."

"Nothing you'll see in this lifetime," Lucifer said. "It'll take time. You're killing the myth to rise again, resurrected as reason incarnate."

Jesus slumped into his chair. "Last time I checked, there were millions of so-called voices of reason. No one listens."

"They're listening," Lucifer said. "Your verified return without the 'rapture' simultaneously confirms and contradicts beliefs."

"Then wh—?"

"You're back," Lucifer said. "But nothing has happened. What should they think? What should they believe? Should they scrape off their bumper stickers?" Lucifer leaned forward. "And you're here to tell them."

"Yeah," Jesus grumbled. "It's a win-win."

"You could have continued the charade. You could have left it to your child. But you 'manned up,' so to speak." Lucifer smiled. "You denied thy father and refused thy name. It's inspired. Shakespearean, really."

"It feels doomed."

"Only in the beginning," Lucifer said. "The more entrenched someone is in their belief, the more they dig in their heels when confronted by facts proving their belief is wrong. For people who believe rather than think, which characterizes most of your flock, the reality of you is unwelcome. Your life will be filled with resentment, open hatred, betrayal, and assassination attempts. Much like your first time around."

"Thanks for the positive spin," Jesus muttered, staring at the floor.

"You're proof the truth will work, Josh. It took two thousand years for you to see the proverbial light, but here you are. You've shed your myth like swaddling clothes. No longer a boy."

"I don't know if I can do it. My post-epiphany glow is wearing off."

The orchestra's prelude music ended. Sharp-dressed ushers escorted wedding attendees to their seats. Palm trees swayed over still sand dunes. Lucifer thought of Temptation in a nearby room. He pushed her from his mind and said, "It's time."

Sergio Pumello watched the ceremony's beginnings from the oasis' edge when a faint *thunka-thunka* reached his ears. At first he didn't search for the sound's source because he had more immediate concerns. The Santa Ana winds were sculpting a small dune on the windward side of his feet, threatening to bury his expensive new dress shoes. He hoped the wedding would be short.

But the escalating beat didn't belong in the scene before him. That morning he'd passed a nondescript van near the community's guarded gates while returning from his hydrotherapy session. Outside the van were stacked equipment cases and one well-dressed individual amongst a small cadre of slovenly crew-types. He tapped his nose and scratched his shoulder. He'd seen a remote news team, the *thunka-thunka* came from a news helicopter, and word of the Wedding of the Millennium had leaked. It also screamed the culprit was Mathias Bundt.

For reasons Pumello found unfathomable, Lucifer had invited the televangelist to conduct the ceremony. Why they needed a clergy of any color was a mystery to Pumello. The church's authority came from God, Who did not exist—or so said His biblical son in Pumello's latest interview. Therefore, no power invested in Bundt. But there he was, up front, ready to officiate, aching to slip in choice Bundt-isms between the ceremony's scripted portions. Today was pure spectacle for the reverend, and Pumello guessed Bundt would earn his keep. There were ninety-seven of Bundt's *Circle of Angels* attending, and if standing within fifty feet of Jesus Christ himself while still above ground wasn't enough to justify the million dollar donation the reverend had exacted from each one for the privilege to attend, by God Mathias Bundt would baptize his every syllable with righteous and rarefied passion.

What was Lucifer trying to achieve?

Pumello was surprised to be here. Jesus had refused to speak in Pumello's presence since their last interview, and Lucifer had been absent without explanation whenever Pumello visited Bundt's estate. Temptation, as usual, treated him with kindness and respect. She had invited him to the wedding.

The approaching helicopter became impossible to ignore. More than one pair of eyes scanned the sky while, in a departure from wedding tradition, Temptation and Jesus strolled together down the aisle toward Bundt. A camel bellowed and the elephant stomped, the jeweled carriage on its back shuddering with the animal's violent movements.

The news chopper dipped low and circled above the ceremony, *Channel 9* emblazoned on its side. Pumello looked down. His feet were buried in a small sand dune. He shifted his weight and tried to lift one foot, but couldn't dislodge himself. Confusion swept through him as the sand around him began to spin, sweeping up nearby sand, churning into a cyclone around him. Grit and dust whipped through the air. Shouts and cries of panic carried through the whirling sand. A palm tree swayed twice and toppled to the ground between Jesus and Temptation. Frightened guests ran for the tent while the camels bellowed and the elephant stomped and the donkeys kicked and complained. Jesus protected his almost-bride with his body and ushered her toward the tent as full-scale pandemonium took hold. Engulfed in the eye's quiet but unable to move his feet, Pumello glimpsed crashing palm trees through breaks in the spinning cyclone surrounding him.

In the days and months and years to follow, Sergio Pumello would decide the coconut striking his head was undeniable proof the God Whose existence Jesus denied had a plan for him, he was an integral link in an unstoppable chain of events, and his was the voice of the times. He would come to believe the articles and exposés written about him, positive or evenhanded or eviscerating, were part of the plan, and his existence and actions went further to describe why a new messiah and different message were necessary than did any of the underground, so-called "people's gospels." But when the coconut clipped his temple he knew none of this, and he went into the blackness wondering why.

★

Pumello awoke in a desert.

A moon far too big painted the undulating dunes in blue and black. The night was calm and smelled of the earth, the warm air a sheath around him, wrapping him and weighting him down. He pushed himself to his feet and searched in all directions, his eyes coming to rest on a solitary form crossing the sand, heading toward him.

It was a camel and rider. The camel loped across the sand, its steady pace bringing them to Pumello quicker than possible. Now they were before him, and the camel stopped, blinking its long eyelashes. The Rider lowered Himself to the sand.

The Rider, a boy, stood five feet tall. He wore comfortable clothing, hiking boots, and a blue baseball cap. A bright red backpack hung from His shoulder. Pumello placed Him in His late teens.

"Hello," Pumello said, at ease despite finding himself in a desert with no way out but this Boy and His camel.

"Hello, Sergio," the Boy said, His voice booming.

"You know my name?" Pumello said. "Who are You?"

"I am Doug."

"Sorry. Have we met?"

"It depends upon what you mean."

Pumello squinted. "It's just… I don't recognize You."

Doug smiled and took off His backpack. He unzipped a pocket and rummaged around inside. He found two round, pink objects wrapped in cellophane.

"Would you care to split some Sno-Balls?" Doug asked. "They're delicious."

Dazed, Pumello took one. It was eye-searing pink. The camel bellowed.

"You were hit in the head by a coconut," Doug said.

Pumello took a bite of his Sno-Ball. "Am I dead?"

"No. You're buried under an inch of sand."

Pumello frowned. He was definitely standing.

"At the wedding," Doug said.

Pumello took another bite. Doug was right. It was delicious. He recalled the wedding now. Jesus. Temptation. The helicopter. The sandstorm. The coconut must have fallen from a palm tree. "Hey," he said, "this has—"

"Coconut," Doug said. "Everything is of a piece."

"So I'm dreaming?"

"Not exactly. You're having a vision."

"What's the difference?"

"The source of a dream is from within."

"Where do You come from?"

"From where I am." Doug stuffed the empty snack cake wrapping into His backpack and slung the pack over His shoulder. "You're about to wake, Sergio Pumello, so heed My words." His voice came from all directions, echoing across the sands. "Deliver Jesus, his woman, and the Dark Angel from the land of stallions and fairways—"

"Deliver? Like Moses and the Jews?"

"—To the realm of the painted sky," Doug said. He seemed amused, holding back laughter.

"I don't know where that is," Pumello said.

"Travel north," Doug said. "When you can go no farther, there you shall be."

"What do You mean? Am I supposed to guess?"

Doug made a clicking sound and the camel kneeled. He mounted the beast with ease. Another clicking sound brought the camel to its feet. Doug and the camel headed for the horizon.

"Wait," Pumello said. "Are we meeting You there?"

"Trust in Me," came the reply on the wind. The camel trotted across the blue dunes.

"Wait!" Pumello shouted, but it was no use. Doug was gone. A giant moon hung above the empty desert. Was his vision over? There was nothing else? He studied the pink coconut-covered snack cake in his hand. Enough for one more bite.

He popped it into his mouth.

This bite tasted terrible. Dry. Grainy. Had he dropped it? Where was the yummy coconut flavor?

With a start he came to, chewing the sand covering him from head to toe. He sat up, spitting sand. Coughing. Shaking out his hair. Wiping at his eyes. Blinking hard. He felt odd, lightheaded.

Helicopters circled overhead in the twilight. A crew cleaned up the destroyed oasis. Music floated from the tent. Sergio Pumello the Newly Serious Journalist rose, steadying himself in the sand. Dizzy, a little giddy. He brushed off all the sand he could see.

He grinned. He was on a mission from Doug.

Pumello headed for the tent.

OPERATION LAND ARK

It was past midnight, and Sergio Pumello stared at the centerline with sleep craving eyes. On the road for three hours in his Rook XIV, they were north of Los Angeles, shooting up the I-5 freeway through an area of hills and valleys known as The Grapevine.

A succession of reflective road signs passed his windshield, testifying to progress Pumello wasn't feeling. The grind of his task had dulled his initial enthusiasm, so he downed an energy shot to revive his sense of purpose.

In his rearview mirror trailed the lights of countless cars and vans, comprised of news crews, religious fanatics, Mathias Bundt, and Bundt's faithful. More cars, more pickups, more buses filled with the hopeful and frightened and curious joined at every exit. He couldn't see the helicopters above or the churning hillsides beyond the darkness, but he knew they were there, too.

"I'm tired," he said to Lucifer.

"Noah piloted the ark for over a year and you didn't hear him complain."

Jesus made a face in the darkness for his own benefit, annoyed Lucifer had talked him into riding with the journalist in this ridiculous armored truck. "Keep in mind I *know* Noah," he said from the back-seat. "I guarantee you he was bitching."

"The point is," Lucifer said, "Sergio had a vision. He has a mission to deliver you. It's his show, his ark, and I'm not going to interfere."

"Yeah," Jesus said, "that would be so unlike you."

"Do you really think it was God?" Pumello asked.

Lucifer closed the road atlas he'd brought along and peered out the window. "He's always looked like a Doug to me."

Pumello's eyes were wide and shining in the instrument lighting. God had ridden a camel across the dimensions to speak to *him*. God trusted *him* to deliver... Pumello's face darkened. What had Jesus said? He hadn't said God didn't *exist*, only He wasn't the God of the Bible. That was good news. *That* God was a tyrant. The Boy on the camel had been helpful, though He hadn't said where they were going, just *north*. Then trust in Him. Through Pumello's mind flashed the blackest night, a storm to end all storms, hurricane winds, fiery rain, a hail of locusts and toads. Hope lost. A brilliant golden light shone from above, illuminating the path as he led the self-renounced Son of God, the Prince of Darkness, and the Stripper of Manhattan to the Realm of the Painted Sky. He'd be lauded. Revered. He would live out his years a man of wealth and piety. Would he be canonized? Why not? He'd had a vision, and already worked one miracle when he stopped the rain on the Queensboro Bridge. He needed one more miracle. *Saint Sergio.* Say it again.

"Saint Sergio," he whispered in the darkness, grinning. It *sang*. After he'd had his saintly portrait painted in oil on canvas a few dozen times and printed several series of limited-edition serigraphs, he'd parlay his bestselling non-fiction hardcover into an international book tour to rival Sodom and Gomorrah. More than once Lucifer had inferred he would spend significant time in Hell, so what was there to lose? He made a mental note to insist on scheduled stops at Catholic girls' colleges.

It had all been so easy. Tracking Jesus and Lucifer. Making the recordings. The BBC special. Blackmailing Jesus to do the interviews and auctioning them for millions. Bugging the pool deck. And after he'd described his vision to Temptation, not an hour had passed before they were in the Rook, northbound. He assumed Jesus and Lucifer sensed the spirit of God within him, had peered into his eyes and *known*. He checked himself in the rearview mirror. His eyes indeed were bluer. Blue like the desert in his vision. He shivered, freaked out. It was too coincidental not to mean something.

"Why did you bring a map?" he asked Lucifer, and patted the steering wheel. "This has a state-of-the-art navigation system that will maintain course under artillery fire and air-to-ground missile attack."

Lucifer raised the atlas. "Something tells me we're going to need it."

Pumello's eyes went wide with alarm.

"Something," Jesus mumbled, "or Someone?"

"That might be difficult to deconstruct."

The white lines of the 5 flashed past as they drove on, the night becoming morning, the sun rising in the Northern California sky. Armed surveillance drones kept eyes and ears on nearby movement and communications. Codenamed *Operation Land Ark* and justified to Congress and the American people as a "one-time circumvention" of the Posse Comitatus Act of 1878 due to "extraordinary circumstances," Delta Force, SEAL, and FBI HRT units on Blackhawk helicopters rotated between protection detail and forward recon along the convoy's expected route. Though Pentagon officials were satisfied with the Rook XIV's practical indestructibility, no one was going to assassinate Jesus Christ—resurrected or cloned, Son of God or not—on the U.S. military's watch.

They stopped for gas every few hundred miles. The drones and news helicopters circled, and lines formed at the pumps. The media surrounded the armored vehicle with cameras and microphones. Pilgrims watched from a respectful distance, standing on their mini-vans and RVs and domestic sedans with tears in their eyes. Special forces soldiers disguised as station attendants kept order and gave Lucifer a wide berth whenever he exited the Rook to restock with chips, candy, root beer, and water. Pumello pumped the gas while the newlyweds honeymooned behind darkened windows.

★

Reggie Blake of Plummer, Montana, rescued a quartet of brewskies from his fridge. It was early for beer, but this was a vigil, and such a thing required exceptions of the beverage kind. He sprinkled more evergreen potpourri into the saucepan simmering on the stove and grabbed two econo-bags of sea salt & vinegar potato chips. On his way to the TV room he popped the bottle tops in the doorjamb's strike plate.

A mammoth wall-hung, curved-screen television dominated the TV room. A brown leather couch Reggie had built more than twenty years ago occupied the room's command position. Stacks of books lined the walls, spines in clear view: *Being and Nothingness. A Tale of Two Cities. Advanced Portuguese.* Four-of-a-kind lamps Reggie had created with a metalworker friend's help thrust upward from the room's corners at varying angles, their rusted industrial appearance belying their ability to transform the room from cave to clinical with the flick of a switch. Along one wall hung the filigreed certificates from Reggie's online PhDs in philosophy and architectural studies. On the opposite wall were successive framed photos of a little girl becoming a young woman.

"Much obliged, Reg," his buddy Chester "Chaz" Wilcox said. Chaz set down one bottle and peered through the other's green glass at the silent television, tuned to the 24-hour cable news channel Reggie deemed least biased.

"If you ain't gonna drink it, Chaz..." Reggie said, sitting next to his friend.

"Don't you worry. They say they gonna look right through the windows of that tank they're drivin'." He continued to stare through the green glass. "I don't think they gonna see nothin'."

Reggie gave his own bottle a good, hard once-over. "They've got cameras that'll see through anything. You should try a science channel every once in a while."

"Ain't got time. Some of us gotta work for a livin'. It's obvious to me you got all the time in the world."

They waited. The network's news ticker scrolled below the erectile dysfunction commercial: *NASA scientists warn major coronal mass ejection (CME) could strike earth within next day... Carrington-class solar storm may disrupt satellites, communications, electronics...*

"Said it'd come on right after the commercial," Chaz said.

"How're we gonna know when it comes on if you have the damn thing on mute?"

"I'll turn it up when the commercials are done. Them things'll turn your mind to mush."

"Sometimes it's the best programming on TV," Reggie said. "I gotta tell you, Chaz, if you ever find yourself dead in the morning, it's because some of us got sick of you muting the damn commercials. Now I ain't saying which ones exactly, just some of us."

"The progressive mind is rarely appreciated in its own time," Chaz said. "Here they come now." He un-muted the television. "You'll be a mute convert yet, Reg. Or 'parently, I'll die tryin'."

They grinned at each other and dug into their potato chips as the commentator informed viewers the convoy had stopped for gas, as projected earlier using the Rook's mileage figures cross-referenced with gasoline stations along their current route. The special camera utilized military technology to pierce the tinted windows, choose among thousands of algorithms to assign contours and colors based on contrast and relative ambience inside and outside the vehicle, and "remove" the darkness to generate video the quality of a low-end consumer-grade camcorder modified with an ill-chosen color wash.

As the commentator informed viewers they were seeing Josh Nazareth aka Jesus Christ and the woman presumed to be his blushing bride and the alleged new messiah's mother, Chaz glanced at Reggie.

"Looks like Becca."

Reggie took a long pull of beer. "Yup."

"Looks *a lot* like Becca."

Information on the identity of Jesus' bride mounted, phoned in by people who were watching, who knew her or had known her.

She lived in New York.

Above a bagel shop.

She kept to herself.

She worked in a nightclub in Manhattan.

The nightclub was a burlesque club—but this was unconfirmed.

Soon it was confirmed.

Reggie set down his beer.

She was known there as Temptation.

"Maybe it ain't her," Chaz said.

Reggie cleared his throat and swallowed. "It's Becca."

Several callers had known her in high school.

The high school was in Plummer, Montana.

Her name was Rebecca Blake.

Reggie Blake's phone rang.

"You want me to get that?" Chaz asked.

"Nah," Reggie said, picking up the receiver. "This is Reg." He listened. "Thanks, Manny. Me, too." He hung up.

The phone rang again.

"This is Reg." He listened. "Uh-huh. That's where the postmarks are from." The voice on the other end said a few more things. "I appreciate that. You too, Grace." He replaced the receiver.

The phone rang.

"Maybe we should head on over to my house," Chaz said. "Before the news folk come."

Reggie nodded, distracted.

"Eight years?" Chaz asked.

"Yup."

"Long time. But now you know."

An unreadable smile came to Reggie Blake's face. "That's my pumpkin."

Chaz stood and pulled up his britches. "This new messiah thing… it's nothin' trivial."

"No it ain't," Reggie said, collecting his chips and beer.

In the kitchen, Chaz studied his friend. "You okay, Reg?"

Reggie put his beer on the counter and shrugged on his hunting coat. "You got gas in your truck?"

"Filled up yesterday."

"All right," Reggie said. "Let's get going."

★

Throughout the morning Temptation's former occupation polarized the world. The non-religious found her past amusing and acceptable, while the religious deemed it blasphemous and infuriating. Both sides weighed in on every news program, talk show, and special report, played off one another by the networks with vicious, relentless intent. Each major news outlet had an exclusive with this exotic dancer or that bartender, which revealed little about Temptation and much about the network's politics, the interviewer's prejudices, and the interviewee's ignorance of the most basic question-avoidance strategies.

"She kept to herself," one of Temptation's fellow dancers, Desire, said to the pretty reporter from the war mongering, politically conservative news network, who wore a mask of superiority and distaste throughout the interview despite her drug habit and self-loathing. "Like, you know, she had another life, or she was hiding something or whatever."

"She liked Kir Royales," the club's bartender, Jordan, said to a west coast morning show running an *Explicit Content – may not be suitable for some viewers* warning after every commercial break. "She tipped me for them."

"What kind of tip?" the leering host with the public indecency conviction asked.

Jordan struggled to not grasp the host's inference. "Cash," he said, glaring into the lens. "Like everyone else."

"It's burlesque," another of Temptation's co-dancers, Chastity, said to the reporter who couldn't drive courtesy of a pending DUI hearing. "There's a difference. We're artists."

"She was a good employee," the club's Saudi owner said to a local news anchor. "Always on time, popular with the regulars, finished her shift. Until the day she left. No notice. An employee should always give two weeks. It's good business. *Respectful* business. But what can I do? It is not my place to forgive. That is Allah's job."

When asked for her opinion on Temptation, Svetlana Babakov donned her oversized sunglasses and said, "I wish much happiness."

In a press release, the Vatican announced their intention to conduct an independent investigation into Temptation's past, to determine the veracity of claims the alleged new messiah's alleged mother was indeed an exotic dancer. They would publish their findings, based on the pontiff's infallible interpretations of available evidence, with the title *Ipsa Tentatio*. The pope would narrate the audiobook in Latin and Aramaic.

The Vatican's announcement did not mention frantic efforts to push back uncontrollable crowds in St. Peter's Square threatening to storm the Basilica.

Vicious, career-defining battles raged in glass-walled corporate media boardrooms. Was Jesus Christ the story? His bride and her past? Their child? Or that he said there was no God? Where *was* God in all of this? What about the estimated eight thousand deaths worldwide per day attributable to Jesus' earthly presence? Or the destruction and communications blackout in Paris? And there was Canada. Did Jesus Christ recognize geopolitical boundaries? If the convoy reached the border, how would Canada handle so many vehicles? On-air pundits surmised there might be tense negotiations occurring between various agencies suspected to be in communication.

"One thing differentiates Josh Nazareth from every Jesus nut on the corner mumbling about the end of times," the author of the hastily self-published e-book *Christ the Clone* said. "He's a clone. What else could he be? Who did it? *That's* the story."

The global brand news factories drained the pool of interviewees and experts, in a desperate, gasping swirl to the bottom. All sides weighed in. They broadcast dark, teasing undercover strip club footage, accompanied by ominous parental guidance warnings and scandalized voiceovers. Opinions were put forth, crucified, buried. Competing network philosophies shaped identical information and images into dissimilar segments with opposing conclusions. Burlesque and striptease were defined and delineated until the casual viewer might conclude they were warring ideologies with differences as subtle and divisive as those of the Abrahamic religions.

And to the satisfaction of both God and the media, Temptation's scandalous past reeled in the stragglers not yet eye-cuffed to their televisions.

★

Noon came, and they were in Oregon.

The road sliced a bright scorched strip through an expanse of endless green, from the rain-fed grass lining the shoulder to the impenetrable forest, looming close enough to reach with a slingshot. Miles passed with little change, the only conversation intimate whispers between Jesus and Temptation.

Pumello might have driven past the Hitchhiker if not for the blue ball cap and bright red backpack, jarring him like a slap from the heavens. This wasn't a vision, nor a voice, but God on foot in the form of Doug, sans camel, here to join the journey north. *Trust in Me.* You bet I will, Pumello thought, confident more signs and instructions were imminent. It was all coming together for him, like the dramatic, revelation-laden life of a New Age enlightenment seeker. He slowed the Rook and pulled to the shoulder. It took a minute for the Hitchhiker to reach them, and Pumello stared straight ahead, unblinking, his heart accelerating as the crunching sound of hiking boots on gravel grew louder. Expectant and terrified, Pumello smiled when the door opened and the Hitchhiker climbed in.

It was a teenage girl.

She had brilliant green eyes, braided black hair, cocoa skin. She smiled with disarming ease. She appeared to be the same age as Doug, but their apparent similarities stopped there.

Pumello faced the road, unsure, a bit numb, his face dripping with sweat. A girl? He looked into the rearview mirror at his other passengers, but their expressions offered neither surprise nor suggestions. He dropped his eyes to the road ahead. *Trust in Me.* Uncertain but lacking a preferable alternative, he shifted into gear and drove off. Behind him the followers pulled back onto the highway.

"Thanks for the lift," She said.

"You're welcome," he said. Had he screwed up? He checked the mirror again. Lucifer was relaxed, as usual. Jesus appeared on edge, but he was an expectant father. He kissed Temptation while she read her book of baby names.

The Hitchhiker dug into Her backpack. "Sno-Ball?" She asked Pumello.

Pumello's stomach lurched and his hands jerked on the wheel.

"Easy, Sergio," Lucifer said from the second row of seats.

Pumello took the pink cake. "Thanks."

"I'm Dionne," She said, biting into the second Sno-Ball as if She hadn't eaten in days.

"That's Sergio," Lucifer said.

"Thanks for stopping, Serg," Dionne said. "What's with all the cars following ya'll?"

"Jesus Christ is in the back," Lucifer said. "With Temptation, his bride. She's pregnant with the new messiah."

"As if You need an explanation," Jesus said.

Dionne glanced at Jesus, at Temptation and her book.

"Sorry," Jesus said. "Am I supposed to play along?"

"This is good," Dionne said, holding up the Sno-Ball. "How 'bout Athena?" She called to Temptation while smiling at Jesus, which annoyed him.

"It's probably a boy," Jesus said.

"You never know," Dionne said.

"Don't You?" Jesus asked, and Lucifer laughed.

"I like it," Temptation said. "I'll put it on the list."

"You do that," Dionne whispered. She finished the snack cake and gazed out Her window at the Pacific Northwest's wooded fringes. Why was this never enough?

When Dionne entered the Rook XIV, the media ejaculated as one.

Picking up a Hitchhiker provided experts and not-so-experts with a solid hour of breathless "We know nothing… We still know nothing… Nothing is yet known…" non-information with which to work.

Not one observer asked how chopper-borne Special Forces had overlooked a Hitchhiker wearing a bright red backpack.

The networks replayed Dionne's minute-long walk to the armored vehicle repeatedly. A grainy, extreme-zoom, freeze-frame image of Her, taken before She climbed into the Rook, was displayed on all stations with requests for calls from anyone who could shed light on the mysterious Hitchhiker's identity. Conditioned for years to expose, criticize, and inspire fear, the press opted to label the Hitchhiker a potential threat to Temptation's unborn baby, though prior to every statement the Hitchhiker's accusers denied Her skin color and their suppressed racism were the sole reasons for their suspicions.

Later in the day, a surprising change of drivers ignited a minor frenzy—"It is uncertain who the driver is"—but other than an unintentionally accurate "God Is My Pilot" bit on the Blessed Broadcasting Network, the new driver went the way of the mysterious Hitchhiker and became one with the repetitive drone.

Around the world, people of all faiths and no faith followed the Rook's northward progress. However, in the western United States there were two distinct groups of pilgrims: those speeding across the hinterland to join the convoy, and those charging to Las Vegas, where casino crowds and betting rivaled the Super Bowl, NCAA Final Four, and World Cup combined. As the convoy neared the Canadian border and thousands upon thousands of wagers rained down upon the houses, odds dropped for place of birth and date of birth, while child's gender remained steady at 1/3 male, 3/1 female—a statistical aberration progressive analysts attributed to patriarchal tyranny. The category of *New Messiah's Name* pulled heavy betting and astronomical odds for the more unusual female names, as most casinos were taking write-ins, with spelling to be exact, thank you very much. The jackpot at the MGM Grand for a unique Place/Date/Gender/Name *Prophecta* promised $5-75 million dollars to the winning prophet(s), based on the betting pool and the date the winner(s) placed the wager(s).

With a bite-sized portion of the $97 million acquired from "attendance donations" for Jesus' sandstorm wedding, Mathias Bundt made the Blessed Broadcasting Network an offer they couldn't refuse and purchased every non-commercial minute until twenty-four hours post-birth. He broadcast live from his chartered *Bus of Hope*. Piloting the bus was a disgraced stock car driver who had accepted Jesus Christ as his savior while imprisoned for vehicular manslaughter. The *Bus of Hope* was first in line behind the Rook, their position unchallenged since a white-knuckle incident south of San Francisco.

Exhibiting practicality, expedience, and sanity, Canadian Border Services opened wide the gates to their beautiful country, but did not allow the Blackhawks to cross into Canadian airspace. All involved drove into British Columbia with minimal delay.

Meanwhile, Sergio Pumello sat in third period lecture wearing a pleated skirt, knee high stockings, and Mary Jane's. His English 3040 instructor, a camel-bodied nun who went by the name Sister Hump, pointed out that Sergio had split his infinitives yet again. He insisted his editor took care of such transgressions, but the teacher refused to listen. While the other girls laughed, Sister Hump trotted to Pumello's desk, backed her prodigious rump right up to Sergio's nose and, with gastrointestinal foulness heard from St Kate's to Mount Mary, proceeded to—

Pumello woke with a start. The Rook swerved right, left, and right again onto the shoulder. He grabbed for the overhead handhold as the big brakes bit hard and the front end dipped, huge tires tearing into loose gravel. With a rocky screech they shuddered to a stop.

"Nicely done," Lucifer said from behind.

Dionne smiled at Lucifer in the mirror. "Thanks."

Pumello blinked to clear the sleep from his head, trembling, struggling to gain his bearings. In every direction were trees, thick and dark and of endless depth. The woods blocked the sun's last throes, and the evergreens took on a misty charcoal cast. Ahead the narrow road twisted into the gloom. Behind them Mathias Bundt's bus idled. The metallic stench of burned brakes and rubber filled the cabin. Pumello read the sign next to his window:

CAMEL PASS – 60 MILES

"Where are we?" Pumello asked.

"Canada," Lucifer said, exiting the Rook with the road atlas.

Temptation hissed from the back seat and Pumello whirled. "What's going on?" he cried, seeing Temptation's strained, deep breathing and Jesus' preternatural concentration on his wristwatch.

"Seven minutes," Jesus called out.

"She's having contractions," Dionne said. "Started a while ago. We had to leave the freeway to get to the doctor."

Pumello read the sign again. "There's a doctor in Camel Pass."

"You got it."

Lucifer climbed back in, gripping the rolled-up atlas.

"Both rear tires?" Dionne asked.

"Both."

"But it's indestructible," Pumello said.

"Only one spare," She said. "Guess we're walking."

Pumello scanned the trees. "It's sixty miles."

"In the direction we're heading, yes," Lucifer said. "But it's seven miles that way." With the atlas he pointed to their left, across the road and into the forest.

"Wait a second," Pumello said. "Sorry. Why don't we get a ride on Bundt's bus? Commandeer it, like you did the plane. That's standard operating procedure, isn't it?"

There was a tap on Lucifer's window. Mathias Bundt waited outside in a rumpled black suit jacket and unbuttoned shirt. Lucifer pressed a button and the window rolled down.

"Yes?" Lucifer asked.

"Do you…" Bundt said before faltering. "Do you need anything?"

"No," Lucifer said. He closed the window. Bundt remained while fear, humiliation, and relief fought for primacy on his face, before straightening and returning to his bus.

"But she's having contractions," Pumello said to Lucifer, struggling to maintain a reasonable tone. "The doctor's an hour away. She can't walk seven miles through the woods. How long will that take?"

"Two or three hours," Lucifer said.

"Through *forest*?" Pumello cried. "At *night*?"

"Late afternoon," Dionne said.

"Sorry. It'll be night soon," Pumello said. "And what's between here and there anyway? Where's the road straight through? If it's so easy there'd be a road."

"Good points all," Lucifer said. "But the map says there isn't. So we're walking."

"But *why?*" Pumello shrieked.

"Because," Dionne said, pulling on Her cap, "that's how it'll be."

Pumello met Her certain green-eyed gaze and saw a forest of blue behind Her, leading into the unknown.

"Trust Me, Serg," She said, patting his hand. "We're heading out."

An electrified honeycomb of cameras clicked and flashed as they exited the Rook. Following a brief exchange between Jesus and Dionne, the fivesome crossed the road and headed into the forest. Jesus led the way. Confusion ensued before the swarm followed, trailed by several news vans whose drivers deemed themselves on par with Britain's wildlife documentarians, capable of wending their underpowered, small-tired, electronics-laden lunchboxes through the nighttime Canadian woods like Range Rovers across the Serengeti. Mathias Bundt deemed this lunacy, and opted for one video camera, a skeleton crew, and every battery pack and mobile light they could lug off the *Bus of Hope*. He prayed clear footage of the new messiah's birth might buy back his soul.

EVE AND THE APPLE

Glaring lights illuminating silhouetted figures and an endless succession of evergreen branches were the images burned into the world's consciousness over the next hour, augmented by a God's eye view courtesy of Vancouver news helicopters circuiting the forest with massive searchlights, presenting a visual smacking of burglars with penlights in an asparagus warehouse.

Mathias Bundt and his production team led the flock following Jesus Christ et al. Maintaining a trailing distance of twenty yards to soften the harsh glare of their camera-mounted floodlight while providing a "buffer of dread" between Lucifer and the reverend, Bundt and his crew transmitted around the globe, vaulting *Mathias Bundt's Bus of Hope* to the highest ratings in television history. Meanwhile, a second team of ministry employees raced to build a roadside bookstore, featuring a commemorative t-shirt in Bible black or dove white, children's and adult's sizes XS-XXXXL, priced at a brotherly $65, tax inclusive.

As the march entered its second hour and the night deepened, the army of humanity walking in Jesus' footsteps numbered in the tens of thousands, with droves streaming from the road into the forest, desperate to join what promised to be, in the words of one newscaster, "the year's biggest event." Heedful of solar storm warnings and anxious to put wheels to ground before the dazzling red northern lights hit stride and shifted to green, a private pilot landed his chartered jet on a straight section of road and whisked his wealthy passengers to the forest entry via on-board golf cart. This proved a minor boon for Bundt's bookstore. The jetsetters hadn't worn proper footwear for a nighttime wilderness trek, and the bookstore teemed with imitation leather *Salvation Sandals*. Thus a dozen of Boston's elite found themselves deep in the Canadian wild wearing cheap sandals, expensive dress slacks, and overpriced concert-style t-shirts. In total, over two hundred thousand people crashed through the trees and brush, their wake a microcosm of modern humanity's heavy steps upon the earth, though no commentator drew the parallel.

Jesus led Temptation through the woods, over gnarled underbrush, through the maze of trees, doting on her, protecting her. Lucifer walked with Dionne, and Sergio Pumello brought up the rear, tapping his nose, scratching his shoulder, and scribbling notes into a thick spiral-bound journal.

Temptation stopped to ride out a contraction, and enjoyed a comforting potpourri of decaying wood and fresh pine.

Jesus checked his watch. "One and a half minutes," he called out, voice stressed. He squeezed Temptation's hand and walked back to Lucifer and Dionne.

"This leading-them-through-the-woods sequence has a real hackneyed feel to it," Jesus said. "Don't You think it lacks Your usual depth and complexity?"

Pumello drew closer as Dionne said, without Her usual breeziness, "This is simple causality."

Jesus snorted and pointed at Pumello. "You appeared to him in a dream."

"Sorry," Pumello said. "It was a vision."

"Whatever," Jesus shot back, annoyed at being interrupted. "We wouldn't be here if not for You."

"I am uninvolved," Dionne said.

"Then why this little charade?" Jesus said, waving his finger at Dionne from head to toe.

"I wish to be at the beginning of something. As a participant."

"I knew it!" Pumello cried. "I *knew* it!"

Dionne smiled at Pumello. "Without the world knowing of My presence."

Pumello nodded, frightened, electrified. He scratched notes in his journal, flipping backward through the pages, erasing without hesitation of thought or pen.

"Josh, are you having a setback?" Lucifer asked.

"This is supposed to be my time," Jesus grumbled.

"It is your time," Dionne said, inclining Her head. "I am here to be here."

"What does that even mean?"

Temptation groaned and stopped, leaning against a broad tree trunk. Jesus scowled at Dionne and raced back to his bride.

Above, the helicopters' beating rotors wavered. They doused their searchlights and veered from their established circle, revealing the beautiful aurora above, a flow of reds and greens. They flew west, their silhouettes shrinking against the aurora's once-in-a-millennium colors. Thousands came to a halt, heads tilted upward, followed by *oohs* and *aahs* of wonder.

Dionne joined Jesus and Temptation at the tree.

"I can't go any farther," Temptation whispered.

"You'll be happy you did," Dionne said.

Temptation hissed at the pain. "I don't think I can."

Jesus closed his eyes, summoning calm. "We're down to a minute now."

Dionne placed a comforting hand on Temptation's belly, meeting the pregnant woman's pained gaze with a mixture of compassion and certainty. "We're close."

Vibrations flowed through Temptation, as if her baby sang to the hum of her bones.

Jesus drew close to Temptation. "Why can't we stop here?"

"Because we're almost there," Dionne said. In the darkness Lucifer chuckled.

"Is that a metaphysical riddle?" Jesus asked. "You said You were uninvolved."

"As little as My all-encompassing nature allows." Dionne took Temptation's hand. "Not long now."

They continued through the brush, and Pumello eased over to Lucifer. "Sorry. Would it be all right if I asked you a question?"

Lucifer studied him in the flashing lights. "Is now the proper time?"

"I—" Pumello began. He peered ahead, into the dark, and asked, "Am I going to Hell?"

"You're still young. It's dicey to conclude one way or another."

"So if I live the rest of my life without sin, I might not?"

"Sin is a manmade construct," Lucifer said. "It doesn't factor into your fate."

"But what if I do? Live without sin, that is?"

"You're not listening," Lucifer said with a laugh. "Rather than living without sin, consider living without fear. Consider this is all you get, that nothing follows."

The journalist's face filled with suspicion. "Sorry. I think you're leading me astray. You and the others must come from somewhere."

"Maybe this is all a grand hoax."

Pumello scoffed. "No. I don't believe that. I think there's a path to where you are, and another to where they live." He pointed at Jesus and Dionne.

"But what if you choose the wrong way?" Lucifer asked. "What if the right path is living life to its fullest? What if you should say yes to everything instead of no? Or what if your earthly deeds don't matter? What if it's a popularity contest?"

Pumello frowned. "How would I know?"

"You wouldn't. Nobody does. It's insane to believe there is something or someone paying attention to your naughties and nices, prepared to damn you to a fiery eternity like a malevolent Santa Claus."

Pumello eyed him. "But Santa Claus isn't real. You are. And I don't want to go to Hell."

Lucifer sighed a mighty sigh encompassing the whole of humanity. "Live your life," he said. "The overwhelming odds are you're not going anywhere."

Lucifer and Pumello turned to the crunch of boots. Mathias Bundt approached with a big man who looked like a backwoods Buddha. His hair was shaved to a few millimeters, and he wore a flannel shirt under a camouflage jacket, heavy blue jeans, dark brown hunting boots, and a determined expression.

"Excuse me," Bundt said, shaking with fear at being so close to the Serpent. "This is—"

"I know," Lucifer said, his tone dismissive of Bundt.

Reggie Blake recognized Lucifer, knew his voice. His presence was the *X* on a mental map Reggie had followed since leaving Montana. But Reggie wasn't a man who put credence in fate or the supernatural or what have you. He was an educated man, a philosopher. He couldn't explain the facts he'd shot skeet with this man near Bozeman a couple of years back, or ran into him again while wade fishing in Madison Junction last October, but suspected it wasn't because an explanation didn't exist. He simply grasped neither the nature nor the mechanism. He filed it under *Jungian* for future consideration.

"It's been awhile," Lucifer said to the big man.

"Yup."

"Still got the Perazzi?"

Reggie nodded.

Lucifer motioned for Reggie to follow him. "She's this way."

Temptation shut her eyes as the pain rose. It was too sharp, too intense, and maintained a maddening edge. Tears rolled down her face. "Can you do something?"

Dionne's expression didn't change.

"Maybe," Jesus muttered, "She hasn't let go of Eve and the apple."

Dionne and Jesus shared a long look. "There was no Eve," Dionne said, "and no apple. The pain of childbirth is natural. Why are you holding on?"

"I'm not trying to," Jesus said, frustrated with himself. "It's just all so new."

Temptation clenched her teeth against the pain. "Make it *stop*."

"She can't," Lucifer said, emerging from the dark with the big man as Temptation cried in agony.

Reggie crossed the space between himself and his daughter with startling speed and took her hand in his massive palm. Hurt and joy reflected from father to daughter to father as if caught between mirrors. What had and hadn't been drifted between them and away, inconsequential, like dust through sunlight. He was there, she was there, there was nothing else.

"Daddy?" she said, confused, elated, ashamed, safe.

"Hi, pumpkin." Reggie used his free hand to swipe at a threatening tear, so overwhelmed he felt like he hadn't experienced an emotion since Becca left eight years ago. The moments between then and now felt forever lost, meaningless, done and gone.

"What are you doing here? How'd you know where to find me?"

"Not sure," Reggie said. "How you doin'?"

"It hurts," she said, wincing.

"Hello," the green-eyed Girl with the braided black hair said to Reggie, "I'm Dionne."

Reggie shook Her hand. Vibrating warmth poured into him, as if he'd grabbed hold of an existential live wire. He saw and heard things beyond the limits of his sensorial spectrum. He felt rooted and soaring at once, connected to all that was and is. He released Her hand, and filed Her under *nature of God* for future consideration.

Dionne laid a reassuring hand on Temptation's shoulder and coaxed her from the tree. "A little farther."

Behind them the crashing of thousands of feet resumed, drowning out Temptation's lesser groans. Television lights, sliced by trees into haphazard beams, darkened the path and made the nighttime forest a series of sudden and dangerous wooden encounters.

Temptation gripped her father's hand, three steps behind Jesus. Dionne walked beside her. "Tell me it's not about original sin," she whispered.

"Original sin is man's creation," Dionne said. "As is the epidural. Occasionally reason triumphs."

"What about nuclear weapons?"

"How a civilization uses a near-limitless power source says a lot about that civilization's future."

Ahead, Jesus stiffened, startled. "Stay out of my head!" he shouted, continuing on. "I don't need divine guidance."

"That was me," Lucifer said.

"Get thee—" Jesus began, but stopped to move aside a tangle of branches. "Oh, forget it."

"Let him be," Dionne said to Lucifer. "He's having difficulty adapting to a life not preordained."

"I heard that," Jesus said.

The immaterial beings in attendance exchanged smiles.

"Are we close?" Temptation groaned. Her father wrapped his arm around her to support her.

"We are," Dionne whispered. "In fact," She said, stopping next to Jesus at a clearing in the forest, "we're here."

Grasses and wildflowers blanketed the clearing, a perfect circle some hundred yards across. A breeze blew through the open space. The northern lights blazed across the sky, providing light enough to read a book, an emotion, an intention.

"Uunnnnhh," Temptation cried, doubling over. Jesus rushed to her and helped Reggie hold her up. As one they advanced into the clearing. The surrounding trees flashed as countless camera phones fired behind them.

"Striking!" The clearing blazed into view courtesy of Mathias Bundt's portable production lights.

Reggie met Jesus' eyes and took his measure, as fathers have throughout time. He squeezed his daughter's hand and let go.

Jesus helped Temptation to the center of the clearing. His inner artist rebelled against the aesthetics this remote place demanded—the harsh, glaring lights and the too-black shadows. Despite every ounce of reason within him he felt abandoned yet again, based on the assumption his faux Father could have visited a prophecy upon a competent filmmaker to ensure a professionally lit birth. Evidently God was *not* in the details. Jesus made his umpteenth mental note regarding how not to run the universe before reminding himself, yet again, he was a man and would never be the beginning and end of all things. For chrissakes, had he once said that? He filled with shame and aimless, impotent wrath. But the feelings drained away when Temptation groaned. Soon there would be something bigger than himself, in the form of his child. Jesus helped his bride to the ground, yearning for no more than the golden sunlight and soothing earth tones of his crucifixion.

★

Temptation lay in the tall grass, surrounded by Jesus Christ, Luis Enfuego, Sergio Pumello, the Unidentified Mountain Man, and the Mysterious Hitchhiker. Phone cameras flashed. Television screens flickered and flared. The glaring video lights washed out the wildflowers' brilliant color. Bundt's cameraman trained his lens on Temptation, her dress providing only a wisp of modesty.

The solar flare's main body reached earth, battering satellites and striking the atmosphere. The geomagnetic storm hit its peak and the aurora's charged particles burned, painting the sky a vivid, trembling green.

The network anchors announced the birth like a sporting event, with an assortment of doctors, midwives, homeopathic physicians, placentophagists, and natural birth proponents providing color commentary, including this unintended gem: "Given the lack of modern narcotics and sterile procedures in the meadow, this is what Mary must have gone through in the manger."

Watching from her hotel room in Dubai, Domina laughed.

No real warning came before it happened. Several in-studio commentators who shared the common background of having cut their teeth on Los Angeles televised freeway car chases—a wall-to-wall narration style that assumes the viewing audience are visual agnosics—announced the Mysterious Hitchhiker had spoken to Sergio Pumello and Pumello had thrust his hand to the sky, striking the pose of an embattled hero in 1970s-era science fiction movie posters.

Within the next breath television screens around the world went black, their digital souls summoned in a global electro-rapture.

Billions of voices rose in a unified, "*WHAT?*"

In the world's professional video facilities and master control rooms there burst forth a mighty howl. Techs tested and replaced lines. Producers threatened careers. Legions pushed buttons and switched drives and tapes. There were anguished screams and lamentations. Firings scorched the land. It was the Apocalypse. Yet despite the heroic worldwide efforts of television's best minds, not one network or outlet or source could resurrect the picture. No savior rose to the occasion. From an ironic, somewhat cynical perspective, it was a miracle.

★

The aurora borealis shimmered and flexed, massive and luminescent, filling the sky with a harsh green brilliance and beauty not seen since the days of Charlemagne.

The crowd clamored for position, each person jockeying for an unobstructed view, a place to witness something magnificent, a spot to take a valuable photo. The camera phone flashes fired off so incessantly they became fill light for Mathias Bundt's broadcast camera.

Until they stopped.

Bundt's cameraman grunted in shock when his television lights extinguished and sparks flew from the camera. His viewfinder went dead. He pushed buttons and raced through his restart checklist as confusion swept through the suddenly bright green clearing. Many present had never experienced life without the freedom to record it. A symphony of thumbs striking hardened glass rose to a frantic crescendo and fell to a betrayed diminuendo. Bundt's cameraman repeatedly broke the second commandment.

Jesus gazed at Temptation, her straining face and the perspiration beading on her forehead bathed in the aurora's ethereal, award-worthy light. For decades cinematographers had argued the color of night. Was it green or gray or blue? Now Jesus had no doubt. Night was green.

Amongst the wildflowers and trembling grasses Temptation cried in pain, her eyes shut tight. She gripped Jesus' hand and pushed, hoping for a quick birth, believing there were billions of eyes trained between her legs, ensuring the most public birth in history while rendering her former career modest by contrast. She struggled to focus as myriad voices rose to a bellowing "Breeeathe!" and "Puuuuuush!"

Temptation summoned a monumental push against an immovable ball of pain, gritting her teeth, her neck and stomach shaking with the effort, sweat pouring from her, hair matted against her forehead. She imagined a quieting in the meadow, an expectant stillness, before everything gave, flowing, as if the world itself poured from her. She knew it was over, she'd done it, and she lifted her head, swept along by euphoria.

Jesus held the tiny wet child in his hands, not certain what to do but satisfied the meadow's lighting was perfect. Lucifer grinned with delight. Temptation's father produced a hunting knife for the umbilical cord.

Dionne looked on.

Jesus' gaze moved from the bawling baby to Temptation. She held his eyes, her spirit reaching for him, naked and overwhelming. Wildflowers swayed in the aurora's shifting light. A single drum beat an ancient rhythm. He raised his arms and offered his newborn babe to the sky.

The crowd roared.

OVER 100 MILLION ENLIGHTENED

Hours later, thousands of witnesses comprised a mass exodus from the forest, following a shimmering, colorful path lit by the astounding aurora. Giddy expectation and an urge to celebrate energized the march. Many collected tree bark, crushed leaves, and flowers for online auction while mentally allocating the millions sure to come their way via book deals, multiple language translations, and vicious Hollywood bidding wars.

Temptation, her father, and the baby were with a doctor in Camel Pass, leaving Jesus and Dionne to walk alone through the trees.

"Though I accept it's not the nature of our relationship," Jesus said, stepping over a fallen branch, "I'd be more comfortable if You'd assume a paternal form."

A wash of pine needles and twigs flowed under foot, crunching and snapping with their every step. Small animals moved in the cool darkness. Shadows and light from the aurora shifted about them, veiling and revealing branches, trunks, and the occasional granite outcropping.

Once God returned Himself to His mid-50s, handsome male look, in hiking gear, sturdy pants, and boots, Jesus asked, "Did it go as You expected?"

God studied Jesus, who did not raise his eyes from the forest floor. He sensed Jesus was uninterested in what He expected, but searching for another answer.

"Few could have handled what you've experienced with such courage and grace," God said. "You lived admirably, you died horribly, you manifested into an existence of unfathomable expectation, only to learn it was a charade and you, therefore, were a charlatan."

"That's maybe a little harsh," Jesus said, caught between wounded and delighted with God's evaluation. "I never said I was Your son."

"You didn't deny it."

Jesus smiled. So went conversations with One Who possessed a measure of omniscience.

"Your father will be proud of you," God said.

Jesus concentrated on the swing of his arms and the placement of his feet. God may have spoken further, but Jesus didn't hear. He walked with wavering legs through a dreamlike void, with sound and color painted in as remembered necessities, cradling the fragile, hopeful place within him God's words had created. Behind his blasé veneer stormed emotions he'd never experienced. He groped through years of fruitless attempts at self-analysis to find what the words had triggered, separating the pearls from the inane and self-serving, and deduced he was experiencing what he'd searched for since manifesting in the City. And though his external senses were subdued, within him grew a sensation of energetic growth and boundless possibility. As he mocked himself for pilfering the Bible's allegorical tendencies, the image of a Joshua tree after a rare desert rain bloomed in his mind, each waxy white flower like the revelatory brush of restoration on a centuries-old master's painting, revealing the underlying brilliance of his life. He was not who he had been or what he'd endured or what others thought he was or should be, but who he *could be* and what he might mean someday.

God said, "My hope is you and your daughter will lead your world from foolish myths toward reality, so one day humanity will find the means to outlive their sun."

With a rush of sound Jesus became aware of his body again, the crunch of needles under his waterproof boots, the footfalls in time with his own. "Why do You care?"

"You know why."

Jesus reveled in the radiant sky, and ached to be with his little family in Camel Pass. "Maybe one being's needs aren't so different than another's," he said, "even when One happens to encompass all of existence."

"I don't know."

"I find that difficult to believe."

"As do I," God said, not without humor.

"Any advice?" Jesus asked. "Last words? Almighty riddles?"

God shook His head. "I leave it to you."

After weeks of rumors, Walter Dunphy of Camel Pass, British Columbia, pitted television networks against multinational corporations and the world's richest individuals when he announced his intention to take bids for the sole recording of the new messiah's birth, filmed with an old 8mm spring-driven camera. The camera, unaffected by the solar storm, had filmed the night's crucial seven minutes and thirty-four seconds. After confirming authenticity by sending twelve qualified bidders a single frame from the grainy film, Dunphy's blind auction opened and closed in less than an hour, fetching an astronomical amount from an unidentified private collector, while proving nobody had more money than God.

The Canadian government enlisted the help of a renowned log cabin architect to build a rustic home for Jesus' family in the forest clearing, declaring the path from the main road to the birthplace "lost terrain" and donating the trees to the project. The government offered tax incentives, comprehensive health care, and fast-tracked citizenship in an aggressive campaign to make the log cabin the family's primary earthbound residence. In return, the government asked for permission to market Jesus' newborn daughter, Aurora, as a Canadian.

The lost terrain designation cleared the way for a new four-lane paved road, christened the Nazarene Parkway, along which a succession of investors bought land. Amongst the fast food behemoths and global coffee brands was the first location of a curious new franchise:

Realization | Realist + Civilization

On the night of Aurora's birth, every major network around the globe had transmitted Mathias Bundt's live signal, after wiring heavenly amounts to Bundt's offshore bank accounts. A small portion benefited the world's poor and hungry, and a share found its way into the Blessed Broadcasting Network's coffers. The vast majority of the four-and-a-half billion dollars in revenue generated from the most riveting ninety minutes in television history was applied to real estate purchases for Realization's worldwide, reality-based, science-championing philosophy. Men and women of any race, creed, and orientation could, for a small franchise fee, purchase the rights to sell the philosophy of Bundt and his silent partner—rumored to be a Spaniard living in the Tuscan countryside. Emulating the most successful restaurant and retail chains, Mathias Bundt bought the real estate, leased it back to the franchisees at a significant markup, and produced a series of five- and ten-minute personal enrichment videos, which franchisees sold for the price of a hamburger, fries, and chocolate shake. *Over 100 Million Enlightened...*

Courtesy of a powerhouse, many-layered performance in the international blockbuster *Vostok* (a minor role expanded by the soon-to-be-divorced director during filming), Svetlana Babakov found herself at the top of every movie producer's A-list. Considered the leading contender for best supporting actress, all of Hollywood was "truly shocked" and "blown away" when she failed to make the list of nominees.

In a widely publicized story of luck and windfall from which those who put credence on the destinies of names and number combinations experienced full-body rapture, a high-rolling gambler by the name of Gabriel Angelo walked into the MGM Grand after Aurora's birth and presented the cashier with his winning Prophecta ticket. He'd placed his bet on the first day MGM had offered the Prophecta, and his was the only winning Prophecta ticket. It was worth $73 million. After collecting his sudden fortune, Mr. Angelo placed a sentimental wager on the Chicago Cubs to win it all and retired to his penthouse suite at the Bellagio.

"Und how are you adjusting to zee challenges of fozzerhood?" Freud asked, squeezing a lime over his blackened salmon taco. "Und simultaneous mortal und immortal existence?"

"Conversion is a strange process, but overall it suits me," Jesus said, pleasant and satisfied. They sat on the second floor deck of *El Pescador*, home of the best fish tacos in the Garden. Jesus munched on an ahi burrito in the cool shade of an oversized dark green umbrella. "We spent yesterday in Montana. Becca's father is teaching me to fish."

"Zat is intriguing—"

Jesus cut him off. "It's a misinterpretation of my myth."

"Hmmph."

"Anyway," Jesus said, smiling at the memory, "the fish weren't biting, and the sun was setting. It may have been the most beautiful sunset I've ever seen. But I couldn't take my eyes off Aurora."

"Zere is often a special connection between a fozzer und his daughter," Freud said, finishing his frozen kiwi margarita.

Jesus peered at the psychiatrist. "The Electra Complex is a slapped-together counterpart theory, and further reveals the male gender-dominance beliefs of its creator."

Freud scowled and bit into his taco before mumbling, "I believe it to be an inherited trait." He wagged a knowing finger at Jesus. "Und you experienced strong Oedipal tendencies."

Jesus lowered his burrito. "I most certainly did not."

"You described visions of conjugal relations wiz your muzzer."

"They were *dreams*. And I'd just watched that damn music video where she laps milk like a cat."

"Zat is interesting."

Jesus glared at him. "Leave it alone, Siggy."

"Once again I must warn you of risking transference," Freud said. "Und you have always harbored resentment toward your Fozzer."

"Not my real father, and *not* because I wanted mom for myself."

Freud removed his glasses and polished them with his handkerchief. "I feel it is, as yet, unresolved." He tsk-tsked.

"And so it shall stay," Jesus said. "This is my last session." He took a big bite of his burrito.

"Why?" Freud asked. "Why do you do zis to yourself?"

"I've found my place," Jesus said, and took a quick swig of kiwi margarita. "I'm not the Son of God. I'm Aurora's father, and Becca's man. The divine link has been broken." He smiled at Freud. "I've transcended therapy."

"Zat is ridiculous. One does not rise above psychoanalysis. Zee mere assertion of such suggests a delusional mentality. You are not well."

"I'm as well as I'm ever going to be."

"Do you see? Do you see? Zat negative, fatalist attitude is a defense mechanism, an indication of an unhealzy, overdeveloped Ego."

Jesus stood, wadding up the burrito wrapper. "I need to convert and catch a plane to Brazil," he said. He tossed the wrapper in a nearby trashcan and extended his hand. "I appreciate what you've done for me."

Freud shook his former patient's hand. "Is it zat traitor Jung?"

Jesus laughed, clapping him on the shoulder as he passed by.

"It is not funny!" Freud called after him. "He is wizzout loyalty!"

Freud remained at the table, lips pressed together. He set down his taco and placed his trembling hands flat on his knees. When they were steady he rubbed his eyes. He watched Jesus catch a falling apple at the Tree of Knowledge, and poured himself another margarita.

Freud sat back beneath a cloudless sky, frozen drink in hand. For years he'd psychoanalyzed Jesus. The information from which to draw was incomparable, compelling. His insight might—

He stopped himself, shaking his head. He could not violate doctor-patient trust. He sipped the margarita, pondering.

Perhaps a book based on his conclusions, containing no overt references to their sessions…

✷

Their canoe eased across a small, quiet lagoon a few tributaries off the Amazon River. Becca's father impaled a small catfish on a circle hook and cast it toward a spot where the water's surface had frothed, vibrated, gone smooth—confirming the presence of a giant arapaima, silver and beautiful and dangerous. She watched her father's eyes, intent and focused, and was pulled back through time, now a little girl munching an apple beside a small Montana creek, her father casting his fly while she traced its delicate arc through the air with her finger.

She breathed the thick jungle air through her nose to avoid swallowing a monster mosquito. She was vaccinated and slathered with insect repellent, but malaria hung over the Amazon like a second canopy and Lucifer had reminded her she and Aurora had this one life. Manifestation and self-awareness remained beyond his influence.

Becca smiled to herself. She was in Brazil. Domina had loaned them her jet for the flight to South America, and had stayed behind to take care of her baby granddaughter. Judging by her mother-in-law's demeanor, equal parts frantic and overwhelmed, caring for a baby had changed little in two thousand years. She stifled laughter to avoid alerting the arapaima across the lagoon. Her father glanced back, not pleased with the small noise. He motioned with his eyes at something behind her. She pushed the canoe away from a gnarled ball of branches and resumed scanning the lagoon for interested caimans.

Twenty yards away, the water exploded.

"Here we go, pumpkin," Reggie said, shifting his weight while he let the fish run.

The line sliced through the water. Soon it was tight and her father pointed his rod where the line disappeared beneath the lagoon's dull, gray-green surface. The fish stopped where a kapok tree's massive roots flowed from the bank into the water.

"Did the hook set?" she asked.

"Yup," Reggie said. "It's just thinking."

She found the paddle between her feet.

"We'll give it a minute," Reggie said. "Let it run, work our way over to the bank there." He made a small motion with his head, indicating a narrow strip of mud and rocks across the lagoon.

"How hard do you want me to paddle?"

"Like you're making a friendly suggestion," he said, turning the reel bit by bit with a safecracker's finesse, feeling for the optimal tension. "The fish'll go where it wants."

A king vulture landed on a branch across the lagoon and settled in to watch the struggle. Something small bolted to a better hiding place. The lagoon stilled.

"What do you suppose it's thinking?" she asked.

"Don't know," her father said. "That might be a question for your friend Lou."

She smiled. Thoughts of Lou had made way for the baby, and the interviews, and this Brazilian beginning to her lifelong walkabout. "Dionne said awareness and thought are proportional to something's complexity."

"Did she."

Becca nodded, though she knew her father wasn't looking. She wanted to tell him everything. "And consciousness evolved."

"Figured so," Reggie said, filing it under *mechanism of consciousness* for future consideration. "Had to."

"She—"

"Pumpkin," Reggie said, interrupting her. "If it's okay with you, I'd like to work it out myself."

"I know, but—"

"If you just give it to me," he said, amused and certain, "I ain't gonna appreciate what's between where I am now and where I need to be." He smiled at her. "But if I get stuck, I'll come to you."

"Okay," she said, grinning and settling her gaze on the spot where the kapok tree's roots entered the water. What separated her from the arapaima? A few hundred million years? In the ten *months* since she'd met Josh, her life was unrecognizable.

The fish burst from the lagoon and shot toward them. She had the paddle in the water and was adjusting the canoe's position in relation to the arapaima's violent orbit before realizing she'd acted. She worked the paddle, coordinating sight and sound and feel with the canoe's momentum and the water's resistance. Words were unnecessary. Her father battled the giant fish and her eyes blurred as childhood memories floated to the surface. She noted movement at her nine o'clock and guessed a caiman was in the water. She blinked rapidly, clearing her eyes. Her father swung the rod over her head as the fish shot beneath the canoe. She whirled to the other side, digging the paddle into the water, adjusting the canoe, suggesting the arapaima head toward their preferred shore. The heavy heat pressed down on her. The fish was strong. The caimans and mosquitoes circled. Her father strained against the desperate arapaima. It would be a long, hard, wet fight.

She was so happy she could scream.

God sat with Lucifer in his Tuscan villa, sipping peppermint hot cocoa. The room's coolness contributed to the mugs' satisfying warmth and the minty steam rising from the cocoa's surface. A television was tuned to an interview with Domina.

The interviewer asked, "What are you working on now?"

"I'm developing an original Christmas album, written from Mary's point of view."

Domina began to strum an acoustic guitar, singing a rough version of a song from the future album, a song confessing a womanly love for God, a love not so innocent, her voice throaty and impassioned. At song's end, she broke into another tune, this one portraying an ascended Mary, alone and yearning.

God tapped His finger on a manuscript. "I am disappointed with Sergio's account. It's focused on the supernatural despite his access to you. It's too allegorical and open to misinterpretation."

"It's an early draft," Lucifer said. "There's too much *Sergio* in Sergio's book."

"He's not the first writer with deific delusions."

"He's playing a part. He's waiting for the Catholic Church to designate the bridge incident and the blackout on the night of Aurora's birth as miracles," Lucifer said. "He wants to be a saint."

God drummed His fingers. "Hopefully, sainthood will have diminishing value."

"In more relevant news," Lucifer said, "forty-one percent of adults, ages eighteen to forty, were able to pick Aurora from a random lineup of celebrity babies."

"Why do you waste your time with marketing research?" God asked. "Why not tap into the collective?"

"I'm a man of my time."

"I see."

"Aurora's qualitative emotional index reads like a famous child actor's would."

"What about Josh?" God asked.

"An over-the-hill rock star on a comeback tour."

"He'll hate that."

"I can't wait to tell him," Lucifer said. "Polls, algorithms, regression formulas. As a cultural barometer, they're infallible."

God chuckled, imagining Jesus' irritation.

"Have you decided how long You'll stay?" Lucifer asked, too casually.

"Not long," God said. "Expanding from My current form will require an epoch by your clock."

Lucifer dipped a cinnamon cookie into the cocoa, not pretending to understand. "What does such a rapid, massive expansion feel like?" he asked.

God smiled, imagining, anticipating, and said, "It's never enough."

CALL ME YESHUA

Jesus settled into a giant overstuffed red pillow and blew sweet smoke into the air. It burned the back of his throat a little on the way out, which he attributed to the years since he'd last smoked shisha. The smoke rose, pale and formless against the ceiling's geometric blacks and reds. He handed the hookah's gold-threaded hose to Muhammad, who took a deep pull, closed his eyes, and held in the smoke.

"This was a good choice," Jesus said. "What is it?"

Muhammad eased himself into the big pillows but didn't reply.

"What are you doing?" Jesus asked.

Muhammad let the smoke escape, forming three perfect circles in the air with his lips, before blowing a thin stream of smoke through the circles' centers.

"Listening to the smoke, my friend," Muhammad said.

"What did it say?"

"God is great."

Jesus laughed.

"I do not speak for the smoke," Muhammad said. "I listen." The prophet pointed at the hookah. "It is infused with grapefruit, watermelon, and mint."

"It's delicious," Jesus said, reaching for the hose. He took a deep pull and held it in, listening. He heard nothing but his heartbeat beneath the shisha bar's music, an energetic dutar arrangement, with hard-plucked strings and the foreign element of electronic feedback, but smooth and—

"Is this Jimi Hendrix?" Jesus asked. He knew Jimi frequented Paradise City's shisha bars. Maybe he'd taken up the dutar.

"You have a good ear, Nazarene," Muhammad said with a smile. He glanced into a heavy pot on the table before them and adjusted the flame. "He taught himself to play several years ago, on a Herati. Fourteen strings. Not traditional."

A woman stopped before their table, the seventh to do so in less than an hour. She wore a sweep of white clothing over her shimmering olive skin, and he sensed she was beautiful but couldn't be sure. Her face was vague, like a stranger's face in a dream. Though he'd missed spending time with Muhammad, inside the walls of Paradise City creepiness abounded. The stone streets and alleys burst with young women like the one before them—white-robed and faceless—and few men.

The olive-skinned woman offered herself to them with an elegant turn of her palms, as if presenting a fine bottle of chardonnay. Muhammad waved her away. She turned her featureless face to Jesus, who shivered. She vanished into the shadows like shisha smoke.

Jesus put the mouthpiece between his lips and breathed in the sweet smoke, hoping it would calm his nerves. He held it in, delaying the inevitable burn. He knew he might have broken shisha etiquette by not passing the hose to Muhammad, but he didn't care. He blew out the smoke before giving the hose to his friend.

"God told me He isn't my Father," Jesus said.

Muhammad watched the trembling liquid in the heavy pot. The first small bubbles burst at the surface and he lifted the pot. Half a minute passed before he returned the pot to the flame and said, "Gabriel did not say He was."

Jesus studied Muhammad, annoyed and amused. "It's okay to break character on occasion. It's just you and me here." When Muhammad said nothing, Jesus said, "Anyway, that's not my point." Jesus closed his eyes, aware he was coming off as defensive. Once calm, he recounted what had happened, finishing with, "He said my virgin birth was impossible."

"It seemed unlikely," Muhammad said, lifting the pot from the flame again and waiting for a short time before setting it back on the fire. "Times were simpler." He set down the hose and watched the heavy pot. As the water began to boil for a third time he lifted the pot. He arranged two small porcelain cups on the table and poured the coffee into the first, raising the pot as he poured. He did the same for the second cup. He compared them and handed Jesus the cup with more foam.

"I added cardamom today," Muhammad said.

"And lots of sugar, I hope."

Muhammad smiled. "Of course."

They lifted their cups and drank. Hot, rich, perfect. Muhammad made the best Turkish coffee in Paradise City. They relaxed in the pillows, lost in thought.

"Why have you told me this?" Muhammad asked.

"I thought you'd want to know."

"I see. Why did you think that?"

"Because we have a responsibility."

"We do?"

"Yes."

"Hmm. And what is our responsibility?"

"To undo what we've done."

"What have we done?"

Jesus sat up. "We've misled billions of people. We inspire wars and genocide."

Muhammad shrugged. "I am misinterpreted."

"Are you?"

Muhammad's smile hovered between entertained and offended. "I am aware you again walk among men."

Jesus said nothing.

"Are you proposing I do so, too?" Muhammad asked.

Jesus picked up the hose and smoked the hookah. He blew out the smoke and watched it obscure the ceiling's complex patterns. "Lou will convert you to mortal, if you're willing."

"I am a prophet," Muhammad said, "not a messiah. It is not my role to return."

"Mo," Jesus said, surprised by his friend's obstinacy, "I have *met* God. I have *spoken* with Him."

"As have I, Isa."

"Are you referring to your night journey?" Jesus asked. "Look around. Do you see anything shrouded in unspeakable mystery? It was, at most, a vision."

"By your biographer's words," Muhammad said, unruffled, "this is how God appears."

Jesus stared at Muhammad, incredulous. Hendrix's dutar riffs rose toward a crescendo, plucking his thoughts like chords, distracting and irritating him. Was that *Purple Haze*? It didn't work on a dutar.

Things would be harder, and dangerous, without the prophet's help. Jesus passed the hookah to Muhammad. "Pumello's not my biographer, but touché, I suppose."

Muhammad pointed at Jesus with the gold-threaded hookah hose. "They will kill you. They would do worse to me."

Jesus stood and spread his hands to emphasize the insanity, the sheer obviousness of their situation, though he knew it was futile. "What else do you have to do?"

Muhammad smoked the shisha and rose from the pillows. They embraced.

"Peace be upon you," Jesus said.

"And you, my friend," Muhammad said. "Come back when they are finished with you."

After negotiating his way through the legions of white-clad, faceless women milling about Paradise City, Jesus walked along the retaining wall to a narrow low-walled street, lined on both sides with small, simple stone houses, flat-roofed, wind-washed. Most had been empty for centuries. Few Old Testament characters had attained self-consciousness, and fewer had chosen to remain here in Tanakh. But he had to walk through the narrow, winding, shifting slum of Tanakh to get to Messiania.

Jesus crossed Tanakh at a fast clip, his head on a swivel, ears tuned for footsteps beyond his peripheral vision. Lot's daughters roamed Tanakh like lustful barmaids, swigging wine like water, and today of all days he wanted to avoid a confrontation with the scheming pair.

Once out of Tanakh and into Messiania, he passed the home his brothers had lived in before they'd dissolved in time, none having approached any kind of self-direction or understanding of their existence. His "brothers" were little more than moving forms, shadows of the boys and men he'd grown up with. His two remaining apostles besides Peter—John and Judas—lived nearby. Elsewhere in Messiania were Herod, John the Baptist, Matthew, Mark, Luke, and Pontius Pilate. The Magi stumbled around like three faceless zombies connected at the hips. Jesus didn't know them by name and hoped he wouldn't see them today. Beings like the Magi and Paradise City's women struck him with dread for what he might encounter today at his destination.

Jesus ascended an easy hill and rounded a street corner, following a vague route burned into his mind for centuries. Though he wasn't certain where he was headed, he trusted he would know when he found it.

He came upon it all too soon.

The house sat along an otherwise empty street. It was an expansive, single-floored, flat-roofed dwelling, made of limestone. Its presence stretched across a thousand years of memory as if built for him to find. It called to him like a beacon, embodying the idea of "home" despite a few modern add-ons: a glass wall extending the home's entire depth and a backyard infinity pool.

Jesus walked down the dusty street. Above him the sky arced from one manifested horizon to Paradise City's high black stone wall. His bones felt leaden. He willed himself not to turn and run.

He stopped when he reached the front door, waiting for a sign or a gentle shove of courage. So much time had passed, and he felt all wrong, overdressed, foolish. He couldn't do this looking like a dandy. He threw his sport coat behind a bush. He slipped off his nubuck hiking shoes and removed his dress shirt, becoming more himself with each item discarded. A breeze wrapped around his back, and dust settled between his toes. He scooped up a handful of dust and rubbed it onto his shoulders and pants.

Jesus lifted the rough, spherical iron knocker. He knocked it twice against the iron plate screwed into the heavy cedar door, which was stained and oiled a deep reddish-brown. Footsteps approached from the other side. Irrational fear blinded him to the home's detailed, subtle design, the infinity pool's perfection, the determination and lucidity required to envision and build the door before him. He steeled himself for a vague face lost to time.

The door swung open and Jesus gasped. His eyes welled with tears of shame and joy, flooding through him like sheets of rain, washing away the millennia between this place and the empty, unfinished room in which he'd last spoken to the lifeless body of the man standing before him, whose demanding nature had pushed him toward his destiny. Here was the sculpted, nuanced face he remembered, the hard and quiet confidence, the stoic presence undimmed by time.

"Yeshua," Joseph said.

Jesus' legs gave and he began to fall, but Joseph caught him, embracing him as if he had waited two thousand years for his son to come to his senses and come home, which he had. He patted his boy's back and ruffled his hair. There was too much and nothing to say.

Jesus wept, whispering, "Father."